Governess's GUIDE TO SPELLS and managing Misfit Marquesses

The Parasol Academy series by Amy Rose Bennett

*The Nanny's Handbook to Magic and
Managing Difficult Dukes*

*The Governess's Guide to Spells and
Managing Misfit Marquesses*

The Governess's Guide to Spells and Managing Misfit Marquesses

Amy Rose Bennett

KENSINGTON PUBLISHING CORP.

kensingtonbooks.com

Content warning: representations of stammering and speech challenges. Children in peril, sexual content, discussed death of family members, body/size/appetite shaming, and self-consciousness.

KENSINGTON BOOKS are published by

Kensington Publishing Corp.
900 Third Avenue
New York, NY 10022

Copyright © 2026 by Amy Rose Bennett

All rights reserved. No part of this book may be reproduced in any form or by any means without the prior written consent of the Publisher, excepting brief quotes used in reviews.

Without limiting the author's and publisher's exclusive rights, any unauthorized use of this publication to train generative artificial intelligence (AI) technologies is expressly prohibited.

All Kensington titles, imprints, and distributed lines are available at special quantity discounts for bulk purchases for sales promotion, premiums, fund-raising, educational, or institutional use.

This book is a work of fiction. Names, characters, businesses, organizations, places, events, and incidents either are the product of the author's imagination or are used fictitiously. Any resemblance to actual persons, living or dead, events, or locales is entirely coincidental.

To the extent that the image or images on the cover of this book depict a person or persons, such person or persons are merely models, and are not intended to portray any character or characters featured in the book.

Special book excerpts or customized printings can also be created to fit specific needs. For details, write or phone the office of the Kensington Sales Manager: Kensington Publishing Corp., 900 Third Avenue, New York, NY 10022. Attn. Sales Department. Phone: 1-800-221-2647.

KENSINGTON and the K with book logo Reg. US Pat. & TM Off.

ISBN: 978-1-4967-5443-1
ISBN: 978-1-4967-5444-8 (ebook)

First Kensington Trade Edition: April 2026

10 9 8 7 6 5 4 3 2 1

Printed in the United States of America

The authorized representative in the EU for product safety and compliance is eucomply OU, Parnu mnt 139b-14, Apt 123
Tallinn, Berlin 11317, hello@eucompliancepartner.com

*To my family, I could never do any of this without you.
Thank you for being my warm blanket.
And to Winston, forever in my heart.*

The Parasol Governess's Essential Guide to the Education and Protection of Children and Adolescents

The Practical Merits of Pockets, Potions, Parasols, and Spells

From the magical pockets in a governess's Academy uniform that will yield practically anything useful in the moment (including, but not limited to, pencils and linen plasters and sweets and Fae potions), to the spells contained within the *Parasol Academy Handbook*, to the Point-of-Confusion at the end of a trusty Academy-issued parasol or umbrella, every Parasol governess knows she will *always* have precisely what she needs at hand to care for and protect her charges from the vicissitudes of youth, and any and all threats (both human and supernatural).

The Importance of Resilience

Whether it's weathering the glares and retorts of a rebellious child who refuses to apply themselves to an arithmetic problem, a sullen adolescent girl in a snit because one caught her making eyes at a footman, or one's employer is particularly exacting, one must stiffen one's spine and firm one's chin and keep one's calm in difficult moments. Resilience, just like maintaining a prim and proper appearance, is paramount.

Preparedness versus Improvisation

Plans are all well and good, but a Parasol Academy governess should be prepared for anything and everything. Always keep in mind that one should expect the unexpected when caring for children. Flexibility (both mental and physical) is key and allows one to rise to any occasion when one's carefully laid plans get hurled out the window faster than a tantruming charge can lob a plate of Brussels sprouts across the room. Pivoting at a moment's notice (especially when dodging said Brussels sprouts, or heaven forbid, a would-be-kidnapper's punch) is just as important as planning ahead, if not more so.

Chapter 1

In Which a Governess Takes Matters into Her Own Hands; A Ship is Slyly Boarded; Walruses, Polar Bears, and Sardines are Featured; And the Merits of Certain Expletives are Considered . . .

St Augustine's Reach, Port of Bristol, England
August 1851

Miss Mina Davenport, a proudly prim and proper Parasol Academy governess, never set out to break the rules. But oh, when she did so, it was in a truly *spectacular* fashion.

Yes, this is definitely an I'm-never-ever-going-to-explain-this-away sort of incident if anyone ever finds out, thought Mina as she discreetly opened her capacious Parasol Academy–issued umbrella then whispered the magic incantation, "*Cloakify*" to make her entire person, and her umbrella, disappear from view. Though with any luck, now she was completely invisible to anyone bustling about on Bristol's crowded quay, she might just get away with the felonious crime she was about to commit.

Of course, kidnapping a child was not customary for Mina by any means. And without a shadow of a doubt, it was strictly proscribed in the *Parasol Academy Handbook*, which governed all areas of a licensed graduate's practice. It was a handbook that Mina had always adhered to, to the letter. To the very *T*. Indeed, she knew the handbook's every regulation better than she knew the back of her own hand (or even the staunchly guarded secret yearnings of her heart). But when one's former charge—a seven-year-old viscount—was being forced to embark on a perilous sea voyage by his glory-seeking guardian (a supposed "gentleman" explorer by the name of Sir Bedivere Ponsonby)—one must go above and beyond and do what one must.

After all, a mere month ago, Mina had made a deathbed promise to the Dowager Countess Grenfell, young Lord Fitzwilliam's late godmother, that she would protect the boy's life at all costs. *No matter how. No matter what.*

No matter how presently involved sneaking aboard Sir Bedivere's newly acquired survey ship—a majestic, three-masted beast of a vessel, the *Valiant*—and rescuing the young viscount from an inherently dangerous situation. Lady Grenfell had been convinced that the prophetic dream she'd had in the week before her death—that her godson would meet an untimely end in a frozen Arctic wasteland—was indeed correct. Not only that, but she'd very much feared that the real reason behind Sir Bedivere's callous disregard for his ward's well-being, was that the baronet had been ensorcelled by a cursed family heirloom. A silver and obsidian ring that had once belonged to the ill-fated King of England—a rumored Fae changeling—Charles I.

No doubt Lord Fitzwilliam—sweet boy that he was—was somewhere on board the *Valiant*, alone and afraid, shivering in his small kid boots.

Well, not for much longer, whispered Mina beneath her breath. She might not be Lord Fitzwilliam's governess in an official capacity anymore—the high-handed Sir Bedivere had summarily dismissed her a fortnight ago for no discernible reason—but she must do what was morally right.

What she'd promised Lady Grenfell she would do.

"No matter what," Mina whispered to herself. Even if the viscount's godmother had been mistaken and Sir Bedivere's ring *wasn't* cursed and her dream had simply been a nightmare and not a genuine portent of impending doom, common sense dictated that the North Pole was *no* place for a child.

Ignoring the frantic tripping of her heart, and determinedly crushing down any second thoughts, Mina picked up the navy wool skirts of her Parasol Academy uniform, stepped out of the deep shadows of a quayside warehouse, then studied the steady stream of laden carts and passersby, looking for a clear path to Sir Bedivere Ponsonby's ship. The *Valiant*'s gangplank was still down, but she was almost ready to launch. A waiting tugboat chugged away at the prow and there was a small crowd—including Sir Bedivere—gathered on the quarterdeck. Although, as far as Mina could tell, there was no sign of little Lord Fitzwilliam. His fair head was nowhere to be seen.

She needed to make haste, but carefully.

Although Mina was invisible, it was always best to be cautious when employing the *Cloakify* spell. Even an inadvertent collision might knock her umbrella and its protective shadow askew, exposing part of her person. The unexpected appearance of a disembodied body part, or even an untoward billow of her bell-like skirts, would be sure to draw attention; attention that she could ill afford to attract.

Subterfuge, just like an immaculate uniform and perfectly professional demeanor, was paramount.

When Mina at last spied a relatively unobstructed gap in the crowd, she marched smartly across the quay heading straight for the *Valiant*. She trusted that no one would detect the light tap of her heeled boots on the cobblestones. Or her gasp, then muttered curse, when a sailor lugging an enormous sack almost ran into her.

Just sneak aboard, find Lord Fitzwilliam, hide him beneath your umbrella, then disembark. Sir Bedivere will be so caught up in the hubbub of the Valiant's *launch, he won't notice his ward is missing until it's too late.* At least, that's what Mina told herself as she swiftly scaled the gangplank—thanks to her Parasol Academy training, she had *excellent* balance—and gained the main deck of the ship without incident.

As she began to creep along the portside railing toward the fair-headed Sir Bedivere—all the while hoping to catch sight of her former charge—an inopportune wind swept across the deck, and for a few fraught moments, Mina fought against the bullying breeze, struggling to keep her umbrella in place.

Drat and darn! She did *not* need this.

Then, thank goodness, the wind abated with a gusty sigh, and Mina couldn't help but breathe her own huge sigh of relief.

Sir Bedivere—he was quite the braggadocio—suddenly released a hearty laugh, catching Mina's attention. "Right-o, Captain," he boomed, clapping the shoulder of a pewter-haired gentleman beside him. In the afternoon sunlight, the baronet's silver and obsidian ring flashed, momentarily blinding Mina. "Let's get this vessel underway! The Northwest Passage awaits!"

Oh, double drat. Mina huffed out an exasperated sigh. There was no time to lose.

She hurried toward the quarterdeck, frantically scanning everywhere for a small fair-headed boy—but Lord Fitzwilliam was *definitely* not on deck.

He *must* be below. Unless Mina's source of intelligence—Napier, the steadfast butler at Fitzwilliam House in London, an upstanding character who'd been loyal to Lady Grenfell—had been wrong about his young master's whereabouts. Though Napier had been right about the details of the *Valiant*'s imminent launch—her maiden expedition to the Arctic since Sir Bedivere had acquired her . . . with his ward's money.

At that moment, the *Valiant*'s captain barked an order and the crew leapt into action—seamen unfurled the mainmast's sails, unhitched the mooring ropes tethering the ship to the quay, then hauled up the gangplank. When the tugboat sounded its horn, the *Valiant* creaked and shuddered and lurched and began moving ponderously along the River Avon, on its way to the river mouth and the Bristol Channel.

Well, now you're definitely too late to beat a hasty retreat on foot. Mina curled her gloved fingers around the railing to help maintain her balance. All was not lost, though. She had other magical means, courtesy of her Parasol Academy training, at her disposal to effect an escape.

As long as she could find Lord Fitzwilliam and avoid detection. That was her priority.

But where could the boy be? Locked in the captain's cabin or below deck in a cabin of his own or Sir Bedivere's?

There was only one way to find out.

As the City of Bristol slid past, Mina turned her attention to the "lay of the land"—or perhaps she should say, the "shape of the ship"? Unfortunately, her knowledge of all things nautical was rudimentary at best. A doorway bracketed by two sets of stairs leading up to the quarterdeck was directly ahead. The captain's cabin was usually at the stern of the ship not too far below deck—or so Mina thought—and the quarters for passengers and higher-ranking crew members wouldn't be *too* far from that, surely.

Mina started forward, making a beeline for the door... only to discover that there was no way on earth her umbrella was going to fit through such a narrow space, let alone the passageway—really a chute—with its ladder in lieu of stairs that led below. It would be akin to stuffing a whole Victoria sponge into a mouse-sized mouth—physically impossible.

Why, her skirts would barely fit.

Glancing about the deck, Mina made sure no one was looking her way, and of course, that no one was lurking below the ladder, before she drew a deep breath and in one smooth maneuver, turned neatly and balanced on the topmost rung. Then, she swiftly closed her umbrella, tucked it firmly beneath her arm, and gently drew the door closed.

Upon descending the ladder, she found herself in a low-ceilinged, shadowy passageway—deserted, thank goodness—that opened onto a relatively spacious cabin with a fine mahogany dining table, matching dresser, and several large chests. The officers' and gentlemen's mess perhaps?

So far, so good.

All she could hear—apart from the rapid tattoo of her own heart—was the creak of timbers, the susurration of waves, the muted calls of the crew above, and the occasional thud or clank or scrape. Dare she try her luck and call out to Lord Fitzwilliam? Surely most hands would "be on deck"—apart from those on duty in the galley.

What she *couldn't* afford to do was dither, flapping about like a faint-hearted flibbertigibbet. According to Chapter 3, Section 2, Subsection 4 of the *Parasol Academy Handbook*, a nanny or governess "must always act precisely and with assuredness. Dillydallying, or any form of shilly-shallying, can waste precious minutes, especially in a precarious situation where a child's safety is at stake. Assess, decide, take action. Above all, carry on."

No matter what.

And then Mina heard another sound beneath everything else like a soft, heartbreaking undercurrent.

The sobs of a child.

Mina's heart clenched. It was Lord Fitzwilliam. She'd know the sound of his weeping anywhere. Hadn't she provided comfort to the boy on numerous occasions over the past six months? Like the time he'd scraped his knee in Hyde Park. And when he'd badly cut his finger with a pen knife in the schoolroom of Fitzwilliam House. The occasion when he'd suffered from a stomachache.

And then of course, when his beloved godmother, Lady

Grenfell, passed away but a month ago, and she, Mina, had been the one who'd had to break the terrible news to her charge.

She hastened through the mess, following the sound into another narrow passage. There, to the right—or should she say, on the starboard side?—were three wooden doors, perhaps leading to cabins; the weeping seemed to be emanating from the middle one.

Oh, my poor little lord.

Mina rushed over. "Lord Fitzwilliam?" she called in a hushed voice as she tried the polished brass handle—of course, it was locked, but she'd been expecting that. "It's me, Miss Davenport. Can you open the door, my lord?"

The crying ceased and the young viscount whispered through the keyhole. "Miss D-Davenport?" There was a sniffle then a hiccupped breath. "Is-is that really you?"

"Yes," Mina whispered back in the most reassuring voice she could muster. "'Tis I, my lord." She glanced about. The coast was still clear. "I've come to fetch you. Is there a key in the lock? On your side?"

Another hiccup. "No . . ." Another small whimper ensued. "Sir Bedivere locked me in. He-he said I had to stay down here where . . . where it's safe."

Mina's lips tightened as she scoffed inwardly. *Safe?* Who in their right mind wanted to take a child on a rough-sea voyage to such a far-flung and inhospitable place as the Northwest Passage? A notoriously treacherous, essentially uncharted sea route that had claimed the lives of many intrepid sailors. As Lady Grenfell had once put it, "Sir Bedivere suddenly fancies himself as a modern-day Sir Walter Raleigh. He's got it in his head that he wants to blaze a trail across the Arctic Ocean where no man has blazed a trail before. Come what may."

More than ever, Mina was convinced she was doing the right thing in fulfilling her promise to Lord Fitzwilliam's godmother. She *must* whisk Lord Fitzwilliam away to safety.

"Don't worry, my lord," Mina murmured through the door's panels. Reaching into the pocket of her governess's uniform, she found her Academy-issued pewter leyport key, which could serve as a "skeleton" key if required. Even through the fabric of her gloves, she could feel a light tingling, buzzing sensation in her fingers as the magic sparked. "I can open the door."

Which she did, at once. Inserting the key, she tumbled the lock as she whispered the incantation, "*Opendium*," and then she was entering Lord Fitzwilliam's cabin.

As soon as she crossed the threshold, the little boy threw himself at her, his arms catching her about the waist like she was a lifebuoy in a stormy sea. "Oh, Miss Davenport, I've missed you so much. I'm so glad you're here. I don't want to go to the North Pole to see the-the walruses with their big pointy tusks, or the polar bears with their sharp pointy teeth. I want to go home."

"There, there, my lord. Everything will be all right," said Mina in her most soothing tone. Beneath the tumble of the boy's overly long blond curls, she gently patted his narrow back. "I'm here now. And I will get us both off this ship. I don't particularly wish to meet a walrus or polar bear either."

"Really?" Lord Fitzwilliam lifted his watery blue gaze to Mina's. The hope in his eyes sent a sharp pang through Mina's heart.

"Yes, really," she said firmly, then worried at her lower lip as another thought occurred to her. It would take at least an hour for the *Valiant* to reach the mouth of the River Avon and thence the notoriously rough Bristol Channel. While her initial plan had been to sneak Lord Fitzwilliam away as soon as she boarded the ship, perhaps it would be better if she stayed a while longer. If Sir Bedivere believed his ward had been "lost at sea" rather than snatched from the vessel while it was docked—especially by a "lowly" and apparently demure, play-by-the-rules governess—he probably wouldn't bother to mount a search for his ward on the mainland ... which would suit Mina.

On the other hand, if he *did* suspect that his ward had been kidnapped, he *would* mount a search. Lady Grenfell had made it clear that the terms of the guardianship were such that the young viscount had to reside with one of his appointed guardians in order for them to access the family trust. Sir Bedivere, now Lord Fitzwilliam's sole guardian since the passing of Lady Grenfell, would certainly not want to give up that sort of carte blanche access, not if it meant he had to curtail extravagant expeditions like this one.

But of course, the longer Mina stayed on board, the greater the chances were that she would be discovered. And she couldn't have that. Because not only would Lord Fitzwilliam still be stuck in a highly dangerous situation, but her name and reputation, and that of the Parasol Academy, would be muddier than a mud lark grubbing along the mudflats of the River Avon.

She'd lose her Parasol Academy license and her means to earn a living, not to mention the fact that she'd likely be sentenced to a life in prison.

It *was* rather a pity that she didn't have permission from the Parasol Academy's headmistress to conduct this rescue mission. Indeed, Mrs. Felicity Temple knew nothing about *any* of this ... But whether or not she should confide in Mrs. Temple was a matter Mina would contend with later.

Right now, it was essential to teleport—or te-ley-port— both herself and Lord Fitzwilliam off this ship.

Mina knelt down so she could look Lord Fitzwilliam in the eye to explain what they were about to do next. "My lord—" she began, then broke off as a male voice she didn't recognize drifted in from the corridor.

"My Lord Fitzwilliam ..."

Mina's pulse leapt as the thud of heavy, masculine footsteps approached. *Ack.*

"It's my new tutor, Mr. Meecham," whispered the young lord, his bottom lip protruding in a doleful pout. "I don't like him. He's always cross and raps me on the knuckles with his cane if I spell a word wrong. Or make a mistake with my sums."

Mina fought to keep her expression neutral while inside she was ablaze with anger and righteous indignation. How dare a teacher do such a terrible thing? It was unconscionable. No child should be treated in such a cruel way.

But moral outrage would do her no good if she were caught. Her gaze darted about the cabin. She couldn't hide under the small single bed—the space beneath contained built-in drawers. There was a narrow closet in one corner, but she feared she wouldn't quite fit. And while she *could* put up her umbrella and cast the *Cloakify* spell, if this Mr. Meecham entered the cabin, he would be sure to bump into her.

There was only one thing for it: She'd have to use her Parasol Academy umbrella in another way.

At that moment, the door opened. "Mr. Meecham?" Even though she was inwardly seething, Mina somehow managed to greet the astonished-looking tutor—a bespectacled man of middle-age with a balding pate—with her most winsome smile. As she slid her umbrella from beneath her arm, she added in an approximation of amiable, "How do you do? Lord Fitzwilliam was just telling me all about you."

The tutor's mouth, which had dropped open, slammed shut, then opened again, reminding Mina of a snapping turtle. "What . . . ? Who . . . ? How . . . ?" he sputtered. Then he rallied and his expression shifted into the territory of cantankerous with a good dash of suspicion thrown in. "What is the meaning of this? Who are you?" he demanded, tapping his cane against his thigh. "You have no right—"

Mina affected a sigh. "I know. I know, it's all rather confusing, finding a strange woman in his lordship's cabin, isn't it, Mr. Meecham? But I think you'll find that this will help."

And then she gave the bristling tutor a short, sharp jab in the middle with the end of her umbrella—the magical Point-of-Confusion, to be exact—at the same time she uttered beneath her breath, "*Perplexio.*"

Almost at once, the tutor's furious demeanor melted into pleasantly puzzled. He blinked a few times and then rubbed a hand across his rumpled brow. "I... Excuse me, miss... There was something... I seem to have forgotten..." His bewildered gaze drifted to Lord Fitzwilliam. "My lord... I came to..." The tutor looked at Mina again as if asking for help.

She smiled. Thank goodness the confusion spell had taken. Although, it would only work for a few minutes. "You came to check on Lord Fitzwilliam," she said, affecting a politeness she in no way felt, "and now you're going to find Sir Bedivere and tell him that everything is perfectly fine. That his ward is alone in his cabin and is diligently completing the mathematical problems you set. Best you make haste and get back on deck."

Mr. Meecham gave an eager nod. "Ah yes. Quite. That's it. Jolly good." He bowed to Lord Fitzwilliam. "I shall see you anon, my lord." And then he turned on his heel and quit the cabin with nary a backward glance.

Mina permitted herself a small sigh of relief as she shut the cabin door. Even though Mr. Meecham had been responsive to her suggestion—and with any luck, would forget the whole encounter entirely—there was no time to lose. Bending down, she caught Lord Fitzwilliam's gaze. "Right. It's time for us to go, my lord. Is there anything you would like to bring with you? Mr. Hopwell, your velvet rabbit perhaps?"

Lord Fitzwilliam nodded. "Yes, but..." His expression grew fearful. "I-I can't swim, Miss Davenport."

Mina smiled reassuringly. "Oh, we're not going to swim. We're going to..." She trailed off. How best to explain the concept of teleporting to a child? "We're going to step inside a magic cupboard, and when we exit the other side, we'll have arrived somewhere safe."

"Highwood Hall?" Lord Fitzwilliam asked hopefully.

Mina's chest cramped. Highwood Hall was the young viscount's ancestral home in Hertfordshire. The house where he'd been born and where he'd lived with his parents before they'd tragically passed away a year ago in a carriage accident. Lady Grenfell had lived with her godson there too. As had Mina when she'd taken up her post as the viscount's governess in March. "I'm afraid not," she said gently. "At least not for the moment. We're going to visit my own mama and sister instead. They live in the country too. In a pretty little cottage by the woods. Sir Bedivere will not think to look for you there. I also think it would be best if I introduce you to everyone we meet as Master Christopher, rather than by your title, or 'my lord.' Keeping your true identity a secret will make it almost impossible for your guardian to find you. If that's all right with you."

Lord Fitzwilliam nodded. "All right. I agree. That all sounds eminently sensible."

While Mina hastily packed a small valise for the boy—she threw in a few changes of clothes that she found in his traveling trunk—he pulled his velvet rabbit from beneath the pillow on the narrow bed. "I'm ready, Miss Davenport," the young viscount said gravely. "But where is this magic cupboard?" He nodded at the one in the corner. "This one is rather ordinary."

Mina smiled. "Ah, but I have a special key that will wake up the magic. Would you like to see how it works?"

The young viscount nodded eagerly. "Yes, please."

Firmly tamping down any last-minute conniptions, Mina again retrieved her leyport key from her magical governess's pocket. In theory, she could use her leyport key in any door to open a leyline portal, but she preferred using cupboards and wardrobes rather than regular doors between rooms. Aside from the fact it was a relatively discreet way to te-ley-port, there was something about the whole act of unlocking the door and discovering the tiny white leylight in the shadowy depths of a cupboard that helped Mina to focus her energy when casting the teleportation incantation.

Once she'd unlocked the cupboard door (it wasn't really locked, but she needed to use the key to awaken the Fae leyline magic), she beckoned Lord Fitzwilliam over. "See that small white light, flickering like a candle flame? In the back corner?"

The boy crinkled his nose as he squinted into the dimly lit recess. "I think so?"

"Well," continued Mina, "after we climb in the cupboard, I'm going to make the light bigger, so it surrounds us. For a moment or two, it will feel like we're caught in a big gust of wind, but then we'll find ourselves at my mama's house, Rose Cottage. The trip will feel a little strange—you might want to close your eyes to shield them from the bright light. You might even feel a bit dizzy because the wind is quite strong. But I promise you"—she gave the boy's shoulder a reassuring pat—"everything will be all right. You have nothing to fear."

Lord Fitzwilliam nodded as he hugged his velvet rabbit to his thin chest. "I trust you, Miss Davenport. My godmama told me that you are a good person and will always look after me."

Mina smiled. "I will. Now, let us away."

As she took one of Lord Fitzwilliam's small hands, she trained all her attention on the leylight. In her mind, she pictured where she and Lord Fitzwilliam needed to be—the ancient oak wardrobe in her bedroom in Rose Cottage in Ablington, the tiny village in Gloucestershire where she'd grown up. Her bedchamber was the safest place she could imagine.

It was a much-needed haven in a storm.

With her umbrella tucked beneath one arm, she picked up Lord Fitzwilliam's valise then drew the boy into the cupboard, holding him close for reassurance (and of course, the cupboard was so tiny, one had to pack into it like sardines in a tin can to fit at all). As soon as she whispered the required magical incantation, "*Vortexio*," they were both engulfed in a brilliant white light. An overwhelming rushing and swirling sensation, akin to being swept up in a giant whirlpool, washed over Mina, stealing her breath . . . and then just as suddenly the whooshing stopped.

Even though she was a tad dazzled by the fading leylight, she was aware Lord Fitzwilliam was still with her and that they were in another cramped and dimly lit space. Her wardrobe at Rose Cottage?

"Are we there yet?" whispered the young viscount. He was tightly clutching Mr. Hopwell and Mina's arm. "Can I open my eyes?"

Mina gave one of the boy's shoulders a light squeeze. "Yes, we are. And it's safe to look." But then a frisson of apprehension slid down Mina's spine when she realized that something was wrong. *Very* wrong . . .

The enclosed space they were squashed into—another wardrobe, given the presence of massive cloaks and coats hanging from hooks—was *moving*. The floor beneath Mina's feet was pitching and rolling, and the sound of creaking wood and surging water—waves perhaps—filled her ears.

Oh no! Mina pushed a decidedly masculine coat sleeve that smelled of sandalwood and pine needles away from her cheek. They were clearly *not* in her bedroom at Rose Cottage, but still on a ship.

Sir Bedivere's ship? Were they in *his* cabin on the *Valiant* or in some other gentleman's quarters?

Oh no, no, no. What a disaster!

She'd obviously been so nervous and distracted, she'd made a monumental teleportation blunder. Mina had *never* made one before, but they did happen on the odd occasion. Her good friend Emmeline Chase (actually now Emmeline Mason, the Duchess of St Lawrence) a former Parasol Academy nanny, had once ended up in the Thames during her training.

At least they hadn't landed in the sea!

Lord Fitzwilliam reached for the wardrobe's handle. "Can we hop out?" he whispered. "It's awfully squishy in here."

"I... um..." Mina swallowed. She was so rattled by the whole business of being teleported, and of course, her terrible error, she was momentarily lost in indecision. The sensible thing to do would be to step out of the wardrobe to ascertain where they'd actually ended up. She could try again to teleport them to her bedroom in Ablington. But what if they ended up somewhere odd a second time? Someplace worse than a ship? Like in the rough waters of the Bristol Channel or the Irish Sea or the North Pole itself?

At moments like these, Mina really wished she could let fly a whole host of expletives to release her frustration. "Darn" and "drat" and "my goodness me," while socially acceptable for ladies to use—and permitted by the Parasol Academy when in the presence of a child—suddenly seemed completely inadequate right now.

"Miss Davenport?" prompted Lord Fitzwilliam.

Mina rallied. "Yes, of course we should hop—"

She got no further as the wardrobe door suddenly flew open and a tall, dark-haired man with mountainous shoulders, a sharply hewn jaw, and eyes as green as the sea, gaped at her. Tucked beneath the man's muscle-bound arm was a stout, snub-nosed dog—a pug.

"Wh-what the feck?" exclaimed the stranger in the lilting accent of an Irishman. And then the pug gave a short sharp bark and a low growl.

What the feck indeed.

Chapter 2

Involving a Discussion on Manners; the Lack of Bones, Sausages, Digestive Biscuits, and Extra Arms (Either Human or Octopoid) Is Lamented; Medicine Is Taken and a Stern Rebuke Is Administered; Followed by an Offer of Cake.

Wh-what the feck?

Mina gaped back at the hulk of a man, in pure horror. Aside from his extraordinary size and breath-stealing physique (his shoulders were seriously, impossibly wide) she couldn't help but notice he had a slightly crooked nose and one of his thick dark eyebrows was bisected by a scar. Apart from the fact he was *very* well dressed—his coat, waistcoat, and form-fitting breeches were superbly tailored—he was quite handsome in a rugged sort of way. How could a man appear to be both a gentleman and a ruffian at the same time?

She opened her mouth to speak—to at least utter a greeting (according to the Academy handbook, manners *never* go astray, especially when trying to smooth over an awkward situation)—but the pug let out another short bark, cutting her off.

"Now, now, B-Brutus," admonished the stranger in that graveled but softly accented voice of his that brought to mind appealing, masculine things like whisky and leather and shaving soap, "that is n-no way to greet . . . to greet a young lady and her-her child." His wide mouth quirked with the hint of a smile. "Even though they appear to be stow-stowaways."

Stowaways?
Her *child?*
Heat flooded Mina's cheeks. "Oh no. He's not—" she began, then bit her lip, swallowing her words. This man clearly didn't recognize Lord Fitzwilliam, so they mustn't be on the *Valiant*. Not only that, but the *Valiant* would still be navigating the River Avon, whereas it was evident that this vessel was riding a rough sea.

But what was she to tell this man, who was looking at her and Lord Fitzwilliam with such keen interest? Or was it suspicion? While he hadn't growled or barked at them like his irascible pug, surely he must be put out at least a little. After all, he'd found two strangers—apparent stowaways—lurking in his wardrobe, hiding amongst his personal things.

Gathering her scattered thoughts, Mina decided that a half-truth was better than an outright lie. "I sincerely apologize for . . . for trespassing in your quarters, sir. We never intended to. And we're not really stowaways. We-we just got on the wrong boat."

The pug growled. *A likely story*, he thought tetchily, and Mina couldn't suppress a frown. Certain Parasol Academy students, when exposed to Fae magic, became "animal whisperers" and could communicate with particular creatures via thought alone. Mina, as well as her best friend, Emmeline, had developed this ability. *Most* of the time, it was a useful skill to have. Of course, on the odd occasion, one heard things that were not intended for one's ears.

Before Mina could respond to Brutus's skeptical remark, his master said, "You-you got on the wrong b-b-boat?" He cocked an eyebrow in query.

Mina blinked. It only just occurred to her that this man had a stammer. Goodness. She didn't know a great deal about the condition, but she imagined it would be frustrating—to know exactly what you wanted to say, but then your mouth wouldn't cooperate. And to have people look askance at you when you hesitated or stumbled or got stuck altogether would be horrid too.

Praying she wasn't looking askance at the man now, she summoned her most amiable smile. "Kind sir," she said. "Would it be all right with you if we conduct this conversation . . . outside of your wardrobe?"

"O' c-c-course." The man immediately stepped back, allowing Mina and Lord Fitzwilliam space to emerge.

Now that the stranger had moved aside—his large frame had really quite obliterated the view—Mina could see they were in a spacious cabin. One might even say it was sumptuous. The rugs and fabrics—silks and satins and brocades—were rich in luster and hue; a mixture of deep greens and blues and antique gold. The wood was polished and the brass finishings gleamed. And then there was the large bed dominating the center of the room.

Mina quickly averted her gaze from *that* particular piece of furniture.

Hoping her face wasn't as red as a boiled lobster, she ventured, "Perhaps we could begin again with some introductions. We've met Brutus." She nodded at the pug, who continued to eye her suspiciously. "And you are . . . ?"

The man stroked the pug's head with a large hand. "Ph-Ph-Phineas O'Connell."

Brutus yipped and then Mina heard the dog mentally grumble, *Jaysus Christ, say the rest.*

Perhaps heeding the pug's nudging bark, Phineas O'Connell added, "The Mar-Mar-Mar-quess o' K-K-Kinsale."

The Marquess of Kinsale? If Mina's face had been red before, she was certain it was now as white as the snowy linen sheets on the nobleman's bed. "My lord," she murmured, dipping into a curtsy—which was no mean feat considering she was still juggling Lord Fitzwilliam's valise and her Academy umbrella, and the darn floor was constantly moving. "I had no idea."

He shrugged nonchalantly, seemingly unbothered. "How w-w-were you to know, lass?" He paused and his gaze drifted over her uniform. "And if you d-don't mind me askin', you are . . . ?"

Oh, heavens, she *really* ought to have worked out her story before she'd blithely suggested that they all share their names. "Mina. I mean, Hermina Davenport," she said. "And this is . . ." She glanced down at Lord Fitzwilliam and placed a hand on his shoulder. "This is . . . Christopher."

If she were game enough to attempt another teleportation to Rose Cottage, she'd probably never see Lord Kinsale ever again. So what did it matter if he learned her name? Supplying Lord Fitzwilliam's Christian name, as they'd agreed, would hardly connect the young viscount to his title. After all, there must be thousands upon thousands of boys, from all walks of life, named Christopher throughout the British Isles.

Lord Kinsale inclined his head. "I'm pleased to m-m-make your acquaintance then, Mrs. Hermina Dav-Dav-Davenport." He smiled at Lord Fitzwilliam. "Christopher Dav—"

Lord Fitzwilliam began to speak, "Oh, I'm not Christopher Daven—" but Mina interrupted him.

"Master Christopher will do nicely, my lord," she said to the marquess as she bobbed another small curtsy. When she could manage it, she would have another quiet word to the young viscount about the crucial need for subterfuge for now.

It was also evident that the Irish nobleman had assumed she was married. Which was only natural if he believed that Lord Fitzwilliam was her son. She didn't see any point in correcting the marquess either. Because that would be far too awkward for words and perhaps even call into question her virtue if she stated she was actually a "miss." Neither could she openly admit that Christopher *wasn't* her son and that he was actually Viscount Fitzwilliam.

What she really *needed* to do was get off this ship. If she could just manage to get away from Lord Kinsale for a few minutes, she could attempt another teleportation. She could always use her umbrella's Point-of-Confusion again, or even employ a befuddling potion on the marquess, but then she'd also have to deal with the feisty Brutus. Perhaps her uniform pocket might yield a nice juicy bone to distract the animal.

"As I mentioned before, my lord, we've obviously boarded the wrong vessel," Mina began as she put down Lord Fitzwilliam's valise, then reached into her pocket, all the while simultaneously adjusting her hold on her umbrella so the metal tip was facing forward for a strategic jab. (Sometimes, she really wished she could utter a spell—something like "*Armus Octopi*"—which would supply her with a few more arms.) "An honest mistake—"

"With all d-due respect, Mrs. Dav-Davenport," said the marquess, his dark brows sliding into a frown, "I-I don't see how. This is a privately owned vessel. M-m-my clipper, the *Kinsale Cloud*. Not many ships set out from K-Kinsale Harbor yesterday evenin'. And you cannot be tellin' me that you and your lad here have been hidin' in me war-war-wardrobe, all this time."

Brutus yapped in agreement. *Only a feckin' fool would buy such a load o' bollocks.*

Mina sent the impudent pug a quelling look—heavens, such language!—and felt around in her pocket again, but nothing—not a bone, nor a sausage, not even a digestive biscuit—had materialized. *Drat it.* She was going to have to talk her way out of this situation. "Well, no, my lord. We haven't," she agreed. "Honestly, we do not wish to be a bother. If you could just direct us to somewhere quiet and out of the way, I dare say we'll be out of your hair in no time at all."

Lord Kinsale put down Brutus, who'd begun to wriggle, then rubbed a hand across the back of his neck. "Well, if you've hop-hopped on the wrong boat, lass, it f-f-follows that you might very well end up in the wrong p-place." He gave her a searching look. "The *Kinsale Cloud* is headed for Bris-Bristol and accordin' to me ship's captain, we'll be there in a c-c-couple of hours. Three at most. Is Bristol where you really w-w-wanted to go?"

Mina considered Lord Kinsale's question. There could be *worse* destinations than simply ending up where one started. Sir Bedivere had already departed the port, so it wasn't likely that she'd bump into him again. If the marquess—who *seemed* like a reasonable man, all things considered—permitted her and Lord Fitzwilliam to stay on board the *Kinsale Cloud*, she wouldn't have to worry about messing up another teleportation attempt while at sea.

Indeed, it bothered her that she still really had no idea *why* the leyline magic hadn't worked as it should. Unless it had something to do with the fact that she'd cast the spell while on the water. Could it be that the flow of the river beneath the boat had somehow interfered with the leyline energy emanating from the earth? There was nothing like that mentioned in the *Parasol Academy Handbook*, but perhaps such a theory had never really been tested before.

If that were the case, surely the choppy waters of the Bristol Channel would make another teleportation go awry a second time. Yes, maybe it *would* be safer to teleport while on dry land. Conversely, she and Lord Fitzwilliam could always catch the train to Ablington. It wasn't so very far. Why, they'd probably arrive at Rose Cottage in time for dinner.

Mina was about to confirm that yes, both she and Christopher *did* wish to travel to Bristol, when Lord Fitzwilliam clutched at her skirts. "I'm sorry, but I... I don't feel very well," he murmured.

One look at the boy's pea-green pallor and Mina knew he was seasick. And no wonder. The ship was pitching and rolling terribly. The whole experience of being whirled around and around during the teleportation process had no doubt contributed to the young viscount's unsettled internal state too.

Lord Kinsale's forehead creased with concern. "The sea is par-particularly rough, this-this afternoon, lad. It might be b-best if we go up on deck. The fresh air m-m-might help." He nodded at Mina's umbrella and Lord Fitzwilliam's valise. "You m-might like to leave your be-belongings here though, Mrs. Dav-Davenport. So you c-c-can hang on to the railings."

"Of course, Lord Kinsale," agreed Mina, depositing her things by the cabin door. "And yes, taking some fresh air sounds like a very good idea."

Once they were on deck, perhaps there'd be a moment when the marquess was distracted. Then she could produce a bottle of medicine from her governess's pocket that would alleviate Lord Fitzwilliam's nausea. Such was the nature of the Parasol Academy uniform's "magical" pockets. They somehow provided a nanny or governess with whatever a child needed. You just reached right in, and there it was.

The marquess and Brutus led the way, and within a minute, they were all up on the rear poop deck of the *Kinsale Cloud*. Any number of curious glances were cast her way and Lord Fitzwilliam's by the marquess's crew. Especially the captain—Lord Kinsale had stopped to have a brief word with the man as they'd traversed the quarterdeck. Mina tried to ignore the stares and whispers. No doubt the men were all wondering where she and the young viscount had come from.

"Hold-hold on to the taffrail, lad." Lord Kinsale nodded at the polished wooden railing. The Irishman stood nearby, booted feet planted as wide as his shoulders, hands on his buckskin-clad lean hips. Even though the wild wind kept whipping locks of his dark brown hair into his eyes, he was watchful, standing guard as though he'd dive into the Channel itself to rescue little Lord Fitzwilliam if he went overboard. "And k-k-keep your eyes on the horizon," he added. "That always helps m-m-me whenever I feel seasick."

Lord Fitzwilliam nodded. "Yes, sir."

"You... you're not feelin' unwell, Mrs. Dav-Davenport?" asked the marquess, his voice as deep and rolling as the sea itself.

Mina summoned a smile. "I'm quite fine, my lord," she replied, fighting to be heard over the snatching wind and crashing waves. But that wasn't the worst of it; she was also highly conscious of the fact that her skirts were plastered against her hips and legs in a most unseemly manner. Not only that, but she feared her coal-scuttle bonnet might be torn from her head at any moment, and only heaven knew how much havoc the gale would wreak upon her perfectly coiled and precisely pinned hair if that happened. The very idea of not meeting the Parasol Academy's strict uniform protocols at all times bothered her no end.

As if the wind were listening to her thoughts, and had indeed decided to taunt her, it suddenly caught at her bonnet and whipped it from her head. It went bowling along the deck, Brutus in hot pursuit, like a hound after a rabbit.

"Brutus!" bellowed Lord Kinsale, turning away and striding after the dog. "Don't you even think about eatin' that hat!"

Now was Mina's chance to produce the medicine Lord Fitzwilliam needed. As she sank to her knees, she pulled a small, clear glass bottle from her pocket. "My lord," she murmured. "I have a special cordial here that will help ease the sick feeling in your stomach."

The boy pouted as he hugged Mr. Hopwell closer to his chest. "I don't like medicine, but if it will make this horrid feeling go away, I'll drink it."

"Very good, my lord." Mina reached into her pocket again and withdrew a silver spoon. "You don't need to drink a lot." She uncorked the bottle then somehow managed to pour out a generous spoonful of the pale honey-hued medicine without spilling any. "Just this much."

Lord Fitzwilliam obediently swallowed the liquid. Then he smiled. "It's delicious," he declared brightly. "Not dreadful at all. It tastes like all my favorite things. Gingerbread and chocolate and ice-cream and boiled sweets."

"Oh good. I'm glad." Mina repocketed the spoon and the medicine bottle. As she climbed to her feet, the marquess returned to her side, brandishing her bonnet.

"Here you are, Mrs. Dav-Davenport," he said with a smile that was almost bashful. "B-bonnet rescued from the elements and me p-p-pug. I suspect you'll be wantin' it to protect your fair complexion."

Mina curtsied, partly to show her thanks and partly to hide her blush. Good Lord, she'd turned into a giddy schoolgirl, all because a gentleman with wide shoulders was paying her a smidgeon of attention. For all she knew, he could be married with children. If that was the case, she shouldn't be admiring the man's physique at all. "Thank you, my lord. I'm most grateful. Not just for this"—she gestured at her errant bonnet before she slid it over her undoubtedly ruined coiffure—"but for your consideration and forbearance given the circumstances."

Lord Kinsale leaned against the railing and crossed his arms. The pose emphasized his bulging biceps and Mina fought to keep her eyes on the marquess's face. "I hope you'll f-f-forgive me for sayin' so, but I still don't quite understand how you c-came to be on me b-boat. How did you m-m-manage to evade me ship's crew?"

Oh dear. Mina wished the marquess would let this matter go because she really didn't have any explanation that he would believe. She hated telling lies, but she certainly couldn't tell him the truth. About anything.

She gave an inward sigh then marshalled an apologetic smile.

"As I said, we mistakenly boarded the wrong vessel and, well... I suppose your crew were so busy, they didn't regard us?" She recalled something that the marquess had said earlier about the *Kinsale Cloud*'s departure, so she added, "Night *was* falling. Perhaps they didn't see us in the fading light."

Oh, she was a terrible liar. Even to her own ears, her reasoning sounded implausible. But it was all she had.

Lord Kinsale frowned. "Hmmm. Perhaps... Although, how did you end up in me p-p-private quarters, of all places?"

Now Mina *did* feel a trifle ill. "My lord," she began, hoping her embarrassment and guilt weren't showing, "I know it was entirely inappropriate and indeed, positively rude of me to take refuge in your wardrobe with Christopher. It was, without a doubt, a gross invasion of your privacy, but"—she drew a breath—"as soon as we boarded, I knew I'd made a terrible mistake, but the ship had set sail. So Christopher and I took refuge below deck for some time until..." She blushed. "We went in search of the necessary, so to speak. And sustenance. But then, I'm afraid, we ended up in your cabin. I'm so dreadfully sorry. About everything."

Drat it. She was not a convincing liar, by any means. She tried again. "All I can do is apologize. You must believe me; it truly was an honest mistake that we boarded the *Kinsale Cloud*. A quirk of fate if you will." She reached into her pocket and her fingers closed about her coin purse. "I-I can pay you a fare, to cover the cost of ferrying Christopher and me to Bristol—"

Lord Kinsale waved a dismissive hand. "Good Lord. I don't want your m-m-money, Mrs. Dav-Davenport. And you ain't in any trouble for stow-stowin' away if that's what you're worried about."

"Thank you, my lord," said Mina, relief washing through her. "I'm most relieved you don't think ill of me. I'm most grateful."

"Think noth-nothin' of it, lass." The marquess's deep green

eyes narrowed a fraction as he studied her face. "Th-though, I cannot help b-but think that somethin' is wrong. Are you sure you and your young lad aren't in any other kind o' trouble? Perhaps I could help."

Good heavens, was the fact she was in the process of stealing a child away from his guardian written all over her face with indelible ink? "Ah, no. Nothing's wrong." Mina folded her hands together at her waist so she wouldn't fidget nervously. "I think perhaps that I'm simply weary from . . . from the journey."

"Are you hungry? Thirsty? I-I can get the galley to prepare somethin' for you and wee Christopher here."

Even though Mina had no appetite for anything at all, Lord Fitzwilliam might want something to eat or drink, especially now that his nausea had abated. And it might be a way to stop Lord Kinsale questioning her. It was hard to talk when one's mouth was full. "Yes, please," she said. "If it's not too much trouble."

"O' course not." Lord Kinsale swung away, striding a few yards across the deck to speak with a crew member.

As soon as the marquess's back was turned, Brutus gave a disgruntled growl. *Trouble? Ye're nothing but trouble if ye ask me,* he mumbled to himself. *Everythin' that comes out o' yer mouth is feckin' codswallop.*

Mina had suddenly had enough of the dog's insolent manner. Everyone was entitled to their own opinions of course—and she hadn't *meant* to eavesdrop—but the pug's mental musings were unusually loud. *Codswallop?* she repeated, arching an eyebrow as she stared back at the pug. *I won't stoop so low as to repeat the other profanity you used. I think you should mind your language around women and children, Mr. Brutus.*

The pug blinked at her. *Dog's teeth. Ye can hear me thoughts? How is such a thing possible?*

Yes, I can, replied Mina. *Quite clearly. And to answer your second question, some people learn to speak Latin, or Swahili, or*

Icelandic, or Gaelic. Well, I've learned the language of animals, especially dogs. Birds and horses too. Cats occasionally. I once had an exceedingly pleasant conversation with a pair of elephants at the London Zoo.

Sweet Jaysus. The pug cocked his head and eyed her with renewed interest. *Ye're an odd one then, ain't ye?*

No odder than you, rejoined Mina. *And I assure you, I'm not a threat to you or your master. So if you'd reduce the growling and snarling, I would appreciate it. I'd rather you didn't frighten young Christopher.*

Humph. The pug puffed out his chest. *I'll consider it. But it's not the boy I object to.* Brutus shot Mr. Hopwell a baleful glare. *It's his rabbit. There's somethin' not quite right about it.*

It's a toy! exclaimed Mina indignantly.

Brutus's already wrinkled brow furrowed even more. *It's still a feckin' rabbit. Why, if I get hold of it, I'll rip its ears off and chew off its tail and pull out its stuffin'—*

You'll do no such thing.

Are you always so bossy?

Are you always so rude? returned Mina in her best governess's voice.

At that moment, Lord Kinsale returned. He smiled at Lord Fitzwilliam. "How d-d-does pound cake sound with a side of ginger b-beer, Chris-Christopher? There might even be a few Bath b-b-buns."

The young viscount's face lit up. "Oh yes, please, sir. That sounds delightful."

Oh, indeed it did. Mina's mouth began to water. Cake, of any kind, was her Achilles heel. Out of habit though, she stuffed her craving down as she recalled her mother's oft-quoted adage: *A lady must always remember that a moment on the lips becomes forever on one's hips.*

But then, she reminded herself as she and Lord Fitzwilliam followed the marquess, it would be the height of bad manners if she *didn't* take afternoon tea with the Irish peer. She'd already decided that it might not be safe to teleport when aboard a ship. So really, it wasn't remiss of her to at least have a small serve of pound cake. Just a finger-width slice. Just to be sociable. After all, Lord Kinsale had gone to all the trouble of organizing it.

And really, what harm would it do if she enjoyed herself, even just for a little while?

Chapter 3

In Which Tea Is Taken with a Pugnacious Pug; Polite Wedges and Impolite Table Manners (Including Plate Licking) Are Featured; And a Spot of Icing Causes a Spot of Bother . . .

Phineas O'Connell, lately known as Lord Kinsale, would admit to feeling somewhat bemused, if not altogether at sea, as he led his ship's surprise stowaways below deck to the gentlemen's mess. His ever-faithful but perennially pugnacious pug, Brutus, brought up the rear.

How the hell did Mrs. Hermina Davenport and her son, Christopher, end up on the *Kinsale Cloud*? Phinn thought to himself as the lovely young woman and the lad took seats at the mahogany dining table—a table that had been set with polished silverware and delicate porcelain tea paraphernalia. Highly impractical on a ship navigating rough waters, to Phinn's way of thinking, but the ship's cook could not be reasoned with. Phinn was a marquess, and a marquess should only dine off fine bone-china plates, no matter how wild the sea state.

Phinn seriously doubted that his ship's stowaways had simply wandered on board "by mistake" just before the *Kinsale Cloud* departed Kinsale Harbor yesterday evening. Unless one of the ship's crew had helped Mrs. Davenport and her son to sneak on. Of course, he *could* ask his ship's captain to question the crew once they reached Bristol. He'd already had a quick word with the man when Phinn had first taken Mrs. Davenport and her son up on deck. But the captain had no idea how they'd managed to steal onto the ship undetected.

It was a mystery indeed.

The woman and the lad certainly couldn't have flown onto the ship like a pair of seagulls. Or sailed alongside in some other vessel and then scaled the sides of the *Kinsale Cloud* in the middle of the night like a pair of pirates or Viking marauders. On the other hand, if Mrs. Davenport were a *maighdean mhara*—some sort of selkie or mermaid...

Phinn smiled inwardly at the fantastical albeit appealing thought. While he might have a healthy dose of superstition running through his Irish veins—as a lad, his mam had regaled him with countless fireside tales about ghosts and púca and Éire's "wee folk," the *aos sí*; he even suspected his childhood home had been close to a *sidhe*, an underground faery fort— logic dictated that Mrs. Davenport *couldn't* have materialized on his ship just by waving a magic wand like a witch. Now *that* idea was utterly nonsensical.

Wasn't it?

But then, did it really matter how Mrs. Davenport and her child came to be on board? It wasn't as though they were dangerous or an inconvenience. If anything, they were a welcome diversion.

Especially Mrs. Davenport...

At that moment, the young woman broke into Phinn's thoughts. "Would you like me to pour, Lord Kinsale?" she asked as she gestured at the teapot and cut-crystal pitcher of ginger beer.

Phinn nodded, transfixed by the loveliness of the young woman's voice and her perfectly enunciated words. She was clearly a genteelly bred Englishwoman with impeccable manners. Why, she hadn't even commented on the fact that Brutus was also at the table, seated upon his customary cushion-stacked chair, his large black eyes fixed on the pound cake and currant-studded Bath buns.

"Aye. Th-Thank you," he managed after an awkward moment in which he fought to loosen his tongue. *Damn it.* Sometimes he really hated the fact that he could barely get a word out, that he stumbled over far too many sounds and syllables. Especially when he wanted to make a favorable impression and not come across as a giant lummox.

He was also all thumbs and largely clueless when it came to performing any refined sort of ritual such as dispensing tea. What with his big brutish paws and their scarred, misshapen knuckles, picking up a teacup without snapping the handle off was a feat in and of itself. And in what order did one do things? Did the tea go in the cup first? Or the milk? Did one have lemon *and* sugar or just one? Before Phinn had unexpectedly inherited his marquessate less than a year ago, he'd never even drunk tea. As a lowly Irish prizefighter, coffee and ale and sometimes whisky and rum had been his beverages of choice. And all he had been able to afford.

Mrs. Davenport had no issues at all when it came to serving afternoon tea.

Phinn knew he was staring as she removed her neat white gloves then adeptly prepared the tea. After depositing several spoonfuls of tea leaves into the china teapot, she added boiling water from the silver urn. And all without spilling a single drop (which was quite remarkable considering the constant rolling of the ship). While the leaves steeped, Mrs. Davenport poured a glass of ginger beer for young Christopher, served up slices of pound cake—Phinn noticed she only cut a very slender "polite" wedge for herself—then dispensed the tea with the poise of an accomplished gentlewoman. He requested milk with two sugar lumps, while she poured herself black tea and added only a sliver of lemon.

And, devil take him, didn't his tea taste damn fine?

When he said so, Mrs. Davenport blushed prettily. "Why thank you, my lord," she murmured before raising her eyes to his. "While I'd like to take the credit, I suspect it's your cook who's the one to thank for providing such a delicious blend. Darjeeling perhaps?"

Now Phinn felt as though his face was as hot as the silver urn. "I-I have n-no idea," he admitted. "I'm usually hap-happy to eat or drink whatever's p-p-put in front o' me. I'm a m-man o' simple tastes."

"Well, there's nothing wrong with that," said Mrs. Davenport with a shy smile. Then her gaze fell to her plate. "I must say, this pound cake is rather good too."

Christopher nodded enthusiastically. "It is indeed." This was followed by two short yips from Brutus.

Phinn laughed. "I know it's a tad un-unconventional. But would you m-mind cutting a p-piece o' c-c-cake for Brutus, Mrs. Dav-Davenport?"

The pug made a disgruntled sound in his throat, which sounded very much like, *It's about time.*

Mrs. Davenport smiled. "Of course I wouldn't mind," she said as she proceeded to deftly serve up another slice of pound cake. "I'm sure Mr. Brutus has delightful table manners."

Phinn snorted. "Well, if you don't mind a wee b-b-bit o' drool and snuffling and c-crumbs. Although he's sure to lick all those up."

Mrs. Davenport laughed as she slid the plated cake toward Brutus. "I'm sure he will. To be perfectly frank, I think we'd all like to indulge in a bit of plate licking if it was at all socially acceptable."

Now Phinn was laughing. He couldn't deny that he had licked a plate or two clean in his time. Brutus was certainly licking the porcelain with gusto. But holy hell, now Phinn was thinking about licking things just as Mrs. Davenport daintily licked away a tiny fleck of lemon icing from the corner of her mouth. The way the pink tip of her tongue slipped out then left behind a light sheen of moisture on her softly plump lower lip made a groan rise in Phinn's throat.

Feck . . . That wasn't the only thing that was rising. His temperature had shot into the realm of "blazing hot."

The problem was, try as he might, Phinn couldn't stop himself from staring at the young woman as she continued to nibble delicately at her cake and take measured sips of her tea. But then who *wouldn't* enjoy looking at Mrs. Davenport?

She was uncommonly pretty, with large hazel eyes fringed with long dark lashes, and her lovely face with its straight nose, generous mouth, and peaches-and-cream complexion, was framed by rich chestnut hair. When the wind had stolen her bonnet, he'd been gifted with the sight of it—it was thick and lustrous like the polished wood of the table before them. It was the sort of hair he'd love to let loose, and after it fell in glossy waves over her shoulders and down her back, he'd sift his fingers through it. Perhaps even bury his face in it to savor the fragrance of the soap she used. When she'd brushed past him to take her seat at the table, he was certain he'd caught the scent of flowers—roses, perhaps?

Get a grip, O'Connell, Phinn's mind growled as he took a gulp of his tea. *You have no business thinking of the poor woman like that. And in front of her child for Christ's sake! Aside from that, she's married!*

Or was she? Phinn glanced at her bare left hand. There *wasn't* a wedding band upon the woman's slender ring finger, so perhaps there wasn't a Mr. Davenport in the picture, so to speak. Indeed, from the moment Hermina Davenport had stepped from his wardrobe, Phinn had noted that the woman's attire— a navy wool gown with black trim here and there—was well cut and of good quality but rather somber and utilitarian rather than fashionable. Perhaps she was a widow and in mourning or half mourning?

Phinn's gaze returned to Mrs. Davenport's countenance. She

was young to be a widow, to be sure. She couldn't have been more than five-and-twenty; six-and-twenty at most. And the boy looked to be about six or seven. But then again, there were many young women in her position, particularly back home in Ireland after the Great Famine.

Phinn frowned as he helped himself to a Bath bun and tore off a large chunk—it was gone in three bites and he feared he might have worse table manners than Brutus. But when Phinn had lived a hand-to-mouth existence in Dublin before he'd become a prizefighter—when he hadn't known where his next meal was coming from, or if it would come at all—he'd developed the tendency to wolf down anything in front of him. And yes, to lick his plate clean. Old habits were hard to break.

If Mrs. Davenport thought him ill-mannered, she displayed no outward signs of disapproval—either by deed or facial expression. Although, there was something about her manner that suggested to Phinn that something wasn't quite right in *her* world. A wariness behind her eyes perhaps? A studied watchfulness? A tightness in her smile?

He couldn't quite put his finger on what was wrong precisely, but he sensed that Mrs. Davenport might be in trouble, despite her earlier denial. Something didn't feel right about her situation and her story. And of course, he had no idea how to broach such a topic in a sensitive way. He was not the most eloquent of men, even when he *did* manage to control his stammer. Which was rarely.

In any event, in a handful of hours they would reach Bristol and he would be farewelling the woman and her child. He'd never see them again.

For no fathomable reason, the idea made him feel disgruntled, like he had a pebble stuck in his shoe.

Once afternoon tea was over, they all returned to the poop deck and were greeted with the sight of rolling green hills on either side of the *Kinsale Cloud*. It wouldn't be long before they reached the mouth of the River Avon. The sea had calmed a fraction and young Christopher Davenport seemed to have completely recovered from his bout of seasickness. Indeed, he appeared to be in fine spirits; standing a few feet away, his purple rabbit clutched in his arms as he was laughing at Brutus's antics. A trio of seagulls had decided to swoop down and chase the pug, but Brutus didn't seem to mind. In fact, he was having the time of his life, racing about the deck, yapping and jumping and generally creating a rumpus.

Mrs. Davenport was laughing too, her expression alight with mirth. In the afternoon sunlight, her hazel eyes glowed like amber-hued honey that was flecked with glints of green and gold. Phinn could get lost in those eyes if he let himself. Then and there, he decided that Mr. Davenport—whoever he was—had been one lucky bastard to have wed someone as lovely as this woman.

His attention wandered back to Mrs. Davenport's son. "You've a f-f-fine lad there," he observed. Then some devil took hold of his tongue and he added, "You and your hus-husband must be p-p-proud o' him."

Phinn would have liked to have claimed that he was only concerned about Mrs. Davenport's situation—that he wasn't actually fishing for information about her marital status—but that was a total lie. He was wildly curious about this woman. And really, he shouldn't have been at all surprised when Mrs. Davenport's smile immediately faded and she turned her head in such a way that her bonnet shielded her countenance. It was like the sun had gone behind a cloud and Phinn could have kicked himself for dimming her light.

"Yes, very proud," she murmured, her gaze trained steadfastly on the horizon. "He's a sweet boy." Her gloved hands gripped the railing tightly. "I'm sorry if I seem rude, my lord, but the subject of Christopher's father is one that I'd rather not discuss. If that's all right with you."

"O' course," said Phinn.

They lapsed into an uncomfortable silence for a few minutes—Phinn wasn't sure at all how to repair the damage he'd done—but at length, Mrs. Davenport ventured in a tone laced with regret, "I've gone and made things all awkward, haven't I?" Turning to face him, she continued, "The truth is, my lord, Christopher's father passed away only a year ago and if Christopher overhears—"

"No, that's-that's quite all right, Mrs. Davenport," said Phinn as guilt pinched inside his chest. He hated the idea that he'd inadvertently caused the young woman any sort of emotional distress because he'd been nosy. He especially didn't want to upset her son. "I'm sorry for your loss. And it was my fault en-entirely for bringin' up the subject. It-it was tactless of m-m-me. And o' course, it's none o' me b-business."

"Thank you for your understanding, my lord." Mrs. Davenport offered him a shy smile. "And for your generosity of spirit. Given that Christopher and I are interlopers, I'm most grateful that you've been nothing but kindness itself. You are a true nobleman."

Phinn inclined his head at the compliment. He didn't think anyone had ever said anything quite so *nice* to him before. Truth to tell, his tongue had suddenly become hopelessly tied in knots and he couldn't, for the moment, loosen it. He had the horrid feeling that he might be blushing again—his face was unaccountably hot. *Say thank you, O'Connell, you great clodpole*, his inner voice urged. *You can at least do that.*

But as his mouth at last began to cooperate, the *Kinsale Cloud* suddenly hit a patch of rough swell. The ship lurched and Mrs. Davenport stumbled toward Phinn, straight into his arms. As they collided, she emitted a soft sound like "ooft" and her delicious floral scent immediately drifted around him. He was acutely aware of the press of her soft, generous curves against his body . . .

It was the most exquisite of tortures. "I've got you, Mrs. Daven... Mrs. Davenport," he murmured gruffly as he strove to hold her steady, his hands about her waist. For one moment, he thought he might lose his balance too until he braced himself against the taffrail. Glancing past Mrs. Davenport, he could see that young Christopher was safe enough—the boy had managed to catch hold of the railing by the stairs leading to the quarterdeck—and he told her so.

"Oh... Oh good," Mrs. Davenport said. To Phinn's ears, she sounded a trifle breathless. But then, he was feeling that way too. Looking over her shoulder, she checked on her son before turning back to meet his gaze. "Thank you for catching me, my lord."

"'Twas not... 'twas not a b-b-bother," he managed. Although that was a lie. He was bothered all over, from the top of his head, down to his toes and everywhere else in between. His throat felt tight, his pulse was racing, strange tingles of awareness were rushing across his skin. What's more, he couldn't seem to relinquish his hold on the woman. Or stop himself from studying her pretty face and the way a rose-hued blush had flooded her cheeks. Or the way her perfect white teeth were pressing into the soft plump pillow of her lower lip.

Her sweet, sweet lips... Phinn swallowed and inwardly cursed himself for even thinking about kissing the woman. Jaysus, she might be a widow, she might be gorgeous, but that didn't give him the right to harbor lustful thoughts about her. Why, only a minute ago she'd been praising him for being "noble." Then he frowned as he noticed a small white smear at the corner of her mouth. "You-you have a wee bit o' somethin'..." He gestured at the spot and Mrs. Davenport's blush deepened. "I-icing perhaps?"

"Oh," she murmured, and one of her hands disappeared into the pocket of her voluminous skirts. "How embarrassing.

Thank you for mentioning it." She withdrew a fine lawn handkerchief and dabbed at the mark. Then she smiled. "Better?"

"Aye," said Phinn. "All b-b-better." He made himself let go of Mrs. Davenport's waist and took a step back. At that moment, Brutus caught his eye. The dog was running about the poop deck, barking excitedly as he chased something that the wind had caught. Something small and off-white and rectangular—a scrap of old paper perhaps. Just as the paper fluttered toward them, Brutus leapt up and caught it in his teeth.

"I'd best check on Christopher," said Mrs. Davenport, reclaiming Phinn's attention. "It might be safer if we go below again." She gave a little laugh. "I'd hate to think that one of us might go overboard just as we're nearing Bristol."

"Aye. O' course," said Phinn. "W-w-would you like me to escort you b-back to the gentlemen's mess? You're we-welcome to order another pot o' tea from the g-galley."

But Mrs. Davenport shook her head. "Thank you, but I'm sure we'll be fine, my lord. I know the way."

She bobbed a curtsy then crossed to Christopher, who took her hand. And then they disappeared down the stairs to the quarterdeck where the entry to the gentlemen's mess lay.

Phinn sighed heavily and scrubbed a hand down his face. He couldn't blame Mrs. Davenport for wanting to distance herself from him. Good God, he'd been flirting with the idea of kissing a woman he barely knew! No doubt she would have detected the intent look in his eyes when his gaze had fallen to her mouth. He was not very good at masking his emotions.

He tended to wear his heart on his sleeve. Not that his heart was in danger by any means when it came to the fairer sex. Surviving in the backstreets of Dublin, becoming "Cutthroat O'Connell," a much-vaunted prizefighter, he'd learned that he couldn't afford to be sentimental. His capacity to care deeply for anyone, apart from his dearly departed family—his da, ma, and sister, who'd perished during the Great Famine—had been crushed to dust a long time ago.

No, I'm merely in the grip of a wave of brutish lust, Phinn told himself as he watched Brutus prancing about the deck with his prize "scrap" of paper in his mouth. It had been a long time since Phinn had been with a woman, and it seemed the hint of a soft smile or the slightest trace of a floral scent could stir the base male in him. He really needed to exercise more self-control. Think and act like the gentleman he was now supposed to be, not a randy dog.

Brutus came trotting over and straightaway, Phinn saw that the pug was carrying something that looked very much like a business or calling card. The edges glinted, as though they'd been dipped in gold. "What have you g-got there, me feisty wee friend?" he asked, bending down to the dog's level and putting out his hand. Brutus immediately dropped the slightly bent and chewed card into his waiting palm, and that's when Phinn noticed it was covered in fine black script. In fact, it *was* a business card.

How odd. As Phinn straightened, he read the print on the front.

The Parasol Academy
Bespoke Nanny and Governess Services
51 Sloane Square, Chelsea

Turning the card over, he read:

Come rain, hail, or shine, everything will be perfectly fine!
Whether your offspring are big or small, expert staff will be at your beck and call.
For all your child rearing and youth educational needs, in London or farther afield, contact the Headmistress of the Parasol Academy for Exceptional Nannies and Governesses, Mrs. F. Temple, for an obligation-free consultation.
(Confidentiality and the utmost discretion guaranteed.)

Phinn rubbed his jaw. *The Parasol Academy?*

Had Mrs. Davenport dropped the card when she'd pulled out her kerchief? Was she, in fact, a nanny or governess? Or was she in need of one? If Phinn hadn't been intrigued by his beguiling stowaway before, he certainly was now.

He descended to the gentlemen's mess, Brutus at his heels, where he found Mrs. Davenport and Christopher seated at the table. The boy was nibbling on a Bath bun while his mother was enjoying a cup of tea.

"My lord?" Mrs. Davenport began to climb to her feet to curtsy, but Phinn waved her back down.

"There's no need for-for any o' that," he said. Then he held out the slightly mangled business card. "I might be wrong, but I think this might have fallen out o' your pocket, Mrs. Dav-Davenport. I'm sorry it's a b-bit worse for w-w-wear. Brutus was play-playing with it."

"Oh." She took it from him and a blush crept across her face. "Yes. I must have dropped it. Thank you for returning it."

Phinn watched her as she dropped her gaze and pushed the card into her pocket. "Are-are you after a n-n-nanny or governess for young Christopher?"

"Oh, I already have one," said Christopher, smiling up at his mother. "You're *my* governess, aren't you, Mis—"

"Yes, I'm a governess, my lord," said Mrs. Davenport, smoothing her son's windblown blond ringlets with a gentle hand. "Moreover, I'm a graduate of the Parasol Academy. But looking after Christopher is my main priority at present." She cast Phinn a smile that didn't quite meet her eyes. "I'm . . . I'm in between posts." Then she tilted her head, her expression curious. "Do you need a nanny or governess, my lord? I've been presuming you're a bachelor, but perhaps not? Is there a Lady Kinsale?"

Brutus gave three short barks as though he were chuckling at the very notion of his master being a married man.

Phinn cocked a brow. "Aye, I'm a ba-bachelor. And no, I don't need a nanny or g-g-governess. But if I ever did, I'd be sure to call on the Pa-Parasol Academy first."

This time when Mrs. Davenport smiled, her hazel eyes were bright with amusement. "Well, maybe you might need one in a few years' time."

Phinn shrugged and an answering smile tugged at the corner of his mouth. "Perhaps. I'm-I'm only eight-and-twenty so there's no . . . no rush." He imagined he might wed one day . . . if he found the right woman. Someone who would accept him for who he was. Who wasn't bothered by all his imperfections. Someone who really cared about him and not just his title and wealth.

Someone who could put up with his irascible pet pug who appeared to have an *unquenchable* appetite for cake. The dog was back on his chair, looking expectantly at the widow.

Phinn's gaze settled on Mrs. Davenport too. She hadn't once looked at him askance because he stuttered. And that was a rare thing indeed. He suddenly wished the woman would confide in him about her situation.

He pushed his hands into the pockets of his coat and rocked back on his heels. "I know you d-don't know me from a bar o' soap, Mrs. Dav-Davenport, b-but if you need any sort o' assistance, I'll do me b-best to offer a helping hand. Like, if you need a way to get back to this Parasol Academy in London, you only n-n-need to ask."

But Mrs. Davenport shook her head. "Thank you, Lord Kinsale. But you really have done more than enough already. I'm just grateful that you've kindly agreed to ferry us the rest of the way to Bristol."

Phinn glanced out the porthole. "It-it looks like we're about to enter the m-m-mouth of the Avon, so we'll be d-d-docking in about an hour."

Mrs. Davenport's gaze wandered to the porthole too. "No doubt you'll be glad to see the back of us," she said quietly.

But Phinn wasn't so sure about that. There was something about this woman, beyond her fine whisky-hued eyes, rich chestnut hair, and delectable figure, that intrigued him. She was a bright, beckoning flame while he was but a blundering moth, captivated by her light and warmth.

Yes, he would be more than a little disappointed to be bidding Mrs. Davenport goodbye. Although, he rather suspected that the young widow—a "bespoke" governess, no less—might be relieved to see the back of *him*. No doubt she was tired of his far-too-many curious questions.

Wherever she went after the *Kinsale Cloud* docked in Bristol, Phinn wished her and her son well.

CHAPTER 4

Concerning Unpermitted Swooning, a Wardrobe, and Potpourri; Floral Explosions; And a Candid Discussion about Boiled Beef and Cabbage, and Pettifogging Shrews...

As Mina trooped down the *Kinsale Cloud's* gangplank with Lord Fitzwilliam—his small hand grasped firmly in hers so there was no chance of him slipping into the River Avon—she couldn't help but breathe a momentous sigh of relief. Not just because she'd reached terra firma safely. She was also relieved that she'd never see Lord Kinsale again.

The Irish marquess was too charming for words and had upset her equilibrium in a most disconcerting way. Heavens, with his lilting Irish accent and emerald-green eyes and far too attractive smile, he'd set her to the blush far too many times. And then of course, there were his mountainous shoulders and thighs like tree trunks, and strong hands that could practically span her waist (and she certainly didn't have the smallest waist in the whole world... even when it was ruthlessly cinched in by her boned Parasol Academy corset). He'd practically made her swoon, and swooning, according to the *Parasol Academy Handbook*, was not permitted at all, *especially* when one was in uniform.

That wasn't the only reason Mina was glad to say goodbye

to Lord Kinsale. While he was undoubtedly kind and possessed a magnanimous nature, his not-so-subtle questions about her "situation" had made her feel decidedly uncomfortable. She hated lying. Not only was it proscribed by the Parasol Academy (unless of course you found yourself in a life-and-death situation and you needed to use "whatever means necessary" to ensure the safety of your charge), but pretending that Christopher was her child and that she was a widow felt *horribly* deceitful. But to protect Christopher, and herself for that matter, she'd had to employ subterfuge. "A necessary evil" to prevent Sir Bedivere finding his ward and taking him on a perilous voyage to a frozen wasteland. An undertaking that was sure to end in disaster.

As Mina began to thread her way through the traffic on the bustling dock, she glanced back at the ship, and Lord Kinsale was still watching her. A commanding figure, one couldn't fail to notice the man. The marquess raised a hand and waved and she would have done the same if she hadn't been juggling a valise and her umbrella, all whilst holding onto Christopher's hand. The most she could do was incline her head before she turned and led her charge away from the docks, hoping they'd soon be swallowed up by the crowd.

It was unfortunate indeed that a Parasol Academy business card had fallen from her pocket. Mina still wasn't quite sure how *that* had happened. Even though the marquess now knew she was a Parasol Academy governess, hopefully it wouldn't matter because the man was a bachelor and didn't require the services of someone like her. *Yes, he'll soon forget me*, thought Mina. A mere governess. A veritable nobody.

But he wanted to kiss you, Mina Davenport, whispered a tiny voice inside her head. *You* know *it*.

Mina's heart performed a strange little flip-flop at the memory. A man like Lord Kinsale could have any woman he wanted, yet he'd been tempted by *her*. The terrible thing was,

Mina had been tempted to ignore all dictates of decorum and professionalism and kiss the Irishman back, despite the fact her charge was nearby and they were in full view of the *Kinsale Cloud*'s crew!

She understood the reason why, though. She was six-and-twenty and fast approaching spinsterhood and she'd never, ever been kissed before. Not properly. She didn't count the quick peck the new vicar of Ablington had bestowed when he'd caught her under the mistletoe at the vicarage last Christmas Eve. Her pulse certainly hadn't fluttered or raced or done anything at all other than plod along like it usually did when his lips had fleetingly touched hers. Which hadn't been the case when Lord Kinsale had looked at her mouth with keen, if not altogether smoldering interest in his deep green eyes. Her pulse had bolted clean away like a runaway horse. Even now, she swore she could still feel the firm press of the marquess's large hands about her waist when he'd caught her to stop her from falling.

Mina sighed. Fate had been cruel indeed to deposit her on the *Kinsale Cloud*, because now the charming Lord Kinsale would inhabit her dreams. *He* might not give her another thought, but she was going to have a very difficult time forgetting the marquess.

"Where are we going?" Christopher asked as she steered him away from the waterfront and in the direction of the towering Bristol Cathedral. Its spire rose majestically above all the other buildings lining the docks.

"Remember I told you about my childhood home? Rose Cottage?" said Mina. "We're going there."

"Oh." The boy pouted and clutched his velvet rabbit, Mr. Hopwell, to his chest. "Will we travel on the train? Or in a carriage?"

Oh dear. No doubt Christopher hadn't liked the experience of being teleported. Mina couldn't say that she blamed him. It was *rather* discombobulating. Disregarding her first-ever teleportation misfire, it was the fastest way she knew to get from one point to another.

"Would it be all right if we hopped in a magic cupboard again?" she asked as they paused on the edge of a busy street, waiting for a break in the traffic. Not far from the cathedral, there was a police box that she could use to teleport. Because the Parasol Academy had been granted a Royal Charter by Queen Victoria, an agreement had been established with the Metropolitan Police that Academy graduates could make use of police boxes "in the line of duty."

"I promise we'll end up at my house, not on a ship," she added. "And it will only take a minute, not several hours to get there. It means we'll arrive in plenty of time for dinner."

Christopher sighed. "All right. Although all the whooshing and spinning made me feel a bit ill."

Mina squeezed the boy's hand for reassurance. "If that should happen again, I promise you that you can have a bit more of the seasickness medicine you liked so much."

Once she and Christopher were safely inside the police box—she was quietly relieved that there were no bobbies about because she really couldn't risk being questioned—she performed the teleportation spell that would spirit them away to Rose Cottage.

Like last time, both she and Christopher were swept up in a maelstrom of bright light that spun them around and around like leaves caught in the wind. And just like last time, they found themselves in a small shadowy space—the interior of another wardrobe. But this time, Mina and her charge weren't surrounded by men's clothes and the scent of woodsy cologne. No, the wardrobe was practically empty save for several old gowns that Mina immediately recognized as her own.

She released a huge sigh of relief. "We've arrived safely," she whispered to Christopher. "You can open your eyes now."

"Oh, good," said the boy. "I liked Lord Kinsale. But I wasn't so sure about his dog. He kept looking at Mr. Hopwell like he wanted to eat him."

Mina laughed softly to herself. The young viscount wasn't wrong at all.

She opened the door to her wardrobe and ushered Christopher into her old bedroom. The boy wrinkled his nose. "Is this where I'll be staying?" he asked. "It's very pink and flowery."

Mina was inclined to agree. Indeed, it looked like a rose garden had exploded in her bedchamber. It had been her mother's choice to decorate the room with rose-patterned wallpaper, curtains featuring pink and red rosebuds, and an Aubusson rug covered in a cabbage rose design. And then of course, there was Mina's bed. The rose-pink brocade counterpane was embroidered with yet more roses, as were the silk cushions piled against the pillows.

"I shall have the guest bedroom made up for you," she said, putting Christopher's valise down by the door. She then deposited her Parasol Academy umbrella on the rosewood dressing table; the removal of her gloves and bonnet swiftly followed. "But first, I must take you downstairs to introduce you to my mama, Mrs. Davenport, and my sister, Miss Dorothea. I'll ask them to call you Master Christopher rather than Lord Fitzwilliam if that's still all right with you. Just in case your guardian looks for you here. I don't think he will, but it's best to exercise caution. Just to be on the safe side."

Christopher nodded, then frowned. "What should I call you now? Mrs. or Miss Davenport? Because I've always called you miss. But Lord Kinsale called you missus."

"I know it's confusing," said Mina. "But Lord Kinsale thought I was your mama rather than your governess. So he called me Mrs. Davenport as he believed I was married."

Christopher fiddled with one of Mr. Hopwell's long floppy ears. "But you're neither of those things. You're not my mama. *Nor* are you married."

Mina smiled. "No, I'm not. So you can keep calling me

Miss Davenport. There is one thing though, that must remain our special secret. We mustn't talk about the magic cupboard, just like we must not mention Sir Bedivere. Or that you are Viscount Fitzwilliam. In fact, we might need to give you a different last name for a little while." Mina gestured at Christopher's toy rabbit. "What about Hopwell? Christopher Hopwell."

The boy smiled and nodded. "Ooh, I like that. And I understand. I don't want to go to the North Pole, so I won't say anything about the cupboard or horrid Sir Bedivere or who I really am." Then he crossed to the window and looked down to the rose garden below. "How long will I have to live here, Miss Davenport? It's nice but it's not like Highwood Hall or Fitzwilliam House." He turned back to look at Mina, his gaze melancholy. "I miss my room and my things."

The young viscount asked a very good question. If Sir Bedivere didn't perish on his Arctic expedition, if he did make it back to England in one piece, Mina would have a rather large dilemma on her hands. If Lady Grenfell had been right and the baronet was under the influence of an ensorcelled ring—a ring that made him act in such a way that put his ward in danger—Mina's grave concerns for Lord Fitzwilliam's safety would not be resolved by any means. But she couldn't keep the viscount here at Rose Cottage forever.

At some point she *would* have to enlist the support of others. Her best friend, Emmeline, a former Parasol Academy nanny, was now a duchess—she'd wed her employer, the very clever and very wealthy Duke of St Lawrence—and she would no doubt provide Mina with help and advice. But Emmeline had only married recently and Mina had just heard she was expecting. Of course, Mina was over-the-moon thrilled for her friend and her husband, but that meant that Mina was also reluctant to drag Emmeline into anything that would definitely be deemed illegal.

She could also present her case to the Parasol Academy's

headmistress. The problem was, Mina really wasn't sure how Mrs. Temple would react to the news that she'd taken it upon herself to remove Lord Fitzwilliam from Sir Bedivere's guardianship. And all because Lady Grenfell had had a bad dream.

Mrs. Temple was once a nanny in the Royal Nursery, so she might have some influence with Queen Victoria if things went awry for Mina. If the Queen could be convinced that the young viscount was in danger and decided to champion his cause, if Her Majesty could convince the Court of Chancery to appoint another guardian... But those were a lot of ifs. Mrs. Temple could very well take against Mina for breaking the Academy's sacrosanct rules *and* the law. She might see it as her duty to protect the Academy and *not* Mina. If that were the case, Mina would lose her licence to practice. She could be arrested and hauled off to prison and incarcerated to the end of her days.

At this juncture, it was too dangerous a prospect to reveal everything to Mrs. Temple. As awful as it sounded, part of Mina prayed that fate or Mother Nature might deal with the threat of Sir Bedivere before she had to. As far as Mina knew, no one had ever navigated the Northwest Passage and lived to tell the tale.

Of course, Mina couldn't share any of this with Lord Fitzwilliam. *No, Master Christopher Hopwell*, she reminded herself. Leaning down, she caught the boy's solemn blue gaze and gave him the best explanation she could. "Until I can make other arrangements, I'm afraid Rose Cottage will have to be your home for the time being. I'm not sure how long it will take me to find another safe place for you to stay, but I will try. I'm sorry, I don't have a better answer. But that's the truth. Now"—Mina straightened and held out her hand—"let's go and meet my mama and sister and then we can sort out your new bedroom. I'm sure we can dig out a blue quilt and matching sheets from the linen press. Something that's not quite so pink. But I can't promise there won't be flowers." Last time

Mina had checked, the guest room was covered in fabric patterned with blue-hued pansies.

Christopher smiled. "Blue is my favorite color, so that would be most satisfactory." Then he whispered in his stuffed rabbit's ear. "It's all right, Mr. Hopwell. You know I really love mauve too."

Mina led Christopher down the stairs—they were narrow and every step creaked, so Mina was worried her mother and sister might hear them. But there wasn't much she could do about that. She certainly wasn't going to tell her family that courtesy of the Fae's leyline magic, she'd teleported into her wardrobe. As far as her mama and sister knew, Mina was just an ordinary sort of governess. Indeed, if her mother ever found out that her eldest daughter could perform magic, she'd surely expire on the spot.

It was no surprise to Mina that as soon as she and Christopher entered the drawing room, her mother was all aghast. Casting aside her embroidery, Edwina Davenport leapt out of her "peony" chintz upholstered armchair. "Hermina! What are you doing here?" she cried, hands flapping about and eyebrows climbing toward the lace fringe of her mob cap. "I didn't hear you arrive. How did you get here?" Then her copper-brown eyes darted to Christopher. "And who is this?"

"Goodness, so many questions all at once, Mama," said Mina with a nervous laugh. Her mother was a curious mixture of excess and parsimony, flightiness and firmness. She had decided opinions and there was no naysaying her once she'd made her mind up about something. For Mina's plan to work, she'd somehow have to win her mother over. But she did have a secret weapon up her sleeve. (Well, really in her Parasol Academy pocket, but she wouldn't employ it until the right moment.)

"It's lovely to see you, Mina," said Dorothea—or Thea, as Mina called her—rising to her feet as well. She was three years younger than Mina and possessed a sweet, caring disposition. Two years ago, when Mina had commenced her studies at the Parasol Academy, Thea had begun teaching at the local parish school that their late father had established. She enjoyed the work and it also afforded her the opportunity to escape the frighteningly floral confines of Rose Cottage.

Thea's soft brown eyes glowed with warmth as she smiled at Christopher. "I see you've brought a visitor."

Her mother touched the cameo brooch at her throat. "But how *did* you get here?" she demanded.

"The train, of course," lied Mina. "And you didn't hear us arrive because we came through the kitchen." She summoned a smile as she laid a hand upon Christopher's shoulder to reassure the boy in the face of Edwina Davenport's persnickety manner. "What does it matter anyway? You're always telling me in your letters how much you miss me."

Her mother gave a haughty sniff. "You still haven't introduced the boy?" she said, aiming a pointed look at Christopher. "I thought you were between posts."

"I am," said Mina. "And this is Master Christopher Hopwell. I'm looking after him as a favor for a friend. Just for a little while."

Her mother gave a humph this time. "So what you really mean is that you want your poor put-upon mother and sister to look after the boy."

Mina's smile tightened. "His name is Christopher. And it will only be for a few weeks. Until I can make other arrangements for him. Possibly with my friend Emmeline, the Duchess of St Lawrence, when she returns to London. I also need to return to the Parasol Academy to secure a new position."

Edwina Davenport did not look amused to be reminded that Mina's friend had been elevated to the heights of a duchessdom whereas Mina was presently unemployed. "Because you were sacked," her mother said bluntly.

Mina stiffened and squared her shoulders. "My last employer decided that he wished to employ a tutor for his ward, rather than a governess. There wasn't anything wrong with the way I discharged my duties."

Her mother leveled a considering stare at Christopher. "I take it he is well-behaved and says his prayers every night before bed and knows his catechism by heart."

"He does," said Mina. "He can even read and write and play the pianoforte. And *he* has a name too. Christopher."

Edwina Davenport's mouth flattened. "Sarcasm does not become you, my child."

Thea, perhaps sensing that her mother and sister were about to butt heads like two disgruntled nanny goats, bravely stepped into the fray. "Well, welcome to Rose Cottage, Christopher," she said brightly. "You may call me Miss Dorothea when we're at home and Miss Davenport when we're at school." Her gaze transferred to Mina. "I take it you would like Christopher to attend the parish school during the day to continue his education?"

Christopher bounced on his toes. "Oooh, I would like that." He looked up at Mina with beseeching eyes. "I should like to go to school and meet other children. May I go, Miss Davenport?"

Mina's heart clenched with sympathy. She'd sensed for some time that the young viscount might be lonely. While it would be safer for Christopher to stay largely hidden within the environs of Rose Cottage, she didn't have the heart to say no. She smiled at the boy. "Of course." To her sister she said, "Thank you, Thea."

Edwina Davenport gave a huff. "It sounds like it's all decided then," she remarked. Then her gaze narrowed. "Let it not be said that I have an uncharitable nature, but who's going to pay for Master Christopher's board? You know I'm not made of money, Hermina. Not since your father, God rest his soul, passed away."

Mina *knew* that her mother would bring up the subject of board money. When Mina's father had died five years ago, the family had been obliged to move from the Ablington Vicarage into the much smaller Rose Cottage. Edwina Davenport had a small widow's jointure. But while she was quite parsimonious about many things—particularly when it came to meals (and most definitely when it came to dessert or anything sweet)—her penchant for decorating her new home in wildly extravagant floral-themed décor had cost her a pretty penny. And Mina and Thea felt obliged to contribute to the cottage's "upkeep" when they could afford to... if only to keep their mother in an agreeable mood. Because when Edwina Davenport was not agreeable—Mina inwardly shuddered—she could be quite the shrew.

Mina knew it was time to deploy her secret weapon. "Have no fear on that score, Mama," she said, reaching into her pocket for her coin purse. "One of Christopher's relatives entrusted me with a small bequest, so I can afford to pay his board." It wasn't a lie—well, except for the bit about the bequest being "small" because it was actually rather substantial. At least to Mina. Not long before she'd passed away, Lady Grenfell had given Mina a diamond-encrusted brooch to sell so she would have sufficient funds to take care of the dowager countess's godson. "How does three shillings per week sound?"

Her mother's brown eyes gleamed like copper pennies. "Oh, that should do nicely," she said with a sugared smile. She beckoned to Christopher. "Come, dear child. I do believe dinner is almost ready. We're having corned beef, white sauce, boiled potatoes, and cabbage."

After everyone was seated at the oak dining table, and Edwina began to supervise the cook and the housemaid—she was very particular about how dishes were set out and how the beef should be sliced and served—Christopher whispered to Mina, "I'm sorry, Miss Davenport, but I'm not very fond of corned beef or cabbage."

Mina sympathized because she wasn't fond of them either. In fact, she detested them. "Eat a little if you can," she said in a low voice, "and when you're all settled in your room, I'll see if I can procure a boiled egg and toast soldiers from the kitchen. Would that do?"

Christopher nodded. "It would." Then his expression slid into resigned territory. "I know I shouldn't complain. I'm truly grateful that I'm here at Rose Cottage and that I won't meet any polar bears or walruses."

At that moment, Mina's mother snapped at the maid, Lizzie, for dropping a sliver of boiled cabbage on the hitherto pristine tablecloth of pressed white linen. Mina couldn't suppress a wry smile as she smoothed her napkin over her skirts. While it was true that there was a decided absence of fearsome Arctic beasts in Ablington, she couldn't say the same when it came to pettifogging shrews on the odd occasion.

She hoped that things would work out here for young Lord Fitzwilliam. If they didn't, Mina would certainly be paying a visit to the newly wedded Duchess of St Lawrence sooner rather than later.

CHAPTER 5

Concerning Blooming Bruises; Belgravian and Backstreet Boxing; a Lion and Lamb, Sewer Rats, and Alley Cats; And the Luck o' the Irish (or a Street Urchin . . .)

"Is it noticeable?" asked Marcus, Viscount Hartwell, gingerly pressing his gloved fingertips against his jaw where a dark purple bruise was blooming. "I look like I've been brawling, don't I?"

Phinn grimaced in sympathy. The light spilling from the gas lamp above the doorway of the gentlemen's club, Boodle's, was enough for him to discern that the facer he'd landed on Lord Hartwell during their friendly bout of boxing at the Belgravia Boxing Saloon an hour ago had been harder than he'd intended. "Aye. I'm-I'm afraid it sticks out like a sore thumb," he said ruefully. "There's no hi-hidin' it. My apol-apologies."

The viscount clapped him on the back. "No hard feelings, old chap. It's entirely my fault. My hubris led me to believe I stood a fighting chance against Cutthroat O'Connell. Of course, I did not. I deserved the right royal trouncing that I received. I am a mere mortal whereas you are a prizefighting god."

Phinn laughed. "I'll teach you to d-duck and weave fa-fa-faster. All the same, I should o' held back a wee b-b-bit." Lord Hartwell was one of the few British peers of his acquaintance who made Phinn feel welcome and not like an outsider. Who didn't openly look down his nose at the newly minted Marquess of Kinsale or offer him a smile that bordered on a supercilious sneer. Or whisper behind his back that they had no idea how a misfit like him had inherited a title and fortune.

Peers of the realm shouldn't have Irish accents or hail from the squalid backstreets of Dublin. Nor should they have the physique of a laborer, or have scarred knuckles, a broken nose, or a stammer. Phinn wasn't just a fish out of water. He was a whale out of water. He would never walk into a gentlemen's club like Boodle's or White's unless he was in Lord Hartwell's company. He knew the viscount had his back.

Marcus led the way into the club. Once they'd divested their coats, hats, and gloves into the care of a pretentious doorman—even the servant snootily regarded Phinn's greatcoat as though it was an outlandish piece of apparel because of its sheer volume and weight—Marcus suggested that they repair to the library for a brandy or two. "It's darker in there than the gaming room," he said sotto voce as he lifted a hand in greeting to a silver-haired gentleman who was exiting the club. "And I don't know about you, but I'm not quite ready for dinner yet."

Phinn was actually quite famished after his extended exercise session at the boxing saloon. But he was used to ignoring a rumbling belly. The brandy would suffice.

They found a pair of green leather wing chairs in a quiet corner not far from a black marble fireplace where a fire burnt brightly. Even though it was still summer, the evenings were getting cooler—the nip of autumn was in the air. After Marcus ordered brandies for them both—even summoning the words to place a simple order could be an ordeal for Phinn and he appreciated that his friend knew this—they fell to talking about Phinn's recent trip to Kinsale to inspect his estate and new home, Kinsale Castle.

Phinn still couldn't quite believe that he'd inherited a title let alone a whole feckin' castle, but he had. An uncle on his late da's side of the family had died without a direct heir, and apparently Phinn had been the next in line.

He examined the gold and emerald signet ring on his little finger that bore the crest of the O'Connell clan—a stag surrounded by three shamrocks—and his mouth curved in a wry smile. The heir presumptive had been a nobody from the slums of Dublin. But he wasn't about to look a gift horse in the mouth. He'd take what he'd been given and he'd make the most of it. Not just for himself, but for the people on his land. And beyond.

"I know you want to make a difference in the lives of your tenants," said Marcus after Phinn had lamented the fact that most Irish tenant farmers had barely any rights. "Indeed, it goes without saying that I'll lend my support to any new bills you try to introduce in that regard. But I fear you'll face stiff opposition."

Phinn agreed. "I-I'm well aware that it will be an uphill b-b-battle to change the status quo. One thing I've learned firsthand is that the rulin' classes do n-not readily like to give up p-p-power and their riches in f-favor of supportin' the work-workin' poor."

"That's very true," said Marcus, swirling his brandy around in his glass. "But I trust that there are some peers who want to make amends for what happened during the Great Famine. Your people have suffered greatly and I, for one, think it's unconscionable."

"Aye." A hard note had seeped into Phinn's voice. His bone-deep resentment, his roiling anger for what the English had put Ireland through for six long, hellish years, could not easily be set aside. And he wouldn't set it aside. *Could* not. There'd been too much cruelty and neglect. Too many unnecessary deaths, and Phinn had witnessed it all firsthand. His fingers tightened around his brandy glass until his scarred knuckles turned white. He'd lost his mother and sister because of it. His da, too.

And these men—Phinn cast his fulminating gaze around the room—these *English* men who were born with silver spoons in their mouths and were cloaked in privilege, some of whom owned vast estates in Ireland and had taken everything that fair isle had had to give and more. They *would* listen to him.

They must.

But that was going to be a virtually impossible mountain to climb because of the monumental cock-up that Phinn had made of his maiden parliamentary speech when he'd taken his seat in the House of Lords in May. He'd been so nervous, so unsure of himself, he'd hardly been able to get a word out. He could still hear the sniggers of his so-called peers in his head as his stammer had rendered him practically speechless, with his mouth twisted up, and his face turning red. He'd wished the floor of the chamber had opened and swallowed him up whole.

Even now, as flaming mortification engulfed him anew, Phinn could sense superior, judgmental glances being aimed his way. Across the room was the Duke of Albemarle. When Phinn's gaze connected with the middle-aged nobleman's, the man's lip curled into a sneer. In fact, Albemarle had been the peer who'd started jeering at Phinn during his maiden speech. Even though Phinn knew the bastard was nothing more than a king-sized bully, it didn't help that it was men like him who had the Queen's ear. That a word from the duke could quite possibly crush any of Phinn's proposed reforms if he came across as an imbecile.

Of course he wasn't. But perception mattered. It's why Phinn's boxing manager had dubbed him Cutthroat O'Connell. The coarse Irishman's words echoed through Phinn's mind as he tossed back a mouthful of brandy. *Remember, O'Connell, yer opponents need to be scared o' you before ye even enter the ring. Prize fightin' is a game o' the mind as much as a game o' the fists. Never forget that.*

While Phinn was nothing but relieved that his boxing days were over, one thing he'd learned about himself was that he was a fighter. He would not be silenced by the likes of Albemarle. The House of Lords was simply a new sort of boxing ring that he had to adapt to. Failure was not an option.

Clearing his throat, he turned his attention back to Marcus. "I can-cannot sit on my hands and d-do nothin'," he said, his voice gruff with determination. "If I can m-m-make sure that Irish tenants can-cannot be so easily moved off the land, if I-I can advocate for agra-agrarian reform, I will feel I've made g-good use of me newly f-f-f-found influence. While I don't... while I don't want to be an absentee land-landlord, I know I n-n-need to be here, in London, m-makin' me voice heard in the House... in the House of Lords." His mouth slid into a rueful grin. "After I grow b-b-big enough bollocks to show me f-f-face again and attempt to make another speech."

Marcus laughed at that. "I'm sure that not a single man in the House of Lords would doubt the size of your bollocks, my friend."

Phinn wasn't so sure about that. Parliament's autumn session was due to start in October, but despite the fire in his belly, he would be foolish indeed to think that he wouldn't be ridiculed when he entered the chamber again. Or even worse, ignored completely.

Marcus, Lord Hartwell, on the other hand, was the epitome of urbane and appeared to be well-liked by his peers. Their mutual friend, Xavier Mason, the Duke of St Lawrence, was a horologist of great renown. Indeed, the Astronomer Royal had recently announced that the duke had won the commission for the grand clock design—the "King of Clocks"—that would grace the top of St Stephen's Tower at the new Palace of Westminster. In Phinn's opinion, the Duke of St Lawrence was as clever as ten professors. Not only that, but he possessed a natural gravitas and a manner that was more cultured than Irish butter. People *noticed* the duke when he walked into a room. He commanded attention.

Phinn sighed heavily. He was irritated no end that he was usually noticed for all the wrong reasons and then just as quickly dismissed. "Be that as it m-may, the size of m-me bollocks won't c-count for much if no one is willin' to take me serious-seriously." He snorted. "I can't... I can't even t-t-tell the difference be-between a toasting f-fork and a f-f-fish fork. I have an army of servants, yet I'm al-always openin' the feckin' door for meself instead of lettin' the footmen do it. I swear me val-valet, well-meanin' though he is, thinks I'm an eejit because I care little about me war-wardrobe. I've n-n-never even been taught to ride a blood-bloody horse. Not prop-properly. Not like a gen-gentleman. I've g-g-got a whole goddamn stable full of Thoroughbred horses at Kin-Kinsale Castle and there are umpteen horses stabled in the mews behind Kin-Kinsale House here in London. But me grooms n-need to exer-exercise them because me horse-horsemanship skills are w-w-woeful. I can't even trot without bruisin' me arse."

Marcus waved a hand. "All that sort of thing can be learned. And I can certainly help on the horse-riding front. If I'd known, I would have been dragging you along to Hyde Park at the crack of dawn every morning."

Phinn released a hearty laugh that drew annoyed glances and a raised eyebrow or two (one of which was Albemarle's). "Even if you've been carousin' all night?" Lord Hartwell did have quite the reputation for frequenting clubs, gaming hells, and the beds of women of all persuasions until the wee small hours.

The viscount grinned sheepishly. "Touché. We'll go riding on the days I'm not hungover or sleep deprived."

Phinn grinned. "So once per m-m-month then?"

Marcus laughed. "That sounds about right. Although"—he took a swig of his brandy then grimaced—"that might all be about to change soon." A shadow crossed the viscount's aristocratically handsome face. "I've heard the Queen is growing tired of my antics and has requested my presence at Buckingham Palace in the not-too-distant future. I believe she's going to ask me to"—he tugged at his collar and black cravat as though they suddenly felt too tight—"get leg-shackled."

"Leg... leg-shackled?" repeated Phinn. "I d-don't take your meanin'. B-b-but whatever it is, it sounds feckin' aw-awful."

"Oh, it is," agreed Marcus. "I'm certain Her Majesty is going to command me to get married."

Phinn's mouth fell open. "The Queen can-can do that?"

"Oh, yes indeed," said Marcus, waving over a footman so their brandy could be replenished. "It seems too many scandalous rumors about my wild behavior have reached her ears, so my punishment is to be matrimony."

Phinn chuckled. "You poor sod." While Phinn had no immediate plans to wed, he'd never viewed marriage as a form of punishment. A few months ago, the Duke of St Lawrence had married a vivacious redhead—a lovely young woman who'd served as a nanny for the duke's three young wards—and he certainly seemed happy with the arrangement.

If Phinn's memory served him correctly, the duke's new wife had been a graduate from some much-esteemed college or academy for nannies and governesses.

The Parasol Academy? He believed it might have been.

Phinn stared into his amber-hued brandy and it immediately reminded him of the *Kinsale Cloud*'s fair stowaway and her fine hazel eyes. It had been five days since he'd farewelled the lovely young woman. Five days, in which at odd moments, his thoughts kept returning to the few hours they'd spent together.

In all honesty, he'd been completely captivated by Mrs. Hermina Davenport. He still suspected that she'd been hiding the real reason that she'd ended up on the *Kinsale Cloud*—his ship's crew had had no idea at all. And he still couldn't fathom how she and her son had magically materialized in his wardrobe, as if from nowhere. But after all was said and done, no harm had come to anyone. He just hoped that Mrs. Davenport and her son were faring well.

"Penny for your thoughts, Lord Kinsale?" said Marcus. Then he grinned. "I know that look. You're thinking about a woman, aren't you?" He gave Phinn's patent leather shoe a nudge with his own. "Come on, man. Out with it."

Good Lord. Phinn's cheeks suddenly felt rather hot and he only just resisted the urge to run a finger around his suddenly too-tight collar. "Ac-actually, I was thinkin' about somethin' you said before. About how the things I d-don't know about or can-cannot do can b-b-be learned. My m-most pressin' concern is me in-inability to speak with-without stammering. I want to b-be able to con-confidently deliver a sp-sp-speech in the House of Lords. N-not sound like an in-inarticulate clodpole."

Marcus gave a sympathetic wince. "I wish I could help you, my friend. But I wouldn't know where to start."

Phinn sighed and examined his brandy glass again. "It's a pit-pity I cannot hire someone from the ac-academy that Xavier's w-w-wife attended. Some-someone who could t-t-teach me about etiquette and provide el-elocution lessons."

Marcus cocked an eyebrow. "Well, why don't you? Seems like a capital idea to me."

Phinn gave a snort of laughter. "You really think that this ac-academy w-w-would let me employ a gov-governess wh-when I don't have a child? At least Xavier had three w-w-wards."

"Mmmm. On second thought, you do make a good point," conceded Marcus. "It would look rather odd, all things considered."

"Just a wee bit." And then of course, Phinn probably wouldn't be satisfied if he employed anyone else other than Hermina

Davenport. He'd liked her forthright yet gentle manner. How she hadn't looked down at him when he'd stammered. *But all of that is beside the point, Phineas O'Connell*, he reminded himself, *when you don't have a wee 'un. Besides, she might have secured another position already.*

Two hours later, after Phinn and Marcus had repaired to Boodle's dining room and feasted on foie gras and pheasant, then pears poached in red wine with crème anglaise for pudding — Marcus ordered, as Phinn had no idea about anything — Marcus had bundled him into a hansom cab. Not to take them home to Belgravia, but to ferry them to another sort of "gentlemen's club" in Covent Garden where an evening of bawdier entertainment than what was on offer at Boodle's could be had.

Except when they climbed out of the cab, Phinn had decided he was not really in the mood for that sort of thing. He wasn't a prude by any means, but tonight, the idea of fraternizing with women who were paid to pay attention to him, didn't sit well with him. Or perhaps it was the foie gras and French red wine. It certainly couldn't have anything to do with a chestnut-haired governess with large hazel eyes. In any event, he told Marcus that he'd changed his mind.

"I feel the need to w-w-walk off all that rich f-food," he explained as Marcus cocked an eyebrow, his expression laden with skepticism. "So I'll stroll home to Ea-Eaton Square. The fresh air will d-do me g-good too."

Marcus laughed at that. "You won't find much fresh air in London. I'd say take care, but anyone who tried to take you on would deserve whatever you dished out." He rubbed his bruised jaw. "Hopefully this won't put off the ladies."

"I'm sure it w-won't," said Phinn. Lord Hartwell received admiring female glances wherever he went. Phinn received his fair share as well. But interest in him — unless he was paying a woman for her company — often waned whenever he spoke.

While he was used to that happening, it didn't mean the rejection didn't sting.

Marcus farewelled him, then Phinn, gloved hands buried in the pockets of his greatcoat, strode along Garrick Street, heading in the direction of Leicester Square. It was only two miles to Belgravia and he'd be home in less than an hour.

A thick pea-souper had begun to roll in and the sickly yellow light of the streetlamps barely penetrated the roiling fog that enveloped the thoroughfares and obscured the surrounding buildings. Whenever he crossed a street, Phinn had to pick his way carefully, not only looking out for carriages and hansom cabs and carts, but piles of manure. He'd been walking for only five minutes when he thought he detected the footsteps of someone who seemed far too close.

Unless it was a trick of the fog? But then, heavy fog tended to muffle sound, which meant that whoever was behind Phinn must be almost breathing-down-the-back-of-his-neck close.

Well, feck that. Phinn pulled his hands from his pockets and cracked his knuckles before balling them into fists. It would be a brave man indeed—or a colossal eejit—who tried to take on Cutthroat O'Connell.

Muscles tense, all senses on high alert, Phinn swung around to face his stalker, but in the shifting gray miasma, he could see no one. He couldn't hear the footsteps anymore either.

Had he been imagining things?

An omnibus rumbled past and then the clatter of an approaching hansom cab came from a different direction. A dog barked and something scuttled past his feet. A rat no doubt.

Phinn waited a moment or two more, but the only pedestrians who passed by were a well-to-do couple.

With a sigh, Phinn turned away. Just to make sure he wouldn't be followed, he ducked down a narrow side street. If he took a circuitous route home, he'd lose any sort of foolish footpad in the fog.

He'd only been walking for another few minutes when the sounds of merrymaking—a chorus of wild drunken whoops, disembodied laughter, and a lively air played on a fiddle—echoed down the laneway. A public house lay ahead.

Within a minute, the Lion and Lamb emerged from the fog. The gaslight spilling out from the doorway and the establishment's large bay window revealed that the pub was packed with rough, working-class men. It was the sort of pub that Phinn used to frequent before some strange twist of fate had turned him into a marquess.

He was almost tempted to push his way through the crowd into the taproom and order a pint of ale, except his expensive attire would mark him as someone who didn't belong even if his Irish brogue and bulky physical build screamed lowborn. And he just wasn't in the mood to deal with drunken louts who might decide to "have a go" at him because they thought he was a toff.

But you are a toff, O'Connell, whether you like it or not, Phinn reminded himself as he lingered in the murky shadows on the opposite side of the street. He'd paused at the entrance of an alley that was littered with refuse piles and only heaven knew what else. There was a soft noise—a muffled scuffing sound behind him—but when Phinn glanced over his shoulder, he saw nothing and no one. And that's when he felt the lightest tug on his greatcoat—a movement that was barely perceptible.

Feck! Had he been marked as a target by a feckin' pickpocket?

Phinn shot out a hand and his fingers closed around a scrawny limb—an arm that was half-buried in his coat's pocket.

"Oi, sod off, you bleedin' sod. Let me go," cried the owner of the arm. A street urchin by the looks of him. He twisted and kicked out, but given Phinn's size and strength, the boy would've had better luck pushing over a brick wall. "You're bleedin' hurtin' me, you bloody bastard."

Phinn immediately adjusted his hold so he was gripping the boy's collar, but he wasn't about to let go. "Hasn't anyone t-told you that it's bad m-manners to steal? If you needed m-m-money, you could've just asked. I'd be ha-happy to give you some." It wasn't a lie. There was nothing worse in this world than seeing children deprived of the basic necessities. To see them so desperate, they had to resort to thievery in order to survive.

He understood because in Dublin, *he'd* been desperate and hungry too.

The boy stilled and squinted up at Phinn from beneath a shock of matted brown hair. Then he spat on Phinn's boot. "A likely bloody story. Why should I believe the likes o' you?"

Phinn bent down and stared straight into the urchin's eyes. Fear lurked behind the bravado. He knew the feeling well. "Be-because believe it or n-not, just like you, I've stolen to survive."

"You're nuffink like me. You're Irish," accused the boy, planting his grubby hands on his hips. "A bleedin' potato-eatin' Paddy."

"There's nothin' wrong with p-potatoes. Or the eatin' o' them," said Phinn. "Especially roasted in g-goose fat until they're crispy and g-golden. Or slathered in lashings o' b-b-butter. Or m-mashed with cream and bacon and ca-cabbage to make col-cannon."

As Phinn described his favorite potato dishes, he swore the boy's mouth began to water. At least his eyes gleamed with a yearning that was hard to hide. And then the lad's stomach rumbled louder than the omnibus that had trundled past not ten minutes ago.

Phinn's grip slid to the lad's shoulder and he gave it a pat. "I'd warrant you're starvin'." He glanced at the public house, but that was no place to take a child. Of course, he could give the boy money, but pickpockets, more often than not, worked in gangs and the leader would take most, if not all of the proceeds their young thieves managed to pilfer. Although, this particular boy seemed to be on his own. Phinn frowned. "Do you have a f-family? Do you w-work for someone? Are you in a gang o' pickpockets?"

The urchin crossed his arms. "I ain't tellin' you nuffink," he retorted. Then his expression grew fierce and he took a step back. "'Ere, you ain't one o' those dirty geezers who likes dustbin-lids, are you? 'Cause if you are, I'll rip your bleedin' nuts off and feed 'em to some butcher's mongrel. Or some mangy tomcat down the alley." He gestured with a thumb over his shoulder. "Or some sewer rats down the Fleet Ditch. Or—"

"All right. All right," said Phinn. "I t-take your point. And no. I'm not one o' those 'geezers' as you c-call them. If you know anyone like that, p-point me in his direction and I'll knock his block off." And he meant it. While Phinn's chest tightened in sympathy for the boy, his guts churned with anger. To think what this child must have seen while living on the streets. No doubt he was wise beyond his years. It was difficult to tell his exact age in the uncertain light—that and the fact his face was smudged with grime—but Phinn estimated him to be about seven or eight years old.

And then a novel thought struck Phinn like a lightning bolt from above. "What's your n-name, lad?"

The urchin's eyes narrowed. "I told you, I ain't tellin' you—"

"I know, I know. You're not go-goin' to tell me anythin'." Phinn crossed his arms, mirroring the boy's stance. "Until you decide to tell me your n-n-name, I'll call you Tom Fleet. In honor of the alley c-cats and sewer rats you men-mentioned." Then he drew a breath. "So, Tom, why don't you come b-back to me house in Eaton Square, and I'll have me cook f-f-fix a meal for you. And if you like it well enough there, you c-can stay. You'll have your own bedroom. N-new clothes. You won't be hungry or c-c-cold or have c-cause to fear anythin' at all."

The boy hiked up his chin, his gaze sharp with suspicion. "Why? Why would you do somefink like that? Why should I believe a toff like you? Your sort usually cuff ragamuffin children like me around the ears before you try to 'aul me off to the coppers."

Phinn rubbed the back of his neck. There was no sense in lying, not to this streetwise child. Honesty would be the best policy. "Even though I'm wealthy and wear f-fancy clothes, I sta-sta-stammer. And I want to hire a gov-governess to help me cor-correct it. The problem is, I'm not . . . I'm not married and haven't any children, so I need a w-w-ward. And by the looks o' things, you n-n-need a safe place to stay."

The boy scowled. "I don't want to take no bleedin' lessons from no snooty governess."

"You w-won't have to," said Phinn. "She'll be t-t-teachin' me."

"You do 'ave a bleedin' awful stammer," agreed the boy. "Makes you sound like a right pillock. *And* you're Irish. No wonder you don't 'ave a wife."

Phinn spread his hands. "So you see my prob-problem."

"I s'pose I do." The urchin scrunched up his nose. "All right then. I'll visit your 'ouse, mister. I'll take a look around." But then he pointed a finger at Phinn. "But listen 'ere and listen well. I've got a 'at pin 'idden on me person. And if I don't like anyfink that you do, I reserve the right to stick you wiv it."

Phinn bowed his head. "And rightly so. I . . . I would-wouldn't want it any other way. My n-n-name is Phin-Phineas O'Connell, by the way. Lord K-K-Kinsale."

The boy's eyes turned into saucers. "Cor blimey. You *are* a bleedin' toff." He began to walk alongside Phinn as they followed the laneway back toward the road that would lead them to Leicester Square. "You can call me Tom Fleet. I reckon it's as good a name as any seein' as I was born in the Fleet Ditch."

"Very well then, Tom Fleet," said Phinn. "I was b-born in a tiny village in County Cork in Ireland. Bally-Ballybrook. I've lived in the b-b-backstreets o' Dublin too."

"'Ow'd you get to be a toff then?" asked Tom.

"You know, that's a very good ques-question," said Phinn as they paused on the corner of Cranbourn Street and Charing Cross Road and Phinn hailed a hansom cab. Tom Fleet's clothes were threadbare and he wasn't wearing any shoes. Phinn couldn't, in all good conscience, make the boy walk two miles to Belgravia. Grinning down at Tom Fleet, he answered the boy as best as he could. "To be sure, it m-m-must be the luck o' the Irish."

Chapter 6

In Which an Unexpected Arrival Results in a Series of Unexpected Events Including a Request to Help Navigate Potentially Treacherous Waters; And an Unfortunate Bout of Ninnyhammer-itis Ensues...

One of the *Parasol Academy Handbook*'s tenets—from Chapter 2, Section 7, paragraph 3(c) to be exact—was that a Parasol nanny or governess should *always* expect the unexpected. And of course, adapt accordingly. Thinking on one's feet, being flexible (both physically and mentally) were core components of a Parasol student's training. Whether a tantrum-throwing toddler decided to lob a rattle or bowl of custard at one's person, or one caught one's rebellious adolescent female charge kissing the handsome young gardener in the greenhouse, or a would-be kidnapper mounted an attempt to steal away a child in one's care, a Parasol nanny or governess was expected to handle any sort of situation with delicacy and aplomb (or decided evasive action, and perhaps even a well-aimed kick or punch or two in the event of an attempted kidnapping) to circumvent any potential disaster.

Mina prided herself on her ability to make split-second decisions and swiftly change course as the occasion demanded. At least that's what she told herself as a leygram or te-*ley*-gram—a magical telegram sent via the Fae's mystical leylines that ran through the earth—suddenly materialized on the mat in her dormitory room at the Parasol Academy.

Reaching into her uniform's pocket, Mina withdrew her leyspectacles and slid them on. The Academy-issued glasses of delicately wrought silver contained lenses made from azure-blue Fae glass. Without them, it would be impossible to read the leygram; the text would look like utter nonsense otherwise.

While any Parasol Academy staff member, student, or fellow graduate could send a leygram, Mina had a feeling that *this* one had been sent by Mrs. Temple. If that were the case, it could not be ignored, no matter its contents. No matter that Mina's fingers all but trembled as she picked up the magical missive that shimmered with a blue pearlescent glow.

If the leygram *had* been sent by the Academy's headmistress, hopefully it was about an interview and nothing else.

It had been several days since Mina had left Ablington and returned to London. Even though she'd been reluctant to leave Christopher behind, she'd had to in order to secure another governess's position. Not only for the income, but she didn't want to arouse Mrs. Temple's suspicions that anything might be amiss—if "amiss" meant "I've effectively stolen Sir Bedivere Ponsonby's ward out from under his nose and hidden him away in the country until I work out what to do next." Waiting for the sword of Damocles to fall because of what she'd done was nerve-wracking indeed, especially since she was staying at the Parasol Academy. It was hard to maintain a calm veneer in front of the Academy's formidable headmistress when you were quaking on the inside, worrying that the crime you'd committed would be discovered.

It was safe to say that Mina still wasn't sure if she should confide in Mrs. Temple or not. To confess or not to confess: that was the question. The problem was, it was simply impossible to predict what the headmistress—a staunch proponent of upholding the Parasol Academy's rules—would do. And so, Mina continued to prevaricate about what *she* should do.

Of course, right now you should stop faffing about and open this leygram, Mina sternly told herself. Indeed, the parchment buzzed against her fingertips as though urging her to make haste and read it.

Inhaling a fortifying breath, she ripped open the envelope... and then exhaled in relief. Yes, the leygram *was* from Mrs. Temple. But she didn't want to haul Mina over the coals about anything at all. The headmistress simply wanted to talk to her about a prospective employer "as soon as possible" as the gentleman—a nobleman, in fact—was presently waiting in the headmistress's sitting room along with his ward.

Excellent. Good. This is good. This is what you want, Mina reassured herself as she put away her spectacles and crossed to the looking glass to check her appearance. Her hair was secured in a sleek coil at the back of her head. Her navy-blue governess's uniform of fine merino wool was perfectly pressed, her crinoline skirts falling in neat pleats to the floor. Her black kid half boots were buttoned up and polished. Her Parasol Academy issued knife was sheathed to her ankle (one never knew when one might need to fend off an attacker or cut through a hopelessly knotted pair of leading strings or a kite string). As Mina was a governess rather than a nanny, she wasn't required to wear a white cotton pinafore or lacy cap. All she needed to do was don her white silk gloves and she'd be ready.

Of course, she was a *teensy* bit nervous—indeed, she had difficulty doing up the tiny pearl buttons that secured her gloves. But despite her fumbling fingers and the tripping of her heart, Mina trusted that she would be able to convey the required air of amiable poise that would convince this nobleman waiting to see her that she was eminently qualified to care for and educate his ward.

When Mina entered Mrs. Temple's office a short time later, she found the headmistress at her desk, examining her reflection in a silver and crystal encrusted hand mirror. She had to clear her throat to secure the blond woman's attention.

"Oh, Miss Davenport," exclaimed Mrs. Temple as though she hadn't been the one to ask Mina to "come in" only a moment beforehand. She placed the mirror down on the purple leather blotter on her desk, then beckoned her closer. "There you are. Let me fill you in on your prospective employer and his eight-year-old ward before I make the introductions."

"Of course, Mrs. Temple. I'm most eager to begin working again." As Mina approached the ornate mahogany desk, she studied the headmistress. Mrs. Felicity Temple—who was really a "miss" but had adopted the honorific of "missus" to clearly indicate she was a serious woman of business—was a petite, attractive woman who was only four years older than Mina. Her heart-shaped face was framed by clusters of immaculately styled pale blond ringlets and her gray eyes held a shrewd light. While the Parasol Academy's headmistress was nothing but committed when it came to upholding the Academy's high standards and protecting its reputation for excellence, her steely determination was tempered with wisdom and kindness. Once employed in the Royal Nursery, Felicity Temple even commanded Queen Victoria's respect. In fact, it was well-known that Mrs. Temple had physically protected three of the Queen's children during an attempted assassination attempt on the Queen herself. Without a doubt, the Parasol Academy's current headmistress was a force to be reckoned with.

Considering the fact that Sir Bedivere Ponsonby had sacked Mina three weeks ago, Mina considered herself fortunate indeed that Mrs. Temple still had faith in her as a governess. "I also wanted to thank you for . . . for giving me another opportunity to prove myself, Mrs. Temple," Mina said. "I've been so terribly worried that my recent dismissal has resulted in an enormous blot upon my résumé. That my professional reputation has been irrevocably stained."

The headmistress waved a hand as though she were batting away a pesky gnat. "There are no blots, small or otherwise, Miss Davenport. I know that you are an excellent governess. Lady Grenfell, God rest her soul, certainly sang your praises. And I'm well aware that Sir Bedivere is a completely different kettle of fish. Your competence has never been brought into question, so worry no more on that score."

Mina's lungs tightened and her heart thudded uncomfortably against her ribs. Was now the time to confess to Mrs. Temple that she'd spirited Lord Fitzwilliam off the *Valiant* at the urging of Lady Grenfell? That Sir Bedivere might be under the influence of an ensorcelled ring that was making him act out of character? Perhaps Mrs. Temple might be able to shed some light on Lady Grenfell's prophetic dream.

But as Mina grappled with all the arguments for and against speaking out versus staying tight-lipped about what she'd done to protect Lord Fitzwilliam, Mrs. Temple was speaking again.

"Now that we've put all your concerns to bed," continued the headmistress, "let me tell you about the nobleman presently waiting to speak with you. He's actually an Irish marquess and he's asked for you by name, Miss Davenport! Although," she added after a moment, "there seems to be some confusion about your marital status. He asked for *Mrs.* Davenport."

An Irish marquess? He wanted to see Mrs. *Davenport?*

Oh no! No . . . It couldn't be Lord Kinsale, could it?

But it *must* be.

Mina strove to keep her manner as composed as the Queen's, even though her pulse was leaping about like a startled rabbit. If . . . if Lord Kinsale was here, what had he told Mrs. Temple? Had he mentioned their recent encounter on the *Kinsale Cloud*? And the fact that she apparently had a fair-haired son by the name of Christopher? Mrs. Temple had met young Lord Fitzwilliam before and knew his Christian name. She was a most canny woman—indeed her insight almost bordered on preternatural at times. It would be quite easy for her to put two and two together...

Before Mina could harness her runaway thoughts, Mrs. Temple spoke. "I understand this marquess—Lord Kinsale to be exact—is acquainted with the Duke of St Lawrence. So perhaps your old alumna, dear Emmeline Chase, recommended you for the post. I know you and the newly wedded Duchess of St Lawrence have always been firm friends."

A wave of relief whooshed through Mina. "Yes. Yes, that must be how this Lord Kinsale heard of me and the Parasol Academy. I must write to darling Emmeline and thank her for the endorsement."

"Please pass on my fond regards to Her Grace," said Mrs. Temple with a smile.

"Oh, I will," said Mina. She would indeed write to her friend—an exchange of confidences was long overdue—but first things first. She needed to secure this position.

Now that the initial shock had worn off, Mina would be lying to herself if she didn't acknowledge that she was just a tad excited about the prospect of seeing Lord Kinsale again. She did think it slightly odd that he hadn't mentioned his ward when they'd been discussing the fact he was unmarried and hadn't any children. Unless she'd somehow misinterpreted the conversation...

No. No, he'd clearly told her that he *didn't* need a nanny or governess. But that had been almost a week ago, Mina reminded herself. Evidently the marquess's situation had changed in the interim.

"Lord Kinsale's ward," began Mina, "I would be keen to learn a little about the child before the interview. Just so I have an idea of what to expect."

"Of course," said Mrs. Temple, folding her hands together on her desk. "His name is Tom Fleet, and as I mentioned before he's eight years old. I'm not entirely sure of the relationship between the marquess and young Tom, but I gather the guardianship has all come about rather suddenly and both Lord Kinsale and his ward are still finding their way."

Mina nodded. That aligned with what she already knew about the marquess. "I take it that Master Tom is an orphan?"

Mrs. Temple's brow wrinkled slightly. "I believe so? The boy himself has been rather quiet and has barely said a word in my presence. I wasn't able to ascertain if he's received any formal education to date, but I have the feeling his circumstances have been somewhat"—she drummed her fingers on the blotter for a moment as though looking for the right word—"straitened, shall we say? Although, he does seem to have rather a hearty appetite and has polished off most of the afternoon tea tray. After I've taken you through to my sitting room, I shall repair to the Academy kitchen to arrange another plate of sandwiches and a fresh pot of tea."

"And the marquess? Is there anything I should know about him?" ventured Mina. It would be useful to hear what Mrs. Temple thought of the Irishman.

"Oh, Lord Kinsale is quite lovely. Although, he does seem a trifle uncertain about his own situation," said Mrs. Temple. Leaning forward, she lowered her voice. "He disclosed to me that he inherited the marquessate quite recently and unexpectedly—in fact, he used to be a prizefighter of some renown back in Ireland—so he's still learning how to navigate the waters of the upper class... and finding them particularly treacherous. Which is all perfectly understandable given his background."

A prizefighter? Heavens, no wonder Lord Kinsale possessed such a magnificent muscular build. Steadfastly steering her thoughts away from the marquess's admirable physique because she was bound to blush, Mina said, "Yes, I can imagine it would be very difficult if you hadn't been brought up with the expectation that you would be a nobleman one day and were then suddenly forced to deal with all the responsibilities that go along with that. It would certainly be a daunting prospect. But perhaps the Duke and Duchess of St Lawrence will be able to provide Lord Kinsale with support in that regard. When they return from the seaside."

The headmistress inclined her head. "No doubt they will. I'm sure you might have some pearls of wisdom to dispense, too, Miss Davenport. Who better than a Parasol Academy governess to know the ins and outs of the nobility's social conventions?"

"I'm more than happy to help my employer and his new ward in whatever way that I can," said Mina. Then she gave a little laugh. "If the marquess does indeed wish to employ me as a governess."

Mrs. Temple rose to her feet. "There's only one way to find out, Miss Davenport. I think it's time I made the introductions."

As soon as the headmistress ushered Mina into the adjoining sitting room and she laid eyes on the marquess, Mina felt as though she'd been struck by a virulent bout of ninnyhammeritis. She was tongue-tied and as witless as a newborn kitten as the dark-haired Irishman rose from his seat and inclined his head in greeting. Her week-old memories hadn't done the nobleman justice.

She'd forgotten how tall he was. How ruggedly handsome. His tailor, whoever he was, did a sterling job. The marquess's clothes looked like they'd been painted on, framing his muscular boxer's body to perfection: his herculean shoulders, the swell of his substantial biceps, the breadth of his chest and taut middle, his thick, muscular thighs. Mina's gaze traveled over the man in quiet awe . . . until Mrs. Temple cleared her throat.

"Miss Davenport," she prompted. "This is Lord Kinsale."

And then she threw her a meaningful look as she affected the tiniest bob—a cue to remind Mina to curtsy.

"Oh. Yes... my lord." Even though she suddenly felt as unsteady as she had on the marquess's ship, Mina managed to execute a passable curtsy. "It's an honor and a pleasure to meet you, my lord. How do you do, my lord?"

Ugh. Had she really just said "my lord" three times in a row? She felt as though she'd lost control of her mouth and far too many words had tumbled out all at once. And she hadn't even acknowledged the marquess's ward, which was very rude of her.

Although, the boy didn't appear to mind. He was presently seated upon a wing chair, his feet propped on a footstool while he munched away on a jam-and-cream-slathered scone. From beneath a shaggy mop of sandy-brown hair, his dark eyes regarded her with keen interest.

"M-M-Miss Daven-Davenport," said the marquess with a smile. And was that a mischievous twinkle in his emerald-green eyes? "Mrs. T-Temple has been... has been telling m-m-me all about you."

"Lord Kinsale 'as a stammer," said the marquess's ward. He put down his plate, climbed to his feet, and placed his fisted hands on his thin hips. "But don't let it bovver you none. 'E's a decent geezer for a nob."

Mina blinked at the boy in astonishment. She had not expected him to speak with a cockney accent. Or to be so waiflike. His clothes virtually hung off his slight frame. No wonder he'd been wolfing down whatever he could lay his hands on. "I... er... You must be Tom," she said.

"Tom Fleet," declared the boy with a tidy bow. "Pleased to meet you, miss."

"Well then," said Mrs. Temple brightly. "Now that you're all acquainted, I will repair to the kitchen to organize another afternoon tea tray. If that is all right with you, Lord Kinsale?"

The marquess nodded. "Aye. It-it is."

"I wouldn't say no to more o' those li'l tarts wiv the cherries on 'em," said Tom. Then after Lord Kinsale exchanged a speaking look with him, the boy continued, "Please. If you wouldn't mind. I don't want to be a bovver."

"Oh, it's no bother at all. The tray won't be too long," said Mrs. Temple. Catching Mina's eye she added, "Just ring if you need anything else."

As soon as the door snicked shut, Mina smiled at the marquess and his ward. "Well," she said, "this is a pleasant surprise." She met Lord Kinsale's gaze. "I had no idea that you had a ward, my lord."

"It's... it's a re-recent development," said the marquess. "So while I did-didn't need a gov-governess a week ago, it seems I d-d-do now. O' course, I im-immediately thought of you, Mrs."—his mouth hitched in a conspiratorial smile—"I mean *Miss* Dav-Davenport."

Mina winced. Glancing at Tom, she noticed that he seemed engrossed in helping himself to another scone so she ventured in a low voice, "Christopher is presently staying with my mother and sister in the country, my lord. I don't like keeping secrets, but I would be most grateful if you didn't say anything to Mrs. Temple. She doesn't know about him, and I'm not sure where I would stand with the Parasol Academy if it came to light that I had transgressed—" She broke off and dropped her gaze to the floor. "Here at the Parasol Academy, moral integrity and decorum are valued very highly. After all, our unofficial motto is 'we're prim, proper, and prepared for anything.' So, I hope you understand why I let you believe I was a widow with a child rather than sharing the truth." She leaned even closer to Lord Kinsale so Tom wouldn't hear. "As forward-thinking as the Parasol Academy is, nannies and governesses who are unwed mothers are probably not in keeping with the organization's pristine reputation."

She hated lying to the marquess by only sharing half the story and implying things that were utterly false—that she'd had a child out of wedlock. But the alternative—confessing that Christopher wasn't actually her son but Sir Bedivere's ward, who she'd essentially kidnapped—was something she just simply could not do.

Chapter 7

Concerning Tumbles and Mishaps and Misses (Not Missus); A Discussion about Fleecing, the Fleet Ditch, Nobsville and Toffstown; And Needs Must, the Smoothing of Wrinkles, and Flip-Flops and Somersaults...

Mina, aside from being plagued by guilt about her dishonesty, didn't need to fret about where the marquess's allegiance lay for long.

"Do-do not fear, Miss Dav-Davenport," he said gently, his green eyes alight with such soft compassion Mina's heart performed an odd little tumble. "Your secret is safe with m-m-me." A slight flush crept into his cheeks as he added after a beat of awkward silence, "I hope you c-c-can f-f-forgive me for asking, b-b-but considering what you just dis-disclosed, should I... should I continue to refer to you as 'miss'?"

Heat scorched Mina's entire face. "Yes," she said. "Miss Davenport will do. I'm not, and have never been, married." At least *that* was the truth.

Lord Kinsale nodded then glanced at his ward, but the boy was presently engrossed in picking through the sandwiches. When the marquess spoke again, his voice was low, his words meant only for her. "I under-understand that these sorts of mishaps hap-happen sometimes, Miss Dav-Davenport. I would... I would n-n-never think badly of a woman who f-f-found herself in such a situation."

Then he smiled and gestured for her to take a seat. "Please join us. I w-w-would like to dis-discuss our circumstances—both yours and mine—further."

Mina smiled and chose the shepherdess chair beside Tom Fleet's. Lord Kinsale sat opposite them. "Would you like a spot... a spot o' tea? Or somethin' to eat?" he asked. Then he frowned. "Although, I expect your Mrs. Temple will be b-back soon with a fresh p-p-pot. And I'm afraid there's n-not much left of anythin' else." He tilted his head toward Tom and grinned. "It seems some-someone has quite the appetite."

Mina smiled back. "I'm perfectly content, my lord."

Lord Kinsale gave a nod then blew out a breath. "Right then." He scrubbed a hand down his face and Mina gained the distinct impression the Irishman was uncomfortable. Of course, the shepherdess chair he was sitting on with its spindly gilt legs and delicately fashioned arms looked far too small to accommodate his long muscular legs and wide shoulders. But given his pained facial expression, she rather gathered that he was having difficulty finding the right words to talk about something that was on his mind.

Mina clasped her hands in her lap and cleared her throat. "I imagine you would like to go through what you're looking for in a governess, my lord," she observed, "and more specifically, what I can offer to ensure that I will suit. I'm sure that Mrs. Temple mentioned that here at the Parasol Academy, we aim to provide our clients with a bespoke service." Then she caught Tom Fleet's eye. "Would that be all right with you, Master Tom? If Lord Kinsale and I discuss your educational needs?"

The boy shrugged a thin shoulder. "Wha'ever, miss. I've never 'ad lessons before an' can't read or write or do nuffink like that. I know me numbers though. And all about coins an' such." He tapped the side of his head. "Mark me words, I can tell the difference between a farving an' a penny an' a shillin' an' a crown. It ain't easy to fleece Tom Fleet."

Mina smiled encouragingly. "Well, that certainly gives me a good understanding of where to begin, Master Tom. If you don't mind me asking, where do you hail from?"

The boy chuckled. "I don't fink it will surprise you to learn that I'm no' from Nobsville or Toffstown." Then he puffed out his thin chest. "I was born in the Fleet Ditch an' I've lived around Saffron 'ill an' Spi'alfields and Cheapside. All over." A grin spread across his thin face. "Where all the best geezers 'ail from."

"Oh, one of my best friends, Emmeline, grew up in Cheapside," said Mina. "In fact, she used to be a Parasol Academy nanny."

Lord Kinsale raised a brow. "Do you . . . do you mean Emmeline, the Duchess of St Lawrence? I've recently be-become friends with her hus-husband, Xavier."

"Why yes," said Mina. "Her Grace and I shared a dormitory here before we graduated."

"Cor blimey! Your friend is a duchess?" exclaimed Tom.

"She is indeed," said Mina. Further discussion about the St Lawrences was curtailed by the arrival of a maid bearing a laden tea tray. Once the empty plates and old teapot had been cleared away and the maid had taken her leave, Mina offered to pour fresh cups for everyone. Tom declared he'd never had tea before today, but he liked it with lots of milk and three sugar lumps. Mina recalled that Lord Kinsale liked his tea with milk and sugar as well.

"You remembered," the Irishman said as she carefully added the sugar.

Mina laughed. "I did. But then it was only six days ago." As she passed him a brimming cup, the marquess's fingers brushed hers and a warm tingle, not unlike the magical buzz she felt when she picked up a leygram rushed over her. Her cheeks grew warm and she feared they were as red as the cherries on the tarts on the tea tray.

Goodness, she really must try to curb these silly, schoolgirlish reactions to this man. How was she to work for him if she couldn't maintain a professional demeanor around him? *At least you'll be spending most of your time with young Tom*, she reminded herself. The poor boy was eight and it didn't sound as though he could even write his name. He clearly had a lot to learn and she would do her best to help him acquire the literacy skills he would need to make his way in life.

Mina busied herself with pouring her own cup of tea, and after she'd taken a few sips, Lord Kinsale's eyes caught hers. His expression was solemn as he said, "Miss Dav-Davenport, you said earlier that you do . . . do not like k-keeping secrets. And neither do I. To that end, I . . . I feel that it is im-important for me to disclose certain things. About m-m-me situation and Tom's. Things you should know be-because they are directly related to the du-duties I'll be asking you to p-p-perform. Duties you might find a bit . . . unusual."

"Unusual?" Mina repeated, watching the marquess's face. He suddenly seemed so . . . so somber, awkward even, and concern fluttered inside her. She didn't like seeing him so subdued and serious, not when he always seemed to have a ready smile.

Hoping to dispel the gathering tension in the air, to perhaps even make the Irishman smile, she said lightly, "Is this when you tell me that I must take Brutus for walks every day, my lord? While I would quite happily undertake such a duty, I'm not sure Brutus would agree. He did seem a trifle growly and grumbly in my presence. Even after I served him cake."

Lord Kinsale's wide mouth tipped into a smile. "Me pug is can-cantankerous around everyone, Miss Dav-Davenport," he said. "But no, I w-w-won't ask you to do that." His shoulders rose as he drew a breath. "I feel that you should know that Ma-Master Tom isn't technically me ward. He and I . . . I met him just last night, not f-f-far from Co-Covent Garden."

Tom Fleet licked the jam off his fingers. "I'm a pickpocket."

"Oh... I see," said Mina, even though she didn't. Well, she could certainly believe that Tom Fleet was a pickpocket. "And your family? Might they be worried about you, Tom?"

The boy frowned. "I might be an orphan? I ain't got a clue 'oo me sire was, and me mum..." He shrugged. "I ain't seen 'ide nor 'air of 'er since she left me at the work 'ouse. That was when I was four? Maybe five." Another shrug. "I 'ardly remember 'er, to be honest."

Oh heavens. To be abandoned at such a young age was heartbreaking. Mina bit her lip as a wave of compassion for this boy and all he'd endured threatened to undo her.

Lord Kinsale leaned forward in his seat, his forearms resting on the bulk of his thighs. "I-I know it doesn't look quite right," he said, his expression earnest, "me p-p-pickin' a random child off the streets. But I n-n-needed a reason to... to hire you, Miss Dav-Davenport. O' course, Tom is welcome to stay with me f-f-for as long as he likes. And receive less-lessons if he wants them. But I... but I have need o' you too."

Mina frowned as she struggled to makes sense of what the marquess was trying to tell her. *Was this the unusual duties he'd been referring to?* Mrs. Temple had mentioned the Irish peer seemed uncertain about taking up the reins of his new role in life... But there seemed little point in speculating, so Mina said, "I don't quite take your meaning, Lord Kinsale. Why would *you*, a grown man, need a governess?"

The marquess's gaze was steady as it held hers. "Be-because I have terrible stam-stammer, Miss Dav-Davenport. And an Irish accent. I m-m-might have inherited a title and a for-fortune, but I know next to nothin' about the rules o' high so-society. Nothin' about et-etiquette. I have a household—actually several households including a whole c-c-castle—full o' servants b-b-but I have no-no idea who does what or what half the rooms are f-f-for. In a mat-matter o' weeks, I'm due to make a speech in the House of Lords, a speech that will ad-advocate for the rights of Irish tenants back home. I w-w-want to make a real diff-difference in their lives. But no one will . . . no one will listen to me, let alone take me ser-seriously if I t-t-talk like this. If they think that I'm . . . I'm a blitherin' Irish eejit."

Mina's heart cramped with sympathy. How could she have been so oblivious? So insensitive? Even though she accepted the way Lord Kinsale spoke as part of who he was, that didn't mean it didn't bother him. Especially when others looked at him with judgment in their eyes. "Yes, I could see how all of that might be a problem, my lord," she said gently. "But I should point out that while I do know a good deal about the rules of polite society, and teaching etiquette to young ladies, and how to a manage a household, I do not know how to treat a stammer. I feel that I might not have the required skills to help you."

Lord Kinsale straightened in his chair. "But you t-teach el-elocution, don't you? A gov-governess would do that, would-wouldn't she?"

"Yes," said Mina. "I do. I can. But I suspect elocution lessons and the techniques used to reduce stammering are not quite the same. I do not want to promise you that I can help when perhaps I cannot. That would not be fair to you." She could not recall anything at all beyond rudimentary references to stammering in the *Parasol Academy Handbook*. But the Parasol Academy's extensive library might have another guide she could access.

"I understand," said the marquess. "But all . . . but all I'm askin' you to do is try. I have no-no idea who else I could poss-possibly ask." Then he smiled and his green eyes gleamed. "I'm go-goin' to propose a deal, Miss Dav-Davenport. If you agree to w-w-work for me, I would be quite happy for young Chris-Christopher to reside with you at Kin-Kinsale House here in Lon-London. During the day he can t-t-take lessons with Tom if that would suit. And in the evenin', perhaps . . . perhaps you could help m-m-me. With me . . . with me speech. And w-w-with etiquette lessons. You could trans-transform me into a silver-tongued toff."

Oh. Oh my. Mina inhaled a quick breath. Such a position, one in which she could keep Lord Fitzwilliam close by her side, would be welcome indeed. While she knew her mother and sister would do their best to care for the young viscount, she couldn't help but worry that something might go wrong. That Sir Bedivere might somehow work out that she'd had something to do with his ward's disappearance.

The tutor, Mr. Meecham, might recall some of their exchange aboard the *Valiant* if the effects of the confusion spell had dissipated quickly, which it sometimes did. And if Sir Bedivere decided to return to England's fair shores instead of pushing onto the Arctic, if he came looking for Lord Fitzwilliam at Rose Cottage—not an impossibility by any means if he hired a private detective—her mother and sister would be ill-equipped to protect the boy. She kept hoping that such a thing wouldn't happen, but the doubt kept pricking away at the back of her mind.

Of course, if Sir Bedivere began nosing about London, it followed that he might discover where Mina was working and that Lord Fitzwilliam was with her. It was a risk, but Mina also had an array of magical weapons at her disposal. If the worst should happen—if Sir Bedivere came knocking on the Marquess of Kinsale's door, at least she could effect another escape.

Accepting Lord Kinsale's offer made sense. Although, she would have to continue to lie to the poor man to conceal the young viscount's identity. She'd have to employ some other kind of ruse to explain how she and Christopher were related. One that wouldn't arouse suspicion or cause the marquess's staff to look askance at her. But she'd work it out later.

Praying she wouldn't be sent to Fae hell for being so duplicitous, Mina summoned a smile. "My lord, I think such an arrangement would suit both Christopher and me perfectly. I will gladly serve as a governess within your household."

Lord Kinsale's mouth tilted into a heart-stopping smile. "Ex-excellent. You've m-m-made this Irishman very happy, Miss Dav-Davenport."

Tom did not seem to share in the sentiment though. His nose scrunched up. "Bleedin' 'ell. Does that mean I have to learn to read an' write an' talk proper?" he asked around a mouthful of cherry tart.

"Being able to read and write are useful skills to have," said Mina. "And I would endeavor to make the process as entertaining as possible. As for the way you talk, a few less oaths referencing hell and blood would be welcome. But I would never try to change that unless you want to."

Tom shrugged. "All right then, miss. I'll 'ave a go."

Lord Kinsale gave his new ward a nod of approval. "That's the sp-spirit, Tom." Then he looked at Mina. "Wh-when Mrs. Temple returns, I imagine I will n-n-need to talk to her about the t-t-terms of your con-contract."

As if summoned by magic—for surely someone as prim and proper as Mrs. Felicity Temple wouldn't have been listening at the keyhole—the headmistress entered the sitting room and the marquess announced that he would love to hire Miss Davenport. Mrs. Temple, all charm and smiles, then ushered Lord Kinsale into her office to go through the required paperwork.

And as easy as that, it seemed that Mina had secured a new post—one that was a perfect fit. *If only I didn't feel so riddled with guilt,* she thought as she took a sip of her tea. But needs must and all that. She was certain there was something along those lines in the Academy's handbook.

When she glanced over to the marquess's ward, there was a decided clinking—a metallic rattling—as he leaned forward to select another cherry tart from the plate.

Hmmm... Mina wasn't sure whether to smile or frown as she said, "Now Master Tom, I know that up until now you've had to pick pockets in order to make a living, but really, I must ask you not to filch the Parasol Academy's silver." She held out her hand. "I would like all the teaspoons and cake forks back, please."

Tom gave a dramatic sigh. "All right," he said, reaching into his pocket. " 'Ow did you know?"

Mina smiled as he placed four teaspoons and three cake forks into her waiting palm. "I'm a Parasol Academy governess, Master Tom Fleet. I might not see all, but I do notice rather a lot including the tomfoolery, shall we say, of light-fingered children. But thank you for being honest when I called you out."

"Honest?" snorted Tom. "I ain't ever been called that before, miss. Or been fanked. Maybe you ain't as snooty as I fought you might be."

"Well, I should hope not," said Mina. "A Parasol Academy governess might appear to be prim and proper in many respects, but snootiness is definitely frowned upon. One thing you can trust me to be, Tom, is fair. And I will always listen to my charges and do my best to care for them."

"Huh. Maybe I might stick around for a bit then," said Tom.

"Well, why would-wouldn't you?" declared Lord Kinsale as he reentered the room. His green eyes met Mina's. "Mrs. Temple and I were dis-discussing your start date, and it occurred to m-m-me that it might be b-best to check with you. When-when would it be con-convenient for *you* to move into Kinsale House, Mrs. ... I mean, Miss Dav-Davenport? I'm aware that you might have a mat-matter or two to take care of f-f-first."

Oh, why was the marquess such a considerate man? It made it even harder for Mina to continue to play the role of "Unwed Mother."

Ignoring the sliver of guilt piercing her chest, Mina smoothed her expression much as she would smooth the wrinkles from her skirts. "Would tomorrow afternoon suit you, my lord? Around one o'clock? I could arrange for my things here at the Academy to be sent over first thing in the morning. And then I will arrive at Kinsale House as soon as I am able to." She lowered her voice. "I'll need to collect Christopher from my mother's house in the country. The early train should arrive in London by noon."

It would be easy enough for her to teleport from the Parasol Academy to her bedroom in Rose Cottage. But she couldn't very well teleport straight back to the Academy with Christopher. And until she'd visited Kinsale House and learned the "lay of the land," she would be reluctant to teleport there. All things considered, it would be better to catch the train back to London with her "son." No doubt, Christopher would prefer that too.

Lord Kinsale smiled. "That would be per-perfect," he said. Before he disappeared back into Mrs. Temple's office, he gifted Mina with that wide smile of his that made her heart perform all manner of odd flips and flops and somersaults. "I have a good f-f-feeling about our arrangement, Miss Dav-Davenport."

Oh, Mina wished with all her heart that their arrangement would work out. Lord Kinsale was a good man and up until recently, she had considered herself to be a virtuous woman. But circumstances beyond her control were pushing her to do things she never thought she'd have to do. To make choices she'd never imagined she'd have to make.

One careful step at a time, Mina, she told herself. *You are smart. You are resourceful. And you are only trying to keep Lord Fitzwilliam safe, just as you promised Lady Grenfell you would do.*

That was the part that was most important. That was what mattered the most.

And if Mrs. Temple found out what Mina had done, and was continuing to do, that would be her defense. Protecting children—whether that be from earthly or supernatural dangers—was the Parasol Academy's key purpose, after all.

Mina just prayed that argument would be enough to save herself from toppling headlong into ruin.

Chapter 8

In Which Several Important Disclosures are Made; And Tea and Toast Are Taken While Some, but Not All the Tea Is Spilled...

The sun was only just putting in an appearance at Rose Cottage when Mina made an appearance in her old bedchamber. As she stepped from the wardrobe into the room, the early morning sunlight gilded the edges of the rose-patterned curtains. The soft scent of dew-dusted roses drifted up from the garden below and Mina inhaled the sweet freshness. The Gloucestershire countryside was nothing like gritty, bustling, and oftentimes malodorous London.

Despite the fact this wasn't the Vicarage where she'd grown up, Mina always felt a wonderful sense of homecoming whenever she was in this cozy house. Her mother might be persnickety on occasion—and have an unappeasable appetite for anything flower-related—but Mina knew that she was loved. Her father, God rest his soul, had loved her too. She also had a kindred spirit in her sister, who loved teaching at the Ablington Parish School.

As Mina crossed to the bedroom door, she wondered how Christopher had been getting on. It had been so very hard for him—he'd lost his dear mama and papa but a year ago and his godmother just last month. Mina was aware she was the only anchor in his shifting, uncertain world. While she was loath to unmoor him yet again and take him to London, she trusted she would be able to provide the care he needed while keeping him safe from his guardian. All going well, the boy would find a friend in Tom Fleet. They were polar opposites when it came to their upbringings thus far, but Mina had hope they would find some common ground and form an amicable bond. She would do everything in her power to make it work.

Just as she would do her very best to please Lord Kinsale. She still wasn't certain how best to help the marquess with his stammer—a search of the Parasol Academy's library had yielded nothing that would be of use. But etiquette lessons would be easy enough to provide. *As long as you don't blush and become tongue-tied every time Lord Kinsale even looks at you, Mina Davenport.*

Any sort of dalliance with one's employer was *definitely* frowned upon by the Parasol Academy. One's license to practice as a Parasol nanny or governess would be immediately revoked if it ever became evident that one had strayed "above stairs."

Although, exceptions were made on the odd occasion. Mina's friend, Emmeline Chase, had not been censured for fraternizing with (really hopelessly falling in love with) then marrying the Duke of St Lawrence earlier in the year. Apparently there was an obscure subclause in the *Parasol Academy Handbook* that had applied to Emmeline's particular set of circumstances. Mina gathered Good Queen Maeve herself had granted Emmeline a special dispensation for her marriage to her former employer. Mrs. Temple had even attended the wedding.

But Mina suspected that marriage wasn't in her stars. She was six-and-twenty, and while she'd once harbored girlish dreams about falling in love and marrying a prince of a man, and perhaps being blessed with children of her own one day, life had taken her down a different path. She hadn't met the right man, and now she was caring for the children of others. But being a Parasol Academy governess was fulfilling in its own way. Her career was enough.

As long as you still have a career, whispered "Apprehensive Hermina" at the back of her mind. *As long as Sir Bedivere and anyone else doesn't find out what you've done.*

The hall outside Mina's room was very quiet save for the ponderous ticking of a longcase clock. No one would be up at this hour save for Rose Cottage's servants. Mina decided she would descend to the kitchen and enjoy a spot of tea and perhaps a slice of toast with marmalade before waking Christopher to get him ready for the train journey back to London.

As she approached the top of the stairs, a soft sound—a muffled sob—drifted out into the hall from the nearby guest bedroom.

Christopher?

Oh no! What could be wrong? Was he ill? Was he having a bad dream? Was he feeling abandoned and lost?

Her heart squeezing tight with anxiety, Mina rushed forward and knocked gently on her charge's door. "Christopher... Lord Fitzwilliam? It's me, Miss Davenport. May I come in?"

The crying ceased and a moment later, the door creaked open revealing a woebegone-looking Christopher in his nightgown with Mr. Hopwell clutched to his chest. His cheeks were flushed and tear-stained, his eyes were red and swollen, and his overly long blond locks were... gone!

Someone had lopped off the young viscount's distinctive ringlets that had made him look like a cherubic child from a Restoration painting.

"Christopher..." Mina sank to her knees and took one of the boy's hands in hers. "What's wrong? What's happened? What can I do to help?"

The boy's bottom lip wobbled. "Your mama cut my hair last night. She said it was too hard for anyone to look after. That it was too knotty and too difficult to comb. And that I looked"—a tear slid down his cheek—"silly. Like a... a foppish milksop. And that all the children at the parish school were laughing at me behind my back." Christopher hiccupped. "But I swear no one was."

Mina's blood began to boil. Her mother could be casually cruel and far too blunt sometimes. "I'm so sorry," she said gently as she pulled a kerchief from her uniform's pocket and offered it to Christopher. "My mama was wrong to say those things. But, I do think your hair was getting a little too long and needed a bit of a cut. And it *will* be a lot easier to comb. And I do think it looks quite smart. In fact, you look rather grown-up."

Christopher sniffed and dragged the kerchief across his drippy nose. "I do?"

"Most definitely," said Mina. "Now"—she rose to her feet—"why don't I tell you why I've come to see you? I think you'll like my news."

She ushered Christopher into the room and found a flannel by the wash basin. "I know I said you would need to stay at Rose Cottage for a while," she began as she dampened the washcloth. "But how would you like it if we went to London and stayed at the Marquess of Kinsale's house? You remember Lord Kinsale, don't you? And his pug, Brutus?"

Christopher's eyes lit up like firecrackers on Guy Fawkes Night. "Of course I do! I had such fun aboard his ship. And the ginger beer and pound cake and Bath buns were wonderful. Might I have ginger beer and cake and Bath buns again?"

Mina wiped the boy's face, then reached for his comb. "I think that could be arranged."

Half a minute of silence passed as Mina began to tidy Christopher's sleep-tousled hair. Then the boy ventured, "Are you going to marry Lord Kinsale?"

Mina's cheeks grew decidedly warm. "Oh no. Nothing like that. Lord Kinsale is employing me as a governess for his new ward. An eight-year-old boy named Tom. You'll have lessons together."

"Oh . . ." Christopher bit his lip while he smoothed the velvet nap on Mr. Hopwell's ears. "I should like a friend. Do you think we might be friends?"

Mina smiled encouragingly. "I don't see why not. Although Tom has lived quite a different life to you. He hasn't any family and has had to live by his own wits on the streets of London for some time. Because of that, he hasn't received any sort of lessons."

Christopher's expression grew solemn. "That sounds dreadful."

Mina gave the boy's shoulder a light squeeze. "I suspect it's been more dreadful than we can even imagine. But thanks to Lord Kinsale, Tom's fortune is about to change. And we will help him adjust to his new circumstances. Which reminds me . . ."

Mina caught Christopher's eye. "While we're living at Kinsale House, I'm afraid I must ask you to . . . to use yet another last name. You see, the marquess believes that we . . . that we are related to each other. That is why he has invited you to stay as well."

Christopher's brow furrowed. "Are you going to pretend to be my mother? Do you want me to call you 'mama'?"

"Oh no. Nothing like that." Mina gave an inward sigh. This was becoming very complicated, fabricating a truth to keep Lord Fitzwilliam's true identity hidden. "We will pretend that you are . . . that you are my cousin. Or second cousin. Or something like that. So, you will be Christopher Davenport for now."

The boy's frown deepened. "So not Christopher Hopwell anymore?"

"That's right," said Mina. "I think it will make things simpler."

Christopher sighed. "All right. And what shall I call you? Cousin Hermina? Or Miss Davenport still?"

Mina smiled. "Either will do. I don't expect anyone will notice all that much. Although Tom will call me Miss Davenport, so you could do the same." Of course, she'd have to have a quiet word with the marquess about this new "lie"—that she was passing Christopher off as a distant cousin—when she arrived at Kinsale House. But Lord Kinsale seemed like such a kindhearted man, she was certain he would go along with the ruse to preserve her reputation in front of his other servants.

Crossing to the small chest of drawers beside the bed, Mina continued, "Why don't you get dressed while I pack your valise. Then after we've had breakfast, we'll set off for London. How does that sound?"

Christopher chewed on his lower lip. "We're not going to use a magic cupboard again, are we? I don't like it very much. It makes me feel dizzy and ill."

Mina sympathized. "No, we'll catch the train."

Christopher nodded eagerly. "I think that sounds most agreeable. Especially the breakfast part." The boy took the fresh pair of knickerbocker trousers, stockings, and a shirt that Mina offered, then darted behind the screen. "I'm ever so hungry. I only had bread and an apple for dinner last night. I'm not fond of jellied tongue and sprouts."

Mina pressed her hand to her mouth as her stomach lurched in sympathy. *Oh dear.* She understood why her mother was so frugal when it came to meals—she was a widow with limited means and had a genuine fear of sliding into genteel poverty. But really, jellied tongue and Brussels sprouts? "I'll make sure

Cook gives you an extra slice of toast with your boiled egg," she said. "And there'll be toast with marmalade too."

"Hurrah!" cried Christopher from behind the screen.

Fifteen minutes later, Mina was escorting Christopher downstairs to the parlor-cum-morning-room beside the kitchen. The cook, Mrs. Appleton, and the housemaid, Lizzie, who were sitting at the scrubbed oak kitchen table enjoying their own early morning cup of tea, gasped in unison when Mina popped through the door.

"Miss Davenport," exclaimed the cook, jumping to her feet. "We weren't expecting you back 'ere at Rose Cottage for another week or two. Is everything all right?"

"Oh, yes, perfectly all right," said Mina with a smile. "Although there's been a change of plan. I've come to collect young Christopher and will take him back to London."

The cook nodded sagely. "I expect that's for the best, miss. What with the gentleman who called 'ere yesterday evenin', askin' about you an' the boy."

Mina's blood ran colder than the water in the Arctic Circle. "What do you mean?" She pressed a hand to her chest, where her heart had begun to gallop most unsteadily. "What sort of gentleman? Did he identify himself? Did he ask for Christopher by name?"

"I don't rightly know, miss. It was Lizzie"—she nodded at the housemaid—"who answered the door. And then your mother spoke to 'im. The upshot of it is, Mrs. Davenport sent 'im away wiv a flea in 'is ear, and the gentleman was none the wiser. About you or young Master Christopher."

Mina sank onto one of the vacant kitchen chairs as relief flooded her. "What can you tell me, Lizzie?"

The girl twisted her apron in her hands. "Not much more, miss. The fellow didn't leave a card, an' I've forgotten 'is name. First, 'e wanted to know if you were 'ere an' if you 'ad brought a young boy wiv long blond curls and a purple toy rabbit to stay. 'E even 'ad a photograph of you. Taken from a newspaper by the looks o' it. When you was at that fancy weddin' of your duchess friend a few months ago. But then Mrs. Davenport came to the door and told 'im you was in London and she knew nuffink about any boy. So 'e could push off." Then the maid blushed. "Well, o' course she didn't tell 'im to push off exactly. But you know what I mean. Your mother would not be bullied by no fancy gentleman from London."

Fancy gentleman? Mina swallowed to moisten her mouth, which suddenly felt as dry as the ashes in the grate. "What did he look like, Lizzie?"

The girl's brow dipped into a frown. "'E was tall an' 'ad salt-an'-pepper 'air an' the bushiest eyebrows an' muttonchops I've ever seen, miss. An' 'e wore silver spectacles."

So *not* Sir Bedivere Ponsonby. Mina breathed a sigh of relief. The baronet had blond hair that was only graying a little at the temples. He also sported a distinctive goatee beard and a thin mustache that his valet curled at the ends with wax à la Sir Walter Raleigh. And he didn't wear spectacles, not even when he was reading.

But that didn't mean Sir Bedivere hadn't employed a private detective or two to scour the countryside for his ward.

Thank heavens her mother had had both the pluck and the gumption to not give away anything pertaining to Christopher.

Mina thanked Mrs. Appleton and Lizzie for sharing their intelligence. While Christopher was taking breakfast, she would speak discreetly with her mother. The sooner she and Christopher were on their way to London, the better.

A short time later, when Christopher was happily tucking into his boiled egg with a battalion of buttery toast soldiers, and Mina was deciding whether to pour herself another cup of tea or go in search of her mother upstairs, Edwina Davenport appeared. She burst into the morning room in a flurry of violet-patterned silk, fluttering hands, and exclamations of surprise that Mina had turned up so unexpectedly.

Once Mina had poured her mother a cup of tea, she quickly explained the reason for her unscheduled visit—that she'd come to collect Christopher because she had a new governess's post and her employer was more than happy for the boy to reside with her; Christopher would be company for the gentleman's ward who was about the same age. She then ascertained that Lizzie and Mrs. Appleton's summation of the mysterious "fancy" gentleman's visit to Rose Cottage the day before had been accurate.

"What sort of mess have you gotten yourself mixed up in, Hermina?" asked her mother, once she'd recounted her own conversation with the far-too-nosy bespectacled stranger. "Starting a new position in London is all well and good, but really, whatever this favor is that you're doing for a so-called friend"—she nodded at Christopher who, thankfully, seemed completely engrossed in dunking his toast soldiers into his runny golden egg yolk—"is it really worth it?" Her face suddenly blanched whiter than the linen of her widow's cap. "You're not involved in anything illegal are you?" she whispered urgently. "That man yesterday—I think he said his name was Cheavers—he had a weasely look about him. Like he was sly and up to no good." She nodded at Christopher. "That's why I cut the boy's hair. Because that man was looking for a child with long ringlets."

So her mother hadn't lopped off Christopher's curls just for the sake of it. "I appreciate the fact that you were only trying to keep Christopher safe," said Mina in a low voice. "Although, you might have spared his feelings. Calling him a silly milksop was unkind and of course, not true."

Her mother sniffed. "The boy was being difficult about it,

and it was the only thing I could think of to say to get him to cooperate. I'd rather have him believe that I'm horrid than risk him getting taken away by that iffy fellow, Cheavers. The man had the meanest eyes."

"Thank you for fending him off," said Mina. "Hopefully he won't bother you again. As soon as Christopher has finished his breakfast, we'll be on our way."

To Mina's surprise, her mother suddenly reached out across the breakfast table and squeezed her arm. "You'll take care, won't you, Hermina? I know you can look after yourself, but... I can't help but feel something *is* wrong. Call it a mother's intuition."

Touched—Edwina Davenport hardly ever displayed affection—Mina covered her mother's hand with her own. "I'll be careful, Mama. The gentleman I'll be working for is most kind. And generous. You mustn't worry."

"You didn't give his name earlier when you were talking about your new position," said her mother. Her brown eyes brightened. "I'm sure he's wealthy. But you only mentioned he has a ward, not children of his own. Does that mean he's not married?"

"No, he isn't married," said Mina, praying that the warmth in her cheeks wouldn't betray the fact that she might be harboring a teeny-tiny tendre for the Irish marquess. "But he's a nobleman, Mama. And I am but a governess and a lowly vicar's daughter. Besides, you know as well as I that the hired help should not fraternize with their employers. The Parasol Academy expressly forbids it."

"That didn't stop your friend Emmeline, who's now a duchess," remarked her mother with an arch of her brow. "*And* I've read *Jane Eyre*. Stranger things have happened..."

Mina would have been less shocked if her mother had slapped her across the face with a wet codfish. She'd read *Jane*

Eyre? Her mother occasionally browsed through magazines like *Blackwood's Lady's Magazine* or *The New Monthly Belle Assemblée* (which she borrowed from Dorothea) but Mina had never seen her read a *novel*. Perhaps Edwina Davenport's straitlaced attitude was softening as she got older.

"Emmeline's situation was different," said Mina with a decided nod of her head. "And *Jane Eyre* is a work of fiction."

"I'm well aware," her mother said, her manner suddenly as stiff as the starched linen tablecloth. "But I've only ever wanted good things for you, Hermina. And your sister. It's why I've always asked you to be mindful of what you eat." Her gaze dropped to Mina's bread-and-butter plate where her marmalade toast crumbs lay. "I hope you only had one piece of toast. Because, mark my words, most men prefer wasp-waisted women. Your employer, whoever he is, won't look twice at you if you gain too many pounds."

"Well, given the fact I have a career and I don't wish to marry, I hardly think the circumference of my waist signifies," said Mina equally as stiffly as she rose from the table. Disappointment sat in her belly like a cold hard stone. "If you're finished, Christopher, then it might be time for us to be on our way. We don't want to miss the nine o'clock train."

The boy smiled and put down his napkin. "Very well," he said brightly, hopping to his feet.

Another shadow of fear crossed her mother's features as she glanced at the child. "I don't know what you are embroiled in, Hermina, but I don't like it. Not one little bit."

"I know, Mama. I know." Mina sighed as she held out her hand for Christopher. "But rest assured, I will work out a way to resolve this . . . situation. All I ask is that you don't tell anyone about . . ." She nodded at the young viscount standing beside her, hugging his velvet rabbit. "The less others know about any of this, the better."

Her mother shook her head. "I'm starting to think I'd rather know nothing at all." As she touched the curls escaping from her cap, she released a weary sigh. "I swear I'm getting more gray hairs by the day, my Hermina. Promise me you'll stay safe."

"I will," said Mina, sending her mother a reassuring smile as she and Christopher headed for the door. "I'm a Parasol Academy-trained governess and trust me, we're prepared for anything."

Chapter 9

Wherein an Encounter with a Cat Yields Limited Results; And a Magical Pocket Yields Results Which Are Unexpected...

The distance from Rose Cottage to Ablington's railway station was but a short walk of one mile down quiet, winding country laneways. Nevertheless, Mina couldn't help but peer over her shoulder and around corners and into the deep green shadows as she and Christopher passed by towering yew hedgerows and thick copses of oak and elm and beech trees.

She wasn't expecting the weaselly bespectacled gentleman, Cheavers, to jump out and accost her and Christopher, but it was always best to be on one's guard. Mina was also silently berating herself for not bringing her Parasol Academy umbrella along. She could have used it to cloak her and Christopher in a shroud of invisibility, or briefly bamboozle the fellow with the Point-of-Confusion to give them a chance to escape. At the very least, she could use it to fend off the man if he tried to grab her or Christopher. One thing Mina had learned at the Academy was that one should never underestimate the power of a good umbrella thwacking.

Of course, she wasn't completely defenseless. Her trusty knife was strapped to her ankle, and at a pinch, she could always wield Christopher's valise as a weapon. She could also pack a decent punch when the occasion called for it. But she'd rather not become caught up in a physical altercation. Particularly not in front of Christopher. The boy was bound to be frightened.

They arrived in the main village without incident, but Mina, having had more time to ponder the situation, determined that it might be best to proceed with caution for the rest of the journey. Instead of waiting on the platform for the London train—where they would be exposed like sitting ducks—she decided that it would be safer if they took cover beneath a large horse chestnut with low-hanging branches that wasn't far from the railway station's entrance.

There was no doubt in Mina's mind that Sir Bedivere had employed a private detective. Mr. Meecham, Christopher's tutor, must have recalled enough about their brief encounter aboard the *Valiant* to rouse the baronet's suspicions. If this Cheavers character planned to visit the parish school later on in the day to look for Christopher, he *might* have stayed overnight at Ablington's inn, which was at the opposite end of the village green and only a few hundred yards from the station.

At least Christopher won't be at school today . . . Mina shivered in the deep shade of the horse chestnut. It had been a week since she'd taken Christopher and who knew how desperate Sir Bedivere had become in his quest to locate his ward. She'd clearly been naive to think the baronet *wouldn't* look for the boy.

Although, if it were discovered that Christopher no longer resided with Sir Bedivere, the baronet's access to the Fitzwilliam fortune would be curtailed. Such were the terms of the guardianship. But in order for Sir Bedivere to conduct his ambitious expedition—to navigate the Northwest Passage or anywhere at all—he *needed* that fortune. So really, it made sense that the baronet would want the search for Christopher to be conducted discreetly. He certainly couldn't afford a scandal.

Yes, Mina was relatively confident that Sir Bedivere wouldn't go to Scotland Yard and create a hullabaloo. He'd continue to use private investigators. Mina just had to be careful to avoid them.

Mina glanced at the front of the railway station. According to the clock above the arched brick entrance, it was ten minutes to nine. She needed to purchase tickets for the journey, but she would only do so at the last possible minute. A handful of villagers were already making their way into the station; she recognized many of them and of those she didn't, none fitted Cheavers's description. That didn't mean the stranger wasn't lurking about somewhere. It was almost as though she could sense him nearby. Waiting. Watching...

Mina began to feel as twitchy as a cat on a hot griddle. Perhaps she could reason with Christopher that it was too dangerous to catch the train and they should teleport to London after all.

At that moment, a large gray tabby—Mr. Quigley, the stationmaster's cat to be precise—appeared on a low stone wall not far from the horse chestnut. Mina knew from experience that he was a most aloof creature and may or may not deign to talk to her. But she would try. Perhaps he'd noticed the stranger. If the coast was clear, she'd venture onto the platform.

Good morning, Mr. Quigley, she offered in a friendly manner. *I haven't seen you for a while. I trust you are well.*

The tabby regarded Mina with his usual superior air. *Do I know you?* he asked, his green-gold eyes glowing. *And there's no need to stare. One would think you'd never seen a cat before.*

None quite so handsome as you, Mr. Quigley, replied Mina. *And I'm surprised you don't remember me. Miss Hermina Davenport's the name. I don't expect you come across many in-*

dividuals in Ablington who can communicate with you by thought alone.
Humph. The cat's tail twitched and his eyes narrowed. *As if a feline would want to communicate with most humans, Miss Davenport. The majority are quite foolish. And annoying. Always wanting to* pat *me. And it's always "puss puss this" and "puss puss that" and "come here, kitty kitty."* He shivered dramatically. *I really wish they'd keep their hands and silly, infantilizing names to themselves.*
Well, I promise I won't ever try to pat you, unless you invite me to, said Mina soothingly. *And I wouldn't dare call you puss or kitty.* Her gaze returned to the entrance of Ablington Station. *I say, you wouldn't have happened to notice a bespectacled gentleman with graying hair and exceedingly bushy eyebrows and muttonchops on the platform this morning, would you?*
No . . . Mr. Quigley's tail began to swish back and forth and his ears flattened as he caught sight of a pigeon strutting past on the footpath. *But I haven't been there the entire time. This feline has better things to do than laze about, watching the comings and goings of strangers all day.*
Of course, said Mina. *I didn't mean to imply you were lazy.*
Perhaps sensing the cat's predatory gaze, the pigeon suddenly took off, winging its way over the gabled roof of the station. The tabby stood and arched his back. *Now look what you've done,* he grumbled.
Mina rolled her eyes. She didn't have the time or inclination to argue with the disgruntled cat. Instead, she thanked Mr. Quigley for his time, took Christopher's hand, then crossed the street to the station. The train was due to arrive in five minutes and a small queue had already formed at the ticket counter. Thankfully, there was no sign of anyone who matched the description of the man looking for Christopher.
Mina had just purchased two fares to London and had

moved to the far end of the platform, when out of the corner of her eye, she caught sight of a middle-aged bespectacled gentleman. *Cheavers?* Her heart hurtling, Mina turned her head to get a better look at the chap and then she almost fainted.

Blast, bother, and oh, I wish I could utter something a lot stronger that begins with B! It *had* to be Cheavers. The man was sporting the most fiercely bristling muttonchops and eyebrows Mina had ever seen in her life. In fact, he looked like his cheeks and jaw were sprouting thick hedgehog prickles, and two fuzzy caterpillars shadowed his eyes.

In one gloved hand, he held a carpetbag, while his other hand delved into his waistcoat pocket to retrieve a pewter pocket watch. But Mina didn't wait to see what the man—he *must* be the private detective—would do next. As quickly and quietly as she could, Mina ushered Christopher around the corner of the station house so they were out of sight.

At that moment, a train whistle—as shrill as a clarion call—sounded in the distance. *Darn.* If Mina missed this train, there wouldn't be another until mid-afternoon. Which meant she'd be late to London and Lord Kinsale was expecting her by one o'clock. She had to get to Kinsale House on time. She must not be late on her first day.

She thrust her hand into her uniform's pocket. She couldn't risk taking Christopher onto the same train as Cheavers. She really had no choice. Despite her charge's reluctance to hop in a "magic cupboard" again, she was going to have to teleport them back to London.

Only... Mina frowned as she dug deeper into her gown's pocket, all the way down to the very bottom. Where on earth was her leyport key? Whenever she needed it, it always, *always* manifested. But it wasn't there. Her fingers closed around nothing. Nothing at all.

Fear clogged Mina's throat. Did the Fae know what she'd done? Had they somehow found out that she had broken the

Academy's rules and removed Christopher from the "care" of his guardian? Was she being punished? But... but the child's life would be endangered if this Cheavers took the young viscount back to Sir Bedivere. *Please*, she whispered in her mind. *Please, Good Queen Maeve. Please do not forsake the safety of this sweet boy. I promised his godmother I would protect him, no matter what.*

And then, all at once, Mina felt something materialize in her palm. It wasn't metallic like a leyport key. It was cold and cylindrical. A small bottle perhaps? And below the bottle she could feel her ley-spectacles.

Mina quickly withdrew her hand from her pocket. Yes, the Fae had provided her with a small, dark blue bottle. And attached to the bottle's neck by a silver thread was a label. Popping on her ley-spectacles, Mina read the fine print.

Drink me.

Drink me? But what would happen if she did?

Mina blinked in surprise. Turning the label over, she discovered more print on the other side...

To don a glamour—an illusory disguise—that will deceive the eyes of others, simply sip the contents of this bottle (one sip per person) then utter, "Glamify." Uttering "Unglamify" will reverse the spell. Please note: Disguises are assigned by chance and chance alone.
Individual results may vary.

Cheavers was no doubt looking for a young woman in a dark blue Parasol Academy uniform with chestnut-brown hair, and a seven-year-old blond boy who carried a mauve velvet rabbit with him wherever he went. But what if drinking this *Glamify* potion could change how they looked?

While Mina had never heard of such a spell, she wasn't going to quibble with the Fae. A Parasol Academy pocket was supposed to provide a governess or nanny with exactly the right thing to care for one's charges. So she would trust this gift.

Besides, there was no time to dally as the train was pulling into the station with a great metallic screeching and clanking and belching of smoke.

Mina hastily put away her ley-spectacles then uncorked the bottle and sniffed the contents. The liquid inside smelled mouthwateringly delicious—like sweet summer berries and vanilla and something spicy like cinnamon. The sort of thing that would taste delicious on pancakes.

"The train's here, Miss Davenport," said Christopher, tugging on her hand.

"I see," said Mina. "But before we hop on, we need to take a sip of . . . of medicine from this bottle."

The boy's brow wrinkled. "Is it the seasickness medicine? Trains don't usually make me feel sick."

"No, it isn't. But it will keep us safe on our trip to London," Mina said. "It's going to . . . to make us look a little different. Just for a little while. Think of it as a magical disguise. It will feel like we're putting on a fancy-dress costume. I'll drink first. Then you. All right?"

Christopher nodded. "All right."

The train's doors had opened and passengers were starting to disembark and collect their luggage. There was no time to lose.

Mina took a sip of the potion—it had the consistency of treacle and tasted like blueberries—then she offered the bottle to Christopher. "Just one small sip," she instructed. As soon as the boy complied, Mina took his hand and murmured, "*Glamify.*"

Almost at once, a shimmering, deep purple mist seemed to engulf her and Christopher, swirling around them like a cloak. It ruffled Mina's hair and skirts and brushed across her face and neck, stroking like gentle feathers. However, when the mist began to dissipate, Christopher looked exactly the same. From what Mina could see of herself, her appearance had not changed either.

Christopher frowned. "Did it work, Miss Davenport? You don't look any different to me."

Panic flared inside Mina as the passengers on the platform had begun to hop on the train. Had the spell really not taken? Had she and Christopher not drunk enough of the magical potion? Was Christopher supposed to have uttered the incantation himself?

And then Mina caught a glimpse of herself and Christopher in one of the station house's windows. Her appearance *had* been transformed and so had the young viscount's. Staring back at her was a stooped, silver-haired woman in a black bonnet and widow's weeds and the boy beside her was actually a tall and gangly red-haired youth with a scattering of freckles across his nose and cheeks. Instead of holding a velvet rabbit, he was cradling a brown leather rugby ball in his arm.

Oh, thank goodness. The *Glamify* spell *had* worked. Just not in the way she'd expected.

"Let's not miss the train," said Mina as she tugged Christopher out from the shadows of the station house and rushed onto the platform toward the closest carriage. "Wait," she called to the conductor who was about to blow his silver whistle to signal the train was going to leave. "We have tickets."

"You're cutting it fine, madam," he said with a stern frown. But nevertheless, the man let her and Christopher hop onto the train. No sooner had they boarded than the conductor's whistle blew, the doors slammed shut, and the train began to chug away from Ablington Station.

Her knees shaking like jelly, Mina placed Christopher's valise in a luggage rack, then she sank onto the bench seat below it. Christopher settled beside her. When she cast her gaze about the carriage, examining the other passengers, she couldn't see any sign of Cheavers. Hopefully he'd stay in the carriage he'd chosen and not move about.

"Why does everything look a bit funny, Miss Davenport?" Christopher asked. He was squinting as he looked about the carriage. "It's like I'm looking through smoke or fog."

"Yes, I see it too," said Mina. "But I wouldn't worry. I expect it's the steam from the train. Or perhaps a mist has rolled in?"

Of course, that wasn't true. It was clearly the glamour. While the spell was actively working, it appeared it affected their perception slightly. When Mina looked down at herself and across to Christopher, she could see their true forms. It was only when she caught her reflection in the carriage window that she saw a stranger staring back at her with a tall, thin, red-headed and freckle-faced youth beside her. Hopefully Christopher wouldn't notice his altered appearance. She didn't want the boy to be alarmed. All going well, they'd be in London and safely installed in Kinsale House within a handful of hours.

In the meantime, perhaps some form of distraction was in order. Reaching into her pocket, Mina found a pack of playing cards. "Why don't I teach you how to play a card game I know," she said brightly. "It's called Old Maid. And afterwards, we could play snap or dominoes or spillikins."

"Oh, that sounds like wizard fun," said Christopher, putting down Mr. Hopwell on the seat beside him. Mina trusted that everyone else saw a football, not a toy rabbit.

After removing three of the queens from the pack, Mina began to shuffle the cards. She was certain the Fae's glamour spell would hold. And clearly, her magical pocket had given her just what she needed to keep Christopher safe at just the right moment. He hadn't wanted to teleport to London, so perhaps that was why she'd been gifted a novel potion and incantation.

Most of all, Mina was relieved she was still able to practice magic in the name of the Fae, upholding the Parasol Academy's key tenet, which was to protect children. Perhaps, in time, she'd seek Mrs. Temple's counsel. Especially if Sir Bedivere persisted in searching for his ward.

Mina dealt out the playing cards. With any luck, the baronet would abandon the cause and soon head off on his expedition to navigate the Northwest Passage. He'd be gone for months and months, and by then, Mina would have worked out what to do next.

Unless he reveals his hand sooner... If it became apparent that the baronet had been ensorcelled, if Mina could procure evidence that would support Lady Grenfell's assertion that Sir Bedivere was being controlled by supernatural forces that meant Christopher harm, perhaps she could go to Mrs. Temple sooner rather than later...

When Mina turned her cards over and fanned them out, the first card that appeared was the queen of hearts. The image of the woman shrouded in red with her imperious glare immediately brought to mind another queen, the evil Fae queen, Mab. If the ring that had once belonged to King Charles I, a rumored changeling, was indeed cursed, then it would follow that Queen Mab might be influencing Sir Bedivere's behavior.

But in what way? Did Queen Mab want another human child of noble birth—a young viscount perhaps—in her Fae Court?

Lady Grenfell had feared that her godson would perish in a frozen wasteland, a place like the Arctic. But what did the Arctic have to do with Evil Queen Mab?

Mina hardly knew. The Parasol Academy's graduates were trained to thwart attempted Fae abductions of young children by Mab or her minions. According to Mrs. Temple, there hadn't been any incidents of human children being kidnapped and then changelings left in their place for quite some time. Although, truth to tell, Mina wasn't sure *why* that would be the case. Had something happened to Queen Mab? Had her influence in the Earthly Realm been curtailed in some way? But what, if anything, did that have to do with Sir Bedivere being ensorcelled and his expedition to the Arctic Circle?

It was all quite mystifying and Mina had no clue what to make of anything. For the foreseeable future, all she could do was continue to protect the child in her care.

Surely no one—neither Fae nor human—could fault her for that.

Chapter 10

Concerning a Yapping Pug and a Twitchy Cock; And Jabs and Crosses and Hooks; Followed by an Exceedingly Impolite Series of Digs . . .

The series of short, sharp raps on the gleaming oak-paneled doors of Kinsale House's ballroom startled both Phinn and Brutus. Brutus began yapping wildly as he leapt down from the window seat and raced over to the double doors, while Phinn jumped so much, water sloshed out of the cut-crystal tumbler that was halfway to his lips and landed on his bare torso.

"Jaysus," he muttered beneath his breath as he pulled off the towel that he'd slung about his neck and swiped at the rivulets running down his chest. He'd just finished a "training" session in the only room that seemed purpose built for his physical exercise needs and had been about to retreat to his suite (a whole feckin' suite of rooms; he still couldn't quite believe it)—to bathe and change before the new governess and her son arrived at one o'clock or thereabouts. It was only a quarter past twelve according to the longcase clock in the corner of the room, so he had plenty of time to get ready and settle his nerves.

Yes, the former prizefighter "Cutthroat O'Connell" was inexplicably nervous. Phinn had decided he needed to work off some of his pent-up energy before he set eyes on the lovely

Mrs.—no, *Miss*—Mina Davenport again. And performing one hundred press-ups before pummeling the hell out of the leather punching bag he'd had suspended from the ballroom's chandelier seemed like the best way to do that. Although, it seemed he was still as twitchy as a cock at dawn.

There was another volley of impatient knocks. "My lord," called a sonorous voice through the panels. "Are you in there?"

Phinn scowled. It was the odious butler he'd inherited with the house and the title of marquess. A smug fellow by the name of Smedley.

Brutus apparently didn't like the far-too-haughty servant either. He was growling now, his upper lip quivering and his teeth bared.

With a sigh, Phinn put down his tumbler on a spindly glass and gilt table that had been pushed against one silk-papered wall, tossed aside the towel, then threw on an emerald-green satin robe. Or "banyan" as Phinn's meticulous valet, Frobisher, called it.

"C-come in," Phinn called, running his linen-wrapped fingers through his sweat-damp hair.

The double doors swung wide and Phinn's mouth dropped open in horror as standing beside the hawk-nosed butler was Miss Davenport and her son.

What the devil? It was clear that the supercilious Smedley was deliberately trying to embarrass both his master and his new employee.

Phinn wouldn't put it past the man as he had the most insufferable sense of self-importance. It was obvious he looked down his nose at the new Marquess of Kinsale with his Irish heritage and lack of refinement... which included (amongst other frowned-upon habits such as cursing) boxing in the ballroom in a state of dishabille.

Young Christopher was seemingly oblivious to the social faux pas that was occurring. Miss Davenport on the other hand, was not. As she dipped into a curtsy, her countenance was aflame and her widened eyes were riveted to Phinn's partially exposed chest and abdomen. Indeed, her shocked gaze slid down his body, over his buckskin breeches to his bare lower legs and feet.

"My lord," said Smedley, "the new governess, Miss Hermina Davenport is here. And *another* child."

This last remark was uttered with such disdain, the governess's attention immediately shifted from Phinn's person to the butler. "What on earth do you mean by that remark, sir?" she asked, a frown of disapproval in her voice. "Are you suggesting my"—she placed a hand on her son's shoulder and caught Phinn's eye—"my young *cousin* is not welcome here? Because Lord Kinsale doesn't have a problem with it."

Ah, so that's how Miss Davenport was going to explain the presence of her child at Kinsale House. A very sensible ruse given she was a miss, not a missus. The servants certainly didn't need to know she was an unwed mother. He'd hate to think they would look down upon her if the truth came out.

Phinn pulled his banyan closed and fastened the tie to secure it in place. "Smedley m-m-means he's not accustomed to havin' children at Kin-Kinsale House, Miss Dav-Davenport," he said, aiming a quelling look at the butler. "But he'll g-g-get used it. Just like he'll get used to his new ma-master and his ways." Phinn cocked a brow. "Wo-won't you, Smedley?"

The butler's expression became as shuttered as a window in a tempest. "Undoubtedly, my lord," he said with a slight tilt of his body—a barely there bow. "Will there be anything else?"

Phinn gave a grunt. He rather thought the butler had done enough for now. Nevertheless, he said, "Could you ask Fro-Fro-Frobisher to draw me a b-b-bath?"

"Of course. Quite, my lord."

But as the butler turned to go, Miss Davenport cleared her throat. "Perhaps you could summon the housekeeper, Mr. Smedley. I believe it's customary for the head female servant to show new staff—particularly fellow female staff—to their quarters. But I'm sure you know that."

Smedley's lip curled ever so slightly as he faced the governess. "Indeed, Miss Davenport," he said. "I'll summon her straightaway. No doubt she'll be here directly." And then he tipped his spare, long-limbed frame into another cursory bow before he stalked off down the hall toward the kitchen where the housekeeper's office and butler's pantry lay.

Phinn, acutely conscious of the fact that he was shockingly underdressed, *and* his butler had been shockingly rude, cast about in his head for the right thing to say at this particular moment. This was not how he'd envisaged his next encounter with Miss Davenport. It didn't help that Brutus was still growling. Although his attention seemed to be focused on the toy rabbit Christopher appeared to be so fond of.

"My lord," said Miss Davenport, "I'm so sorry to...to have interrupted"—she gestured at the ballroom and the punching bag—"your boxing session. Our train arrived earlier than I expected. And, well, I... If I'd known you were otherwise engaged, I would have asked your butler to send for the housekeeper to show us to our quarters. But he insisted that you wished to receive us." She gently touched Christopher's head.

"I'm sorry as w-w-well, Miss Dav-Davenport. Smedley is..." Phinn struggled to find the right word.

"Far too full of himself?" suggested the governess, with a light tinkling laugh that seemed to reach right inside Phinn and turn parts of him into a squishy pudding. "I shall soon knock that out of him." Her gaze transferred to the punching bag. "It might surprise you to learn, Lord Kinsale, that I sometimes engage in a bit of boxing."

What? This lovely young woman, with delicate features and warm hazel eyes, boxed?

Phinn's surprise must have shown on his face as Miss Davenport laughed again. "Surely Mrs. Temple told you that all Parasol Academy nannies and governesses are trained in the art of self-defense. For the protection of our charges of course. I can also fence, and wrestle, and shoot a pistol. I'm rather a good shot if I do say so myself."

"I . . . er . . . I-I had no idea," mumbled Phinn as he tried not to imagine wrestling with the comely governess in ways that were *not* befitting of a gentleman. Especially in the presence of *her child*. Although, Christopher wasn't paying attention to their conversation. The boy had wandered across the ballroom to the other end to examine a magnificent mural depicting nymphs and winged sylphs frolicking about a shaded lily-pond while a small band of centaurs and satyrs playing lutes and pan pipes looked on. Brutus had followed, his large black eyes fixed upon the toy rabbit.

"You look skeptical of my boxing prowess, my lord." The governess grinned. "But I assure you, I can throw a decent punch. Let me show you." Miss Davenport removed her dark blue bonnet, revealing her sleek chestnut hair, placed the hat on the glass and gilt table, then crossed to the punching bag and took up a perfect fighting stance, left foot to the fore. Then she fisted her gloved hands and delivered a neat series of punches— a right jab, a left cross, a right hook, then finished with an even stronger left hook.

Phinn was most impressed and he said so. "But m-m-may I suggest that when you throw a . . . throw a jab or a c-c-cross, rotate your shoul-shoulder a bit more. The punch will be more f-f-forceful."

"I see," said Miss Davenport. Then she bit her lip and frowned. "Might I . . . might I ask you to show me, Lord Kinsale? I hope you don't mind, but Mrs. Temple told me that you used to be a professional boxer. A prizefighter."

"Aye, I was," he said. "And no, I . . . I don't mind." Studying the governess's expression, Phinn suddenly wondered if she might be impressed by his former occupation, rather than shocked. A tiny glow—a flickering warmth—sparked in the center of his chest. One of pride rather than the usual shame he'd come to associate with his past.

Well, if the lass wanted a bit of a demonstration, he would give her one.

As he approached the punching bag, the governess took a few steps back. "It's-it's best to tack-tackle a punch like this," he said. With his left foot forward, he then threw all his not inconsiderable weight behind a series of powerful right jabs at the sand-filled leather bag. "See . . ." He delivered a volley of left and right crosses to the punching bag, then a hook that sent the chandelier above them shaking. "See . . . how I throw me shoulders . . . into each b-blow?"

When he'd finished "showing off," (because deep down, he knew that's exactly what he'd been doing) he was slightly breathless, and he swore Miss Davenport was too. "That's where much of your p-p-power comes from," he said. "Your shoulders."

The governess nodded. "My goodness, you're strong, my lord," she murmured huskily. "And fast." Then she cleared her throat and added, "I'm surprised that many men would have been game to take you on in the ring."

Was it his imagination, or was there actually a note of quiet awe in Miss Davenport's voice? Phinn's chest swelled to think the young woman might admire his physical prowess, if nothing else. He wiped his forearm across his damp forehead, hoping the action might hide the flush he could feel creeping into his cheeks. He cleared his throat. "In the ring, they c-c-called me Cutthroat O'Connell. It's a n-n-name I was never par-particularly fond of, but it drew in the crowds. Which m-m-meant more money for me m-m-manager and me. During the famine, it was the only thing that k-k-kept the w-w-wolf from the door."

Jaysus, why had he disclosed *that* to the prim and proper governess? *She'll view you as some hulking murderous brute*, he chided himself. *Not a hero*. And oh, God's teeth, his feckin' robe—*no, banyan, you dolt*—had come loose and the poor woman was all goggle-eyed and pink-cheeked again as her pretty hazel eyes settled on his bare chest.

"Me-me apologies, Miss Dav-Davenport," he said, jerking the banyan closed. "About me in-indecorous state of dress. I g-g-got carried away with me demonstration. And to be sure, I'm cer-certain you do not want to hear about me box-boxing days."

"Oh, no, my lord. Do not concern yourself about..." Miss Davenport gestured at his banyan. "In fact, I should be thanking you for teaching this governess something new. And for trusting me enough to share some of your history with me. That time in Ireland must have been so very difficult and challenging."

At that moment, there was a knock on the door and the housekeeper, Mrs. Aldershot, appeared. "Miss Davenport," she said as her curious gaze jumped between the governess and Phinn. "I've come to show you and your"—she gestured at Christopher—"your young *cousin*, is it, to your new quarters."

"Christopher is my second cousin, twice removed," explained Miss Davenport.

Christopher returned to Mina's side. "Miss Davenport, am I going to meet Lord Kinsale's ward soon? Tom?"

The governess blushed as her eyes darted to Phinn's. "Oh heavens, I got so caught up with our... our discussion, my lord, I didn't ask after Master Tom."

Phinn shrugged a shoulder. "It's quite... It's quite all right, Miss Dav-Davenport. I expect Tom is some-somewhere about. He's the sort of child who... marches to the b-b-beat of his own drum, as they s-s-say."

Mrs. Aldershot rolled her eyes. "Well, that's one way of

putting it," she muttered. But then she faced the governess and smiled. "Come along then, Miss Davenport. Your room and your cousin's are very close to the old nursery and schoolroom on the second floor. Master Tom's bedchamber is adjacent to young Christopher's as well. I trust that will suit?"

Miss Davenport returned the middle-aged woman's smile. "Thank you, Mrs. Aldershot," she said. "I'm sure it will all be perfect."

The governess collected her bonnet, then turned back to Phinn. "Lord Kinsale," she said as she curtsied before she encouraged her son (no, *cousin* now, Phinn reminded himself) to bow as well. "If there's anything else you need from me, my lord, you only have to ask," she said softly. "I imagine you might like to provide me with more direction on the particulars of the curriculum you'd like to see me teach?"

"Aye, I would, Miss Dav-Davenport. But there's n-n-no rush. Make sure you g-g-get settled first."

Phinn would readily admit that at this particular moment, *he* was feeling particularly *un*settled.

Perhaps he should have asked his valet, Frobisher, to prepare an ice bath for him to cool down.

As Mrs. Aldershot the housekeeper led Christopher and Mina away from the ballroom and down a corridor toward a set of servants' stairs, Mina cursed herself for gawking at her employer like a moonstruck ninnyhammer. Her case of ninnyhammer-itis had been on full display again.

Where was her professionalism for heaven's sake? Where was her self-control?

Of course, it hadn't helped *at all* that Lord Kinsale had been attired only in formfitting buckskin breeches and a silk banyan that had revealed a good deal of his muscled chest and lean torso. Mina swore she'd been able to count the ridges on his abdomen. Six sets of perfectly chiseled stomach muscles. A veritable washboard! She'd never seen such a sight, not even on the Greek and Roman marble statues of gods and warriors at the British Museum.

And then when he'd launched a volley of punches at the punching bag, Mina had almost fallen into a swoon. The way his muscles, slick with sweat, had rippled and flexed... The manner in which the buckskin of his breeches clung to the rock-hard muscles of his thighs. Oh, she'd stared and stared and something deep inside her had fluttered and pulsed and she'd known the feeling was desire.

It had hardly been Lord Kinsale's fault that he'd been caught in such a state of undress. The smarmy butler, Smedley, had clearly known what his employer had been doing in the ballroom, and had brought Mina and Christopher to meet him anyway. It was no doubt a deliberate ploy to not only humiliate Lord Kinsale but disconcert and embarrass his new employee.

And disrespectful and disloyal servants were *not* to be borne. Mina would definitely have to put the butler in his place. No wonder the marquess wanted to enlist the aid of someone like her—someone who understood polite society's rules and could help him settle into his new elevated place in the world. As for the housekeeper, Mrs. Aldershot, Mina wasn't sure where the middle-aged woman's loyalties lay just yet. She supposed time would tell.

"So, I hear you are some fancy governess from some fancy academy," said Mrs. Aldershot as she scaled the narrow servants' stairs with Mina and Christopher following along behind.

"Yes," said Mina. "The Parasol Academy to be exact. Queen Victoria herself granted the college a Royal Charter."

"Oh, how very la-di-da," said the housekeeper. "But I'm afraid you'll have your work cut out for you trying to teach that street urchin the master dragged in."

"Whatever do you mean?" Mina asked mildly, even though she was inwardly railing against the housekeeper's choice of words. She'd managed to insult Lord Kinsale and his ward in one fell swoop and Mina was *not* impressed.

Mrs. Aldershot snorted as they reached the first-floor landing where she'd paused to catch her breath. "Have you not met the lad yet? He's a right piece of work. A sniveling, thieving pickpocket, he is. Our cook, Mrs. Dunkley, caught him trying to nick silverware out of the kitchen last night. And Smedley boxed his ears after he noticed the boy making off with a gilt Boulle clock from the drawing room. A whole clock! Aside from all that, he's hardly ever here. From what I've seen, he comes and goes as he pleases, darting in and out of the house at all hours of the day and night like the sneaky little rat that he is."

Sneaky little rat? Sniveling, thieving pickpocket? Mina bristled like a cat that had been dumped out in the rain. "I beg your pardon, Mrs. Aldershot?" she said crisply in her best schoolmarm's voice. "I'm sure I misheard you just now."

Mrs. Aldershot puffed out her not inconsiderable chest. "You did not, Miss Davenport. The boy is a nasty little rodent who apparently crawled out of the Fleet Ditch and I have no idea why Lord Kinsale decided to bring him into this house. The old master would be turning over in his grave if he could see who inherited his title—an inarticulate, uncouth lout of an Irishman—who for some insane reason has decided to adopt a filthy little ragamuffin who should rightly be cleaning the chimneys or the gutters, *not* living here in splendor."

The unmitigated cheek of the woman! Mina aimed her best fulminating glare at the horrid housekeeper. "Mrs. Aldershot, I'd have a care if I were you. I've met Master Tom Fleet and found him to be a most charming, forthright boy who has much to recommend him. I would urge you not to judge him based on where he was born, or his hitherto straitened circumstances, but to regard him with compassion and treat him kindly. He's but an eight-year-old child. He's hardly going to choose a better path in life if others look down their nose at him and put obstacles in his way. He needs support, not scornful putdowns and boxing about the ears."

The housekeeper glared back. "Well, I never! How dare—" Mina raised an admonitory finger. "Oh, I *do* dare. And furthermore, if I ever hear or see you insult Lord Kinsale again, *you* will be the one out on the streets. The same can be said for that insufferable swell-headed excuse-for-a-butler, Mr. Smedley. Come, Christopher"—Mina held out her hand to the boy—"I'm sure we can find our bedrooms and the schoolroom. And Mrs. Aldershot, I'm sure that from now on, I can trust you to act in a completely professional manner. I don't want to have this discussion again."

Mina swept past the flabbergasted housekeeper with Christopher, but halfway up the next flight of stairs, she called down, "If I need anything, I shall ring for you or one of the other maids."

The housekeeper did not reply other than to slam the door behind her with a resounding bang as she exited the stairwell.

Oh dear (and perhaps a few choice words that Lord Kinsale and Brutus had been known to utter on occasion, but a Parasol governess never would). Mina sighed as she and Christopher pushed through the door at the top of the last flight of stairs into an unfamiliar hallway. She probably should have held her tongue. But ugh. The servants at Fitzwilliam House in London and Highwood Hall in Hertfordshire had never behaved in such a high-handed, disrespectful fashion. No doubt Mina had made enemies of Kinsale House's resident butler and housekeeper, but she rather suspected that a show of strength was the only way to deal with such blatant, bullying behavior.

Yes, Smedley and Mrs. Aldershot were bullies. But they were about to find out that Miss Hermina Davenport of the

Parasol Academy was a force to be reckoned with. A young woman who could pack a powerful wallop or two—at least in a figurative sense—in the defense of others.

In the coming days, Mina would do her best to take care of Christopher and Tom Fleet. And she would also advocate for Lord Kinsale. There was no doubt the marquess was a strong, resourceful man, but he was on unsure ground in unfamiliar territory. She now understood completely why he needed her services, and she would *not* let him down.

Chapter 11

In Which Introductions Are Made and an Opportunity (or a Rabbit) Is Seized; Followed by a Mad Dash in the Rain and a Possible Lightning Strike; And Wistful Thoughts about Shamrocks, Sausages, and Cucumbers Feature...

It was easy enough for Mina to work out which bedroom belonged to Tom, which one had been allocated to Christopher, and which one was the governess's bedchamber.

Of course, it certainly helped that her trunks from the Parasol Academy had already arrived and been deposited in her new room; early that morning, before she'd teleported to Rose Cottage to collect Christopher, she'd sent a message to Kinsale House along with her luggage indicating that she would like to unpack her own things. It wouldn't do for maids to go through her belongings and discover items like her *Parasol Academy Handbook* (even though it would look like it contained nothing but gibberish unless one used a pair of ley-spectacles or a ley-lensed quizzing glass to read the text) or her spare pearl-handled knife. She trusted that no one would wield her Parasol Academy–issued umbrella or parasol in a magical way as they appeared to be perfectly ordinary. And of course, one had to know the precise incantation to use in order to become invisible or render someone temporarily confused.

As Mina settled Christopher into his new room, she couldn't

help but marvel at the fact that the Fae, in their infinite wisdom, had sent her a new type of magic to use. The *Glamify* spell had worked remarkably well, and as the label on the bottle had proclaimed, it was easy to reverse. As soon as Mina and Christopher had arrived at Kinsale House, Mina had simply uttered, "*Unglamify*" and both her physical appearance and Christopher's had gone back to normal before she'd knocked on the door.

There was no way on earth that Cheavers could have followed her and the young viscount to Kinsale House in Eaton Square. The only way Sir Bedivere could find out where Mina was now working—and where his ward was now residing—was if he staked out *all* of London, watching every square and every park around the clock (a virtually impossible feat), or he tried to force the knowledge from Mrs. Temple (an utterly impossible feat). Even if the Parasol Academy headmistress suspected Mina had had a hand in the disappearance of young Lord Fitzwilliam, she would confront Mina about it directly and discreetly. She would not allow the Parasol Academy's reputation to be besmirched because one of its governesses had "gone rogue," taking the law into her own hands.

"Where do you think Tom is, if he isn't here, Miss Davenport?" Christopher asked Mina as she finished putting the boy's clothes away in the oak wardrobe and matching set of drawers. He was sitting in the window seat of the wide sash window that overlooked Kinsale House's lovely rear walled-garden. "Do you think all the mean things the housekeeper said about him are true? That he's a pickpocket?"

Oh goodness. Christopher might be a quiet boy, perhaps even a little shy, but he listened and his powers of observation were keen. Mina turned to face him. "Tom told me himself that he picked pockets. But up until Lord Kinsale took him in, he's had neither family nor home. I imagine he only took from others in order to survive. He's not had an easy time of it."

Christopher fiddled with Mr. Hopwell's ears. "Stealing is wrong," he said.

"I agree," said Mina. "But I don't think Tom had much choice. Now that he'll be living here, I'm certain he won't need to take things that aren't his anymore. Not when Lord Kinsale will give him everything he needs—a warm bed, decent meals, and new clothes. And of course, we can help Tom too by showing him kindness and understanding."

Christopher worried at his lower lip. "Tom won't steal Mr. Hopwell, will he?"

"Well, 'oo's this Mr. 'Opwell geezer, then?"

Mina spun around to discover Lord Kinsale's ward lounging in the doorway of Christopher's room. "Good afternoon, Master Tom," she said with a welcoming smile. "I'm pleased to see you."

The boy doffed his tweed cap, revealing his shaggy mop of sandy-brown hair. "Likewise, Miss Davenport." Looking past her, Tom's gaze settled on Christopher. "So is this the boy I'm goin' to 'ave lessons wiv?"

"Yes. This is my cousin." Mina beckoned Christopher over. "But allow me to make the proper introductions. Tom, this is Christopher Davenport. And Christopher, this is Lord Kinsale's ward, Tom Fleet."

Christopher smiled shyly at the older boy. "How do you do, Tom?" he said.

Tom chuckled. "'Ow do I do? No one's ever asked me that before. I reckon I'm right as rain." The boy marched into the room and plopped himself down onto the window seat beside Christopher. "I still don't know 'oo this 'Opwell fellow is though."

"Oh, this is Mr. Hopwell," said Christopher, presenting his rabbit to the boy for inspection.

Tom scrunched up his nose. "'Ow old are you then? I fought you were seven."

"I am," said Christopher.

"So why are you cartin' a toy rabbit about? An' a purple one at that? Seems like a funny sort o' fing to do."

"I . . ." Christopher bit his lip for a moment. "Mr. Hopwell was a birthday present from my mama and papa," he said. "I've had him since I was four. He . . . he reminds me of them."

"Christopher is an orphan," explained Mina gently.

Tom nodded. "Like me. At least I fink I'm an orphan," he said to Christopher. "I ain't seen me mum for four years, so I may as well be. Don't know 'oo me dad was eiver."

"You can borrow Mr. Hopwell anytime you like if you need a hug," said Christopher. "He's made of velvet, so he's very soft."

"Fanks, but I'm not the huggin' sort," said Tom. His gaze transferred to Mina. "So 'ow's this all goin' to work then? When are we supposed to 'ave these lessons? 'Cause I'm not always 'ere. I'm a busy lad. Got fings to do an' people to see."

"Well, there won't be any lessons today," said Mina in a reassuring tone. "We've only just arrived, and I haven't even taken a look at the schoolroom yet. Who knows what we'll find."

"I'll show you, miss." Tom jumped up. "It's just down from my bedroom and Christopher's. It's got lots o' books an' china knickknacks an' such. Maybe some ink an' pencils an' a bit o' paper in the desk. Not much else though."

"That sounds like a wonderful idea, Tom," said Mina with an approving nod. "Lead the way."

The boy, apparently eager to please, darted out of Christopher's room into the hallway. Mina and Christopher followed. To Mina's surprise, Christopher left Mr. Hopwell behind.

She'd take it as an encouraging sign that perhaps the boy was already starting to feel comfortable in this new house. Indeed, Mina had begun to wonder, in quiet moments, if the boy's close attachment to his stuffed toy was a sign that he was troubled. He was always so quiet and agreeable and well-behaved, but she sensed he felt things deeply. And he'd endured so much disruption of late. His entire world had been effectively turned upside down. Perhaps Tom Fleet would help him to come out of his shell.

The schoolroom was indeed close to the boys' bedrooms. It was a decent-sized parlor-cum-study with a large oak desk—for Mina's use presumably—and an assortment of chairs, occasional tables, a pair of glass-fronted bookcases that flanked the fireplace, and a set of large sash windows dressed with sea-green brocade drapes. A Turkish rug covered the floor's polished oak boards, and the gray marble mantelpiece sported the fine bone-china "knickknacks" Tom had mentioned.

While Christopher explored the room with Tom, Mina crossed to the desk and opened the drawers to ascertain what supplies were at hand and what she might need to ask the marquess for. The bookcase doors were locked—not that that would present any problem if Mina used her leyport key to open them—but from what she could see, the books contained within were old almanacs and ledgers. Kinsale House no doubt had a library somewhere—

A knock on the schoolroom door made Mina jump. Swinging around, she discovered Lord Kinsale—now suitably attired like a gentleman rather than a boxer—leaning one mountainous shoulder against the doorframe. Brutus sat by his master's patent-leather-shoe-clad feet, eyeing her with keen interest.

"Miss Dav-Davenport," the marquess said, greeting her with a wide smile. "I see you've found the school . . . the schoolroom."

Brutus bared his teeth in what might have been the approximation of a canine smile or the precursor to a warning growl; it was a little hard to tell. *Ye cannot keep away from his lordship, eh? First ye stow away on the* Kinsale Cloud, *then ye manage to sweet-talk yer way into a job here.* Cocking his head, he added, *I saw ye drooling over me master in the ballroom. Making big puppy eyes at him. I know what ye're up to,* Miss Davenport. *Ye want to be the next Lady Kinsale, don't ye?*

Mina sighed inwardly. A warning then. Ignoring the pug as the marquess was looking at her expectantly, Mina bobbed a curtsy. "Tom kindly showed me the way. I take it this *is* the room you'd like us to use for lessons?"

Lord Kinsale pushed away from the door and took a few steps into the parlor. His gaze swept over the desk, the furniture by the fireplace, and the boys who were presently studying something in the garden below. Brutus had joined them, his curly tail quivering as he stared out the window too. "Is-is it all right? I w-w-wasn't sure what you might n-n-need. Like Tom, I've never had formal less-lessons myself. Although, me mam t-t-taught me to read and write and do arith-arithmetic."

Mina smiled. "I'm sure she did a fine job, my lord. As for the room . . ." She cast her gaze about the chamber as well. "I think it should suffice. There's certainly enough space and an adequate number of tables and chairs. Although, I might need to purchase a few more books and stationery supplies. You know, suitable text and exercise books and novels as well as slate boards and chalk and pencils and notebooks, et cetera."

Lord Kinsale waved an expansive hand. "O' course. P-p-purchase whatever you n-n-need, Miss Dav-Davenport. I have a man of b-b-business who can set up accounts at var-various stores. Just let me know their n-n-names and I will arrange . . . arrange it."

Mina dipped into another curtsy. "Thank you so much, my lord. Your consideration is very appreciated."

The marquess smiled and Mina's pulse began to frantically flutter about like a butterfly caught in a net. "You're very welwelcome." Moving closer, he then lowered his voice as he added, "I hope you don't m-m-mind, but I've sent for me tailor to visit Kin-Kinsale House tomorrow mornin'. Tom requires m-m-more clothes and . . . I did wonder if your son—" A faint flush suddenly tinted Lord Kinsale's cheekbones. "Par-pardon me, your *cousin*, might need a few more items o' clothing as well."

"Oh . . ." Mina found herself blushing too as she found herself trapped in the Irishman's emerald-green eyes. Could this man be any more thoughtful?

Steeling oneself not to respond to this man's charms was proving to be more difficult by the minute. As soon as Mina returned to her bedchamber to unpack, she would dig out the *Parasol Academy Handbook* and reread the section (in the sternest voice she could muster) on the perils of employee-employer fraternization.

"Miss Dav-Davenport? Would that be all right?" The marquess cocked a dark brow and his mouth tilted into an appealing lopsided grin. The amused twinkle in his eyes (perhaps they were more of a shamrock green than emerald) seemed to say, *I know you're affected by me.*

Damn it!

Damn it? Did I really just think *that?* Mina had never uttered such a vulgar curse in her own head before and she couldn't deny that she was shocked. It seemed that Lord Kinsale was turning her every which way except the right way, and if her countenance was only pink before, surely it was now redder than a boiled beet, considering how hot her face felt.

Mina's voice was mortifyingly husky as she said, "I . . . er . . . Yes, that would be perfectly all right, my lord. And more than generous. What-what time will your tailor be here?"

"Ten . . . ten o'clock," said the marquess. "He'll be seein' me after that. Me valet, Frobisher, insists that I need a few new bits and—"

A shrill cry from Christopher cut Lord Kinsale off.

"Miss Davenport! Miss Davenport!" the boy cried, pointing at the hallway beyond the schoolroom door. His face was pale and his eyes were wide with panic. "Brutus has Mr. Hopwell!"

Oh no!

Mina whirled around and sure enough, the wicked pug had the mauve velvet rabbit in his mouth. The dog's large black eyes gleamed with impudent glee as he pranced on the spot for a moment.

Catch me if ye can, Miss Davenport, Brutus taunted before he took off, disappearing from view.

"Brutus!" bellowed Lord Kinsale as he bolted through the doorway. Mina, close on his heels, was followed by Tom and a distraught Christopher. "Stop, you-you wee dev-devil of a dog!"

But the pug did not heed his master. Mina could see that the dog was already at the end of the hall, near the top of the stairs. *Too slow, Miss Davenport!* he called as he proceeded to leap down the staircase, faster than a rat darting out of the Fleet Ditch.

"Brutus! Stop!" cried Mina in her best schoolmarm's voice. Picking up her skirts, she hurtled after Lord Kinsale and his dog down the stairs. In her mind she added, *What has young Christopher or Mr. Hopwell ever done to you to deserve such ill treatment?*

All feckin' rabbits must die! Brutus rejoined with savage delight as he paused on the first-floor landing. Catching Mina's eye, he then growled and shook the toy, raising a wail from Christopher. *Especially purple velvet ones with floppy ears an' button eyes an' ridiculous fluffy pom-pom tails.*

"You wait 'til I g-g-get my hands on you, you wee bugbugger," growled Lord Kinsale back, as he somehow took the stairs two at a time. "You'll be sleepin' outside and eatin' nothin' but scraps for a whole week."

But nothing would slow Brutus down. He took off again,

barreling down the remaining set of stairs to the entry hall on the ground floor below. And then it sounded as though all hell had broken loose. There was a man's shout, a high-pitched scream, and then a crash.

"Brutus!" yelled the marquess. When Mina reached the bottom of the stairs, she saw that the dog had managed to bowl over a maid, and a few yards beyond, a porcelain bust had been knocked off its pillar and lay fractured upon the marble floor. Smedley looked on, arms crossed, shaking his head in apparent disgust.

"Jaysus," muttered Lord Kinsale in a tone graveled with frustrated anger. He paused to help up the maid, but Mina rushed past.

"Which way did Brutus go, Smedley?" she managed, even though she was more than a tad breathless.

The butler sighed and pointed through a set of open double doors. "Into the drawing room. But the maids were cleaning in there, so I suspect the French doors leading onto the terrace are open."

Blast and blinking hell! Deciding she had no time to admonish herself for mentally firing off yet another round of frowned-upon curses, Mina continued on. "Don't worry. I'll rescue Mr. Hopwell," she called back to Christopher, who'd paused at the bottom of the stairs. He was crying, but Tom had touchingly wrapped his arm around the younger boy's shoulders. Even though Tom had proclaimed he wasn't the "hugging sort," it was lovely to see that he wasn't afraid to comfort another.

By the time Mina reached the French doors, Lord Kinsale had caught up to her.

"I'm so s-s-sorry, Miss Dav-Davenport," he said, his gaze frantically scanning the back garden. It had begun to rain—not heavily, but the light shower made it harder to see into the farthest corners and shadowy places beneath hedges and bushes.

"I d-d-don't know what has got-gotten into Brutus. He's not u-usually like this."

"It's not your fault, my lord," Mina returned as she watched for any sign of movement. Any flash of purple. There were so many potential hidey-holes for a small dog: At the end of a flagstone path in the center of the lawn stood a large and elegant stone fountain; at least a dozen marble statues were positioned like sentinels along the line of two towering hedges at the walled garden's side perimeters; several thickly trunked beech trees shaded the terrace; and a densely planted rose garden lay at the very back. "Dogs will be dogs." In her mind she called out, *Brutus, if you come back to the terrace right now, I'll give you a bone. Maybe even a Bath bun.*

She didn't want to reward bad behavior, but she was beginning to feel desperate.

Huh, as if I'm goin' to believe that malarkey, returned the pug.

Mina moved farther out onto the terrace, squinting into the rain. While she couldn't see Brutus, she sensed he was nearby. *It's not much of a chase if you hide*, she called out. *Where's the fun in that?*

Lord Kinsale suddenly reached out and laid a large hand on Mina's arm. "There," he whispered. "He's be-behind the f-f-fountain. Why don't we try to trap . . . trap him? You round the ri-right side, and I'll appro-approach him from the left. Per-perhaps we can catch him in the mid-middle."

"Good idea, my lord," Mina whispered back. In truth, she was terribly disconcerted by the nearness of the marquess. The light touch of his hand seemed to penetrate the wool sleeve of her uniform, making the skin beneath tingle and burn with awareness.

But how Lord Kinsale made her feel when he was close should not signify. She had to get Mr. Hopwell back in one piece. If that toy rabbit was damaged or even—heaven forbid—completely ruined by Brutus, Mina knew Christopher would be inconsolable.

With a gesture and a nod, Lord Kinsale indicated that both of them should begin their covert rabbit rescue mission.

As stealthily as she could, Mina descended to the rain-misted lawn and began to sneak along the hedge line, making her way toward the fountain. Two chubby-cheeked cherubs wielding bows and arrows—cupids perhaps—sat atop the fountain's central sculpture. Glancing over to the opposite side of the garden, Mina could see that Lord Kinsale was keeping pace with her.

No doubt Brutus could detect their approach. He'd have a keen sense of hearing and smell. Aside from tiptoeing and employing a two-pronged strike, Mina suspected additional ploys would be required to foil the wily pug.

Drat this rain. I really should go back inside and speak with the marquess's cook about the boys' dinner, said Mina in her head, but loud enough for Brutus to hear. *I wonder if there are any sausages in the larder. Big fat juicy ones...*

Sausages? came the excited response. Mina could almost see Brutus's head cocking to one side. *Will there be sausages for dinner?*

Mina and Lord Kinsale were almost level with the fountain now. She paused and put up a hand to halt the marquess's advance. To Brutus, Mina replied, *Only for those who behave themselves. You know what you need to do, Brutus. Hand Mr. Hopwell over to Lord Kinsale or to me—*

A low, frustrated growl emanated from behind the fountain. *Feck, feck, feckity-feck.* Then, *No, I cannot be doin' it. Besides, the master has already declared I'll be gettin' scraps for the week. I might as well be hanged for a sheep as a lamb...*

*Damn, damn, damn. That ruddy dog was probably about to

rip the toy rabbit's head off. Cajoling hadn't worked. It was time for an all-out offensive. Catching Lord Kinsale's eye, Mina gathered up her skirts then called, "Now!"

Both she and the marquess exploded into action, rounding the fountain at the same time—Lord Kinsale from the left and Mina from the right—trying to head Brutus off before he could evade capture.

The pug gave a yip upon seeing them, then shot past Mina like a miniature tan and black cannonball. What occurred next happened so quickly, Mina could scarcely comprehend it. She attempted to slow down so she wouldn't crash into Lord Kinsale, but the flagstones beneath her boots were slick with rain and her feet went out from underneath her. With a startled cry, she fell backward, but instead of hitting the hard ground, Lord Kinsale swooped down and caught her in his strong arms. For one breathless moment, Mina felt like she was suspended in midair, the marquess bending over her, his lips hovering only inches above hers. His startled green gaze searched her eyes. "Are-are you all right, Miss Dav-Davenport?" he asked before he straightened, bringing her with him.

The soft misty rain had darkened the marquess's brown hair to a slick shade of sable and an errant drop of water traced a path from his brow, down the slightly crooked path of his nose to the sharply etched cupid's bow of his top lip.

Mina swallowed. "Aside from being hideously embarrassed, I-I think so," she murmured huskily. "Thank you for catching me. Again. You seem to be remarkably good at it."

She was still clasping Lord Kinsale's substantial biceps (goodness, the man's muscles were as hard as marble) and her bosom was rising and falling with indecent haste that had nothing to with her charge behind the fountain, and everything to do with her current position—being held so closely by the marquess. Was there electricity in the air? Because Mina suddenly felt as though she'd been struck by something hot and sizzling like lightning. Or maybe one of the cherubs atop the fountain had struck her with his arrow. In any event, it was like her entire universe had been knocked sideways and she would never be quite the same again.

"We... we should check on Brutus," she managed as she made herself let go of Lord Kinsale. The marquess's arms, which had wrapped about her shoulders in a protective circle, fell away as he took a step back. Then he scrubbed a hand through his rain-damp hair, ruffling it into sharp spikes that did not lessen his appeal; in fact, the wet, messy look lent the rugged Irishman a roguish air that made Mina feel like she was going to have a fit of the vapors for the second time this afternoon. (Perhaps she should start to carry a bottle of hartshorn about with her. Something that was labeled *Sniff Me* whenever the Marquess of Kinsale walked into the room.)

"That dog." Lord Kinsale shook his head. "I hope to God the rab-rabbit survives. I'll b-b-buy your son a dozen more t-t-toy rabbits to make up for Brutus's mis-misbehavior if needs be."

Guilt pinched Mina. She suspected it would every time the marquess called Christopher her son. "Hopefully it won't come to that," she said as they hastened back toward the townhouse. The rain was getting heavier by the minute and Mina would have to retire to her room and employ the *Unsmirchify* spell to repair her hair and uniform.

There was no sign of Brutus. Or Mr. Hopwell for that matter, intact or otherwise, and Mina's heart sank. Christopher would be beside himself by now. Restoring her appearance to the Parasol Academy's exacting standards of perfectly prim and proper could wait.

The French doors were still wide-open, and as she and Lord Kinsale gained the terrace, Christopher suddenly appeared in the doorway. "Look," he cried, brandishing his mauve velvet rabbit in the air. "I have Mr. Hopwell back!"

Oh, thank the Fae! Mina rushed into the drawing room. "Did Brutus give him back?"

"No," said Christopher. His cheeks might still be tear-streaked, but his face was wreathed with a bright smile. "It was Tom who rescued him. As Brutus ran inside, he pounced on him as quick as anything and Brutus let go."

Tom stepped forward from one of the shadowy corners. "It were nuffink," he said, shrugging off the praise. "I s'pose I just 'ave a talent for nicking fings nice an' quick."

Lord Kinsale, who'd joined them, released a low chuckle. "I suppose you do, Tom," he said. "But I don't think re-returnin' somethin' to its rightful owner c-c-can be classed as stealin'. So thank you, lad."

"Yes, thank you," said Mina with a heartfelt smile.

Christopher handed Mr. Hopwell to Mina. "He's only a little bit wet from the rain. And one of his button eyes is loose. Do you think you can fix it?"

Mina took the rabbit and examined him. "I certainly can and will do so at once," she said. The *Unsmirchify* spell would take care of any dampness or muddy streaks. And it would be easy enough to secure the loose button with a needle and thread. "If that is all right with you, my lord?" she added, catching the marquess's eye.

"O' course," said Lord Kinsale. Then his mouth slanted into a rueful grin. "I'll be track-trackin' down me wee wick-wicked dog to have a stern w-w-word with him so this nev-never happens again." Then his eyes softened and he dropped his voice. "I-I usually dine at eight o'clock, Miss Dav-Davenport. W-w-would it suit you to meet me in the d-d-dining room then so I might dis-discuss your other duties related to . . . to me own par-particular concerns? If the b-b-boys are all settled o' course."

Ah, the etiquette and "elocution" lessons. Mina brushed a

dripping strand of hair away from her suddenly hot cheek. "Yes, absolutely, my lord."

As the marquess strode away, Mina rather suspected that unless and until she learned to keep her composure around the far-too-appealing Irishman, "pink and flustered" rather than "professional and unflappable" would be her permanent state of being.

If only there were a "cool as a cucumber" incantation she could cast. "Something like a *Cucumberfy* spell would be handy," she muttered to herself.

Until then, a bottle of smelling salts would have to do.

CHAPTER 12

*In Which Dinner Is Served; Mock Turtle Soup,
Collywobbles, and Fish Forks and Knives Are Discussed;
And the Merits of Dancing and Singing Are Weighed...*

The towering walnut longcase clock in Kinsale House's grand entry hall was striking the hour of eight o'clock in doleful, ponderous tones when two footmen, at Smedley's signal, threw open the double doors to the opulent dining room and Mina was ushered inside.

Lord Kinsale was already waiting for her. He stood by the fireplace, staring into the bright leaping flames, one long, patent-leather-clad foot resting upon the edge of the tiled hearth, one strong arm braced against the green-veined marble mantelpiece. As soon as she was announced by Smedley, the marquess looked up and smiled so widely, with such genuine pleasure, Mina was tempted to glance behind her to see if his delighted expression was for someone else.

But it wasn't. It seemed Lord Kinsale *was* inordinately pleased to see his new ward's governess because as she sank into a curtsy, he greeted her with a warm, "Good evenin', Miss Dav-Davenport. You look w-w-well."

Smedley gave a small snort and Mina sent him a narrow-eyed look. A warning look. A "that's enough from you" glance that she'd perfected during her Parasol Academy training. In fact, it was facial expression *Number 32* in Chapter 10 of the *Parasol Academy Handbook* entitled "Effective Aspects, Airs, and Stares to Employ in the Line of Duty." It essentially applied to the management of unruly children and adolescents, but Mina rather thought it also worked well when it came to managing disagreeable adults. Particularly officious butlers.

She wasn't wrong as Smedley looked away first.

Mina returned her attention to her employer. "Thank you, my lord," she said brightly. Of course, the marquess was simply being polite when he'd remarked she looked "well" because she was attired in her regulation Parasol Academy uniform of navy blue with its plain black trim. Her hair was perfectly parted and coiled into her customary bun at the back of her head. Indeed, she looked like she usually did. Neat. Professional. Very governess-y and not at all rosy cheeked and giddily girlish and heart fluttery (which is how she felt inside). "I hope... I hope I haven't kept you waiting," she added, not at all breathlessly (well, maybe just a little).

Lord Kinsale straightened. "Not-not at all, Miss Dav-Davenport." His gaze shifted to the butler. "You may leave us, Smed-Smedley." He gestured at the two pairs of attendant footmen, stationed at various intervals around the vast mahogany dining table—a table that was long enough to seat at least sixteen people but was set for only two at the end nearest the fireplace. "You m-m-may all leave us as w-w-well, gentlemen."

Smedley arched a thin black brow. "What of dinner, my lord? I presume you still wish to dine. Who will serve you and Miss Davenport if you've dismissed the footmen?"

The marquess crossed his impressively muscled arms over his equally impressive wide chest and leveled a hard look at the butler. "I think it's ra-rather obvious. When each course... when each course is ready," he said gruffly, "the f-f footmen may bring the dishes in and ser-serve us. Just kn-knock. It's n-n-not that hard."

"And the wine?" persisted the butler, his tone bordering on insolent. At least Mina thought so. "Who will serve that when your glasses need refilling during the dinner?"

Lord Kinsale emitted a low growl, a sound of frustration. "I think I'll manage to p-p-pour it. Even if me m-m-mouth doesn't always work, I have fu-fu-functionin' hands and arms and legs, you know."

Smedley bowed but he didn't look the least bit chastened. "Of course, my lord," he said, his dark eyes gleaming. "You can always ring if you need any assistance."

"I'll expect the f-f-first course in ten minutes."

"Yes, my lord."

As soon as the dining room doors shut firmly behind the odious butler and the four footmen, Lord Kinsale turned to Mina. "I'm-I'm sorry you had to wit-witness that. Smedley is very s-s-set in his w-w-ways. I understand me pre-predecessor liked things just so."

While Mina's heart cramped in sympathy, she couldn't quite extinguish the hot flare of righteous indignation in her blood. "Smedley needs to learn his place. Mrs. Aldershot too. Their blatant disrespect for you, their master... is-is not to be borne."

The corner of Lord Kinsale's wide mouth quirked into a wry smile. "I'm afraid it's not all that un-unusual around here. I'd dismiss both of them, but I'm n-n-not sure I would find anyone b-b-better. It's this feck—" He broke off and a flush rushed into his cheeks. "My-my apol-apologies for bein' so crude, Miss Dav-Davenport. It's me blasted stam-stammer and Irish brogue that m-m-marks me as different. A m-m-man who doesn't deserve the ti-title that a quirk of fate has be-bestowed on him. M-m-most folk no doubt consider me to be a sim-sim-simpleton. A m-m-misfit."

"Oh, my lord. Surely n—"

But the marquess held up a hand, halting Mina's denial. "While I appreciate that you're more than willin' to rush to me defense, Miss Dav-Davenport, we b-b-both know it's the truth. I've lived with this stam-stammer for as long as I c-c-can remember. To be sure, there c-c-can be worse afflictions in life. B-b-but there are some days when I just wish me m-m-mouth would work without ty-ty-tyin' itself in knots."

Mina inclined her head. "I understand, my lord." It wasn't fair of her to deny the truth of Lord Kinsale's situation. That people, by and large, were judgmental and viewed him in a negative light because of the way he spoke. Because he wasn't au fait with the ways of the upper class. He'd hired her to help him with all these things. And she would. To the best of her ability.

"How . . . how would you like to begin?" she asked, gesturing at the table. "Both Tom and Christopher have gone to bed without any fuss, so I'm at your complete disposal for as long as you need." And then she blushed.

Oh dear. Had she really just said that? It made it sound as though she would do virtually anything at all . . . even things that were of a licentious nature.

Perhaps Lord Kinsale thought so too because he smiled the sort of roguish smile that made Mina's blush deepen into the scorching-hot range. "I'm glad the lads are settled in," he said, drawing closer to the dining table. "Brutus, in case you were wonderin', has been ban-banished to the terrace for a few hours. To reflect on his wicked be-behavior. Though to answer your f-f-first question—how would I like to begin—I'll be placin' meself in your very ca-capable hands, Miss Dav-Davenport. I'm ha—I'm happy to go along with anythin' you suggest."

"Ah . . . should we focus on dinner table etiquette first, my lord?" asked Mina. Hoping the gaslights were low enough that her red countenance wouldn't be noticed, she approached the closest place setting; there would be a soup course, an entrée, a main course, then dessert. "Then afterwards, we could address your concerns about your speech and ways that I might be able to assist you in that area." *Yes, focus on the practical. The work you need to do. Not how handsome Lord Kinsale looks in his evening finery.*

"A cap-capital idea." The marquess moved to Mina's side of the table and pulled out her chair. "I know one of me footmen w-w-would normally do the hon-honors, but allow me."

"Thank you." Mina sedately sank onto the plushly upholstered seat. As she slid her palms over her skirts to smooth them, Lord Kinsale crossed to the mahogany sideboard and retrieved two cut-crystal decanters—one filled with red wine, the other with white.

"Would-would you like a glass of somethin', Miss Dav-Davenport?" he asked with a grin.

"Oh . . . I . . ." Mina didn't know what to say. She was not one to imbibe alcohol. Apart from having a sherry at her father's wake, and indulging in a glass of champagne at dear Emmeline's wedding to her duke, she'd never tried anything else. Of course, she knew *of* wine—what one served with certain courses at a dinner party had been covered during her Parasol Academy training. But she was technically working this evening and needed a clear head, so abstaining altogether would be wiser. "I think it might be best if I just had water, my lord," she said at last. "But considering the fact the first course—mock turtle soup—will be served shortly, I dare say a glass of Madeira would be a suitable accompaniment." Mina had checked with the marquess's cook what was on the menu when she'd organized an evening meal for the boys.

"Ah," said Lord Kinsale. "I c-c-can't say I've ever had mock turtle soup be-before, but if Ma-Madeira is the thing to have with it, wh-who am I to say no?"

Once the marquess had poured their respective drinks—

Madeira for himself and water for Mina—he claimed the dining chair opposite hers. "I su-suppose I could have asked a f-f-footman or two to stay," he said as he regarded her over the sea of white linen furnished with gleaming silverware, sparkling crystal glassware, and gilt-edged china, "but to be honest, so many ser-servants hoverin' about, watchin' and listenin', gives me the colly-collywobbles and I . . . I cannot eat."

Mina nodded in sympathy. "I could not blame you, my lord. Being observed, feeling that one is being judged, would be most off-putting. But"—she offered Lord Kinsale a smile—"I will do my very best to help you master the skills you wish to acquire so you might feel comfortable in any situation."

"I-I would appreciate that, Miss Dav-Davenport," replied Lord Kinsale. His expression was sincere. "Since I came into this ti-title, I have dined with me f-f-friend, Lord Har-Hartwell, on the odd oc-occasion at his clubs. I've tried to f-f-follow his lead, but I'm still not entirely clear on which f-f-fork or knife is which. Or how to hold anythin' correctly." He lifted a large hand and turned it, showing Mina his long fingers and scarred, misshapen knuckles. "These paws are a wee b-b-bit clumsy at the best o' times."

"Oh, I don't know about that, my lord," said Mina with a small smile. "Only a few hours ago, those paws of yours—as you call them—delivered a very precise series of blows to the punching bag in your ballroom. I don't think you give yourself enough credit."

At that moment, there was a knock on the double doors—the mock turtle soup had arrived. The footmen served it from a large silver tureen with a minimum of fuss. Neat bread rolls were deposited on side plates and a dish of elegant butter curls was placed between Mina and the marquess. Smedley oversaw all, directing operations—including the unfurling and laying of linen napkins upon laps—with the ruthless efficiency of a sergeant major at a military parade. Or a Parasol Academy tutor during compulsory exercise drills in the Sloane Square headquarters courtyard. After Lord Kinsale informed the butler that he would ring—there was a small crystal bell within his reach on the table—when he wanted the plates to be cleared and the next course served, Smedley bowed and silently quit the room with the attendant footmen.

As soon as the door closed, Lord Kinsale frowned at his soup and his bread roll. "See, I-I know wh-wh-which spoon is for the soup. But do I split m-m-my roll f-f-first? Spread it with b-b-butter? Can I s-s-season my soup with salt and p-p-pepper? It is all so very per-perplexin' for an unrefined man like m-m-me."

Mina met the marquess's gaze. In the golden glow of the gas chandelier above them and the pool of light spilling from a nearby branch of candles, Lord Kinsale's eyes were the deep, soft green of a shadowy glade. They were the sort of eyes one could quite happily stare into for hours. Even get lost in . . .

Good grief, Hermina Davenport. Stop swooning and Cucumberfy *yourself, this instant.*

Professional resolve rallied—if not fully restored—Mina swallowed, picked up her bread roll, then carefully tore it in two. "Tearing one's dinner roll with one's fingers rather than cutting it with a knife is the accepted way of eating it," she said. "And helping oneself to butter is quite acceptable too. Just use the butter knife upon your bread-and-butter plate. Adding a touch of salt or pepper to one's soup is perfectly fine. But the most important thing to remember"—Mina picked up her soup spoon—"is to scoop away from oneself." She carefully slid her spoon from the front of the bowl to the back. "If the soup is too hot, you mustn't blow. Rather, hold it above your bowl for a few moments until it cools. Then gently sip it from the side of your spoon. Like this." Mina demonstrated. "One must *never* slurp."

When she looked up, it was to discover Lord Kinsale's eyes had darkened and all his attention was fixed on her mouth.

Oh my... Mina's own gaze dropped to the marquess's wide handsome mouth. Even though he'd been a boxer, he appeared to have all his teeth and she could not detect any sort of scarring that marred its symmetrical perfection. Perhaps the beauty of his mouth was a testament to his skill as a pugilist.

To dispel the strange spellbinding atmosphere in the room — it was almost as though sparks had escaped from the fireplace and danced between Mina and the marquess — she cleared her throat. "My lord, now you try," she murmured.

Lord Kinsale nodded, then picking up his spoon, he took a perfectly mannered mouthful of his mock turtle soup. "How-how was that, Miss Dav-Davenport?" he asked in a low voice.

"That was very well done, my lord," she replied. "That's all there is to it."

"That's easy for you... for you to say," said Lord Kinsale with a lopsided smile. "I'm more than li-likely to s-s-spill me soup all d-d-down me shirtfront."

But the marquess did not spill a single drop and by the time the soup course was cleared and the fish course had been served, Mina was more than a little convinced that her employer was not as devoid of fine-dining adroitness as he supposed himself to be.

Although, that was *before* Lord Kinsale began to tackle his sole fillet en croûte served with lemon, capers, and parsley butter; it seemed he was *definitely* all thumbs when it came to wielding a delicately wrought silver fish fork and knife.

"A special knife is sometimes provided for the fish course," explained Mina as she neatly sliced off a section of pale succulent fish encased in golden flaky pastry. "But some in society believe it's very bourgeois to use such a utensil. That one should either use a single fork to flake one's fish onto a slice of bread, or use two forks to separate the flesh. But as your cook has prepared sole en croûte this evening, I do not think the use of a knife is unwarranted."

"I just... I just cannot seem to be able to m-m-manage it,"

said Lord Kinsale in exasperation as the fish knife slipped from his grasp and clattered onto the edge of the plate. His brow concertinaed into a fierce frown. "I literally have b-b-butter fingers drippin' with butter."

Oh dear. The marquess did indeed have buttery fingers. "Perhaps the problem is, we're sitting opposite each other," remarked Mina gently. "You're trying to mirror what I'm doing, but what you're observing is all back to front."

"Aye," agreed the marquess grimly as he wiped his fingers on his napkin then tossed the soiled linen onto the table. Sitting back, he sipped his white wine and scowled at his plate.

Mina put down her fork and knife. "We could always sit beside each other," she suggested. "That might help."

"By St Patrick, I think you m-m-might be right." Lord Kinsale's expression immediately lightened. Climbing to his feet, he deftly moved his entire place setting, his meal, and his wine glass to the spot next to Mina.

"All right," he said as he lowered himself into his new chair. "Let's see if this m-m-makes it any easier."

Mina blew out a small breath. With the handsome marquess now sitting so close to her—goodness, if she leaned just a little to the right, their shoulders would brush—she wasn't quite sure if *she* wouldn't be all thumbs now. "Well," she said, picking up her cutlery again. "If you grip your fish knife like this—just lightly, like you would an ordinary knife—you cannot go wrong. A nice neat little trick though, is to just turn your wrist a fraction, then use the flat of the blade to either remove any skin or lift the fish directly off the bones—if your piece hasn't been filleted—or indeed, to help scoop up some of the buttery sauce and then deposit it onto your laden fork. Like this."

Mina took another bite of her sole en croûte, then watched Lord Kinsale as he tried again. "Wonderful," she declared as the marquess took another mouthful without mishap. "You could quite happily dine with the Queen and Prince Albert."

"Per-perhaps," said Lord Kinsale, toying with the stem of his wineglass. "But they'd sure-surely look away as soon as I o-o-opened me mouth. Or regard me with p-p-pity, which in some ways is even w-w-worse. Some might even laugh. It's what I f-f-fear will happen when I speak in Par-Parliament. I can-cannot be effective if no one will lis-listen or take me serious-seriously. Me accent is enough to m-m-mark me as an out-outsider."

Without thinking, Mina laid her hand on the marquess's sleeve. "I promise we will work on your elocution after the meal," she said. In truth, she still wasn't exactly sure *how* she could help Lord Kinsale to overcome his stammer. The *Parasol Academy Handbook* contained minimal guidance in that regard. Every time she looked within its pages, she kept hoping she would see something else. A section she'd missed. But so far, she hadn't.

She could certainly help the marquess to soften his Irish brogue if he wished to do that. But she was virtually all at sea when it came to suggesting exercises that might alleviate some of the marquess's worst articulatory difficulties—his awkward pauses and word and sound repetitions. The terrible tension around his mouth when he struggled to produce particular consonants at all. If she could just pull a magic wand from her governess's pocket and wave it and make the stammer go away, she would. In a heartbeat.

The corner of Lord Kinsale's mouth lifted into a smile. "Miss Dav-Davenport, as much as I enjoy hav-havin' your hand upon me s-s-sleeve, I cannot help but w-w-wonder if such a gesture m-m-might be seen as a breach of eti-etiquette?"

Mina immediately snatched her hand away and buried it in her lap. Heat scalded her cheeks. "My lord. You're right and I'm so, so sorry for behaving in such an overly familiar and unprofessional way. It's behavior that's certainly proscribed in the *Parasol Academy Handbook* and quite unforgiv—"

The marquess turned in his seat and caught her gaze. His green eyes were bright with mirth. "Miss Dav-Davenport. I'm not off-offended in the least. I was merely fun-funnin' you."

"Oh." Mina released a little laugh. "Well then... Even so, I-I shouldn't have. You're my employer. Uninvited touching is not permitted. Neither is invited touching for that matter."

Lord Kinsale's eyes gleamed. "It sounds like this hand-handbook of yours is very com-comprehensive. Though tell me, Miss Dav-Davenport"—the marquess picked up his cutlery and sliced off a neat portion of his sole en croûte—"what if... what if your employer requires dancin' lessons? Because that is a s-s-skill I do not possess and should like to ac-acquire as well. How-how would we pro-proceed if we can-cannot... if we cannot touch?"

Mina suddenly wished her glass contained something a tad stronger than water. Lord Kinsale's gaze was resting on her, and she knew her face was ablaze. She took a hasty sip before replying. "I imagine there are certain situations, particular cases such as yours, where exceptions to the Academy's strict rules can be made," she said carefully. "If said touching is socially acceptable—for instance, when engaging in an activity such as dancing—I don't see why not."

At least, Mina didn't think that what she'd stated was an outright falsehood. The *Handbook*'s chapter on fraternization had never mentioned that dancing was *not* allowed. And it wasn't as though she and Lord Kinsale would be dancing as part of some "courting" ritual. No, it would be part of the suite of etiquette lessons Mina was providing.

"I shall keep that in m-m-mind," said the marquess, placing his fish fork and knife in the precise center of his plate. "Rest assured, I would play the part of a per-perfect gentleman. I w-w-wouldn't want you to get in trouble with the P-P-Parasol Academy." Then he gave a wry smile. "Your Mrs. Temple scares even a b-b-big bruiser o' a man like me."

Mina laughed at that. Considering Lord Kinsale was at least

a whole foot taller than the petite Parasol Academy headmistress, it was an amusing notion indeed. Although, Mina had, on at least one occasion, witnessed Mrs. Temple's "death" glare when several students in Mina and Emmeline's cohort had broken the Academy's rules and snuck out of the dormitory one night—well, teleported out—to Covent Garden to see a play. It was the sort of look Mina never, ever wanted to receive. She was certain she'd fall into a dead faint.

The marquess rang the crystal bell and the servants, including Smedley, immediately appeared. Of course, Smedley's expression grew sly when he observed that the marquess was now seated beside Mina rather than across from her, but for the most part, it was easy to ignore the supercilious butler. In the flurry of activity that ensued—the clearing of used plates and cutlery, the replenishing of wine and water, the serving of the main course (roast beef with mustard sauce and a mélange of seasonal vegetables)—Mina fell to contemplating what exactly she would do with Lord Kinsale after dessert had been served and dinner ended. She imagined they'd repair to the nearby drawing room. Or perhaps the library.

But then what? Chapter 24 of the *Parasol Academy Handbook* had mentioned that singing and reciting nursery rhymes or poetry could assist one's charge with achieving fluent speech, at least temporarily. Praising one's charge for being fluent was also highly recommended. Other than that, providing a calm environment to promote relaxed conversation was the only other recommended strategy.

But Lord Kinsale couldn't very well sing his parliamentary speech. And did he even like to sing? He had a deep, melodious voice and Mina was certain that he'd be lovely to listen to.

As one of the footmen carefully poured mustard sauce over the slices of roast beef on her plate, Mina released a surreptitious sigh and smoothed the linen napkin resting on her lap. She really didn't want to fail Lord Kinsale. But what if—

Mina frowned as her fingers brushed against something hard

in her uniform's pocket. Something small and rectangular like a notebook. Something *she* hadn't placed there.

Something she was sure would be useful even if it wasn't magical...

Glancing at Lord Kinsale, she could see he was distracted as he issued instructions to Smedley about how and when dessert—a steamed treacle pudding with glazed clementines and vanilla custard—should be served. Surely it would be all right to take a peek at what her pocket had provided.

Mina reached in, then withdrew a small, slim, leather-bound volume. On the dark green cover was written in embossed gold lettering:

The Governess's Guide to Fluent Speech Instruction: Practical Exercises to Encourage Clear and Smooth Elocution in Any Social Setting

"Wh-what do you have there, Miss Dav-Davenport?" asked Lord Kinsale. The butler and footmen had gone and she and the marquess were alone once more.

"It's er... It's a new guidebook I found... that might have a few strategies that will help you achieve smoother speech, my lord," she said.

Lord Kinsale's green eyes glimmered with a roguish twinkle. "I'm up for tryin' anythin' if you are, Miss Dav-Davenport."

Mina smiled back. "Anything?" she asked. "I might hold you to that, my lord, because I suspect singing might be on the cards."

The marquess whipped around in his seat to face her. His expression was the textbook definition of "aghast." "Singin'?" he exclaimed. "You m-m-must be jokin' with me."

"Indeed, I'm not," returned Mina. "From what I understand, singing and reciting poetry might help control stammering because one doesn't have to think about the words. And one draws breath at regular intervals. There's a predictable rhythm to it all. If it makes you feel any better, I will sing along with you. Perhaps even accompany you on the pianoforte."

Lord Kinsale's gaze grew curious as he picked up his glass of claret. "Do-do you know 'The Rose of Tralee,' Miss Davenport?"

"I can't say that I do, but I'm a quick study," she said. "Even if you hum the melody first, I should be able to work out the notes to play it."

"I will teach you," he said. "The words and the tune." And then he picked up his knife and fork and sliced into his roast beef with alacrity.

Mina smiled as she did the same. It hadn't escaped her notice that Lord Kinsale had just said her name quite perfectly for the very first time. Indeed, his last two utterances had been completely stammer-free as well.

Perhaps it was a side effect of the wine. (Although, the marquess really hadn't had much at all.) Or maybe it was the convivial atmosphere. Mina couldn't be certain.

Nevertheless, she suddenly had a glimmer of hope in her heart. Perhaps she *could* help Lord Kinsale with his stammer. Even just a little bit would be better than not being able to help him at all.

Chapter 13

Concerning Medieval Torture Dungeons; An Unconventional Use for Napkins; An Unsuccessful Quelling; And Experimental Elocution Exercises (Including the Emission of Linguolabial Trills) Result in Unexpected Consequences...

Following dinner, it was decided—at least Miss Davenport had decided—that they would both repair to the drawing room next door in order to commence Phinn's elocution lessons.

Truth to tell, Phinn was relieved to be putting a wee bit of physical distance between himself and the comely governess. What had started out as a thoroughly pleasant, diverting, and educational evening—the governess's expert instruction on dinner table etiquette was very much appreciated—had rapidly descended into a torture session that any guard in charge of a medieval dungeon would have been proud to preside over. Phinn had clearly miscalculated when he'd impulsively decided to sit beside Miss Davenport at the table. He really *did* think it would help him to master the use of fiddly fish forks and knives and other equally ridiculous pieces of cutlery.

The problem was, he hadn't taken into account that her very nearness would create havoc with his senses and disrupt his ability to think clearly. Not to mention the effect she'd had on a particular, decidedly masculine part of his person that, thankfully, had been obscured by the napkin draped over his lap.

Unfortunately, there had been at least two occasions during dinner when the starched square of linen hadn't been the only stiff thing beneath the table...

Indeed, it had been most disconcerting to discover that the mere drift of Miss Davenport's floral scent, or the accidental brush of her skirts against his thigh, or the mere touch of her hand upon his sleeve, or even the melodic tinkle of her laughter, had set his blood rushing and pumping like he was a randy adolescent catching a glimpse of a woman's cleavage for the very first time.

Phinn was *not* that sort of man. Not usually. Of course, there'd been occasions in the past when he'd enjoyed a good tumble in the hay (at times, quite literally if the only place available to tryst had been a stable at a coaching inn) with a willing woman back in Ireland. Phinn "Cutthroat" O'Connell had not been a saint, by any means, especially when his bloodlust had been up after a fight. But he wasn't a libidinous, rakish sort of fellow like his friend Marcus, Lord Hartwell, either.

Now, as Miss Davenport installed herself on the velvet-upholstered pianoforte stool, and lifted the glossy walnut lid of the instrument, exposing the ivory and ebony keys, Phinn ordered himself to stop admiring the young woman's lovely countenance, to *stop* being so damned physically attracted to her womanly curves (he just *knew* she had a spectacular cleavage hidden beneath her severe Parasol Academy uniform; probably shapely legs and a luscious, peach-shaped derriere too). But he couldn't seem to help himself.

Feck it.

With a grumble that would have done Brutus credit, he crossed to an overly ornate oak sideboard where he kept a decanter of Irish whisky. Of course, Smedley had arched a disdainful brow when Phinn had made the request to have his favorite spirit on hand in both the dining room and drawing room. But damn it. Kinsale House was *his* now. It no longer belonged to his late great-uncle, the former marquess, Columbus O'Connell.

What he needed to do was focus. Pay attention. Listen to all the bits of wisdom this clever governess was about to impart to help him get his cursed stammer under control. She could also help him to soften his accent so he sounded more cultured and refined. More *English*.

But it seemed he was utterly, hopelessly in the woman's thrall. He poured a measure of whisky—the same hue as Hermina Davenport's pretty hazel eyes—into a crystal tumbler and took a sip. He mustn't drink too much. He was already having a devilish time trying to concentrate on what the governess was saying rather than how lovely she was.

But you didn't hire her because she's pretty. You hired her for her knowledge and expertise, Phinn sternly reminded himself as he turned back to face the piano. *So you'd best get your money's worth. It'll be time to make your speech in the House o' Lords before you know it. And to be sure, you don't want to be soundin' like a right royal git like last time.*

Miss Davenport looked up and the smile she sent him didn't help quell Phinn's less-than-gentlemanly thoughts in the slightest. But quell them he must. Quelling was imperative.

Yes, any and all libidinous urges would be so quelled they would cease to exist.

He was a rock. A lump of wood. As impervious to feeling as a sand-filled punching bag.

"Are you ready to try some of the exercises in my elocution guide, my lord?" Miss Davenport asked.

"So we're n-n-not goin' to sing?" While Phinn was not averse to singing, more often than not it had been when he'd been belting out a tune at a public house when he was well in his cups. It had been a long time since he'd sung any sort of hymn. He was not really the church-attending type.

"Oh, we will," said Miss Davenport. She was consulting her

green guidebook. "But it might help if we try a few warm-up exercises first. To that end"—she rose gracefully from her seat and crossed the Turkish rug toward him with light steps—"might I suggest that we . . . that we limber up a bit? Imagine you are about to start a bout of training and need to stretch and loosen your limbs."

What the devil? Phinn put down his whisky. "Limb-limber up?"

"Yes," said Miss Davenport. "My guidebook proposes a theory—that any tension in the muscles in your body, specifically those related to both breathing and speaking—can make it harder for speech to flow smoothly and easily. That the rhythm of talking is more likely to go awry."

Phinn nodded. "That seems log-logical. But limberin' up to b-b-box is surely different to limb-limberin' up to speak."

"Very true," agreed the governess. "To that end, we're going to focus on not just relaxing the muscles of your abdomen and chest and shoulders, but your neck and jaw and tongue and lips."

Phinn couldn't stop his mouth twisting in a wry smile. All this talk of body parts—particularly his lips and tongue—was *not* conducive to relaxing at all. If anything, the tension in the air was increasing with each passing second. And was it getting hot in here? He had to resist the urge to run a finger around his suddenly too-tight collar.

"Now," said Miss Davenport, all business and seemingly oblivious to the fact her employer was battling with his overwhelming attraction to her, "one should stand tall with one's chest lifted but arms hanging loose. One's feet should be comfortably apart, in line with one's hips. Like this."

She demonstrated and Phinn copied her. He kept his eyes steadfastly on her face because he would *not* focus on her admirable bust lifting. Or think about her legs slightly parted beneath her skirts. Or *anything* to do with her womanly hips. That way lay insanity.

"We're also going to practice breathing from our diaphragm," she added after a moment.

Was it Phinn's imagination, or was Miss Davenport suddenly a trifle breathless? "Me-me diaphragm?" he asked, his voice none too steady either.

"Yes. From here." Miss Davenport placed a slender hand on her cinched-in midriff. "Rather than lifting your chest or raising your shoulders, I want you to close your eyes and focus on inhaling and exhaling from this part of your abdomen. Your belly. Just gentle, easy breaths."

Phinn let his eyelids drift down. *Gentle, easy breaths?* He was caught between the urge to laugh and the urge to curse. The desire to bolt from the room and the desire to sweep Miss Hermina Davenport into his arms and taste her sweet, sweet lips.

But he didn't do any of those things. He curled his fingers into his palms and breathed slowly in, trying *not* to lift his chest or shoulders, then slowly out.

"That's very good, my lord." Miss Davenport's voice drifted over him like a warm, barely there caress. "Next, I want you to dip your chin down to your chest, then gently swing your head toward your right shoulder. That's it. Now . . . lift your left hand and stroke down the side of your neck. That's the way. Very good. And again. And now the other side . . ."

Feck. These "exercises" were exquisite torture. Nevertheless, Phinn's pent-up physical tension slowly began to ebb away. His body began to feel languid. His breathing grew deep and even as he diligently followed Miss Davenport's directions. He tipped his head up, then down, then all the way around in a circle. He opened his eyes and pressed his fingertips into the hinge of his jaw until the tightness in the joint lessened. He used his thumbs to massage beneath his chin to loosen the muscles at the base of his tongue.

But when Miss Davenport asked him to open his mouth,

protrude his tongue slightly between his lips and blow a raspberry like a horse, he burst out laughing.

"You-you want me to do what, Miss Dav-Davenport?" he asked, his voice brimming with barely suppressed mirth and incredulity. "How in God's n-n-name is *that* goin' to help ease me stam-stammer?"

Miss Davenport shrugged a shoulder. "I imagine that the exercise—it's apparently called a linguolabial trill—relaxes your tongue and lip muscles. It can't hurt."

Phinn snorted. "Except for the f-f-fact I'll look and sound like a to-total f-f-fool. A king-sized ass."

The governess smiled. "If it makes you feel any better, my lord, I'll do it with you."

"You're jokin'."

"Indeed, I'm not." Miss Davenport put down her guidebook on the table beside Phinn's whisky, then turned to face him. Her expression was nothing but determined. "I trust the guidebook implicitly." Then she arched a delicate brow and her lovely mouth twitched with a mischievous smile. "I'm more than willing to make a fool of myself in aid of a good cause. We can look foolish together."

Phinn shook his head and wiped a hand across his chin. "Very well, Miss Dav-Davenport. I'll have a go."

The governess grinned. "All right. On the count of three, we'll both blow raspberries together for as long as we can. Ready? Breathe in . . . and one, two, three, blow!"

So Phinn did. He poked out his tongue and blew the biggest, fattest, longest raspberry he could. All the while, the usually prim and proper Miss Davenport blew an enormous "linguolabial trill"—or whatever the woman had called it—straight back at him until she was red-cheeked and her eyes were watering. And then, when they were both out of breath, they collapsed onto the nearest sofa, panting and wheezing and laughing.

"Sweet... sweet Jaysus, Miss Davenport. You've... you've almost kill-killed me," gasped Phinn. "I swear... I swear we sounded like Bru-Brutus... when he's eaten too much c-c-cake."

He was sprawling rather than sitting, with one arm extended across the back of the overstuffed sofa. Miss Davenport was beside him, slumped against a pile of silk-covered cushions. She was so close, her crinoline skirts were partly spread across his thigh like a blanket, and if he reached out he was sure he could wind a lock of her glossy chestnut hair—several had escaped her bun—around one of his fingers...

"Oh dear. I'll... I'll take that as a warning... next time there's cake on offer... and your dog comes nosing around." The governess turned her head and her gaze met Phinn's. Her large hazel eyes were bright yet soft at the same time. Like sunlit honey. "I'm... I'm glad that I didn't kill you," she added. She was still breathless, her chest rising and falling with the increased rate of her breathing. "I'm certain... that there's at least one rule in the *Parasol Academy Handbook*... that discourages... such a thing."

"I should ho-hope so," said Phinn. He pushed himself upright. Even if the "limbering up" exercises hadn't improved the fluency of his speech immediately, he couldn't deny that he was enjoying himself. He certainly felt less self-conscious around Miss Davenport.

But perhaps that was due, at least in part, to the fact that she was so accepting of him and the way he spoke. He never felt like she was distracted by the awkward moments when he stumbled over words or got stuck altogether. She listened attentively as if there was nothing amiss with his speech at all. Even if his stammer never went away, he was grateful that his conversations with the governess were nothing but pleasurable.

Miss Davenport sat up straight too. "Do you think you could teach me 'The Rose of Tralee' now, my lord? It would be a shame not to see if singing might be a technique to facilitate smoother speech. At least while you're engaged in it."

Phinn rubbed the back of his neck. "Actually, Miss Dav-Davenport, when I think of all the t-t-times I've joined in a song—if I know the w-w-words—me stam-stammer does tend to dis-disappear."

"Well, the method might have some merit then," said the governess, hopping to her feet. "Let's see what happens this evening."

It didn't take long at all for Miss Davenport to learn the melody and the words to the Irish ballad that Phinn was so fond of; it seemed she had a very good ear.

As the governess played and sang in sweetly mellow tones, he sang along too, his voice mingling with hers. Every time he drew a breath, he attempted to do so from his belly rather than his chest. And to his delight, the words flowed freely like melted butter over a hot scone.

"Though lovely and fair as the Rose of the summer,
Yet 'twas not her beauty alone that won me.
Oh no, 'twas the truth in her eyes ever dawning,
That made me love Mary the Rose of Tralee."

As the song drew to a close and the last notes of the pianoforte drifted away, Phinn smiled down at Miss Davenport. In hindsight he probably shouldn't have chosen such a sentimental ballad; it was full of allusions related to falling head-over-heels in love with a beautiful young woman. And Phinn was *not* going to let himself feel anything soft or tender for the clever governess he'd employed to help him, no matter how bright her hazel eyes or luscious her pink lips or delicious her rose-scented perfume.

Although nothing could suppress the feeling of quiet, budding hope and elation in Phinn's chest. The governess and her little green elocution guidebook had been damn right. He'd never really thought about it in any great depth before, but yes, he *could* sing without stammering. He hadn't stumbled once.

He hadn't got stuck on any particular sound or syllable or word, unable to move on. His breath hadn't frozen in his chest. His tongue hadn't become tangled in hopeless knots. It *was* possible for him to be fluent . . . at least sometimes and in some situations. He opened his mouth to tell Miss Davenport so, but got no further than a stammered, "It-it w-w-worked," as a pitiful howl rent the air.

"*Ah-wooooo . . . Ah-wooooo!*"

Jaysus wept. Phinn swung toward the drawing room's French doors. The curtains hadn't been completely drawn and in the narrow gap, he could see a small black wet nose and blunt muzzle smooshed up against the glass pane.

Miss Davenport had pressed a hand to her mouth. "Oh goodness," she murmured. "Brutus is *not* happy."

Phinn scowled at his pug. "No. But the wicked wee f-f-fiend needs to take his punish-punishment and learn his lesson. He's to stay out there all night."

"*Ah-wooooo . . . Ah-wooooo!*" Brutus continued to howl and Phinn rolled his eyes.

"Forgive me for saying so, my lord," said the governess, "but it's raining and I think he might be cold. I'm sure he's truly repentant and won't take off with Christopher's rabbit again."

Phinn grunted. He didn't want to come across as curmudgeonly. He didn't usually banish his dog to the terrace. But then, Brutus wasn't usually so badly behaved. Phinn wasn't sure what had gotten into the pug, but hopefully the canine's bout of disobedience was only temporary.

"Very well," he said with a sigh. "I'll let . . . let him in." He crossed to the French doors and as soon as he opened them, the pug raced over to the fireside and shook his stumpy body madly, sending raindrops flying everywhere.

Then Brutus flopped down onto the hearthrug on his belly with a grumble and a groan as if to say, *Well, that took you long enough.*

Miss Davenport laughed. "My dear Mr. Brutus, I've never seen such a maudlin face before."

The pug grunted and cocked one eyebrow. The look he sent the governess could only be described as withering.

Phinn frowned. "Brutus, don't tell me you've taken a dis-dislike to Miss Dav-Davenport," he said. "She's the one who pled your-your case to be let back inside, so I should think you should be grate-grateful, not grumpy."

When the dog lifted one buttock cheek and released a sound not dissimilar to a linguolabial trill, Phinn growled. "You foul beast-beastie. Where are your m-m-manners? There's a lady present. It'll be b-b-back out in the rain with you shortly."

But Miss Davenport didn't seem to mind. She'd covered her mouth again as though she were trying to stifle a laugh. Or maybe she was trying to cover her nose. "Honestly, it's quite all right, my lord," she said. "I imagine it's simply a case of Brutus just working out where he sits in the hierarchy of the household now that Christopher and I have come to stay." She caught the dog's eye. "Isn't it, Brutus?"

The pug emitted another grumble and snuffle as he put his head between his front paws then closed his eyes.

Phinn sighed, suddenly feeling weary beyond words too. "I expect... I expect you're right," he said. Glancing at the mantel clock, he could see it was well after half-past ten. "You-you must be exhausted, Miss Dav-Davenport. I shouldn't keep you up any... any longer. You should retire for the n-n-night. No doubt those boys will be a handful on the mo-morrow." He grimaced. "I'm also supposed to be go-goin' riding with Lord Hart-Hartwell in the mornin'. It's part of me 'gentrification' pro-process. I just hope I don't end up ma-makin' a total t-t-tit of myself."

The governess laughed as she rose from the piano stool. "Oh, surely not. But I do hope it's an enjoyable exercise. Hopefully the rain will stop. As for your speech exercises, my lord"—she picked up her elocution guidebook and slid it into her gown's pocket—"I do think you've achieved quite a bit this evening. I thought your rendition of 'The Rose of Tralee' was well sung and wonderfully smooth. It's given us a place to start, knowing what might work for you. I shall study other elocution exercises we can try. And I'll endeavor to come up with ways to soften your accent. Even though some might think it's perfectly charming." With a curtsy and murmured goodnight, she then promptly quit the room.

Phinn couldn't say he blamed her, given that the eye-wateringly malodorous miasma released by Brutus still lingered. It was foul enough to fell a hardened boxer.

Although, he would readily own that he'd been practically felled by Miss Davenport's comment about his Irish accent being charming. If only the rest of polite society and his "peers" in Parliament would think that too.

Chapter 14

Concerning Pudding and Sweets and Bad Dreams and Butterflies...

"Miss Davenport..."

Mina paused in the hall outside her bedchamber and peered into the soft shadows. Even though the gaslights were turned low, she could still discern Tom Fleet sheltering in a curtained window alcove with his knees tucked up to his chest. "Yes, Tom?" she asked. Concern touched her voice as she continued. "Is everything all right?"

The boy slipped from his seat and approached with the silence of a cat. He was dressed in trousers, shirt, coat, and shoes—not in his nightshirt and nightcap—the attire he'd been in when Mina had bid him goodnight in his room three hours ago. "I'm fit as a flea, miss. It's young Christopher 'oo's not. 'E's been cryin' in 'is sleep. I fink 'e might've been 'avin' a nightmare or somefink. I went in an' gave 'im a pat on the shoulder, but 'e didn't wake up. 'E's quieted down now, but I just fought you should know. Considerin' 'e's your cousin an' all."

Concern tugged at Mina. "Thank you for looking out for him, Tom. That's very kind of you."

The boy shrugged and pushed his hands into his pockets.

"That's all right, miss. I figure Christopher ain't like you an' me an' 'is lordship."

"How so?"

"Well, Christopher seems like a milk puddin'. 'E's soft and needs protectin'. Whereas Lord Kinsale an' me, we're 'ard as a rock. Like humbug sweets. Comes from livin' on the streets. Whereas you, miss, you're more like..." He narrowed his gaze. "You're more like a bonbon with a hard outside, but I reckon you've got a gooey middle. You won't put up wiv rubbish from no one, but you've got a good 'eart."

Mina smiled and inclined her head. "I'll take that as a compliment, Tom. By the way, I think you and Lord Kinsale have good hearts too, underneath your tough veneers."

The boy hunched his shoulders and kicked at the delicate gilt leg of a nearby side table. "I dunno about that."

Mina gestured at his attire. "Are you going somewhere?"

"Maybe..." He crossed his arms and eyed her suspiciously. "Are you goin' to stop me?"

"No," said Mina. "But I would remind you that the streets at night are cold and dangerous and you have a safe and warm place right here. I'd prefer it if you'd stay, but I cannot make you."

Tom's expression hardened with defiance as he hoisted up his small chin. "I can take care o' meself."

"I have no doubts at all that you can," replied Mina. "But you don't have to when you're here. It's quite all right to rest awhile. To take a break from life on the streets."

"I s'pose I'm just used to it," he mumbled. "It's in me blood." He gestured at the fine hallway with its plush runner and velvet drapes and flocked wallpaper and gleaming wood and gilt. "I don't feel like I belong 'ere."

"I understand," said Mina. "But it's raining at the moment. At least wait until the shower stops. There's no sense in getting wet if you don't have to."

"I'll fink about it," said the boy. "'Ow you gettin' on wiv 'is lordship then? 'Is stammer is bleedin' awful. I 'ope you can 'elp 'im."

"I do too, Tom," said Mina. After the session in the drawing room, she was quietly confident the guidebook that had manifested in her pocket might actually assist. The marquess could certainly be fluent while singing. The trick would be working out a way to maintain that degree of fluency during different sorts of "speaking" exercises.

She was just about to bid Tom goodnight when there was a muffled cry from Christopher's room. *Oh no.*

"Sounds like your young cousin is 'avin' anovver bad dream," said Tom.

"Yes," said Mina, hastening over to Christopher's door. His life had been so topsy-turvy of late, she shouldn't be surprised that he'd begun to have nightmares. She waved goodnight to Tom, then let herself into her charge's room.

She'd left a gas lamp burning after she'd tucked Christopher in, so could clearly see his small frame beneath the bedcovers. The sheets and pale green counterpane were twisted, and Mr. Hopwell had fallen onto the floor. As Mina approached the bed, Christopher released a whimper and she could see that his cheeks were flushed and damp with tears.

Oh heavens. Mina's heart contracted with pain. The poor boy. She laid a gentle hand on his shoulder. "Christopher," she murmured. "It's me, Miss Davenport. You're safe—"

At that moment, the boy lurched upright and his blue eyes popped wide open. "Make her go away! Make her go away!" he cried.

"Who?" asked Mina. Even though she knew no one else was in the bedchamber with them, she couldn't stop herself from glancing about the room. Of course, there was no one there.

"The horrible white lady . . . with-with black eyes," sobbed Christopher. His terrified gaze met Mina's. "There was snow in her silver hair and she had a sword made of ice. She says she'll find me, one way or another. That she'll have me taken away."

A white lady with black eyes? Mina sat on the edge of the bed and offered a hug to the trembling, weeping child. As she held him and murmured soothing words of comfort, a shiver of foreboding slid down her spine, chilling her to the bone. Lady Grenfell had told Mina that in her prophetic dream, she'd seen her godson in a frozen Arctic wasteland. But she'd never mentioned a dark-eyed, silver-haired woman brandishing an icy sword. But then, the dowager countess had been quite ill and drowsy; her physician had given her laudanum to ease her pain.

Mina suddenly wished she could confide in Mrs. Temple. Despite the fact the Parasol Academy had a Fae Charter and graduates practiced Fae magic to protect the children in their care, she knew little about the Royal Fae sisters, Good Queen Maeve and Evil Queen Mab, other than Mab's influence in the Earthly Realm had dramatically waned since the Parasol Academy had been established ninety years ago by Verity Truelove, Mrs. Temple's great-grandmother.

But what did that mean, really? Mina was starting to think that perhaps someone from the Fae Realm wanted Christopher. *She says she'll find me, one way or another. That she'll have me taken away.*

Could this terrifying woman the boy had just seen in his nightmare be Evil Queen Mab herself? Because surely Queen Maeve, who wanted to protect human children from being kidnapped by her sister, wouldn't manifest in such a fashion. She wouldn't torment a poor child through dreams.

Mina couldn't be sure. But as soon as she returned to her room next door, she would consult the *Parasol Academy Handbook* and look up the chapter on invoking a protection spell. A ward that would put in place a temporary magical barrier around Christopher's bedroom during the dark, nighttime hours when Queen Mab's elvish minions might attempt to visit a child's room to steal him or her away and leave a changeling behind.

It was powerful magic and not commonly employed. From what Mina could recall, one had to ask the Fae for permission to use the spell, and if it *was* deemed to be necessary, the nanny or governess requesting it would be provided with the means to cast it. Rather like the *Decalamitifying* spell that Mina knew her friend Emmeline had employed when she was working as a nanny for the Duke of St Lawrence.

When Christopher's tears stopped and he seemed calmer, Mina tucked him into bed again with Mr. Hopwell. He asked for a bedtime story and a lullaby and Mina readily complied; it was the least she could do to make the boy feel safe. Although, as soon as he'd drifted to sleep, she repaired to her room and dug out her *Parasol Academy Handbook* from her trunk and her ley-spectacles from her pocket.

The blue leather cover of the handbook shimmered as Mina placed the tome on the small satinwood escritoire by the fire. It didn't take her long to locate the protection spell in Chapter 21. Armed with her refreshed knowledge and renewed resolve, Mina returned to Christopher's room. He was curled on his side, still sleeping soundly with his toy velvet rabbit tucked beneath his chin. His cheeks were slightly flushed and his breathing was deep and even.

More than ever, Mina was determined to protect this child from whatever supernatural harm might be lying in wait for him. If Lady Grenfell had been correct about her portentous dream—if Mina's assumption that Evil Queen Mab was the white lady haunting Christopher in his sleep—then surely the Fae would grant her the use of a warding spell to keep the boy safe at night.

She could but try. Drawing a deep breath, Mina slid her hand into her governess's pocket, closed her eyes and entreated the Fae and Good Queen Maeve to gift her the use of the *Guardia Nimbus* spell on behalf of Christopher, Lord Fitzwilliam. That she had reason to believe the young boy was in imminent danger of being taken away from her care.

For a full minute, nothing happened at all and Mina's heart plummeted like a sinking lump of lead. She must be wrong, about everything. She'd believed Lady Grenfell. She'd convinced herself that Sir Bedivere was being controlled by a Fae-ensorcelled ring. She'd been so certain the woman in Christopher's nightmare had been Queen Mab. Tears of frustration and despair pricked at the back of Mina's eyes and she was about to pull her hand from her pocket when she felt a faint flickering sensation against her palm. A soft caress like a sighed breath brushing over her fingertips. And inside her head she heard a barely there, melodic voice that whispered, "Believe."

Hope beat tiny wings in Mina's chest, and when she withdrew her hand and unfurled her fingers, she gasped in delight. There, upon her palm sat a tiny, lilac-winged butterfly. It sat perfectly still, its wings trembling, as though it was waiting for something.

The incantation, Mina Davenport, you ninny. Say the magic words.

So she did. "*Guardia Nimbus,*" Mina whispered. All at once, the butterfly fluttered its wings, sending a tiny puff of faint purple dust into the air. The dust somehow coalesced and became another tiny lilac butterfly and then another butterfly appeared. And then another. Christopher's room was suddenly filled with a hundred or more fluttering butterflies and as they flitted about, they seemed to weave and spin a faint gossamer web that quickly enveloped the entire room in a shimmering silken veil of pale purple light.

And then all the butterflies disappeared except for one, which lit upon the pillow beside Christopher's blond head. Its delicate wings flapped gently, almost lazily, and Mina instinctively knew that while it remained, the ward would stay in place.

Christopher might still have bad dreams, but no supernatural beings—no elves or Fae in service to Queen Mab—could enter the room. For now, the boy was safe.

As for Sir Bedivere... Mina yawned as she began to get ready for bed. He was a problem for another day. She trusted that she and Christopher were safe here at Kinsale House, at least for the moment. Mrs. Temple would never divulge the whereabouts of one of her employees. And Lord Kinsale was not out and about in high society circles all that much. The baronet and the governess of the marquess's new "ward" were not likely to cross paths, if at all.

Mina prayed with all her heart that might truly be the case.

Chapter 15

Wherein the Upper Crust, Cod-Liver Oil, Corinthians, Cucumbers, and Pickles Are Mentioned . . .

The rain had cleared overnight, but that didn't stop Phinn getting soaked the next morning when he went riding with Marcus, Lord Hartwell, in Hyde Park.

"Feck," he muttered as Marcus hauled him out of an enormous mud puddle on Rotten Row. "I mean, b-b-bloody blazing hell," he amended when the viscount cocked an eyebrow as if to say, *Really, old chap? 'Feck' is just not the done thing around London.*

"That's better," said Marcus, confirming Phinn's thoughts. "Curse like you've been to Eton and Oxford or Cambridge and half of the beau monde won't even bat an eyelid at your accent."

"The b-b-beau what?" asked Phinn, looking down at his wet and filthy riding clothes. This had been the third time he'd been unseated this morning and he was freezing cold and his arse and inner thighs were sore and he'd really had enough. He felt like he'd been smashed to bits by an opponent twice his size in a bare-knuckle boxing match. Feckin' horse-riding was not his cup of tea, or tankard of ale, or whole bottle of whisky, or anything at all. He'd rather drink a bottle of cod-liver oil than hop on Marcus's stinking horse again.

"The beau monde. The upper ten thousand. The upper crust. The toffs." Marcus grinned. "Like I said, replace 'feck' with a few other choice words like 'deuced' and 'damned' and 'dash it all' and everyone will be calling you 'chum' and giving you slaps on the back before you know it."

If only it were that simple. Phinn sighed heavily as Marcus clicked his fingers and the mount that had thrown Phinn—a fine gray gelding—trotted over, as docile as you please. "It w-w-would be a feckin'—I mean, a *dashed* sight easier bein' accepted if I didn't have this d-d-deuced stammer."

Marcus cast him a sympathetic look. "It sounds like your new governess might be able to make a difference though."

Phinn gave a wry smile. "Aye. I mean, yes. I hope... I hope so."

He'd told his friend as they'd set out from the mews behind Hartwell House that he'd hired Miss Davenport to give him etiquette and elocution lessons. What he *hadn't* told Marcus was that he was also fighting a damned inconvenient attraction to the young woman. That last night, after he'd gone to bed, he'd stayed awake half the night, tossing and turning while wild fantasies involving Hermina Davenport had cavorted through his head. At this rate, he'd have to take matters into his own hands—or more precisely, one hand—in order to get any peace. It meant that when he encountered Miss Davenport again, he wouldn't be thinking about her in inappropriate ways that did him no credit as her employer. It wasn't fair on the woman that she'd become the object of his salacious desires.

When he got home he'd definitely need a scalding hot bath. The sooner he rid himself of this infernal ache in his loins, the better.

But misbegotten lust wasn't the only reason Phinn's nether regions were aching. As soon as he climbed back onto his borrowed mount, he couldn't hold back an agonized whimper as he lowered his bruised arse into the saddle. *Sweet Jaysus.*

Marcus threw back his head and laughed. "Oh, my friend. I'm so, so sorry."

Phinn clenched his teeth. "This is pay-payback, isn't it?" he gritted out. "For that p-p-punch I landed on your . . . on your jaw."

Marcus's shoulders shook with mirth. "It's not. Truly it's not. But I'm thinking that next time I give you a riding lesson, we keep to walking and avoid trotting altogether. It's not the easiest gait to master for a beginner. I fear we were being overly ambitious."

"What makes you think there'll be a n-n-next time?" grumbled Phinn beneath his breath as they headed in the direction of Hyde Park Gate. Even though it was early, the park was packed with other riders. In only a few hours, Phinn imagined the park would be full of sightseers visiting the Great Exhibition at the Crystal Palace.

He suddenly wondered if Tom and Christopher would like to go. He could show them the Duke of St Lawrence's Queen of Clocks, which had won a prestigious Council Medal in June. And afterwards, perhaps they could drive past the Houses of Parliament where the duke's King of Clocks would grace the very top of St Stephen's Tower one day.

When they reached Belgravia and Hartwell House in Wilton Crescent, Phinn had never been so grateful to have his feet planted firmly on terra firma.

"I don't suppose you'd be up to attending an event with me this evening," said Marcus as he pulled off his leather riding gloves and slapped them against his buckskin breeches.

Phinn took a few steps away from his horse and grimaced as his leg muscles protested. "What sort of . . . what sort of event?"

Marcus sighed. "A deuced ball. I'm doing my best to comply with the Queen's decree that I look for a wife. In fact, she's going to be at this ball. The Duke of Albemarle and his wife are throwing it, and they happen to have an eligible daughter—Lady Sophia Granville. No doubt I'll have to waltz at least once with the girl."

Phinn would rather eat rocks than attend a ball thrown by Albemarle. No doubt Albemarle would like nothing more than to throw rocks at *him* considering the contemptuous looks the arrogant prat had aimed Phinn's way at Boodle's a few nights ago.

He said as much to Marcus but his friend waved a dismissive hand. "Albemarle looks that way at everyone, so I wouldn't worry. And aside from being my righthand man on the battlefield, so to speak, I thought it might give *you* the chance to be seen out and about by Her Majesty. You know, rubbing shoulders with other toffs can't hurt." His expression changed and his eyes gleamed with a decidedly wicked light. "Come on, Lord Kinsale. I know you're no monk and the ladies do like a man with a fine physique—or more specifically the buttocks of a Corinthian." He winked. "You're bound to snare the interest of a willing widow or two at the very least."

Phinn's thoughts immediately went to Miss Davenport. Was she of the same opinion about his behind? She'd certainly seemed transfixed by the sight of his bare torso the day before when she'd come upon him in his banyan and breeches. Aloud he said, "The butt-buttocks of a Cor-what-thian?"

Marcus laughed. "It means you've got a well-shaped, muscular arse, my fine Irish friend."

Phinn snorted. "The only thing m-m-my arse is, at the mo-moment, is bloody bruised. And because of that, I'm afraid I w-w-won't be up to attendin' any b-b-ball tonight, whether the Queen is goin' to be there or n-n-not." He wasn't lying about his backside. He also didn't want to confess that the only dance he knew was an Irish jig. And that he wasn't interested in trysting with willing widows or indeed anyone at all. (Well, that was another lie, but he wasn't going to tryst with his ward's governess. Although, he hoped she'd be up for teaching him how to dance a wee bit at some point. A waltz would be useful to know.)

Marcus sent him a look of sympathy. "That bad, is it?"

"You-you have n-n-no idea," said Phinn. And he wasn't just talking about his abused body. "I think it will be at least a w-w-week before I go ri-ridin' again."

Thank God Kinsale House in Eaton Square wasn't too far off. Because he'd be limping the entire way.

Christopher slept peacefully through the rest of the night and when Mina rose the next morning, she watched the small lilac butterfly on his pillow fade into the shadows as light filtered into the room. Perhaps the protection spell helped to keep bad dreams at bay too. Mina couldn't be certain, but she had her fingers crossed. It couldn't hurt to hope for the best.

At ten o'clock, the marquess's tailor, a Mr. Travers from Savile Row, and his tailor's assistant, arrived at Kinsale House to take Tom and Christopher's measurements for a raft of new clothes. Christopher didn't seem to mind standing still and being poked and prodded and measured, but Tom Fleet was as twitchy as a rabbit in the sights of a fox. He looked like he wished to bolt at any second.

When Mr. Travers was done, he tucked his tailor's chalk in his pocket and draped his tape measure about his neck. "Now, we just need to choose the fabrics," he said, pushing his silver spectacles up his long nose.

Tom Fleet groaned. "I'd ravver stick pins in me eyes," he grumbled.

Mina laughed. "It's all right, Tom. I can take care of that. Why don't you and Christopher go into the schoolroom and wait for me there?"

Another groan. "Don't tell me we're goin' to start lessons today."

"I'll make it as entertaining as possible, I promise. You can show me what you know about coins. How about that?"

"All right," said Tom with a defeated sigh.

Mina reached into the pocket of her governess's uniform and pulled out a pack of playing cards. "While you wait, Christopher can teach you how to play Old Maid."

"It's wizard fun," said Christopher brightly as the boys trooped out of his room into the hallway. "Miss Davenport taught me on the train yesterday and I trounced her three times..."

Turning to the tailor, Mina said, "Right, Mr. Travers. Where are these fabric swatches?"

"Oh, the butler suggested that I leave them with the marquess's valet in the marquess's suite downstairs," said the tailor. "It's quite a hefty bundle and I wasn't keen on lugging them all the way up here. I hope you don't mind accompanying me to his lordship's rooms. Mr. Smedley assured me it would be all right."

"Oh," said Mina. "Oh, of course not." She really had no idea where Lord Kinsale's private rooms were, but she couldn't deny she was wildly curious to at least take a look at the marquess's sitting room. While she didn't trust Smedley, as far as she knew—or what she'd heard from the marquess's valet, Mr. Frobisher, who'd shown the tailor and his assistant to Christopher's room when they'd first arrived—Lord Kinsale was still out on his morning ride. The coast would be clear.

The Marquess of Kinsale's suite, as Mina expected, was spacious and beautifully appointed. The sitting room contained elegantly carved oak furniture, and the curtains, plush rugs, and upholstery were all in complementary shades of rich green and blue and gold.

As soon as Mina, Mr. Travers, and his assistant stepped into the room, Frobisher came rushing out of an adjoining chamber. Before the double doors closed behind him, Mina caught a glimpse of Lord Kinsale's bedroom with its enormous four-poster bed festooned with dark green velvet drapes edged in gold, and a thick Turkish rug in matching jewel tones of peacock blue, turquoise, and rich amber.

"Miss Davenport," said the dapper, dark-haired valet who couldn't have been more than thirty. He appeared quite harried as his concerned gaze darted between Mina and the tailor. "I-I was expecting Mr. Travers and his assistant to return, but not you."

The tailor sniffed. "The governess needs to choose fabrics for the boys' clothes and all the samples are here," he explained with a wave of his hand. Indeed, Mina could see an enormous bundle of swatches and various bolts of fine fabric piled up on an oak table, a pair of dark brown leather wing chairs, and a sofa upholstered in teal brocade.

"I-I won't take long," said Mina, hurrying over to the fireside, where a fire leapt in the hearth. Even though last night's rain had cleared, a definite autumnal chill was in the air. "I'll be gone before Lord Kinsale comes ba—"

At that moment, the door to the marquess's bedchamber opened wide and Lord Kinsale appeared on the threshold wearing nothing but a loosely cinched silk banyan and a look that hovered somewhere between surprise and horror. His dark hair was wet and curling about his ears, and a white towel was draped around his neck.

Gah! Not again! Mina's face felt like it had caught on fire as she stared back in open-mouthed dismay at her near-naked employer . . . and maybe just a little bit of awe because *my goodness,* was the marquess's physique not godlike? She already knew his broad chest and taut abdomen were all sleek, hard muscle, but today she'd also learned that his powerful thighs were dusted with the same dark hair that was scattered over his corded forearms and bare lower legs. Good Lord, even his bare feet were attractive.

How could this have happened—that in the space of two days, she'd seen Lord Kinsale in such a scandalous state of undress? Had Smedley somehow engineered this to humiliate her and Lord Kinsale a second time?

She really should have insisted that Mr. Travers bring his fabric swatches to the schoolroom, then this entirely awkward encounter would not be happening. Because how on earth was she to ever look Lord Kinsale in the eye again, now that she knew what he looked like just after he'd emerged from his bath? Because clearly he'd been bathing before—

Brutus appeared beside the marquess and gave a yip. *What the hell are ye gawkin' at, Miss Davenport? Ye look like ye're about to drop into a dead faint. It's just the master in his bathrobe, not a feckin' ghost.*

Enough, Brutus, returned Mina hotly. She was not in the mood to be taken to task by the obstreperous pug. Dipping into a curtsy, she dropped her gaze to the floor, away from the marquess's face. "My lord, I'm so, so sorry to intrude upon your privates. I mean private"—*Oh sweet Lord, don't even* look *anywhere near that private part of his anatomy, Hermina Davenport*—"your private rooms. I honestly didn't mean to—"

Mr. Travers cut her off with another expansive wave of his hand. "Yes, I'm sorry, my lord. But your new governess insisted that she had to accompany me to your chambers to select fabric for your wards' new clothes. Of course, I suggested that she wait until I'd finished seeing you, but she would not take no—"

"Well, I never," gasped Mina. But then she snapped her mouth shut. It would do her no good to argue like a fishwife in front of Lord Kinsale. As per Chapter 2 of the *Parasol Academy Handbook,* which spelled out nanny and governess etiquette, discretion was always the better part of valor when it came to dealing with one's employer. Better to apologize for any breach of protocol and retreat gracefully rather than stay and fight a losing battle.

When all was said and done, *she* was to blame for this particular blunder. She'd let her curiosity get the better of her. If she were truly honest with herself, a tiny part of her *had* hoped she might bump into the marquess in his suite. But *not* like this. She should never have gone along with the turncoat tailor, Mr. Travers. She should never have trusted Smedley's word.

Oh, dear God, what if Lord Kinsale decided to dismiss her for "conduct unbecoming"? What if she were sacked from her post before she'd even begun?

Crushing down a sudden rush of hot tears along with a surge of panic, Mina sank into another curtsy. "Forgive me, my lord," she murmured in a voice that was none too steady. And then she picked up her skirts and all but fled from the marquess's sitting room without a backward glance.

When she was calmer, when she'd successfully "Cucumberfied" herself, she would seek out the marquess and apologize again. Profusely.

And hopefully Lord Kinsale *would* forgive her. If not, she'd be in the pickliest pickle that had ever been pickled.

Chapter 16

*In Which Knots Are Undone and the Air Is Cleared;
And Plans for the Afternoon Are Made . . .*

Phinn hovered by the door to the schoolroom, his hand poised to knock while he attempted to untangle his tongue, which felt like it was tied in innumerable knots. It had been over an hour since Miss Davenport had fled from his suite in tears. No doubt the sight of him in next to nothing had been an unexpected shock to the poor woman. But feck—no, dash it all—how could he have known she'd be in his sitting room looking at fabric swatches?

He suspected that the tailor, Travers, had been too goddamn lazy to take the samples up to the schoolroom. No doubt he'd been the one to suggest the governess accompany him to the Marquess of Kinsale's rooms, not the other way around.

Phinn needed to apologize to Miss Davenport for startling her so badly. She could hardly have known he'd been taking a bath and would then come barreling into his sitting room with nothing between nudity and a semblance of decorum but a thin piece of green silk.

He was of a mind to dismiss Mr. L. M. Travers of Savile Row and find another tailor. Not only was the man arrogant and judgmental—he was always frowning and tut-tutting about how certain fabrics wouldn't sit the right way on Phinn's frame or how a particular style that was currently the height of fashion and desired by most gentlemen of rank, did not suit such an overly muscular physique, but he would do what he could, et cetera, et cetera—but Phinn could not abide a man who would not take responsibility for his own transgressions. The fact that Travers had talked over Miss Davenport and then thrown her under the omnibus, so to speak, made Phinn feel like knocking the tailor into next week.

Speaking of knocking... Phinn drew a deep breath, gathered his nerve, and at last rapped on the schoolroom door.

Miss Davenport's murmured summons to enter came straightaway. Phinn found her sitting at one of the larger occasional tables with the two boys, a small pile of coins between them all.

Before he could untether his tongue, the governess hurriedly rose to her feet and curtsied. "Oh, Lord Kinsale," she said. "I-I was not expecting to see you so soon after..." Her face turned crimson and she pleated her fingers together in front of her waist. "Mr. Travers... He, er... he sent his assistant up here with some fabric samples. Apparently some of the boys' new clothes—things like shirts and waistcoats—will be ready in a few days, and we should receive everything else—their new trousers and coats—within a week."

Phinn grunted. *I should bloody well hope so*, he thought to himself. *Considering the fee I'm paying the pompous bastard.* His tongue loosened and he at last managed, "I hope... I hope that will s-s-suit."

"Oh yes. Of course. Christopher has a few things that Tom is welcome to borrow in the meantime. And anything that gets too mucky can be laundered." Miss Davenport glanced at the boys. "Christopher, can you show Tom how to write the numbers designating each of the coins in that notebook I gave you?

Then, Tom, can you practice copying those numbers beneath them? I just need to step outside and speak with Lord Kinsale for a few minutes."

Ah, damn it. Miss Davenport wanted to speak with him privately? Phinn prayed the governess wasn't going to resign because of what had happened in his rooms.

With a sigh, he followed her into the hallway.

"Miss Dav-Davenport," he began at the same time the governess said, "Lord Kinsale." And then they both said, "I'm sorry," before breaking off a second time. In the awkward silence that ensued, the governess bit her plump lower lip and damn it . . . now Phinn was distracted by her pretty mouth. And he really couldn't afford to be.

Inhaling a calming breath, he tried again. "Ordinarily, I w-w-would let you speak first, Miss Dav-Davenport. But . . . but I really f-f-feel that I should . . . that I should say somethin'. About the in-incident in my sit-sittin' room."

The governess was twisting her fingers together now. "Yes," she said, her voice little more than a breathless whisper. "Yes . . . I-I wanted to talk to you about that too, my lord."

"Aye . . . I-I m-m-mean yes." Phinn wiped a hand down his face then rubbed the back of his neck as awkwardness assailed him. "Miss Dav-Davenport. There's n-n-no easy way to say this but . . ."

The governess nodded and her expression fell. "I know, my lord," she said, her gaze trained on the hall runner rather than his face. "After what occurred earlier—after I invaded your privacy yet again—clearly there's no other option but to dismiss me. I shouldn't have listened to Mr. Travers, even though Smedley had apparently told him it would be fine. I've been so very foolish."

What? Phinn's mouth dropped open as horror blasted through him. Not because Travers and perhaps Smedley were behind this second misadventure of the sartorial kind. No, it was what the governess had said before that. "N-n-no. No-no, M-M-Miss Dav-Dav-Davenport. I d-d-don't want to dis-dis-dismiss you. I . . ." He drew a steadying breath and fought desperately to make his blasted mouth work properly. "I came to see you to apol-apologize for-for you havin' to see m-m-me in . . . Well, n-n-not dressed as a gentle-gentleman should b-b-be."

"But that was hardly your fault, my lord," said Miss Davenport, at last raising her eyes to his. "How could you have known that I would be there?"

"Just like it w-w-was hardly your fault that I b-b-burst into the room in nothin' but me b-b-bathrobe. Need-needless to say, I'll be havin' a w-w-word with Smedley about the in-incident. His med-meddlin' is not to be borne." He blew out a sigh and attempted a smile. "Honestly, the last thing I w-w-want you to do is leave, Miss Dav-Davenport. I . . . I need you. And that's the God's honest truth of the m-m-matter."

The governess studied his gaze intently for several long moments and Phinn began to wonder if he'd said something he shouldn't have. "Well, that's most reassuring," she said with a soft smile. "Because I certainly don't want to go."

"Oh. Good. Ex-excellent," said Phinn, relief washing through him like sunlight breaking through a bank of dark clouds. "I'm glad we've c-c-cleared up any mis-misunderstandin'."

Miss Davenport's hazel eyes glowed with warmth. "Yes. I am too. And you can rest assured that I will never enter your suite of rooms again."

More's the pity, thought Phinn. Little did Hermina Davenport know that only ten minutes before he'd encountered her in his sitting room, he'd been fantasizing about her entering his bedchamber and joining him in the bathtub.

Thank the Lord she couldn't read minds, so she didn't know what he'd been up to in the bath . . . or more precisely *what* had been up.

"I suppose I should get back to the boys," said Miss Davenport, taking a step toward the schoolroom door.

Even though Phinn should seek out Smedley—he would let the butler know in no uncertain terms that he was *not* pleased—he hesitated to leave. "How is everything go-goin'?" He *was* genuinely interested. "How is . . . how is Tom settlin' in?"

A worried expression crossed the governess's features. "I think he *is* keen to learn, despite his protestations. Only . . ." She lowered her voice. "I'm concerned that he wants to leave the house to wander the streets after dark." She then told Phinn how she'd come across the boy, fully dressed in the hallway when she'd been on her way to bed the night before. "He appeared to reconsider when I reminded him it was raining, and there was no sense in getting wet. But I suspect that he still might be tempted to try again another night."

Phinn sighed. "Unfortunately, I f-f-feel there's little I can do. I'm not really his guard-guardian, so I have no authority over him. I've b-b-been hopin' that with t-t-time he'll learn to trust m-m-me and will want to stay of his own accord."

Miss Davenport nodded. "I think you might be right, my lord. Stopping him from coming and going as he pleases will only cause resentment and rebellion. As you say, he has to *want* to stay. But I will do my best to make him feel like he's welcome here. I do think he's forming a bond with Christopher too. Which is lovely to see."

"You-you mentioned yesterday that you need-needed to purchase various items for the b-b-boys," said Phinn. "Do you n-n-need the carriage at all? You're wel-welcome to send for one at any t-t-time."

Miss Davenport's eyes brightened with eagerness. "Actually, I was rather hoping I could take the boys to Hatchards this afternoon."

"Of course," said Phinn. "Although, m-m-might I c-c-come along too? That way I c-c-can set up an account straightaway, rather than havin' to go through me, I mean *my* man of b-b-business."

"I'd be delighted." The governess blushed prettily. "I mean, I'm sure the boys would be delighted if you joined us. The more the merrier as they say."

"Very good," said Phinn. "After lunch, per-perhaps? Say two-two o'clock? Would that suit?"

"It would be perfect." Miss Davenport cast him a look that Phinn interpreted as shy. "I hope it's all right to ask this, my lord... but, will you require further etiquette and elocution instruction this evening? At dinner and afterwards? If I know in advance, I can devise a lesson plan."

"Yes. Yes, I w-w-would," said Phinn. He paused, searching for the right words. "Last n-n-night I wasn't jest-jestin' when I mentioned I m-m-might require dancin' lessons too. While I was out ridin' with Lord Hart-Hartwell this mornin', he suggested I attend a b-b-ball this evenin' that the Queen herself is attend-attendin'. But I d-d-don't even know how to w-w-waltz. So I can-cannot go. Not yet."

Miss Davenport's cheeks took on a rosy hue. "I would be happy to, my lord. Would you like to begin dance lessons tonight?"

Phinn grimaced. *Damn it.* He'd love to hold Miss Davenport in his arms. And not just because he'd caught her like he'd done on the *Kinsale Cloud* or in the garden yesterday afternoon when she'd slipped on wet flagstones. "I'm afraid not," he said. "I'm... After me... After my ri-ridin' lesson I'm a b-b-bit sore and sorry for myself. I t-t-took a few tum-tumbles and trotting is feck—I mean, damnably hard." He glanced toward the main staircase a bit farther along the hall. "I'm not lookin' forward to go-goin' down the stairs. Promise you w-w-won't laugh if you no-notice me limpin' and cur-cursin'."

The governess pressed her lips together as if she were already trying to suppress a smile. "I promise," she said. Although her eyes were certainly twinkling with mirth.

As Phinn gingerly descended the stairs, his bruised thighs and backside hurting like the very devil, he was sure he heard a soft huff of laughter right before the schoolroom door snicked shut.

It seemed Hermina Davenport had a wee bit of a wicked side lurking beneath her prim and proper exterior . . . and Phinn liked the idea very much.

Chapter 17

Concerning Cocked Legs, Leg-shackles, Bosoms, and Moon-eyes; And a Book Excursion Featuring Unanticipated Traps and Bonnet Blows . . .

At two o'clock, Mina, Christopher, and Tom met Lord Kinsale and Brutus in the grand entry hall of Kinsale House. Smedley gave them all a snooty look and Mina sent him a snooty look right back.

She would *not* be cowed by the man, and she was gratified when the butler was the first to look away. *No one* intimidated a Parasol governess.

Lord Kinsale did not seem to notice the exchange of disdainful looks as he donned a well-cut frock coat, gloves, and top hat. Brutus did, though, and he gave a throaty chuckle.

Ye want me to cock me leg on Smedley? he asked. *Or tear a hole in his trouser leg? I hear he's in the master's bad books after this mornin', so I'd be happy to do it.*

Mina's cheeks warmed at the thought that Lord Kinsale was willing to defend her honor by taking the odious butler to task about the sitting room incident. Nevertheless, she gave a discreet shake of her head as she assisted Christopher and Tom into their coats. *Bad books or not, it will create too much fuss and bother. And Lord Kinsale might feel obliged to discipline* you. You probably won't be allowed to accompany us on this excursion. And surely you don't want to be banished to the terrace again.

I suppose not, replied the pug with a grumble.

Mina gave the dog a smile. *I appreciate the offer though. And at least you and I can at last see eye to eye on something.*

Oh, we are not *bosom friends, by any means*, retorted Brutus with a huff and a backward kick of one small stocky leg then the other. *Ye cannot sweet-talk me like ye can the master.*

What? No one is sweet-talking anyone, protested Mina as she fastened her own Parasol Academy coat over her gown.

Brutus gave a yap. *A likely story. Me master might be all moon-eyed whenever he looks yer way right now, Miss Davenport. But that won't last long. The marquess isn't lookin' to get leg-shackled anytime soon, so you can stop battin' your eyelashes at him. To be sure, like most men, he likes a pretty face an' shapely figure. But don't ye be thinkin' that his admiration goes beyond that.*

Before Mina could retort that she was a career governess and not the sort to dally with her employer, the impudent pug was racing out the front door while the marquess was inviting her and the boys out to the square, where a footman was letting down the steps to the carriage.

It was certainly a novel experience taking a carriage ride with the marquess. The cabin's interior was spacious, with ample room for two adults, two boys, and a pug. But of course, Lord Kinsale's large frame seemed to dominate one entire side of the confined space. Mina, who sat with Tom and Christopher on the opposite leather bench seat, tried very hard not to stare all "moon-eyed" at her employer. But it was hard not to sneak an admiring glance at him every so often, even when Brutus sent her narrow-eyed looks that clearly told her that *he* knew what she was doing. (Even though she wasn't doing anything. Not *really*.)

She was not the simpering, flirtatious type, despite what Brutus thought. Her mind was on the job and nothing else. She would look after Tom and Christopher and find them educational texts and books that would both entertain and engage them and expand their knowledge. That's all she had to do. She was *not* going to stare at Lord Kinsale all afternoon.

At least the journey to Piccadilly wasn't too long. Indeed, within fifteen minutes, they were exiting the carriage, right in front of Hatchards. Lord Kinsale lifted the boys down onto the street and then, to Mina's surprise, he handed her out like she was a fine lady. As his large hand engulfed hers, her skin tingled within her gloves, almost as though she was using magic. Her cheeks might have grown warm too.

Thank goodness Brutus was too busy sniffing around a lamppost and then observing another dog—a pretty golden-brown spaniel—who trotted past with her owner. Mina had had quite enough of the pug's tetchy remarks, thank you very much.

A tug on Mina's sleeve drew her attention. It was Christopher. "Miss Davenport. There's a wizard sweet shop just over there." The boy gestured across Piccadilly toward Burlington Arcade. "Might we visit there first? It's been ages since I had any sweets."

Mina was conscious of the fact that both Lord Kinsale and Tom Fleet were watching the exchange. "It has," she agreed. "But let's visit Hatchards first. We're right here and sticky fingers are not particularly good for leafing through the pages of new books. Perhaps we'll go afterwards if it's all right with Lord Kinsale."

The marquess smiled. "It-it will be per-perfectly fine with me," he said with a grin. "I like . . . I like sweet things too."

Brutus gave a disgusted snuffle. *Ugh. The pair o' ye make me ill even without eatin' any sweets.*

Says the dog who was just making eyes at the pretty spaniel who pranced by not half a minute ago, replied Mina with a small smile. *You don't have a leg to stand on, Brutus.*

The pug snorted then cocked his leg on the lamppost he'd been sniffing. *I beg to differ*, he retorted.

Mina simply rolled her eyes. She knew she should be above such petty squabbles. But really, the pug was most vexing. At this rate, it didn't seem like she and Lord Kinsale's pet dog would be calling a truce anytime soon.

Once their small party was all inside Hatchards—except for Brutus, who stayed outside with the marquess's footmen—Mina led the boys toward the Children's Literature section.

"Now, I want you to have a look through the books shelved on these two bookcases and point out anything that catches your eye," she said. "Picture books are just as valuable as books with text alone. The main thing is, I want you to enjoy reading whatever you choose. Learning doesn't have to be a chore."

Now it was Tom who was looking disgruntled. "I ain't 'ad any use for books in all me eight years. Don't see why I need books now."

"Just have . . . just have a look, lad," said Lord Kinsale. "That's all Miss Dav-Davenport is askin'. You nev-never know. You might find some-somethin' you like."

Tom sighed dramatically. "All right, my lord." He turned away from the marquess but didn't stray far from Mina's side. Christopher joined him, and the boys each selected a book and began to thumb through the pages.

"Thank you, my lord," said Mina, choosing a book herself. It was *An Illustrated History of the British Isles; 1066 to Present Day*. "Do you enjoy reading? Is there anything in particular you'd like to look at in the store?"

The marquess's mouth lifted in a wry grin. "I'm ha-happy right here," he said. "Unless you're tryin' to get rid o' me, Miss Dav-Davenport."

"Oh no," said Mina hurriedly. "I didn't mean that at all, my lord. And I apologize if—"

She stopped when she saw that Lord Kinsale's eyes were gleaming with mischief.

"I'm just jokin' with you," the Irishman said with a soft chuckle that Mina seemed to feel all the way to her toes.

To hide her blush—heavens, she'd never blushed so much in her entire life—she slid the history book back into place then selected another title at random. *Robinson Crusoe*. "I'd still be interested to know if reading is a pastime you enjoy, my lord. Perhaps we could choose something for you to recite from tonight."

Lord Kinsale plucked a book from the shelf—it was a Dickens title—then returned it to its spot. "I can-cannot say I am much of a re-reader. Growing up, me mam—I mean, my mother—did-didn't have anythin' much on hand except a worn-out B-B-Bible and a copy of *Gulliver's Travels*, which I can-cannot say I enjoyed." He grimaced. "She ended up sellin' both for-for food. That was before I took up box-boxin' for money."

"I'm sorry," said Mina. And she meant it. "I didn't mean to bring up painful memories."

"It's not your fault, Miss Dav-Davenport. Do you...do you have any books you'd rec-recommend? A fa-favorite book? I find myself...I find myself wantin' to learn more about you and the things you like."

Oh goodness. Why did Mina's heart flip over at the thought? "I...er. I would say my favorite book is *Jane Eyre* by Charlotte Brontë." She laughed. "Ironically it's about a governess."

"Who falls...who falls in love with her employer?" Smiling, Lord Kinsale leaned an arm against the bookshelf and Mina tried very hard not to ogle the man's bulging biceps muscles, which pushed against the seam of his coat. "I know of it," he continued, seemingly oblivious to Mina's flustered state. "It sounds quite scandalous, Miss Dav-Davenport. Com-completely outrageous."

"Well, obviously that's something that *I* would never do," said Mina, attempting to marshal her professional, never-put-

a-foot-wrong, never-going-to-give-my-heart-away-like-Jane-Eyre-did self. "After all, the Parasol Academy—"
"The Pa-Parasol Academy forbids fraternization? I know. I'm... I'm simply—"
"Teasing me again?" Mina sent the marquess a mock frown. "For shame, my lord. For what it's worth, I also enjoy *Pride and Prejudice* and *Sense and Sensibility* and *Emma* by Jane Austen. And the poems of Elizabeth Barrett Browning. Her *Sonnets from the Portuguese* is quite sublime."
Again, that teasing, bordering-on-rakish smile. "Hmmm, all works with romantic themes if I'm not mis-mistaken."
When Mina cast the marquess a skeptical look—because really, how could a former boxer who purported not to read much at all, know about such things?—he added, "My sis-sister liked Jane Austen's novels too. After I began prize-prize-fightin' and had a bit o' a wee windfall one time, I bought her a subscription at one of the cir-circulatin' libraries in Dublin for her birthday. She could nev-never stop ravin' about how delicious someone n-n-named Mr. Darcy was. Tell me, Miss Dav-Davenport"—Lord Kinsale lowered his voice so perhaps only she could hear him—"are you... are you a romantic at heart? It sounds like you m-m-might be."
Mina paused in her perusal of the titles on display and considered the question. *Heavens, how to respond?* "I suppose I... I simply like happy endings," she said, meeting Lord Kinsale's gaze directly.
His beautiful green eyes glowed softly with a smile. "Well, I can't... I can't say that I blame you."
At that moment, there was a yelp then a howl of pain behind Mina. Spinning around, she discovered Tom was leaping about, waving one arm wildly, squawking like his trousers were on fire. "Get it off! Get it off!" he screeched. A white-faced Christopher was huddled against the bookcase while several other customers sent disapproving looks Tom's way.

Get it off? It was then that Mina spied what the problem was. Several of Tom's fingers were caught in a mousetrap.

A mousetrap? What on—?

Lord Kinsale, registering the cause of Tom's distress too, took action. Stepping forward, he caught the boy's arm with one large hand, then swiftly prized the snap trap off the boy's fingers with the other.

"Ow, ow, ow!" cried Tom. As he massaged his abused fingers, he threw a baleful look at Mina. "'Oo the 'ell keeps a bleedin' mousetrap in their blinkin' pocket?"

Oh . . . Mina suddenly knew what had happened. While she regretted that Tom was hurt—she didn't like seeing him so upset and in pain—she suspected that he'd just learned something *very* valuable: One should never try to pick the pocket of a Parasol Academy governess. Much like a snapping turtle, uniform pockets could bite back to protect their magical contents.

Mina reached into her pocket and found that it had produced a small pot of ointment and a length of linen bandage, almost as though it was trying to make amends for injuring the child. "Here, Tom. I could bind them—"

But the boy shook his head and backed away. "I don't fink so, miss."

Christopher placed a hand on Tom's arm. "It's all right. You can trust Miss Davenport. She's only trying to help."

Guilt pinched Mina's heart. "I'm sorry your fingers got injured, Tom," she said softly. "But picking my pocket wasn't a very good idea."

Tom pouted. "I just wanted to filch a few coins so I could buy some sweets for Christopher."

"Ah, Tom, lad. That's not . . . That's not the way to go about things," said Lord Kinsale, his expression grave. "Re-remember I said that we'd visit the sweet shop after we were fin-finished here?"

"You did," said Tom. "But grown-ups often say fings they don't mean."

It was clear to Mina that Tom was naturally wary after living on the streets for so long. And even though he'd tried to steal from her, it was important to try and build his trust. She would extend an olive branch. "We'll still go to the sweet store," she said. "But after we've concluded our business here. I understand that you might not particularly enjoy looking at books, Tom. But I'm a governess and I need books in order to help you and Christopher learn."

"I *like* books," said Christopher brightly. "And I think I can see one of my favorites, just over there." He pointed to another bookcase a little farther back in the store. "It's called *Little Downy: or, the History of a Field Mouse*. It even has pictures. Do you want to take a look, Tom?"

Tom gave a little shudder. "As long as there's no bleedin' mousetraps in it," he said, and Mina tried very hard not to laugh.

"Oh dear," she said as the boys moved away. "That was rather a lot to deal with."

"I think you d-d-dealt with the situation re-remarkably well," said Lord Kinsale.

Mina permitted herself a small smile. "Thank you, my lord."

"Although..." the marquess added. His expression had grown curious. "I, for one, would... would like to know why you had a mouse-mousetrap in your pocket in the first place. Did you su-suspect Tom might try to pick your p-p-pocket?"

"Ah, no. Not quite," said Mina. Of course, she'd had nothing at all to do with the mousetrap materializing in her pocket. It was Fae magic, and Parasol Academy uniform pockets just happened to produce whatever was needed no matter the situation. But she couldn't very well tell Lord Kinsale that. She'd have to come up with a tiny white lie. Which *was* permissible to protect the Academy's secrets. "I... earlier this morning, I er... I found evidence of a mouse in the schoolroom, so I asked Mrs. Aldershot if there might be a spare mousetrap somewhere. She er... she gave it to me just before we left to go on our book-buying excursion and I put it in my pocket." She shrugged a shoulder. "Tom was just unlucky."

"It w-w-would seem that young Tom has learned an im-important life lesson," returned Lord Kinsale with a grin. "Whatever you do, do *not* muck about with a Parasol govgoverness."

Mina smiled back. "Very true," she said. A sharp yip from outside—it sounded like Brutus—suddenly drew Mina's attention toward one of Hatchards's wide front windows. And then she nearly expired on the spot because there, outside on the pavement, was Sir Bedivere Ponsonby.

Oh God! Christopher's guardian was back in London?

As the golden-haired baronet peered through the store's windowpane at the books on display, he stroked his sleek mustache and goatee beard. The silver and obsidian ring on his finger flashed in the sunlight, seeming to wink at Mina. Ice-cold dread speared through her and her breath froze.

At least Christopher was presently shielded by a bookcase, but what if Sir Bedivere noticed *her*? He'd be sure to come inside and demand to know if she knew the whereabouts of his ward.

Damn and blast and buggeration! (Not words she would usually use but they seemed entirely appropriate for the present situation.) Mina hadn't brought an umbrella or parasol with her, so testing out the Point-of-Confusion on him wasn't an option. And of course, she couldn't very well put up her umbrella or parasol and employ a *Cloakify* spell in the middle of Hatchards anyway. Or use the *Glamify* spell for that matter, even *if* the potion bottle magically materialized in her pocket. A befuddling potion *might* work at a pinch.

Or violence. A swift kick to the baronet's nether regions would disable him long enough to make a getaway with Christopher. But that would create a scene. And there were children present. And Lord Kinsale would be sure to ask questions she didn't want to answer.

All these thoughts raced like quicksilver through Mina's head in a matter of seconds. She had to do something, *anything*, before Sir Bedivere *did* see her.

There was nothing for it. Mina seized upon the only sensible course of action open to her. She'd hide. Duck down. "Excuse me, my lord," she said in a breathless rush. "I need to tie my bootlace."

In one swift movement, she dropped to one knee, lurched forward as she reached for her half boot... and then the very top of her head, coal-scuttle bonnet and all, accidentally smashed into Lord Kinsale's crotch. Hard.

"Feck. Me," wheezed the marquess, stumbling backward a few paces. He'd folded at the waist and was clutching his groin with two gloved hands. And then he toppled like a felled tree, crashing into a nearby elegant oval table stacked with a neat book display.

Oh no! The table went over along with Lord Kinsale. Books went flying and a woman shrieked.

Mina hurriedly tugged off her crumpled bonnet then scrambled on hands and knees over to the marquess. "Oh my God. I'm so, so sorry," she cried, hands hovering about the man's shoulders. She wanted to pat him, offer comfort, but didn't think it would be well received, considering she'd just grievously injured the poor man. She was also highly conscious of the fact that Sir Bedivere might have heard the commotion and had come into the store to investigate.

She prayed that he hadn't. Glancing at the small crowd of half a dozen or so customers who'd already gathered, she couldn't *see* the blond baronet. Not yet at any rate.

Christopher and Tom had joined them. "What's happened to Lord Kinsale?" asked Christopher.

Tom was chuckling. "Miss Davenport head-butted him in the goolies."

"Goolies?" repeated Christopher, clearly confused.

"You know, the cods, knacker bag, stones, nuts, meat and two veg. The bollocks."

"Oh," said Christopher, wincing. "Ouch."

Ouch indeed. Mina prayed she hadn't done her employer any permanent damage. (Unlike her bonnet. Now *that* was completely ruined.)

"Here, what's going on, you lot?" The proprietor of Hatchards had appeared and he was none too happy. A fierce frown was deeply etched into his brow and his mouth was set in a poker-straight line. "I ought to call the police!"

Mina rose to her feet. "Sir, my sincerest apologies for creating a fuss. But my employer, the Marquess of Kinsale, just fainted. Rather than threatening to call the police, perhaps you could offer assistance? Offer his lordship a glass of water and a quiet place to sit until he's recovered his equilibrium?"

The man's eyebrows shot up toward his thinning gray hair. "Marquess of Kinsale, you say?"

"Aye." Lord Kinsale had managed to sit up. His face, which had turned an alarming shade of red when he'd first been hit, was now paler than milk. "I am Lord Kin-Kinsale."

"Oh . . . Oh, my apologies, my lord." The man flapped his hands. "I had no idea. Please. Come and sit in my office. I can have someone bring a pot of tea. I might even have some brandy—"

"No. Its-it's all right," said Lord Kinsale. He pushed to his feet and Mina handed him his top hat, which had gone flying too. "Thank you," he said, running a hand through his tousled dark locks before redonning his hat. (Ugh, why did this man look so good with messy hair? Whereas Mina just looked unkempt.)

"Are you sure you are all right? Can you walk?" she murmured, daring to touch his forearm. He looked down at her hand, then covered it with his own.

"I . . . I am." His mouth inched into a weak smile. "I'm in

the w-w-wars today, aren't I?" he said. "You might want to give me f-f-fair warn-warnin' next time you need to tie your laces though. Give-give a man a chance to step b-b-back first."

Mina scrunched up her nose. "You have no idea how sorry I am, my lord," she said. "I-I don't know what I was thinking. That's no excuse of course. If there's anything I can do to make it up to you . . ."

"Oh, I'm sure I'll think of some-something," he said in a low, velvet-soft voice meant only for her.

Heat flared in Mina's cheeks. Surely he didn't mean—

"I know," he declared. "You must pick out a stack of your fa-favorite novels and perhaps even a book of po-poetry or two, and that's what I'll start recitin' this evenin'."

"All right," said Mina. "That sounds like a wonderful idea."

The coast appeared to be clear. She hadn't spotted Sir Bedivere in the store and he wasn't outside anymore. Perhaps he'd been in the area for a reason that had nothing to do with book browsing. White's and Boodle's were practically around the corner.

It just meant she'd have to take extra care when out and about town. At least until the baronet decided to quit London and head off on another exploratory venture.

Hopefully that wouldn't be too long.

Chapter 18

In Which Physiognomy Is Admired and (Some but Not All) Confidences Are Shared; And the Hue of Irish Whisky Is Reflected Upon . . .

"*H*e had been looking two minutes at the fire . . . and I had been looking the same length of time at him . . . when, turning suddenly . . . he caught my gaze fastened on his physiognomy . . . 'You examine me, Miss Eyre,' said he . . . 'do you think me handsome?' "

Phinn looked up from *Jane Eyre*, the copy Miss Davenport had selected from Hatchards two weeks ago. "Well, what-what do you think, Miss Dav-Davenport?" he asked, catching her gaze which, just like Miss Jane Eyre's, had been resting on his face. They were presently in Kinsale House's library, sitting before the fire. Phinn was reclining in his leather wing chair with Brutus lightly snoring at his feet while the governess was sitting demurely upon the nearby settee, listening to him recite the book aloud, giving him helpful suggestions every now and again to improve the smoothness of his speech.

Miss Davenport blushed, her cheeks almost matching the burgundy velvet of the settee. "I . . . I think you're . . ." She sat up straighter. "Yes, I do. Think your physiognomy is pleasing to the eye." And then the wash of bright color in her cheeks swept across her lovely face and her gaze dropped to her elegant fingers, which lay pleated together in her lap. Then she looked up and Phinn detected a spark of challenge in her fine hazel eyes. "But I'm sure you know that already, my lord." Phinn was being a cad, teasing Miss Davenport so. He knew he was being unfair. He knew he was being a rogue. But he'd never claimed to be a gentleman let alone a saint and, quite simply, he couldn't seem to help himself. The governess's reactions—her fight to retain her composure in the face of a reluctant attraction (and he sensed she *was* attracted to him)—were most gratifying. It meant he wasn't alone in fighting to subdue a highly unruly and inconvenient tendre.

"Oh. I-I wasn't fish-fishin' for compliments about me looks, Miss Dav-Davenport," he said slowly, exercising the techniques contained in her little green elocution guidebook. "I do apologize for the mis-misunderstandin'. I . . . I was seekin' your opinion on the fluency of me . . . I mean my speech and pronun-pronunciation. But thank you all the same. I'm not foolish enough to believe that my . . . that my"—he paused and drew a breath then carefully said—"physiognomy is the epitome of masculine beauty. After livin' the life of a pro-professional boxer"—he pointed at his slightly crooked nose and scarred eyebrow—"I'm cer-certainly no Adonis."

"No, more of a Heathcliff perhaps," she remarked, an impudent twinkle dancing in her eyes. "But not quite so broodingly frowny or vengeful."

"Good God. I should . . . I should hope not. Although," Phinn continued, "considerin' I haven't yet read *Wuther-Wuthering Heights*, I believe you have me at a dis-disadvantage, Miss Davenport . . . Now I don't know whether to take the comparison as a compliment or not."

"Oh, it's definitely a compliment," said the governess. "Heathcliff is dark of hair and in one section of the book, if I recall correctly, is described as a 'tall, athletic, and well-formed man.' And in another part, 'an erect and handsome figure.'"

Phinn grinned. "Well-formed, you say?" He wouldn't dare comment on the "erect" remark. It seemed he was becoming quite infatuated with Miss Hermina Davenport—not just because she was pretty, and he was wildly attracted to her in a physical sense—but because he admired her calm disposition and her intelligence and he liked her sparks of liveliness and her kindness. How patient and good she was with Tom and her own lad, Christopher.

Over the last two weeks all of them had fallen into a routine—Miss Davenport would teach and take care of the boys during the day. (Although Phinn would often accompany them on excursions to the park or the library or a museum or gallery.) But Phinn would readily admit that this quiet time of day, taking dinner with Miss Davenport to perfect his knowledge of dining etiquette, then working on his speech—improving his fluency and softening his brogue a fraction—was his favorite.

In the space of a mere fortnight, he already felt as though she'd made a marked difference when it came to helping him with his speech. He felt as though he could control his stammer to some degree. At least in certain situations. Miss Davenport's exercises and suggestions—she claimed they all came from her elocution guidebook—were simple yet effective. Measures such as making sure his oral musculature and neck and chest and diaphragm were relaxed before his elocution exercises made a world of difference. Little prompts such as, perhaps he should take a deeper breath before a particularly long sentence, or that he should pause in a particular place when reciting a passage to help with the prosodic flow. It might help if he slowed his pace a fraction because talking aloud didn't have to be a race. (That actually helped an *awful* lot, the idea that he didn't have to rush to get all the words out at once because he feared he'd get "stuck.")

What if he tried producing harder consonant sounds with a softer contact of teeth, lips, and tongue? Being gentle with his words.

Of course, reading and reciting poetry, even singing, helped immeasurably. It simplified the overall complexity of speaking when he didn't have to think about *what* was going to come out of his mouth. He could see what was coming so he knew exactly when he needed to take a breath or soften the way he said certain sounds. It relieved the anticipatory pressure—the unhelpful whirligig of thoughts that inevitably tripped him up like, *Oh Jaysus, what should I say, and what if I stumble on that word, or get stuck on that consonant and sound like an utter eejit?* It dispelled some of the panic in his brain.

Miss Davenport ignored his blatantly flirtatious remark. Instead, she gestured at *Jane Eyre*. "Would you like to read more, my lord? Or will you choose something else? You're making excellent progress with your speech, by the way."

Phinn inclined his head in acknowledgment. "Thank you. But it's all . . . it's all because of you, Miss Davenport. I've-I've been meanin' to tell you that even my friend Lord Hartwell has noticed a difference. When we've been out ridin', or when I've visited White's or Boo-Boodle's with him, I've been able to greet . . . to greet other gentlemen without feelin' like I'm makin a total"—he broke off because he'd been about to say "total tit"—"I mean, an ab-absolute fool of myself."

"I'm sure you'd never do that, my lord. But yes, the improvement in your speech—even when you're not reading or singing—is quite noticeable." She smiled softly. "You still have your lovely lilting Irish accent, but I've also observed that you're using less colloquial Irish expressions, and your vocabulary is more 'English' sounding, shall we say?"

Phinn felt a spark of pleasure hearing Miss Davenport describe his Irish accent in such terms. "It's-it's readin' books of poetry and novels like these," he said, holding up *Jane*

Eyre. "I think I'm absorbin' your . . . your Anglified vernacular that way."

It wasn't a lie. He'd been devouring everything Miss Davenport had selected from Hatchards's shelves. While he didn't think he'd ever sound like Mr. Darcy or Mr. Knightley or Edward Rochester, or come up with anything as eloquent as a verse composed by Elizabeth Barrett Browning, reading those books was helping him immeasurably. He endeavored to use "my" for "me" when talking about things that were his. And that he should take care to correctly pronounce the "-ing" on the ends of words—which he remembered to do when reading, at least. And as Marcus had pointed out, when in the company of other gentlemen, curse like he'd studied at Eton or Oxford, even though he hadn't.

"You'll be ready to make your speech when Parliament sits again before you know it," said Miss Davenport.

"Aye . . . I mean yes. Especially if-if I rehearse it. I-I would like to . . . to be more fluent in con-conversation though."

"I feel it will come. With time." She glanced at the mantel clock. It was almost a quarter to eleven. "Speaking of time, I know it's getting late, but would you like to chat with me for a while? The extra practice can't hurt."

Phinn suddenly wondered if the governess was enjoying their shared time together as much as he was. She didn't appear to be in any hurry to leave. "I-I don't want to keep you," he said, giving her the option to retire for the night if she wished to.

"Oh no. I'd be happy to, my lord."

"What do you . . . What do you suggest we talk about?"

Miss Davenport answered straightaway, as though she'd been thinking about just such a thing for some time. "I'd love to learn more about Ireland. Whatever you feel comfortable telling me."

Phinn was touched. Since he'd become a marquess, no one had asked him about his home. It hadn't always been terrible.

One thing he'd learned, especially over the last few years, was that good things could live alongside the bad. "I'm happy to talk... to talk about anythin' to do with my life there. Past or present."

"You have a castle there? In Kinsale?" she said. "Living in something so huge and so grand, I can't even imagine it. I suspect it would take a bit of getting used to."

Phinn laughed. "You have no idea, con-considerin' my humble beginnings. I grew up in the country in Count-County Cork. The village of Ballybrook to be exact. Me da..." He paused. "My father man-managed a public house, The Bally-Brook Arms, that was actually owned by his uncle, the last Marquess of Kinsale. At least until his lordship decided to sell it off—maybe it wasn't as prof-profitable as he would o' liked. So... so then we moved to Dublin... when I was nine. And o' course, like most folk, our fam-family fell on hard times during the Fam-Famine."

A shadow of concern crossed Miss Davenport's features. "We can choose a different topic if this one causes you too much pain."

"No. It's all right." Phinn mustered a smile, even though sadness welled in his heart. "I'd like to talk about my fam-family... to you. I-I don't want to for-forget them."

Mina nodded. "You've spoken of your mother and sister before."

"Aye..." He smiled, recalling them both in his mind's eye. Their dark hair and bright green eyes just like his. His mam's caustic wit and his sister's kind heart. "Me sister was older than me. By two years. Brigit was her name. Me mam—I mean my mother—her name was Maureen. She was originally from Derry in the north. And my father's name was Colin. Like me, he... he was an ox of a man. We'd been happy in Ballybrook. I recall it was as pre-pretty as a picture—all those rollin' green hills and woods and the River Bride run-runnin' through it. It wasn't even so bad in Dublin when we all had reg-regular work. Me mam worked for a fancy milliner, and . . . and when she was old enough, Brigit found employment as a maid-o'-all-work with a well-to-do merchant family. When I was twelve, I began to work along-alongside me da, down at the docks." Phinn's mouth twisted with a wry smile. "Then the Famine arrived and o' course, the work dried up and no one in Ireland was happy except for . . . except for the absentee landlords and their rent collectors o' course."

"That must have been so very hard," the governess remarked, her tone gentle.

Phinn's chest rose and fell on a heavy sigh. "Aye. It was. When jobs became scarcer than hen's teeth, I took up boxin' pro-professionally. It-it was the only sort of work I could find. It paid enough to keep some f-f-food on the ta-table. And to pay the rent for our . . . for our lodgings."

A delicate furrow—the sort of line Phinn wished he could smooth away with his fingertips—appeared between the governess's delicate brows. "Fighting for a living must have been so very difficult, my lord," she said, her voice soft with compassion. "Both physically and mentally demanding."

"It's not the sort o' work I would have chosen for meself, that's true," he said. "But-but I'd been fi-fightin' in amateur matches at a handful of the dockside taverns for a few years. Doin' physical labor from mornin' 'til night when I was a dock worker had tough-toughened me up. And havin' a stammer—being the sub-subject of taunts for so long—had made me learn how to stand up for meself. It . . . it wasn't so very hard."

"All the same," said Miss Davenport, "it can't have been easy. I can't even imagine what you've been through."

Phinn didn't mention that it wasn't until he was an adolescent when he'd sprung up and started to fill out with muscle that things began to change. That he stopped being teased so mercilessly—labelled an "eejit" by all and sundry. "I . . . I survived those years. If I'm being to-totally honest though, losin' me f-f-family—me da and mam and sis-sister—to typhoid fever, which swept through our quarter o' Dublin—was far, far worse."

"I'm so sorry. To lose them all at once must have been truly devastating." Sadness clouded Miss Davenport's eyes. "A terrible fever—our physician called it typhlitis—claimed my father's life as well," she added softly. "Five years ago."

"I'm-I'm sorry too," said Phinn. And he meant it. "Does . . . does your family—you've mentioned your mother and sister—have every-everythin' they need? Do you and Christopher?"

Miss Davenport nodded. "They do. They are content."

"If they ever need anythin'—if *you* and your son ever need anythin', Miss Davenport—you only need to ask. All of this"—he gestured about the room—"is far too much for one man."

The governess plucked at her blue woolen skirts as though something was bothering her. But after a minute, she lifted her eyes to his. "I can understand why you want to do something for your fellow countrymen and -women—to lend them a voice in Parliament—so that sort of suffering never happens again."

"Aye. I'm glad you understand," he said.

Phinn had told the governess about his family. But he'd only shared the barest of details about their lives, particularly after they'd moved to Dublin. He hadn't told Miss Davenport about his father's descent into deep melancholy and drink when he'd suffered a terrible shoulder injury and had been laid off and then couldn't find work anywhere else. Or how his mother and sister ended up taking in odd mending and laundry jobs, working their fingers to the bone, often ironing and darning by the weak light of a single tallow candle into the wee small hours for just a few pennies.

He certainly wouldn't share what it had been like to be a fighter. How ghastly it truly was. How he'd hated profiting off the violence he could deliver so effectively with his fists. He didn't tell her about the pain, the blood and bruises, or the terrible injuries he'd suffered—the cuts and broken ribs and knuckles and a broken nose and cracked cheekbone and jaw and several cracked back teeth. Or the bone-deep feelings of self-loathing when he beat another boxer because he, Cutthroat O'Connell—the name his uncompromising manager had given him to draw in the "crowds"—only made money when he won. The brutal daily training schedule he was put through, even though he barely had enough food to drag himself out of bed let alone put one foot in front of the other. But then the ravening guilt when he did manage to procure some food for himself and his family, when so many fellow Irish folk around them had nothing at all.

Phinn didn't tell Miss Davenport any of this because he didn't want to make her sad. He liked to see her lush mouth curve into a lovely smile and her eyes glow like a glass of whisky held up to the firelight. So like then, back in Ireland, he absorbed the pain of his difficult memories, keeping the ache deep inside him, pushing through it, burying it. Taking it like he'd take a gut punch in the boxing ring. By sheer force of will he ignored how much it hurt. He would not let it take him down.

The clock suddenly struck eleven and Miss Davenport barely stifled a yawn.

Phinn cast her a compassionate smile. "You-you should go to bed, Miss Davenport. The lads keep you busy enough during the day. I don't . . . I don't want to keep you up all night."

Well, that was a blatant lie. Phinn would love to sweep the gorgeous young woman up into his arms and convey her to his bed, where they'd stay for the rest of the night doing things that had naught to do with sleeping, but some thoughts were best kept to oneself.

It was only after Miss Davenport had quit the library that Phinn realized she'd never told him whether *she* had all that she needed.

Had she avoided his question deliberately? He sensed the young woman had secrets. Of course, she'd already disclosed to him that Christopher was her son out of wedlock. And he, for his part, felt so very honored that she'd trusted him enough to share such a private, and no doubt potentially incendiary piece of intelligence. But he was so very sure there was something else going on. Sometimes Hermina Davenport looked... troubled. On edge.

Guilty?

But of what? Phinn really had no idea.

He picked up *Jane Eyre*.

He still hadn't worked out what had happened in Hatchards a fortnight ago. He could have sworn Miss Davenport had been hiding from something or someone, but he hadn't been able to work out what or who. There *had* been a fair-haired man looking in the bookstore window at the time she'd ducked down in apparent alarm and accidentally hit him in the "goolies" as Tom had boldly declared.

What had *first* made Phinn suspicious that something wasn't quite right was when he'd handed Miss Davenport back into his carriage and he'd seen that her boots had a neat row of three buttons along one side. *Not* laces. So either the governess had misspoken when she'd claimed she was tying her bootlace, or she'd needed to hurriedly drop down low behind a bookcase for an entirely different reason that had nothing to do with laces or buttons.

Whatever the case, Phinn hoped that if she really was in some kind of trouble, she'd take him into her confidence.

And then it struck him. The well-dressed gentleman had had blond hair.

Just like Miss Davenport's son, Christopher...

Of course, there were countless blond gentlemen in London. But had Miss Davenport been avoiding *this* particular gentleman?

Phinn frowned into the fire. Miss Davenport never spoke of

the boy's father. Of course, she had no reason to, especially to her employer. And perhaps she simply didn't want to because it pained her to do so. Three weeks ago when Phinn had first discovered Miss Davenport and her son had stowed away on the *Kinsale Cloud*—and he still didn't know *why* she had (not to mention there was something decidedly peculiar about how she'd "magically" ended up on his ship to begin with)—she'd mentioned she didn't wish to talk about Christopher's father. That he'd passed away a year ago.

Unless he hadn't . . .

Whoever Christopher's father had been, he clearly hadn't done the right thing and asked Miss Davenport to marry him.

Phinn couldn't help but wonder if Christopher's da had been an absolute bounder of the highest order and had taken advantage of Hermina Davenport. Christopher was seven, so she must have only been eighteen when she'd found herself in the "family way." Had a young Miss Davenport fallen in love with that man? Had the cad broken her heart?

Phinn's hands curled into tight fists on his thighs as he revisited the memory of the man peering through the front window of Hatchards and Miss Davenport's reaction. *Her fear.* Yes, she'd been afraid. In the moment before she'd dropped down, Phinn had seen her eyes widen with fright. He'd wager his soul that the golden-haired, mustachioed and bearded fellow had had something to do with her sudden need to hide.

But Miss Davenport was no longer alone. Phinn had money and some degree of power now he was a marquess. And he genuinely *liked* the woman. He'd never judge her like polite society would for being an unwed mother. Heaven knew, he was far from perfect. He'd made his fair share of mistakes and had a prizefighting past he'd rather forget.

Yes, he'd help Miss Davenport in whatever way he could. If only she'd trust him enough to ask.

With a sigh, Phinn opened up *Jane Eyre* and found the page

he'd been reading. He might be clueless about many of high society's rules and customs, but he wasn't clueless about class barriers and where the lines were between sharing too much and too little with his employees. From what he'd read so far of the book he held in his hands, Mr. Edward Fairfax Rochester was certainly crossing all kinds of lines with Miss Eyre.

And somehow, she'd fallen in love with the man, despite his physical imperfections and myriad personal flaws.

But Jane Eyre is a book, Phineas O'Connell. And despite the fact you're a marquess, you're not a broodin' Byronic hero or a knight in shinin' armor—the sort of man who's likely to snag the interest of someone as fine as Miss Davenport. Deep down, you're a simple man from County Cork with a scarred physiognomy and a heart that's been bruised and battered by far too much loss. You can barely even say the woman's name without makin' a mess of it.

And then he gave himself a mental shake as he cast the romantic novel aside. What was he thinking? What was all this talk of falling in love? Was the brutish former boxer "Cutthroat O'Connell" really beginning to harbor such finer, tender emotions?

No, he was just "in lust" with pretty Miss Mina Davenport, he reminded himself as he pushed to his feet and crossed to the drinks tray by his desk. There was nothing "fine" or "tender" involved when he had visions of whisking the governess up to his suite. Or what he thought about doing with her in his bed when he was alone at night and couldn't fall asleep.

It's the reason he'd been avoiding dancing lessons with her, even though he desperately needed them. He kept making excuses—that he was far too sore after another riding lesson, or he'd strained his muscles during a far too vigorous boxing session. The truth was, he was worried that if he held the gorgeous governess in his arms, when he stared down into her beautiful face, when he fantasized about sliding his fingers through her glossy chestnut hair and mussing it up, or cupping her smooth-as-satin cheek in the moment before he tasted her mouth, she'd sense how much he wanted her. And then he'd scare her away. And he couldn't do that. He would never take advantage of her or hurt her like Christopher's father clearly had.

Besides, this stammering oaf of an Irishman needed this woman's expert tuition to turn him into an articulate, self-assured gentleman, who, even though he might never pass for an English nobleman, would command attention and respect next time he stood before his "peers" in Parliament.

That's what he needed to focus on. That was all that mattered.

At least that's what Phinn told himself as he poured himself an Irish whisky and compared the glorious deep amber hue to a particular someone's stunning hazel eyes.

Chapter 19

In Which a Governess (or Perhaps a Footman?) Embarks on a Middle-of-the-Night Foray into Enemy Territory . . .

The soft lilac butterfly resting upon Christopher's pillow gently undulated its wings as the boy slept. But his rest wasn't peaceful. He was having another bad dream.

Mina gnawed her bottom lip as she hovered in the doorway of the boy's room, watching as he muttered in his sleep and curled his small fingers tightly into the sheets. It was almost midnight, and she'd only said goodnight to Lord Kinsale in the library a short time ago; she really *should* try to get some sleep herself. But that would be impossible when she was so worried about Christopher.

It had been a whole month since she'd taken the young viscount away from his guardian and three weeks since they'd arrived at Kinsale House. Three weeks since she'd begun casting the *Guardia Nimbus* spell each night to protect the boy from any attempted kidnappings by Queen Mab and her minions. The powerful Fae ward had been able to keep Christopher's nightmares at bay at first. But not tonight or the night before that.

And Mina wasn't sure what more she could do to help. Well,

that wasn't quite true. She could offer Christopher a magical sleeping draught before he went to bed. A concoction she'd read about in the *Parasol Academy Handbook* that while ostensibly safe, would put a child in such a deep slumber he or she wouldn't dream at all. But Mina didn't like that idea. It seemed rather drastic. Not *all* dreams were bad.

Of course, the alternative was equally horrid—that a seven-year-old child would continue to be plagued by nightmares about a woman of snow and ice with black-as-midnight eyes. A being who whispered she would claim Christopher and spirit him back to her kingdom, one way or another.

Christopher whimpered, and as he rolled over, Mr. Hopwell fell to the floor. Mina immediately crossed the room and returned the toy velvet rabbit to the bed, tucking it in beneath the quilt. The *Guardia Nimbus* butterfly fluttered its wings, but it didn't fly away.

There must be *something* Mina could do to ease the boy's distress in sleep. He'd been looking so very tired of late with shadows beneath his blue eyes.

Tom Fleet and even Lord Kinsale himself had been looking tired too. Mina knew Lord Kinsale's ward had still been sneaking out at night and that the marquess sometimes followed the boy to make sure he was safe. Brutus had recently let the thought slip when he'd been complaining about how cold the streets were when he'd accompanied his master on one occasion. It was touching to think this burly bruiser of a man had such a soft spot for a boy who'd been a street urchin.

Christopher sighed in his sleep and hugged his toy rabbit closer. And then Mina had an idea. Something that should have occurred to her sooner. She should visit Fitzwilliam House right now to collect some of her charge's favorite things. Some of his other toys. The books he loved. His clothes. Items that were familiar and would bring him comfort. Things that would make him feel secure.

Even though Sir Bedivere was back in London, she hadn't seen him, thank heavens, since that brief glimpse of him outside Hatchards three weeks ago. She'd been scanning the London broadsheets every single day—surreptitiously, of course, so no one at Kinsale House would notice (especially Lord Kinsale, Smedley, or Mrs. Aldershot)—but she hadn't seen a single article about the baronet setting off for the Northwest Passage on the *Valiant*. Or the fact that his young ward, Viscount Fitzwilliam, was missing and Scotland Yard was scouring the entire country, searching for him.

If she were pragmatic—like every good Parasol Academy nanny or governess should be—she'd also visit Ponsonby House, to glean intelligence about the baronet's plans, then she wouldn't be wondering, tossing and turning half the night. Fretting about being caught.

Although, truth to tell, worrying about Sir Bedivere—and what he may or may not be doing in regard to locating his ward—wasn't the only reason Mina was restless at night.

Her infatuation with Lord Kinsale kept her awake too... well, until wrung out with frustration, she sometimes took matters into her own hands and tried to dispel her thoroughly unprofessional urges under the cover of darkness beneath her bedcovers. She was certain she was breaking the Parasol Academy rules, but no one would ever know, so she did what needed to be done to alleviate her unsatisfied desire. Surely that could be classed as pragmatic?

Of course, Mina enjoyed every moment she spent with her employer during the day—Lord Kinsale often visited the schoolroom to see how Tom was progressing with his lessons. He also accompanied them on jaunts about town. Mina especially adored the time she spent alone with the marquess in the evenings. How he made her laugh. How he took an interest in her. How he made her feel when he smiled at her. (Aside from perpetually blushing, her heart had never performed so many somersaults before.) Lord Kinsale had made so many gains with his speech and with his acquisition of "manners," she was quietly proud of what he'd achieved. He deserved so much respect. He deserved to succeed.

But that made it even harder dealing with the fact that she was lying to her employer every single second of every single day about Christopher's true identity. It hurt her heart to know she was being so duplicitous, that she was betraying the man's trust when he'd shown her nothing but consideration and kindness.

Thank goodness her best friend, Emmeline, was returning to London soon; the newly wedded duchess had sent a telegram—just the regular kind—to Mina the day before, announcing her imminent return, and Mina couldn't wait to visit her friend. Not just to see how she was faring as the wife of the Duke of St Lawrence—Mina was sure she must be blissfully happy—but to seek her advice about the pickliest pickle of a situation she was in.

What would Emmeline do? was a frequent refrain in Mina's head.

Of course, Emmeline would make sure her charge was safe and happy. And then she'd deal with any threat to the child's safety. She wouldn't hide and she wouldn't back down.

So that's what Hermina Davenport will do, decided Mina.

Reassuring herself that Christopher was as safe as he could be for now—Mina trusted the *Guardia Nimbus* ward would stay in place until the sun rose—she retreated to her bedroom to prepare for her foray to Fitzwilliam House. First, she checked that her Parasol Academy–issued knife was firmly strapped to her ankle. Then she collected an empty carpetbag from beneath her bed; she'd need something to put Christopher's toys and books and clothes in so she could easily ferry them back to Kinsale House.

She contemplated taking her Parasol Academy umbrella—

poking a nosy parker with the Point-of-Confusion or casting the *Cloakify* spell while beneath the umbrella's canopy were always handy tools to have at one's disposal when subterfuge was paramount. But given it was midnight and the handful of skeleton staff left at Fitzwilliam House were likely fast asleep in their beds—well, apart from the night footman—there didn't seem much point. Christopher's bedchamber wasn't too far from the governess's quarters; in fact, it was only a short trip down the servants' stairs to the floor below. She'd simply teleport into her old wardrobe, the one that she knew very well—just to make sure she arrived safely.

And on the off chance she *did* happen to bump into another servant, she could always employ a befuddling potion.

Deciding she was as ready as she'd ever be, Mina pulled her pewter leyport key from the pocket of her uniform, then crossed to her wardrobe. With a deep breath, she "unlocked" the door, pushed aside her gowns, then conjured the leylight flame. It flickered in the deep shadows, coaxing her to use its ancient power to spirit her to where she wanted to be. Focusing on the leylight's pale luminescence, Mina pictured her destination... and then she climbed into the cupboard as she determinedly whispered, "*Vortexio.*"

The familiar whirlwind of breath-stealing white light immediately swept Mina away, and in no time at all, she was stepping into her old bedroom at Fitzwilliam House. Thankfully, this teleportation had been a success. (Mina *still* hadn't worked out what had gone wrong when she'd teleported off the *Valiant* with Christopher, but that was a mystery for another day.)

A pale beam of moonlight filtering through the casement window traced a silver path across the neatly made single bed and the slightly worn Aubusson rug on the wooden floor. Mina winced as she tiptoed across the room to the door and the floorboards creaked, but it couldn't be helped. There weren't any servants' bedrooms on the floor below. Just a private study and sitting room that had once belonged to Christopher's father. Lady Grenfell had never used it during Mina's time at Fitzwilliam House, preferring to keep to her own suite at the other end of the townhouse. As far as Mina knew, the late viscount's rooms had been closed up and holland cloths had been thrown over everything. Christopher's bedroom was just a little further along.

The hallway outside her old bedroom was dark and deserted, and within half a minute, Mina had descended the servants' stairs and had entered Christopher's bedchamber. It didn't take her long to fill the carpetbag with some of his favorite clothes—a few pairs of trousers, a blue velvet coat, a comfortable pair of shoes and soft woolen socks—along with toys Mina knew that he'd been missing: a small box of treasured toy soldiers, a kaleidoscope Lady Grenfell had gifted him on his sixth birthday, and half a dozen books that Mina hadn't been able to find at Hatchards. She also squeezed in his favorite pillow.

"Right, time to go," said Mina to herself. Even though she hadn't heard anyone moving about Fitzwilliam House, perhaps she should use Christopher's wardrobe to teleport back to her room in Kinsale House. It would save her having to go back upstairs—

At that moment, a door slammed and Mina froze. She heard voices—male voices—and then a distinctive booming baritone reminiscent of a foghorn.

Sir Bedivere Ponsonby.

Fae help me! Mina pressed a hand to her chest where her heart crashed in uneven thuds against her ribcage. What on earth was *he* doing here?

He had his own house here in London, for goodness' sake!

And then anger sparked. Damn it! Why couldn't the blighter push off and go and blaze a trail through the Northwest Passage?

Because he needs to prove he's residing with his ward to continue to access the Fitzwilliam family fortune, Mina mentally reminded herself. And he'll only be able to pretend Christopher is with him for so long. Before others notice the young viscount is missing. You've been fooling yourself that he'll give up his search.

But he won't. You know he won't.

And now, how will it look if he discovers you here, Lord Fitzwilliam's former governess with a carpetbag full of the boy's belongings in hand?

She needed to get away, right this instant. Lord Fitzwilliam's closet would have to be her "magic cupboard."

But as Mina reached into her pocket to retrieve her leyport key, her fingers wrapped around something small and cold and hard and cylindrical. It wasn't a pewter key, but a bottle, along with her ley spectacles

Had her pocket provided her with a befuddling potion?

For mercy's sake. Using a befuddling potion on more than one person at a time would be a tricky undertaking indeed. Because Sir Bedivere *had* been talking to another man. Their voices had faded, but not completely. Mina suspected that they'd simply moved farther along the hall and had entered the private study of the late Lord Fitzwilliam—Christopher's father—which was on the same floor, not too far from the viscount and viscountess's suite of rooms. Mina knew it well because she used to pass it every day to take Christopher to his godmother's bedchamber and sitting room, which were also on the same floor.

With a frustrated huff, Mina put the carpetbag on the bed, pulled out the bottle, then took it over to the window to examine it in the moonlight. And then genuine surprise flared. It was a dark indigo bottle. Had her pocket provided her with a *Glamify* potion?

Quickly donning her ley-spectacles, she read the label and

confirmed that yes, it was exactly that. And just like last time when she found it in her pocket at the Ablington Railway Station, it said: *Drink me.*

But when Mina turned it over to check the fine print on the other side, she read something slightly different:

> *To don a "bespoke" glamour—an illusory disguise <u>of your choice</u>—that will deceive the eyes of others, simply take two sips of the contents of this bottle then utter, "Glamify," all the while picturing <u>who</u> you want to look like. Uttering "Unglamify" will reverse the spell.*
> *Please note: Individual results may still vary (but only by a little).*

Mina blinked. She could *choose* who she wanted to look like?

What if . . . What if she chose the guise of a servant? A *male* servant. A footman. After all, footmen were always traipsing through corridors and attending to things like checking windows and doors and snuffing out candles and dimming gaslights.

Yes, if she looked like a footman, she'd virtually blend into the woodwork of Fitzwilliam House. She could conduct reconnaissance—gather some intelligence (even eavesdropping at keyholes might prove useful)—with relative safety. It certainly would be helpful to know what Sir Bedivere might be up to. It would be a darn sight better than stumbling about in the dark like she had been doing for weeks on end, wondering when that dashed sword of Damocles might fall.

Two Parasol Academy tenets sprang to mind: *Know thy enemy.* And *Knowledge is power.*

It would be silly not to stay and see what she could learn about Sir Bedivere's agenda, and what he knew or didn't know about his ward's disappearance from the *Valiant*. If she had the chance, maybe she could even befuddle him and attempt to snatch that cursed ring off his finger. Unfortunately, she hadn't had the opportunity to try out the befuddling potion on him—or the Point-of-Confusion for that matter—before she'd been dismissed. It had all happened far too quickly. But maybe she could tonight.

Her decision made, Mina uncapped the bottle.

Closing her eyes, she took two sips of the berry-flavored, treacly potion. Then she conjured a mental image of one of the Fitzwilliam House footmen—a tall young fellow with an easy smile by the name of Tristan—as she whispered, "*Glamify.*"

Just like last time, a shimmering swirling mist enveloped her, gently mussing her uniform and brushing softly over her skin like a warm summer breeze. When she looked down at herself, she looked the same, but a glance in a full-length mirror in the corner of Christopher's room confirmed her appearance had changed—she'd turned into an exact replica of Tristan the footman. Well, almost. Perhaps she wasn't *quite* as tall as the young man, and there was something about her—or was it his?—eyes that weren't quite the same, but the disguise would do.

Righto. In for a penny, in for a pound. Ignoring her galloping pulse, Mina exited Christopher's bedroom. Farther along the dimly lit hallway, the door to the late viscount's private study stood slightly ajar and Sir Bedivere's voice blared out, bellicose and trombone-like. That booming baritone could probably even travel through castle walls.

Another man spoke, but Mina didn't recognize his voice. It was gruff, the cadence harsh and unpleasant, like carriage wheels crunching over rough gravel. Or rusty iron cogs inside a machine grating against each other.

Mina crept closer, keeping to the thick carpet that ran down the center of the hall. A shiver passed over her, but it wasn't simply because she was nervous. The hall was bitingly cold; so much so her breath misted in the air. And was that a glimmer of frost on a nearby windowpane? In September?

Sir Bedivere was still speaking. "I'm not made of money,"

he grumbled as Mina lingered in the deep shadows by the open door. "How many more men do you really need? You're looking for a small blond boy with a purple velvet rabbit, for God's sake. Not a mythical creature like a dragon or phoenix. Or the philosopher's stone or Holy Grail."

The man with the irritatingly harsh voice responded. "Enough to watch all the main parks about Belgravia and Mayfair during the day, my lord. Half a dozen men should do."

"Half a dozen?" Then there was a muttered, "God damn it," and the scrape of a desk drawer. This was followed by the faint scratch of a pen nib on paper. "Here's a thousand pounds. I'm expecting results, Cheavers. If the executor of the trust fund hears that the boy isn't with me, he'll cut off my access to the Fitzwilliam coffers—and I *need* that money to fund my expedition. Not only that, but my name will be mud. My competency as a guardian will be called into question. I can't have just 'lost' little Lord Fitzwilliam. He *must* be found."

Mina dared a peek through the door. Yes, it was the bespectacled man she'd seen on the railway platform in Ablington, with his salt-and-pepper hair, ferocious-looking muttonchops, and caterpillar eyebrows. Cheavers spoke again. "Well, until I do locate your ward—and rest assured I will, sir—I must say, moving into Fitzwilliam House is a sound strategy. That should at least give the impression that everything is all right."

The baronet emitted a snort. "Unless some little snitch on staff here reports the boy missing. I don't trust the butler, Napier, as far as I can throw him. Nor that bloody headmistress at the Parasol Academy. Temple or whatever her name is. I'm certain it was that blasted Parasol Academy governess that somehow stole my ward off the *Valiant*. As soon as Meecham described her, I *knew* Miss Hermina Davenport must be the one behind his disappearance. If I could just find her, I'm sure I'll find the boy."

Mina's blood turned to ice. So Sir Bedivere *did* know—or at least strongly suspected—that she'd been on the *Valiant*. But it sounded as though Mrs. Temple wouldn't disclose her whereabouts, thank goodness.

"I've been keeping an eye out for the governess too, sir," said Cheavers. "I'll be sure to show my men that photograph of Miss Davenport—the one from the newspaper—that you supplied. And they all know she wears a Parasol Academy uniform."

"Good." There was a beat of silence in which it sounded as though someone—perhaps it was Sir Bedivere—was drumming his fingers on the late viscount's desk. Then the baronet said, "Are you going to try breaking into the Parasol Academy again? There must be some sort of record in the headmistress's office about where this Miss Davenport is now working." Something thumped the desk—a fist perhaps. "If she's not in London, I don't know what I'll bloody do."

"Humph. Believe me, I've tried breaking into the Academy," grated out Cheavers. "My men have tried, too. But it's impossible. The place is an impenetrable fortress. You're sure the headmistress won't tell you anything about Miss Davenport's latest post?"

"Not a thing," Sir Bedivere growled. "I've tried bribes... The headmistress won't yield."

"You could try less conventional methods... I know how to make people talk..."

"What, threaten or kidnap the damn woman?" A snort. "From what I hear, this Temple character is friendly with the Queen herself. If she disappears, Scotland Yard is bound to get involved and I can't have them poking around, asking questions about who she's been talking to of late. I'll risk a lot to find my ward, but I won't go that far. No, my name must be kept out of it. I cannot afford any scandal to be attached to my name or reputation."

"I understand, Sir Bedivere."

"Do you? Because I don't know if you truly do," the baronet sniped. "I can't afford to dillydally for much longer. I *need* the boy. I *need* him on my ship. It's imperative that I take him north to Queen—" The baronet broke off. "Never mind."

Queen? Queen who?

Mab?

Mina, who'd wrapped her arms around herself to ward off the bitter cold, leaned toward the door. But as she did so, her shoulder brushed against it, making it creak ever so slightly. *Damn. Damn. Damn.*

"What's that? Who's there?" demanded Sir Bedivere, his voice snapping into the hall like the lash of a whip.

Mina shot across the hallway into the darkened window alcove. *Remember you look like Tristan, the footman*, she reminded herself. *Brazen this encounter out. You can do it.*

When the baronet appeared in the doorway, Mina pulled her shoulders back and lifted her chin as though she had nothing to fear. "It's just me, sir," she squeaked. "Tristan." *Blast.* Her appearance might have changed, but her voice certainly hadn't. She cleared her throat and dropped her voice as low as it could go. "The footman," she mumbled.

Sir Bedivere's brows plunged into a frown deeper than a well. "What the hell are you doing, lurking out here in the hall?" His gaze narrowed in suspicion. "Were you eavesdropping?"

"Oh . . . n-n-no . . . Not me, sir," said Mina, hoping her tone was deep enough to pass for a man's. "I'm-I'm just checking all the doors and windows. Like I usually do. Mr. Napier's orders. I'm the night footman tonight."

The baronet took up a wide stance and folded his arms across his chest. The gaslight emanating from the study illuminated the man's dark golden hair and his obsidian and silver ring glinted. It almost seemed like the stone was winking at Mina. "Come out where I can see you," he ordered, his breath turning to fog in the icy air. "And what's wrong with your voice? You sound like you've swallowed a mouse."

Mina did as she was bid, stepping into the middle of the hallway. At the same time, she reached into her pocket, hoping to find a bottle of befuddling potion, but damn it, nothing was there. Now would have been the perfect time to test it out. "Um... er... more like a frog," she said as gruffly as she could. "I think I'm coming down with a cold." Then she put a fisted hand up to her mouth and affected a cough.

Sir Bedivere immediately took a few paces backward into the study. "Well, begone, man," he commanded, waving his hand. The ring flashed again. "Don't come anywhere near me. I don't want whatever plague you're carrying about."

"Of course, sir." Even though she was stiff with cold, Mina somehow executed a deferential bow. "So sorry to bother—"

She broke off just as the study door slammed shut. But not because of the baronet's rudeness. No, the breath had frozen in Mina's lungs and her voice had failed because in the split second before the door closed, leaving her in the dark, she'd seen something that had chilled her to the very marrow of her bones.

The obsidian stone in the baronet's ring had winked at her, actually *winked* like a cold black eye, and a voice like the harsh north wind in midwinter whispered inside her head, *Spy! I see you.* Then more faintly from behind the closed door, *Tell me your name.*

In that moment, Mina *knew* the midnight-eyed woman of ice and snow frequenting Christopher's nightmares was Mab... and the evil Fae queen had seen straight through the glamour.

Chapter 20

In Which a Governess (and Perhaps a Marquess) Embark on a Second Middle-of-the-Night Foray . . .

Sir Bedivere Ponsonby's ring was ensorcelled. There was no doubt in Mina's mind now as she scurried like a frightened rabbit back to Christopher's bedroom in Fitzwilliam House.

By the time she'd teleported back to her own room at Kinsale House, and *Unglamified* her appearance, she'd also decided that her conclusion was indeed correct: The black eye *had* to belong to Queen Mab. Mina would stake her life on it.

Although, thank heavens Mab hadn't recognized Mina. Even if Mab told Sir Bedivere that he'd been spied upon by a young woman wearing a Fae glamour, even if he put two and two together and deduced that it was his ward's former governess, he still didn't know where she was residing in London. Or if she was even in London at all.

What *was* abundantly clear to Mina now was that the evil Fae queen was controlling Sir Bedivere through the cursed ring. Making him act out of character.

Lady Grenfell and her prophetic dream had been right.

But why did Queen Mab want the baronet to take his ward to the Arctic? Was that where the queen was currently holding court? And what did she really want with Christopher? Why was the young viscount her target?

None of it made any sense to Mina. She was out of her depth and terrified.

She needed help.

As she took the carpetbag of Christopher's things to his bedroom, she wondered what would happen if she went to Mrs. Temple and confessed all. Everything she'd done.

What she'd learned tonight.

The Fae—and Good Queen Maeve—must be on her side at least a little bit because why else would they furnish her with a *Glamify* potion a second time?

But what if you're wrong about the Fae's support? What if it was all just a coincidence that a "bespoke" Glamify potion materialized in your pocket?

Oh, Mina wished Emmeline was back in London.

But really, it wasn't just about what would Emmeline do. It was really about what she, Mina Davenport, would do. The path she took, her next steps, were her responsibility and hers alone.

The pertinent question was, which direction would she take? And of course, where would she end up? Would this risky venture she'd embarked on—all to protect a little boy from dark forces—end well or in utter disaster?

And how long could she keep Christopher safe, all on her own, without any other help?

Mina hardly knew. When she entered Christopher's bedroom, all was well. All was how she'd left it. The little boy was snuggled up with his mauve rabbit and the butterfly rested above his head upon the pillow. It fluttered its lilac-hued wings as though in greeting.

She quickly and quietly unpacked the boy's clothes and toys and placed his favorite pillow on the bedside armchair. The small mantel clock declared the time to be just after half past twelve. She should go to bed and get some sleep, but she also suspected her mind would be abuzz with everything she'd learned tonight. And possible plans about what she should do next to best protect her charge.

A sound in the hallway—a heavy footstep and the creak of a floorboard made Mina jump and her heart stumbled. It couldn't be anyone or anything sinister, she reassured herself. She was simply on edge because of what had just occurred at Fitzwilliam House.

But there was definitely someone outside Christopher's bedroom. Perhaps it was Tom Fleet, venturing out as he sometimes did.

Mina poked her head out the door and instead of encountering Tom, she locked eyes with Lord Kinsale.

Brutus, who was at his heels, gave a gruff little bark. *What would ye be doin' up at this hour?* the pug asked accusingly. *Shouldn't ye be in bed?*

Mina ignored him and instead spoke to his master in a low voice. "Lord Kinsale," she said, exiting Christopher's bedroom and gently closing the door. (She didn't want to disturb Christopher, nor did she want the marquess to notice there was a small purple butterfly on his pillow. Or a soft silvery-lilac haze inside the room.) "I-I didn't expect to see you here."

The marquess's wide mouth tipped into a half smile. "Nor did I ex-expect to see you, Miss Dav-Davenport," he said softly. "It's late."

"It is. Can-can I help you?" she asked.

Lord Kinsale's forehead crinkled with a frown and he awkwardly rubbed the back of his neck with one large hand. "To be sure, I'm not . . . I'm not certain . . ." He sighed, then said, "I came to check . . . to check on Tom. To see if he's slip-slipped out o' the house." His smile became a trifle sheepish. "I would have checked sooner, but after our elocution lesson, I-I fell asleep in front of the li-library fire."

"I'm not surprised you fell asleep," returned Mina gently. "I know you've been going out late at night. To make sure Tom stays safe."

Lord Kinsale cocked an eyebrow. "You do?"

Mina smiled. "Yes. And it's very noble of you to do so. It shows you care."

The marquess gave a small huff and a faint flush flooded his cheeks above his dark night beard. "I've never thought about it like that be-before. Or been called no-noble for that matter. But I thank you, Miss Dav-Davenport. I'll take the com-compliment."

Mina wasn't sure what made her pose her next question, but she did anyway. "Shall we check on Tom together, my lord?"

Brutus snorted. *Ugh. Please, spare me. Ye just want to spend more time with the master, temptin' him with yer feminine wiles. Especially when he's tired an' his guard is down.*

That's not true, returned Mina, sending the pug a narrow look. But she got no further as Lord Kinsale answered her. "Oh, that-that won't be necessary. You-you should go to b-b-bed."

"Oh. It's no bother, my lord. After all, it's part of my job as his governess."

Lord Kinsale inclined his head. "Very well."

Although, upon opening the door to Tom's bedroom, it was immediately apparent the boy wasn't there; his bed was empty.

The marquess sighed heavily. "I wish . . . I wish I knew why Tom kept sneakin' out. But the b-b-boy won't say."

"I've tried questioning him too," said Mina. "But he's very tight-lipped. I imagine that with time, he'll adjust to his new situation. That he'll learn to trust he's safe here."

"Hmmm. Trust," said Lord Kinsale. "Poor lad. I can't . . . I can't even imagine what Tom's life has been like up until now."

Mina looked up at the marquess. Even though the soft golden glow of a nearby gaslight only illuminated half of his ruggedly handsome countenance, she could clearly see he was troubled. On an impulse she said, "Would you like some company when you venture out to look for Tom? Two pairs of eyes are better than one." She could see he was going to say no—that he would be chivalrous and declare it was too dangerous, so she added quickly, "It's my duty to look out for him, my lord. Remember, I'm a Parasol-trained governess. I have skills." Flipping up the hem of her skirts she displayed her ankle. "And I have a knife and I *know* how to use it."

Lord Kinsale chuckled softly as he looked down at the small, holstered dagger that was strapped just above the top of her half boot. And Mina's heart immediately performed an odd little flip-flop.

The real danger wasn't in London's dark streets. The danger to Mina was right here, in front of her, in Kinsale House. She should be alarmed at how rapidly she was falling for this former Irish boxer with his charming smile and tender heart and wickedly dancing green eyes. She should try and put some distance between herself and her employer. But, it seemed she couldn't.

"Very well," he said. "You-you can come along. Although, I would-wouldn't want to take you away from your son."

The usual guilt Mina felt for continually lying to Lord Kinsale about Christopher's true parentage nipped at her heart. "Oh, he's sound asleep and I don't expect him to wake. He'll be safe here in Kinsale House. But perhaps Brutus"—she caught the pug's eye—"could stay here in the hall to keep guard. Just in case." To Brutus she said, *There'll be a sausage in it for you.*

Now ye're talkin'. The pug leapt onto a silk upholstered chair opposite Christopher's door, circled around three times, then settled down with a small grunt.

"It seems Brutus agrees with your plan, Miss Dav-Davenport," said Lord Kinsale. To his dog he said, "Good boy, Brutus. Now don't let anythin' ha-happen to Miss Dav-Davenport's lad." He pointed an admonitory finger. "*Or* his rabbit."

I can't make any promises about that feckin' rabbit, grumbled the pug, looking at Mina. *They're all nasty creatures. With their ridiculously floppy ears and hoppy legs and twitchy noses and stupid little fluffy tails.*

Mina sighed inwardly. There was no convincing Brutus that all rabbits—real *or* toy—shouldn't be obliterated. Of course, she wasn't expecting Sir Bedivere or Cheavers or any of his hired "henchmen" to break into Kinsale House tonight, even if Queen Mab did reveal that Mina had been masquerading as a footman. None of them knew Lord Kinsale had hired her. But, all the same, it was at least a little bit comforting to know that Christopher was protected by both the *Guardia Nimbus* ward and a fierce little guard dog.

To Lord Kinsale she said, "Just let me fetch my cloak and umbrella from my room, my lord."

The marquess frowned. "It's-it's not rainin' though."

Mina smiled knowingly over her shoulder as she headed down the hall. "One never knows what the weather will be in London. Besides, my umbrella can always be used as a weapon. It can deliver a sound thrashing if required."

Of course, Lord Kinsale's answering laugh, deep and low, was music to Mina's smitten ears.

Oh, she truly was a hopeless case.

Phinn and Miss Davenport stood in the deep shadows of the alley near the Lion and Lamb public house, the place where he'd first encountered Tom Fleet.

"So this is where Tom comes at night?" asked the governess in a low voice by Phinn's ear. There was still quite a substantial group of boisterous merrymakers inside the pub, and their voices and laughter echoed off the walls of the surrounding buildings, making it hard to hear unless one drew close. At least that's what Phinn told himself as he felt Mina's deliciously warm breath caress the edge of his stubbled jaw.

He swallowed as his throat tightened with a wave of longing. And then he inwardly berated himself for not focusing on why they were here in Covent Garden to begin with. "Aye. Mostly. I suppose it's what he knows."

"He told me that after he left the workhouse, he was forced to work as a chimney sweep for a while, poor sweet boy," said Miss Davenport, her tone weighted with sadness. "But he ran away and joined a gang of pickpockets. I cannot blame him for doing so."

"Nor can I," agreed Phinn. The life of a chimney sweep was horrendous. Certainly, the cruel—and indeed, inhumane—practice of recruiting young boys because they were small and could fit into tight spaces, should be outlawed as far as he was concerned. It was one of the many social reforms he wanted to work on. "I-I haven't caught him pick-pickpocketing when I've shadowed him at night, but . . . he's very quick."

Miss Davenport nodded. "And I haven't noticed anything odd or out of place in his bedroom. But then, it would be easy enough to conceal money and other small objects like pocket watches and coin purses that he might have pinched."

"He doesn't *need* to steal any long-longer though," said Phinn. "But I suppose it's all he's know-known for so long."

Miss Davenport peered into the alley behind them, scanning the darkness. A London fog had begun to filter through the streets, making it even harder to see anything at all, let alone detect a slight boy. "I do wonder if that's the point. Tom is a canny lad. Perhaps he's worried that when you no longer need *me*, then you won't need him. And he'll have to come back"—she gestured at their surroundings—"to all this. He's never had anyone he can count on. It would be only natural for him to assume that the life he has at Kinsale House might only be temporary."

Good God. Miss Davenport was right. As the horrible truth slammed into Phinn, leaden guilt settled inside his chest. He'd spent some time with Tom in the schoolroom, watching him as he grappled with learning to read and write and spell. While in many ways the boy was a quick study, he also got bored very easily.

Of course, Miss Davenport was endlessly patient and also quite ingenious when it came to engaging both the boy and her son. Somehow she always knew what both boys needed. Phinn supposed that was why she provided a "bespoke" service. She was a governess like no other.

What she'd just said also made Phinn realize that *he* could do much better. In future, he would do his utmost to reassure the boy that he wouldn't have to go back to living on the streets. Not ever. He would *always* have a home with Phinn.

He was about to say all this to Miss Davenport when there was a shout and a curse from across the street not far from the Lion and Lamb. "What the 'ell, you li'l gobshite!" bellowed a man. A coarse laborer by the looks of him, who was at least two—perhaps even three—sheets to the wind. The problem was the "little gobshite" he was referring to was Tom!

The irate stranger was gripping the boy's thin shoulder in one meaty paw while his other ham-sized fist was drawn back as though he were going to punch the child into next week. "'And over wha'ever you nicked from me pocket. Or so 'elp me . . ." He gave Tom a violent shake.

Feck.

Miss Davenport had taken note that Tom was in trouble too. Before Phinn could stop her, she'd raced across the street in a blaze of fiery indignation, swirling wool skirts, and a billowing navy-blue cloak. "Unhand that boy at once," she ordered in a tone so fiercely confident even Phinn was taken aback. The small crowd of patrons outside the Lion and Lamb all turned to look at the drama unfolding.

As Phinn jogged over to intervene—he had no doubt he could easily fell the laborer if he had to—Miss Davenport gave the drunken oaf a swift, sharp poke in the midriff with the end of her umbrella while she muttered one of the strangest words Phinn had ever heard: "*Perplexio.*" And then to Phinn's utter astonishment, the man let go of Tom and took a step back.

What the feck?

"Miss, so sorry to 'ave . . ." The laborer trailed off as he scratched his head and frowned in apparent confusion at Miss Davenport. "Bleedin' 'ell, I fink I've 'ad one too many pints. I forgot wha' I was goin' to say." His attention turned to Phinn. "'Ullo. Do I know you?" he asked with an affable grin plastered on his face. "Wha' can I do you for?"

"No. You don't . . . you don't know me," said Phinn warily. "And I don't need any-anythin'." He wasn't quite sure why the laborer had suddenly decided to obey Miss Davenport. Or why he was acting so flummoxed. Or should he say "perplexed"?

But Phinn wasn't about to look a gift horse in the mouth. To be sure, he was adept with his fists, but he'd prefer not to use them, especially in front of Miss Davenport and Tom.

Miss Davenport sent the unusually agreeable laborer a charming smile. "We're all perfectly fine, sir," she said, laying a hand on Tom's shoulder. "Good evening to you." And then she caught Phinn's eye. "Let us be on our way."

"Aye," agreed Phinn. He offered the governess his arm, which she readily took, and then he escorted her and Tom back across the street.

As soon as they were around the corner, he stopped and bent down to speak to Tom. "Are you . . . are you all right, lad? Did . . . did that brute hurt you?"

Tom sniffed. "Apart from rattlin' me teef a li'l, only me pride is dented," he said. "It's been a while since anyone's caught me pinchin' stuff out o' their pockets."

Phinn huffed. "If-if you recall, lad, *I* did."

"Well, aside from you an' that grumpy old geezer, no one 'as. Not for bleedin' ages." Then the boy sighed. "I must be gettin' soft in me old age. I'm losin' me touch."

Phinn couldn't help but laugh at that. *Old?* The lad must think that he, Phineas O'Connell, a man of eight-and-twenty, was positively ancient.

Once they were all safely installed inside a hansom cab a short time later, Phinn took advantage of the shadowy interior and studied Miss Davenport with no small degree of curiosity and frankly, wonder. She was sitting across from him, back perfectly straight—a portrait of propriety—with a subdued Tom on the bench seat beside her. Her gloved hands lightly clasped her umbrella across her lap.

That umbrella and the peculiar word Miss Davenport had spoken—"Perplexio"—*as she'd poked that drunken brute with the pointed tip . . . What was all that about?*

Phinn would readily own that he was still mightily perplexed himself. Indeed, he could almost believe that Miss Davenport had cast a spell outside the Lion and Lamb. How else to account for the dramatic—dare he call it a magical?—change in the laborer's demeanor. He'd miraculously become as malleable as unfired clay. Pleasantly confused and as docile as a lamb.

Casting his mind back to the moment when he'd unexpectedly encountered Miss Davenport exiting her son's bedroom earlier on, Phinn had also been puzzled by the strange mist he'd glimpsed in the air, just before she'd closed the door. It was almost as though the governess had been veiled in a purple-hued, softly shimmering light; it had given her an ethereal appearance, making him think of otherworldly creatures like the Fae—the *aos sí.*

Of course, the bedroom window could simply have been left open, allowing fog to creep in . . .

Phinn's gaze drifted to the hansom cab's window. But London fog was *not* purple, he reminded himself. It was usually a greenish yellow, just like the pea-souper that was presently cloaking the city's streets.

And then there were those mysterious pockets of hers that

could produce almost anything at all. From kerchiefs to business cards to pencils and marbles. Even mousetraps. And how *did* she end up on the *Kinsale Cloud*?

But how could he possibly ask the governess about any of this? *Miss Davenport, can you perform magic? Are you a witch or a sea maiden or a faery or even an angel?* Even in his mind, the questions sounded nonsensical. If he *was* wrong about her, he couldn't bear it if she regarded him differently. If she looked at him as though he were completely daft or not right in the head. Not when he'd come to value her company so very much.

Maybe his imagination was simply running wild because he was so captivated by this young woman. And of course, he was so very grateful for all that she'd done for him so far. The difference she'd made to his speech and to his confidence in general — turning this simple Irishman into someone who resembled a mannered gentleman — now *that* was nothing short of a miracle.

Yes, it was best that he kept his suspicions to himself and accepted Mina Davenport for who she was at face value. In any event, it mattered not whether she was a magical being or simply human just like himself, as long as she stayed and they could continue — Phinn frowned into the shifting fog outside the window — to explore whatever this relationship was. It didn't much feel like an employer-employee arrangement anymore.

But then, had it ever been just that?

It was Miss Davenport who at last broke the heavy silence in the cab when she asked her charge gently, "Tom, is the reason you've been sneaking out at night related to the idea that you need to . . . to maintain your pickpocketing skills? In case you might need to rely on them again?"

The governess's question was met with silence as Tom fiddled with a torn piece of leather on the cab's bench seat. "Maybe," he mumbled after a few moments. "It's better to be safe than sorry, I always say."

"Oh, Tom," said Miss Davenport, her voice soft with compassion. Looking up, she caught Phinn's eye and he knew straightaway that it was his cue to reassure the lad.

"We'll talk more to-tomorrow, Tom. But... but I want you to know that you don't have to pick pockets anymore. You will al-always have a home with me," said Phinn gravely. "And if I have to swear a blood oath or vow to cross me heart and hope to die to convince you that I'm sincere, and that you can trust me, I'll do it. Whatever it takes, lad. It-it worries me more than I can say that you keep venturin' out at night on your own."

Tom lifted his chin. "I know you've been followin' me some nights, my lord. You're not 'ard to miss, even in the dark."

"Aye, I have." Phinn's voice was gruff with emotion as he added, "It's... it's because I care about you, lad. That's the God's honest truth."

The boy nodded. "I believe you," he said solemnly. Then his mouth kicked into a smile. "Even though you're a bleedin' Irishman."

Chapter 21

Wherein There Are Unmentionable Shivers and Flutters; Confidences Are Shared over Tea and Cake; And an Epiphany About Romantic Novels Is Had...

It was almost half past two in the morning when Mina, Lord Kinsale, and Tom arrived back at Kinsale House. The fog had rolled in heavy and thick, and there was a decided nip in the air as Lord Kinsale helped Mina to alight from the hansom cab. Tom, obviously keen to be back at the place he could now call "home," raced ahead of them into the townhouse, dashing up the stairs to the second floor where his bedroom lay.

Try as she might, Mina couldn't ignore the fact that the touch of the marquess's gloved hand on hers, or upon her elbow, or at the small of her back sent delicious shivers racing over her skin and set up flutters in the vicinity of her "unmentionables"; sensations that had nothing at all to do with the cool night air and everything to do with her hopeless attraction to her far-too-attractive employer.

But then she gave herself a stern talking-to, reminding herself that she must ignore any and all unprofessional shivers and flutterings. It was her duty to see Tom settled for the night and to check on Christopher. Nothing else signified.

Mina was of course relieved to find that her "son" was safe

and sound and fast asleep in his bed, just as she'd left him. The *Guardia Nimbus* ward had stayed in place and so had Brutus. The pug greeted Mina with a terse hullo before demanding his sausage, which Mina quite happily gave him. (Her governess's pocket had quite conveniently supplied one, much to Lord Kinsale's bemusement.) And then the dog had trotted off to the marquess's sitting room where he usually spent the night.

Actually, Mina was quite surprised to find that Lord Kinsale hadn't retired to his own suite when she emerged from Tom's room some ten minutes later; the marquess had evidently waited for her while she'd tucked Tom into bed.

He got to his feet—he'd been reclining in the armchair Brutus had occupied earlier—as soon as he saw her. Sans coat, with his neckcloth loosened and his shirtsleeves rolled up revealing his thickly corded forearms, he was a sight to behold. The sort of sight that set off all Mina's barely quelled shivers and flutters again.

"My lord," she said softly as she closed Tom's door behind her. "I was not expecting to see you here. Did . . . did you wish to speak to me about something?"

Lord Kinsale scrubbed a hand through his thick dark hair, ruffling it into haphazard spikes. "I . . . I . . . Yes, I did," he said. "But . . . but not here."

Mina frowned. "Oh . . . it sounds rather serious."

The marquess's mouth curved into a faint smile. "Not-not really. It's just . . . I know it's late but I-I don't think I can fall asleep quite yet. I wondered if you . . ." He inhaled a breath. "If you'd join me in a drink of . . . of somethin'. I have brandy and sherry and whisky in me sittin' room. But o' course"—he shook his head as though frustrated—"that's not the done thing at all. So ignore that suggestion, Miss Dav-Davenport." He studied her face for a moment as though trying to read her thoughts. "Or we could go to the library? Or draw-drawing room? But then, what am I thinkin'? I know you're not one to tip-tipple..."

Mina's heart squeezed. His indecision and attempts not to offend her—to reassure her in fact—were quite endearing. "I feel the same way. I don't think I can sleep yet either. Why don't we venture down to the kitchen and I'll make us some tea."

Lord Kinsale's smile returned. "That would be per-perfect."

Ten minutes later, Mina had managed to stoke the fire in the kitchen range, boil the kettle, and assemble nearly everything else needed for tea making: a silver teapot, a pair of matching fine bone china cups and saucers, a bowl of sugar lumps, lemon slices, and teaspoons.

"What sort of tea would you like, my lord?" she asked as she studied the array of tea caddies on the top shelf of the kitchen's oak dresser. "There's Earl Grey, Lapsang souchong, Darjeeling, oolong, dandelion, chamomile, peppermint..."

"Whatever you prefer is fine with me, Miss Dav-Davenport," he said.

"Chamomile," said Mina decidedly. "It's best for promoting sleep. Although"—she turned and cast the marquess a beseeching look over her shoulder—"it seems I cannot reach the caddy, even if I stand on tiptoes."

"Allow me." Lord Kinsale pushed away from the kitchen counter where he'd been leaning, arms crossed over his wide chest as he watched her go about preparing the tea. And then Mina found he was right behind her. Indeed, she was flush up against the lean hard body she'd been fantasizing about for weeks on end. Ever since she'd stumbled into Lord Kinsale's arms on the *Kinsale Cloud*, if truth be told.

She closed her eyes and allowed herself to wallow in the sensations engulfing her as his front pressed against her back. Then as one of his thickly muscled arms reached past her and he retrieved the tea caddy. The delicious woodsy scent of his cologne drifted around her, teasing her. Even the heat of his body seemed to penetrate the wool of her gown, and beneath her corset and chemise, her nipples tightened quite shockingly. Her breath caught and her face grew hot and her heart clenched with acute longing.

Mina had never experienced desire like this before. What's more, she had no idea what to do with these sensations hurtling through her, threatening to overwhelm her and trample all over her good sense. Lord Kinsale hadn't moved away—he'd simply put the tea caddy down on the dresser beside her clenched hand—so perhaps he felt the pull of desire too. Indeed, he released a shaky sigh and Mina wondered if he'd been holding his breath, just like she had.

If she dared to turn her head to the side, would her lips brush against his strong stubbled jaw? What would Lord Kinsale do next? Would he lower his head and press his lips to her cheek or her ear or even her neck where her pulse raced wildly? Turn her around? Would he kiss her on the mouth?

Oh... If only he would...

And then Mina's sensible, practical, schoolmarmish side came to the fore.

No, Hermina Davenport. No. You must not even think about such things. That way lies utter ruin. You'll lose your post. You'll be putting Christopher in danger.

Your reputation—both personal and professional—will be destroyed if anyone ever finds out that you shared a romantic entanglement with your employer. You must *not break the Parasol Academy rules... even though you want to smash them all to pieces.*

Inhaling a fortifying breath, she made herself pick up the tea caddy with both hands. "Thank you, my lord," she murmured in a voice that was none too steady.

"It was... it was my pleasure, Miss Dav-Davenport," returned Lord Kinsale gruffly. Then he moved away and Mina heard the scrape of a chair on the kitchen floor's flagstones as he took a seat at the oak table.

Mina barely looked at him as she busied herself with adding several scoops of fragrant chamomile leaves and flowers to the teapot and then pouring the boiled water over the top. Although, she could feel the weight of the marquess's stare like a physical touch.

This had been a huge mistake, agreeing to take tea with him like this. She thought the kitchen would be a mundane environment. It was full of practical, ordinary things and plainly furnished. It was the sort of place where romantic thoughts and feelings shouldn't spark to life. But oh, how wrong she'd been.

The kitchen, at this time of night, was cozy and quiet and warm. The fire in the cast-iron stove and the candles and lamps they'd lit bathed the room's white-washed stone walls and sturdy furniture in a soft golden glow. Copper pots and pans gleamed, and the fragrance of dried herbs—neat bunches hung from the dark ceiling beams above the table—cast a spell of intimacy about the space.

"Would you like something to eat as well, my lord?" Mina asked as she passed the marquess a steaming cup of fragrant tea. "Mrs. Dunkley made a Victoria sponge. It's in the larder."

Lord Kinsale's eyes met hers as he took the cup and saucer. "I can al-always be tempted by cake," he said. "Especially one that's smothered with straw-strawberries and jam and cream."

Oh my. The way the marquess had looked at her when he'd mentioned he could be tempted... Mina feared her cheeks were redder than the strawberries. The man was *definitely* flirting with her.

But as she sat down at the table with her own tea and cake—a very slender slice considering she'd already eaten a gooseberry fool for dessert earlier in the evening when she'd dined with the marquess—she couldn't deny that she was tempted by the man too, despite her stern self-admonishments. She suddenly wondered if Emmeline had felt this way when she'd been working for the Duke of St Lawrence—caught helplessly between duty and desire.

But Emmeline and her duke had fallen in love. And Emmeline had already been married, so she at least had some way to tell the difference between infatuation and fleeting lust and true love. Whereas she, twenty-six-years-old-and-never-been-kissed Mina Davenport, was so terribly confused and out of her depth.

There was no denying that she respected Lord Kinsale and liked him very much. Perhaps *too* much. She was certainly attracted to him in a physical sense. But was she falling in love? Was this giddy, dizzying, wondrous feeling—a sensation that was akin to being caught up in a teleportation whirlwind whenever she was around the man—a sign that her heart was becoming hopelessly engaged?

She hardly knew.

She didn't have time to dwell on her feelings for too long as Lord Kinsale spoke, pulling her away from her convoluted musings. "I've been mean-meanin' to tell you, Miss Dav-Davenport that I was... that I was nothin' but impressed with the way you rushed over to-to protect young Tom outside the Lion and Lamb. Although"—he put down his cake fork and pushed his plate away—"there were a few moments in which I was more than a wee bit worried about what that drunk-drunken lout might do when you told him to let go o' the boy. Especially when you gave him a poke with your umbrella. But what-whatever you did, it worked." He suddenly reached out and put his large hand over hers. "I know you did-didn't need me to intervene, but I... but I would've. The idea that some brute might hurt you, fills me with—" He broke off. "I have power in me fists, Miss Davenport. I don't like to use them, but I would to pro-protect you. And the boys. You all... You all mean so very much to me. I-I wanted you to know that."

Oh. Mina hadn't expected Lord Kinsale to make such a heartfelt disclosure. She was touched, more than she could say. "Thank you," she murmured. She should remove her hand from the marquess's, but it felt so very right feeling the warmth of his calloused palm against the back of her hand. How his long, work-roughened fingers lightly wrapped about hers. "Even though it's my duty as a Parasol governess to ensure the children I look after remain safe, I do find that I've come to care for Tom." *And his master too...* The telling words hovered on the tip of Mina's tongue but she held them back. To steer the conversation in a less dangerous direction she added, "It's obvious that you've always gone out of your way to take care of others. What you did for your family in Ireland, when you lived in Dublin, was no small thing."

Oh dear, she'd said the wrong thing entirely. To Mina's dismay, Lord Kinsale removed his hand from hers and clenched his large fists on the tabletop. Even in the muted lamp and candlelight, the white marks of scars across his misshapen knuckles stood out starkly. These fists were clearly the hands of a fighter. Not a gentleman's hands at all despite the fact he always wore a gold and emerald signet ring on his little finger.

"I... I think about that. Quite a lot," he said in a voice rough with emotion. "What I did b-b-back home. The life of a pro-professional p-p-prizefighter is not an easy one. And I cannot tell a lie, I'm... I'm ashamed of the things that I did, the things I *had* to do, to sur-survive those years. It was a bloody, bru-brutal existence. I loathe v-v-violence, yet it seems I had a t-t-talent for it."

Concern squeezed Mina's chest upon witnessing the shadows of remorse, and yes, an unmistakable flicker of pain in

Lord Kinsale's green eyes. A deep frown was etched between his dark brows and a muscle twitched in his lean cheek. His mouth had twisted as he'd spoken and his stammer, which he constantly made an effort to control, had become noticeably worse. She wished she could reach out and cradle that tense jaw to comfort this man. To lessen the immense guilt that clearly weighed heavily on his heart. But it wasn't her place to soothe him with her touch, so she would try with words.

"My lord," she said softly, "you do not condemn Tom for his pickpocketing. Why should you judge yourself so harshly? Desperate times undoubtedly call for desperate measures. Surely no one would censure you for doing what you needed to do to keep from starving."

One corner of Lord Kinsale's mouth inched into a wry smile. "Aye. That's what I k-k-keep tell-tellin' meself. But then I recall the men I hurt in the ring to earn that m-m-money. Even though it technically wasn't b-b-blood money, Miss Dav-Davenport, me con-conscience says otherwise."

"I know you are a good man," said Mina. "And no one can convince *me* otherwise. You are kind and generous and patient and noble and brave. Why else would you have embarked on a mission to change the laws in Ireland to curb the power of ruthless landlords? To ensure that wealthy landowners never abuse their privilege and cruelly take advantage of their tenants ever again? It takes courage to challenge the status quo. You have my admiration and my support, such that it is."

The expression in Lord Kinsale's green eyes grew fiercely earnest. "You've made so much difference in me life already, Miss Davenport. Hirin' you was the best . . . the best decision I've ever made. I may not be the epitome of a per-perfect gentleman yet, but I'm well on the way. My speech, on the whole, is mark-markedly better. And I owe . . . I owe it all to you. Just think, if you'd never boar-boarded the *Kinsale Cloud*, you and I might never have met. The very thought of that makes this bat-battered heart of mine clench in the oddest way. It's . . . it's the queerest feelin' . . ."

Oh heavens. Was Lord Kinsale alluding to the scene in *Jane Eyre* where the governess bares her heart and soul to her employer? When they sit beneath the chestnut tree in Thornfield Hall's garden, and Mr. Rochester declares that he "sometimes has a queer feeling" with regard to the governess. But the reader *knows* he is really declaring his love for Jane?

Surely not.

But goodness, the way Lord Kinsale was looking at her right now made Mina's heart behave in strange ways too. But unlike the character Jane Eyre, it was she, Hermina Davenport who was harboring terrible secrets, not her employer.

A bittersweet ache—a confusing combination of tender emotion and longing and guilt—penetrated Mina's chest. She wanted to be honest with the marquess about Christopher—that the boy wasn't her son but her former charge. But how could she explain that the boy's guardian was being controlled by an evil Fae queen who had unclear but undoubtedly nefarious designs on the child? That she, Hermina Davenport, possessed magical abilities courtesy of her Parasol Academy training? She couldn't tell Lord Kinsale *any* of it.

She'd committed a crime in the eyes of the law. She'd broken and was continuing to break countless Parasol Academy rules. She was being duplicitous and underhanded and taking advantage of her employer's good nature.

Aside from all of that, if she did decide to throw caution to the wind and confess all to Lord Kinsale, he'd undoubtedly think she was completely, certifiably insane.

So Mina held her tongue about all of these things. Instead she said something that was true. "I'm so very grateful that fate has brought us together, even if it's just for a little while, my lord."

"Aye . . ." Lord Kinsale's expression grew pensive, and

Mina wondered what the man was thinking. "Although, it sounds like Tom, now that he's decided to stay, might need your ser-services for a wee while longer. So I hope you'll con-consider stayin' on for him, even when I . . . when I no longer require fluency or etiquette lessons. He and Chris-Christopher certainly get on well. I feel as though they've be-become firm friends."

"I believe so too," said Mina. "Like us." She dropped her gaze to her plate, where her slice of Victoria sponge sat, barely touched.

"Aye, I like to think we're friends," said Lord Kinsale softly.

Friends? Was the relationship she shared with the Marquess of Kinsale really a friendship? Could an employer of elevated rank and his employee really be friends in the true sense of the word?

They certainly couldn't be lovers. And Lord Kinsale would surely be accused of being as mad as a hatter if he offered marriage to someone like her, a mere governess. He was trying to build his reputation, not ruin it.

Mina dared not look up at Lord Kinsale. To try to read the expression on his handsome face. Instead, she picked up her cake fork and prodded at a plump strawberry. Then she treated herself to a small, ladylike bite of cake.

She adored cake of all kinds, but when her thoughts were troubled, as they were now, she either couldn't eat a thing, or she wanted to eat the whole cake. Not that she *would* eat the whole thing—Mrs. Dunkley's Victoria sponge was a magnificent creation of three light-as-air layers slathered thickly with strawberry jam and cream and decorated with more swirls of cream and glazed strawberries piled on top. But cake offered comfort. It was something Mina *could* have when she couldn't have what—or *who*—she really wanted.

She was still deciding how much cake she *would* eat after

Lord Kinsale quit the room, when the marquess said, "Are-are you going to eat the rest of your sponge, Miss Davenport? I apologize if our rather serious talk has put you off your . . . off your food."

Mina put down her fork. "Oh no, it hasn't, my lord." She offered him a smile. "It's just that I like cake rather too much. One piece seems like it's never enough."

He chuckled softly and the deep sound seemed to reach inside Mina and warm her very soul. "I understand com-completely. But seriously. Why not eat that slice and then have another?"

Mina shook her head. "Oh no, my lord. I couldn't." She placed a hand upon her middle. "As my mama says, 'A lady must always remember that a moment on the lips becomes forever on one's hips.'"

"What?" Lord Kinsale gasped. His expression was caught somewhere between horror and outrage. "Your-your mother really says things like that? To you? To stop . . . to stop you eatin' cake?"

"Yes." Mina blushed. "My waist isn't particularly slender—"

"Miss Davenport, I'll hear no more of such-such rubbish in my house. You are the most gorgeous woman I've ever laid eyes on, and as far . . . as far as I'm concerned, you can eat as much feckin' . . . I mean damn . . . I mean . . ." He waved a hand at the decadent sponge on its silver stand in front of them. "Eat as much as you like. I will not judge you, at all."

Had . . . had Lord Kinsale really just called her gorgeous?

Mina bit her lower lip. She wasn't sure what to say. Indeed, her tongue had become tangled in hopeless knots while something warm and wonderful had unfurled inside her chest. No one—especially a member of the opposite sex—had ever praised her looks before. It was a novel feeling. The giddy, swirling, dizzying feeling she often felt in Lord Kinsale's presence was back and she had no idea what to do with it.

If there was such a thing as a *Cucumberfy* spell in the *Para-*

sol Academy Handbook, now would have been the perfect time to employ it.

"I . . . Thank you, my lord," Mina said at last. "That's very generous and sweet of you to say such things . . . about me."

"There's nothin' sweet or generous about it," said the marquess gruffly. "It's-it's simply true."

"Well . . ." Mina glanced at the clock on the mantel shelf. It was almost three o'clock. "I should probably save any further cake eating until tomorrow and bid you good night, my lord. The boys will likely be up in four hours or so—"

Lord Kinsale immediately climbed to his feet. "Of course, Miss Davenport. I should-shouldn't be keepin' you from your bed."

Mina rose too. "I'm more than happy to converse with you anytime, my lord."

The marquess's mouth curved in a slow and easy smile. "I . . . I could say the same."

He moved toward the kitchen door and Mina followed him. But as he opened it for her and she brushed past him, his large hand captured hers. Their fingers laced together as though they should be intertwined, and in the next instant, the door had closed, and Mina found herself being spun around and trapped between the hard wood panels and Lord Kinsale's equally hard chest.

His fingers gently caught her chin and there was no mistaking the heated look in the marquess's deep green eyes as he stared intently at her mouth. "I-I can't let you go. Not yet," he murmured roughly. "Not . . . not when you have a few cake-cake crumbs and a dollop of cream"—his calloused fingertip brushed fleetingly beside the corner of her mouth—"right here."

"Oh . . . Thank you . . ." Mina raised a hand and wiped the offending remnants of Victoria sponge away. Then, unthinkingly, she flicked her tongue against her own fingertip... and it was like she'd set a lit match to tinder.

The smoldering light in Lord Kinsale's eyes immediately flared with unmistakable lust. "Christ, forgive me, Miss Dav-Davenport," he whispered, his voice ragged with want. "I-I know I'm crossin' a line here, but I... but I so very badly want to kiss you. I... I can't stop thinkin' about it. In fact, I've been think-thinkin' about kissin' you for weeks. I know it's wrong—"

Mina pressed a trembling finger to his lips. "You are not alone." She couldn't lie any longer. Not about this at least. "I've-I've been thinking about it as well. You kissing me. I want that too."

Lord Kinsale groaned. "Thank God." And then, before Mina could even hint that she was a relative novice when it came to the art of kissing—because she absolutely was—his mouth crashed onto hers, sliding hungrily, desperately... and she froze. Her breath caught in her lungs and her fingers gripped Lord Kinsale's shirt.

Nothing in all the romantic novels she'd read—not *Jane Eyre* nor *Wuthering Heights* nor *Pride and Prejudice* nor *Sense and Sensibility*—had ever prepared her for something as wild and visceral and passionate and as completely overwhelming as this!

She had no idea what to do, at all... and Lord Kinsale *knew*.

Silly, silly, Mina. What had she been thinking?!

The marquess ripped his mouth away and stared down at her. His brow was furrowed, and his eyes were clouded with confusion as he whispered her name. "Mina? Miss Davenport? What...?" He wiped a hand down his face. "Don't tell me you've never... never been kissed."

Mina swallowed then nodded. "No. No, I haven't," she murmured thickly. "Not... not properly. I'm sorry. I'm sorry for misleading you. For allowing you to think—" She broke off as hot tears prickled. She couldn't tell him any more than that. She couldn't confess that Christopher wasn't really her son. That she was living a lie. She'd said too much already.

"I should go," she said, pushing ineffectually at his rock-hard chest.

But Lord Kinsale shook his head. "No. Not yet," he said firmly, placing a large hand flat against the door at Mina's back. "Not until I understand what's goin' on."

Chapter 22

Concerning a Disclosure, a Contract, and Unexpected Consequence...

"No. Not yet," said Phinn as he braced his hand on the kitchen door by Hermina Davenport's head. "Not until I understand what's going on."

His mind was awhirl with confusion. He'd just seized this lovely young woman's mouth in a passion-fueled kiss—a kiss she had consented to, had claimed to want—but then she'd frozen like a terrified deer trapped in a hunter's sights.

She's never been kissed... If Phinn had known, he never would have kissed her that way, like a wild, lust-bitten beast. He would have been gentle. He would have gone slowly.

He would have made it so, so sweet...

God, he could still taste her on his lips. The lingering sweetness of vanilla and sugar and strawberries and cream—and he suspected even ambrosia from heaven—could in no way compare to the divine sweetness of Mina Davenport. And Lord help him, he wanted to taste her again.

He swallowed as guilt lanced through his chest. "Mina... Miss Davenport, how can it be that you've never been kissed by anyone before? You have a child... Unless..."

No, no, no! Feck! Phinn's hands curled into tight fists as white-hot blistering anger seared through his veins. "Who hurt you?" he growled. The blond gentleman who'd been looking in Hatchards's front window, was he the dog who'd used Mina so callously and cruelly? "Tell me his name."

But Miss Davenport was shaking her head. Her eyes were wide with alarm as she said in a breathless rush, "Oh no. No, it's not what you think, Lord Kinsale. Nothing untoward has ever happened to me. No one ... no man has ever hurt me, or taken advantage of me, or forced me to-to do anything of a ... of a lascivious nature, if that's what you're thinking." She drew a shaky breath and her eyes locked with his. "I'm sorry I'm being so vague. I'm so sorry I haven't been completely open and honest with you. I wish I could say more, my lord. It's just that ... the situation I find myself in ... with young Christopher ... It's-it's so very, *very* complicated."

Confusion assailed Phinn again. "I cannot lie, but I'm mightily confused, Miss Davenport." He regarded the young woman's face, the line of worry etched between her elegant brows. He'd never known her to be dishonest about anything. Although, that wasn't *quite* true. When they'd met aboard the *Kinsale Cloud*, she'd been vague about her circumstances then too. He'd always suspected that she was in some sort of trouble. It seemed she still was.

Phinn sighed. He wished she would confide in him. One thing he wouldn't do was push her away. Deep in his heart, down to his very bones, he sensed that Mina Davenport was forthright and *good* even if she couldn't divulge her secrets right now. He had no reason to distrust her. He certainly didn't want to make things harder for her than they already were. "I just wish ... I wish I'd known you were so inexperienced when ... when it came to kissing," he said. "I wouldn't have been so-so overzealous. I would have been gentle."

Miss Davenport's hazel eyes brightened with an emotion that Phinn interpreted as relief. "You're not angry with me?"

Phinn smiled down at the governess. *Mina.* "How ... how

could I be?" he said softly, tucking a stray lock of her silken chestnut hair behind her ear. "We're friends, are we not? Friends who care about each other?"

A soft pink blush rose in Miss Davenport's cheeks and her eyelids fluttered downward, shielding the expression in her eyes. "Yes," she whispered. "That's true."

Heartened, Phinn continued. "All . . . all these weeks we've spent in each other's company," he said, "the way you've been helpin' me with me speech and to master society's damnably complicated rules, you've shown me bound-boundless patience and understandin'. And before you tell me it's simply your duty, we both know that's not the case en-entirely."

Miss Davenport didn't say anything. But her eyes had returned to his and Phinn was mesmerized by their whisky-brown glow. "I wasn't lyin' when I said I'd been thinkin' about kissin' you for some time," he said in a low voice. "If I haven't put you off kissin' with me overenthusiastic effort before, I'd . . . I'd like to try again. To redeem meself. To show you how won-wonderful kissin' *can* be."

Miss Davenport's frown was back. "Yes. Yes, I do want that, my lord. I'm six-and-twenty and to be perfectly honest, being kissed—in a romantic way—is something I'd like to experience. Very much. I also strongly feel that if you and I kiss, we'll both stop wondering what it would be like. Our curiosity will be satisfied. At least mine will be. Only . . ." She bit her lip and it took everything in Phinn not to groan as he watched her straight white teeth press into that lush pink pillow. "Part of me is worried you'll think less of me if I do acquiesce. It's not very professional of me to be dallying with my employer. If Mrs. Temple at the Parasol Academy ever found out . . ."

"Well, I won't tell if you don't." Phinn tried to lighten the mood and cast Miss Davenport a rakish smile. "You could . . . you could look upon it as a . . . a kissin' lesson. That way it's a contract of sorts. There are no other obligations. It would be a once-only offer. Tonight only. No . . . no other strings attached."

Miss Davenport's gaze searched his for one long moment. And then she gave a decisive nod. "Very well, my lord," she murmured huskily. "I consent to a kissing lesson. Just one. Just tonight."

Phinn exhaled and a heady feeling akin to exultation flooded his chest. Potent desire rushed through his veins, straight to a decidedly masculine part of his person; a part which twitched with rampant eagerness.

But this time, Phinn would not let lust hold sway. He would take his time with Miss Davenport. He'd meant what he'd said: He wanted to show her how wonderful kissing could be.

"I . . . I will make this experience good for you, Mina," he whispered as he slid a hand behind the young woman's slender back and drew her close against him. Her palms lay flat against his chest, and he wondered if she could feel the wild thud of his heart. "I promise."

With his other hand, he cradled Miss Davenport's soft-as-a-rose-petal cheek. As he did so, her gaze dipped to his mouth and she parted her sweet lips and dear Lord, she was trembling. And he was trembling too. Not with nerves but with sharp want and delicious anticipation. He would not let Hermina Davenport down. This kiss would be everything she'd ever dreamed of and more.

Lowering his head, Phinn ever so gently pressed his mouth to Miss Davenport's . . . and when she followed his lead and moved her plush lips against his, when she leaned into him and her hands wound around his neck, when her fingers tangled in the hair at his nape and she released a soft breathy moan, he was certain he'd found heaven.

So this *is kissing*, Mina thought as Lord Kinsale's mouth moved slowly yet with gentle purpose over hers.

This was nothing like the first wild and far too overwhelming kiss the marquess had bestowed only minutes ago.

This kiss was lingering and heart-meltingly tender. An enticing blend of firmness and subtle coaxing. A combination of teasing brushes and soft silken glides that Mina easily mimicked. It was precisely the sort of swoon-inducing kiss that made one want to moan in a most un-governess-like fashion.

And oh, sweet heaven, Mina *did*. As a breathy, helpless sound tumbled forth, the tip of Lord Kinsale's tongue, warm and slick, boldly swept between her parted lips. And she gasped with surprise. And then his tongue delved a little deeper.

Good Lord, the marquess was *tasting* her. But the sensation of his tongue entering her mouth, the way he gently stroked *her* tongue as though inviting her to taste him back, wasn't unwelcome. At all. In fact, Mina decided she liked what Lord Kinsale was doing, rather a lot, even though it *must* be all kinds of wicked.

Who'd have thought that wickedness had a taste, and it was so, so good.

In fact, it was even better than cake.

It was better than anything Mina had ever experienced in her entire life.

Thrills raced through Mina from head to toe and before too long, she found that her knees were so weak, she had to cling to the marquess's neck lest she fall. Lord Kinsale's hand, the one cradling her cheek, moved to the back of her head and his fingers speared into her hair, scattering pins.

Oh my . . . As their kiss deepened, when Lord Kinsale's tongue boldly caressed hers yet again, Mina dared to accept his invitation. Their tongues entwined in an intimate dance and oh, how wonderful it felt to hear the marquess groan. To know that she'd elicited such a response in such a large, powerful man, to think that he was unraveling, just a little bit because of what she'd done, was heady indeed.

But underneath all the achingly sweet tenderness of Lord Kinsale's kisses—because by now, Mina couldn't deny that what they were sharing was a series of kisses—desire bloomed. Especially when Lord Kinsale's hand, the one at her back, slid forward to splay over her ribcage and his thumb skimmed the underside of her breast. That particular caress, fleeting though it was, provoked a shiver of unbridled delight inside Mina, and her nipples tightened in the most scandalous way. Indeed, it seemed as though Lord Kinsale was effortlessly awakening sensations inside Mina that she'd never experienced before. Delightfully *wicked* flutters that were stirring in secret, entirely feminine places. Mina's limbs felt as soft and malleable as sun-warmed butter, yet other parts of her quivered and pulsed and ached as though they needed to be touched and stroked as well. The places *she* sometimes touched when she was alone in her bed . . .

Oh, how wanton she was becoming. This was supposed to be just a kissing lesson, but Mina sensed that she was learning so much more. Not just about passion and the all-consuming pleasure of being kissed by a man, but about herself and *her* needs . . . and how desperately she wanted Lord Kinsale.

They'd both asserted they were merely friends. That this "academic" exercise in learning to kiss was a once-only event. But Mina knew they'd both been lying to each other and to themselves. This felt like the beginning of something, not the ending. And Mina had no idea what to do about it.

She might be able to deny herself cake on a regular basis. But would she be strong enough to resist the sweet temptation of Lord Kinsale's kisses when she saw the man every single day and night?

Could she stop herself falling headlong into love?

Oh, that would surely be an unmitigated disaster.

Only one thing was certain in her mind as the marquess eventually pulled away and stared down at her, chest heaving, his green eyes glowing with desire and some other emotion Mina was too afraid to put a name to: Losing her heart to her employer was yet another problem she would have to add to her growing list of "Complications Hermina Davenport could really do without."

"Well, how did I do, Miss Davenport?" asked Lord Kinsale. His mouth had curved into a wide satisfied smile that only made Mina's heart swell with even more unwanted longing. "Do you feel as though I fulfilled our contract? Did me lesson meet your expectations?"

Mina exhaled a shaky breath. Lord Kinsale's large hand was still resting lightly on her waist and his lean hips and muscular thighs were still pushing against her skirts, no doubt crushing them, but she didn't have the will or the desire to ask him to move away. Which did not augur well for her ability to resist temptation in the future. "You . . . you certainly did meet my expectations, my lord. Your demonstration was particularly . . . comprehensive." Despite the reservations brewing and bubbling in the back of her mind, she smiled. "I feel as though I've been thoroughly enlightened. I am in the dark no more about kissing."

"Well, perhaps the most important question is"—Lord Kinsale caught a lock of her no doubt disheveled hair and wound it around his finger before letting it slide off—"are you satisfied, Miss Davenport? Because surely satisfaction is the true measure of whether a kiss is everythin' that it should be."

Satisfied? In one sense, yes. Lord Kinsale's kisses had been a dream come true. He'd kissed like a fairy-tale prince and she was the princess he wished to woo and wed. Being in his arms, having his mouth tutor hers so expertly, had been pure bliss.

But in a whole host of other ways, Mina was far from satisfied. Her greedy heart, indeed, her entire body was thrumming with a yearning so intense that surely Lord Kinsale must sense it. She wanted countless blissful kisses. Infinite kisses. She wanted Lord Kinsale to kiss her to the end of her days.

But she couldn't admit to any of that because he was a marquess and she wasn't a princess. She wasn't even a gentlewoman. She was a duplicitous governess with far too many secrets. A happy-ever-after with Lord Kinsale wasn't written in her stars. So Mina answered the marquess's question about whether she was satisfied, the only way she could. She forced another smile and lied. "Completely and utterly."

"Good," Lord Kinsale said. He took a step back and his gaze darted to the kitchen clock. "It's well after three, Miss Davenport. We both need our beauty sleep." Then he released a soft chuckle. "Well, some more than others. Even if I slept for a thousand years"—he gestured at his slightly crooked nose—"I doubt it would make any difference to this battered visage."

Mina dared to reach out and straighten a wrinkle in Lord Kinsale's silk waistcoat. "I don't know. I think ruggedly handsome men with a few battle scars hold a certain appeal for some women."

He cocked a dark brow and his eyes gleamed with amusement and something else, which Mina thought might be wickedness. "You do, do you?"

"Oh, definitely," she returned. Then she drew a brave breath and said something she didn't want to say but most definitely had to. "You'd be surprised, my lord. I'm sure that when you grace high society's ballrooms, you'll have any number of well-bred ladies lining up to waltz with you."

There she'd done it. She'd emphasized how far apart they were in terms of social status. How wide the gulf dividing her class and his really was.

Lord Kinsale's expression changed. His brow furrowed for a moment, but then he smiled. "You still need to give me a dancin' lesson or two before I do that, lass," he said as he reached past her and opened the kitchen door. "But that can wait until the morrow. Or at least until we're both rested." He nodded at the darkened corridor beyond the kitchen. "I'll bid you good night here, Miss Davenport. You go up to your room first. I'll tidy up the tea things."

"Oh no," began Mina. "I couldn't let you do—"

But Lord Kinsale held up his hand. "You wouldn't be arguin' with your employer now, would you, Miss Davenport? Aside from that, I'm sure you wouldn't want any of the other servants wonderin' what you and I have both been up to at this late hour in the kitchen. I know I certainly wouldn't."

"No," said Mina softly. "You're quite right, my lord. Thank you. For everything. And good night."

Had Lord Kinsale noticed the note of regret in her voice? She hardly knew. Lifting her skirts, Mina pushed past him and hurried away before she did something mad and foolish and threw herself back into the man's strong arms again. Before she begged him to kiss her and never let her go.

It was only when Mina was back in her bedroom and had begun to shed her governess's garb that she realized something quite extraordinary.

After their "kissing lesson," when Lord Kinsale had spoken to her, he hadn't stammered. Not once. His speech had been as smooth as his silken waistcoat.

As smooth as his slick-as-butter kisses.

Mina pressed her fingers to her lips, which were still slightly swollen. Could it be that the act of kissing somehow alleviated the marquess's stutter?

Surely not. There'd been nothing in her little green elocution guidebook about "kissing" being a tried-and-true treatment method for remediating stammering.

But . . . but perhaps the act of kissing somehow relaxed the marquess. What if it reduced the tension in his oral musculature and throughout his entire body? What if it calmed his mind?

That made sense to Mina. It couldn't be that their kisses had been "magical."

Well, they had been to her, and she would cherish the experience. Always. She'd lock the precious memory of it in her heart and perhaps one day, when she no longer worked for Lord Kinsale, she would take it out and remember the night when the marquess had made her feel so very special and perfect and wanted.

It wasn't just the night that he'd kissed her. It was the night when he'd whispered her first name, the one those close to her used. *Mina*. She'd only said it to him once. On the occasion when they'd first met aboard the *Kinsale Cloud* in fact.

And he'd *remembered*.

Perhaps that had been the most magical gift of all.

Chapter 23

In Which Coffee Is Taken, Yet More Tea Is Spilled; And an Invitation Is Issued . . .

Mina tried to hide a yawn behind her hand as Mrs. Dunkley, Lord Kinsale's cook, deposited a fresh pot of coffee in front of her. She was sitting at the oak kitchen table, trying not to fall asleep while simultaneously trying not to remember the exquisite kisses she'd shared with her employer, right up against the kitchen door that stood directly across from her.

Had it only been six hours since she'd shared an amorous tryst with Lord Kinsale? No, a "kissing lesson" Mina reminded herself as she pulled a newspaper toward her. It was *The Illustrated London News*.

"Thank you for the coffee," she said to the cook as she carefully refilled her cup.

"No worries at all, pet," said Mrs. Dunkley, crossing over to the larder. "I know 'ow 'ard it is keepin' up wiv those boys you've got to look after." She nodded at the mantel clock. "When did Lord Kinsale say they'd be back from 'Yde Park again? I'll try to time the bakin' o' me scones so they're nice an' warm an' fresh when the master walks in the door wiv those two young scallywags." She emitted a laugh as she returned to the table, her sturdy arms laden with ingredients: flour, baking powder, butter, and a jug of milk. "I fought Lord Kinsale and Brutus were 'ard to fill up. But lawks-a-mercy, ain't that Tom Fleet a bottomless pit an' a 'alf? If Lord Kinsale 'adn't told me first fing this mornin' tha' 'e were the one 'oo got stuck into me Victoria sponge last night, I would've fought it were young Master Tom."

Mina's cheeks warmed. The marquess was the most noble man alive, she was certain of it. Aloud she said, "Tom does have a healthy appetite. But to answer your first question, I believe Lord Kinsale will be back around half past ten. Or thereabouts."

"Excellent," said the cook, depositing a rolling pin, a wooden spoon, and a large china mixing bowl on the table. "Let's get this scone makin' underway."

While Mrs. Dunkley got on with her baking, Mina perused the broadsheet in front of her. She'd already been through the *Times* and various other papers that were issued in the morning. But she'd found nothing in their pages about Sir Bedivere Ponsonby or his missing ward, Lord Fitzwilliam. Thank the Fae.

She didn't regret her visit to Fitzwilliam House, dangerous though it was. Not only had she gleaned valuable intelligence about what the baronet was up to, when Christopher had seen the items she'd collected from his old bedroom—his much-loved toys and books and favorite items of clothing—his blue eyes had immediately brightened with delight. She hoped they would bring him some degree of solace. And hopefully his bad dreams would go away.

Of course, when Lord Kinsale had appeared in the small parlor adjoining the schoolroom where the boys were taking their breakfast and eight o'clock, as was their usual custom, she'd been at sixes and sevens. Part of her was flustered because it had only been a handful of hours since the marquess had held her in his arms. But part of her had been delighted by the undoubtedly foolish notion that the marquess hadn't been able to resist seeing her again. That no sooner had he risen from his bed he'd been simply champing at the bit to seek her out.

Although, it turned out that Lord Kinsale was simply being kind; he'd proposed taking the boys, along with Brutus, for a jaunt about Hyde Park in a new light carriage—a phaeton—he'd recently purchased. His friend, Lord Hartwell, was going to teach him how to drive it. "Christopher and Tom will both be per-perfectly safe," he said. "Christopher shall sit beside me and Tom can take the seat at the back."

"Wicked!" Christopher cried.

"'Ooray!" added Tom.

Mina, who could barely keep her eyes open—her mind had been so abuzz, she'd barely slept a wink even after she'd collapsed into her bed—had not had the stamina to protest. "Very well," she said. Looking at Christopher, she added, "As long as you wear your sailor hat." She'd surmised that the large brim would sufficiently shield his face while he was out and about. And of course, her mother had cut his long blond curls. The child wouldn't be easily recognizable. Besides, it sounded like Sir Bedivere's detective, Cheavers, and his men were mainly on the lookout for Miss Hermina Davenport.

Christopher agreed to Mina's request with an exaggerated sigh. "All right."

"I ain't wearin' no sailor hat," Tom declared. "But I'll wear me cap."

Mina had given a nod of approval. "I'll also look after Mr. Hopwell," she said to Christopher. Cheavers was aware that little Lord Fitzwilliam had a toy purple rabbit—he'd mentioned it when he'd visited Rose Cottage a month ago—so exercising additional care right now was essential. Indeed, since the Hatchards excursion, when Mina had spied Sir Bedivere on Piccadilly, she'd made it a rule that Mr. Hopwell must stay at home.

Spoilsport, Brutus had grumbled from the doorway. He'd accompanied his master upstairs too.

Considering your attitude last night, Mr. Brutus, what did you expect? rejoined Mina. *Pugs who constantly threaten to tear apart toy rabbits are not to be trusted.*

Brutus, being the cantankerous little beastie that he was, had of course retaliated with the dropping of a malodorous "bomb" that made Lord Kinsale curse and the boys laugh and all Mina could do was dab at her watering eyes.

Mina had just finished perusing *The Illustrated London News*—like all the other papers, not a word had been mentioned about Sir Bedivere or Lord Fitzwilliam or Mina herself (thank goodness)—when Smedley stalked into the room.

He sent her a narrow look. "Don't you have better things to do than lazing about, drinking coffee, and reading his lordship's newspapers?" the horrid butler sniped. "Don't you have lessons to plan and pencils to sharpen and chalkboards to clean?"

Mina only just managed to suppress a rebellious eyeroll. "I'm keeping up with current affairs," she said. "According to the *Parasol Academy Handbook*, a good governess is always well-informed."

"A good governess knows her place," returned Smedley with a superior look. "I strongly suggest you visit Mrs. Aldershot in her study. She's sure to find some sort of gainful employment to occupy you until your charges return. You know what they say about idle hands . . ."

Mina plastered a false smile on her face. "As soon as I've finished my coffee I'll drop by," she said brightly. A lie of course. She had no intention of visiting the housekeeper. The woman would no doubt make her sweep out the coal cellar or wash the outside of the windows on the townhouse's uppermost floor. (She could easily manage such a task with a sturdy enough rope and a grappling hook, but perhaps not on less than four hours of restless sleep.)

Smedley slunk away—probably to his lair, the butler's pantry—and Mina breathed a sigh of relief. A minute later, Lord Kinsale's valet, Frobisher, entered the kitchen and greeted her with a smile. He was in search of coffee too.

After helping himself to a cup, he took a seat beside Mina. "Pardon me for saying so, but you're looking rather tired this morning, Miss Davenport," he murmured in a conspiratorial fashion by her ear when Mrs. Dunkley was fussing about with the oven and one of the maids had disappeared into the scullery to wash up the used bowl and rolling pin. "So was Lord Kinsale. And even though you're sure to deny it, I heard you both on the stairs heading for the second floor with young Master Fleet at half past two in the morning."

Mina's cheeks burned. She'd forgotten that the valet's bedroom was not far from his master's suite. But at least Frobisher wasn't aware that she and Lord Kinsale had then sneaked downstairs for tea and cake . . . and kisses. "Honestly, I really don't know what you're talking about, Mr. Frobisher," she said primly. "And even if I did, my lips would be sealed. A governess is always discreet when it comes to matters concerning her employer."

The dark-haired valet nudged her arm and smirked. "Ha! That tells me all I need to know. Late night shenanigans with the master—I love the idea and I'm absolutely in your corner, Miss Davenport." He dropped his voice and whispered, "Your secret is safe with me. I'll even pinky swear to it if you want me to."

Mina's face was positively on fire now. "That won't be necessary," she murmured. "I trust you."

And Mina did indeed. Frobisher had become an unexpected ally since the "bathrobe incident" when she'd visited the marquess's sitting room just as he'd emerged from his bath. Frobisher had laid the blame for the embarrassing, bordering-on-scandalous encounter squarely at the feet of the uppity Mr. Travers, the Savile Row tailor. In fact, Frobisher—who was always immaculately dressed and quite knowledgeable about haute couture—had since convinced Lord Kinsale to engage another tailor who would tut-tut less about his supposedly "far-too-muscular, virtually-impossible-to-cater-for" frame. "Just because Lord Kinsale is built like Hercules, it does not mean he's difficult to dress," Frobisher had once declared to Mina. "The man is a god, and any tailor who's worth his salt should be able to make the marquess look like one without complaining about his bulky biceps." From what Mina had seen of Lord Kinsale's impressive physique, she was very much inclined to agree.

The valet had also confided to Mina in quiet moments that most of the staff liked Lord Kinsale but couldn't stand Smedley or Mrs. Aldershot. In fact, below stairs, the butler was often referred to as "Meddley Smedley" and the housekeeper had earned the moniker of "Alderot."

Talk turned to far more mundane subjects and soon the scullery maid and Mrs. Dunkley had joined the conversation. At ten o'clock, as Mina was contemplating the idea of drifting upstairs to the schoolroom—she was now quite buzzingly awake after drinking three large cups of very strong coffee—one of the footmen walked in with a note for her.

"Oooh, who's sending you mysterious missives on such fancy parchment paper?" said Frobisher, waggling his eyebrows suggestively. "Does the lovely Miss Davenport have a secret admirer?"

Mina laughed and she was about to say, "Hardly," when the footman declared, "It's from the Duchess of St Lawrence accordin' to the liveried footman 'oo delivered it. 'E said I must 'and it to Miss Davenport 'erself. In fact 'e won't leave until 'e 'as an answer."

Mina took the note from the footman, and sure enough the paper was the gilt-edged stationery of the Duchess of St Lawrence, sealed shut with red wax that contained an impression of her personal seal: a coat of arms featuring cherry blossoms, a key (that looked remarkably like a leyport key), and a clock-face.

"Well, go on. Open it," urged Frobisher. "You mustn't keep a duchess waiting."

Mina cracked the seal and folded open the parchment. It was indeed a message from darling Emmeline announcing that at long last, she'd returned to London!

Mina hugged the note to her chest. "You may tell Her Grace's footman that all going well, I will be at St Lawrence House at three o'clock for afternoon tea."

The scullery maid squealed while Mrs. Dunkley fanned herself with her apron and murmured, "Lawks-a-mercy."

Frobisher was grinning knowingly. "I always suspected that you knew people in high places, Miss Davenport. You have that 'refined' sort of look about you. No wonder Meddley Smedley and Alderot are secretly scared of you."

Mina gave a shocked laugh. "Scared of me? You must be joking. I'm just the governess."

"Oh no, I'm not joking," replied the valet. "They absolutely know that you have the master's ear. You say the word"—he snapped his fingers—"his lordship will sack them on the spot."

Mina frowned. "Then why are they so horrid to me and everyone else? *And* disrespectful to Lord Kinsale?"

Mrs. Dunkley's mouth twisted with a wry smile. "Tha' sort don't know any different, pet. Right bullies they are. They fink that if they browbeat all of us enough, we'll be too afraid to say anyfink. And everyone knows 'is lordship is just a big squishy teddy bear underneaf all his beefy Irish brawn. But you're too clever and forthright to put up wiv that sort o' rubbish. An' you're not afraid to give as good as you get. That's why everyone on staff likes you 'ere. Well, everyone except for them two." The cook gestured at the closed kitchen door and the corridor beyond, which led to the butler's and housekeeper's domain.

Well, that certainly gave Mina food for thought. But she didn't have time to dwell on the implications of what Frobisher and Mrs. Dunkley had just disclosed. She had to put plans into action in order to see Emmeline!

As soon as Lord Kinsale returned from his excursion to Hyde Park, she'd ask for the afternoon off to see her dear friend. She was certain he wouldn't say no. At least she *hoped* he wouldn't. It had been three weeks since she'd begun working at Kinsale House, and she hadn't yet spoken to the marquess about taking any time off. And she so badly needed a friend to confide in about *everything*—from "kidnapping" Lord Fitzwilliam, to deceiving Mrs. Temple and Lord Kinsale. And of course, her foolish infatuation with her employer and their ill-advised "kissing lesson" last night.

It was certain to be a *long* afternoon tea.

Chapter 24

In Which Flogging, Caning, Brooding, Prats, and Blatherskites Feature; And a Funny Belly Leads to Rumination . . .

"Hey-ho, steady on, Kinsale. This isn't the Epsom Derby," called Marcus, Lord Hartwell. He was riding one of his horses alongside Phinn's new phaeton as Phinn bowled along Rotten Row in Hyde Park. Christopher, who was sitting beside Phinn, was holding onto his sailor hat and laughing with glee, while Tom, seated at the back of the small carriage, was urging Phinn to go faster. Brutus, sitting between Phinn and Christopher, was grinning his doggy grin as his jowls flapped in the breeze.

"Go on, Lord Kinsale," Tom cried. "We need to flog Lord 'Artwell. Let's beat 'im to the end of the Row!"

"Flog me?" rejoined Marcus in mock outrage. "I'll have you know, m'laddo, that the only one who'll get an absolute caning is Lord Kinsale. Last one to West Carriage Drive is a rotten egg." And then the viscount gave his fine bay gelding a nudge with his heels, and man and horse shot off toward the end of the riding path in a flash.

Phinn laughed. There was not a hope in Hades that they'd be able to catch Lord Hartwell. And there was no way in hell that he'd urge the pair of matched grays pulling his phaeton into anything faster than a brisk trot. Not if Phinn wanted to live to tell the tale. Because if Miss Davenport heard that he'd driven his carriage hell-for-leather down Rotten Row with her son and Tom on board, he wouldn't just receive a flogging. She'd have his guts for garters, of that there was no doubt.

"Awww, why are you going so slow, Lord Kinsale?" asked Christopher. "I'm not afraid to go faster. My papa used to take me—" The boy broke off and Phinn looked down at him.

"Your-your papa used to take you out in his carriage? Some-something like a phaeton? Or a gig or a dog cart?" Phinn knew he shouldn't question the boy about his father, but after his encounter with Miss Davenport last night, he couldn't deny that curiosity was eating away at him about the boy's sire.

But Christopher wouldn't be drawn on the subject.

Phinn sighed inwardly. He supposed it really wasn't any of his business. He just wanted to make sure that no cur had hurt Mina Davenport. He had no reason *not* to believe her assertion that she hadn't been ill-used by a man. But still, she had a son and no husband. And neither Christopher nor his mama would say a word about Christopher's father.

Deciding he'd best leave sleeping dogs lie, Phinn concentrated on driving his phaeton safely to the end of Rotten Row. He was bone-tired, but he needed this excursion to reinvigorate him after his late night. And to take his mind off a certain governess and her sweet kisses.

Sweet Jaysus, Miss Davenport's kisses. Unschooled yet totally perfect. Last night, when Mina Davenport had been in his arms, Phinn's head had been reeling like he'd downed a full bottle of whisky. And the astonishing aftereffects of those kisses . . . Phinn still couldn't quite believe that his stammer had utterly vanished, at least temporarily. It was truly astounding.

Magical.

Even though it would pain him, Phinn would keep his promise that last night's "kissing lesson" would be a once-only occasion. He wouldn't be that man who pressed Mina Davenport for more than she was willing to give, just for his own selfish pleasure or gain.

He would never, ever hurt her. He'd rather put out his own eyes.

Which was why he'd offered to take the boys off her hands this morning. In hindsight he should have given Miss Davenport the whole day off. He was well aware that she hadn't had a rest day since she'd begun working for him. *And* she'd been working day and night. Not only did she teach and take care of Tom and her own son, but she'd also been catering to his needs by providing elocution and etiquette lessons. The poor woman must be exhausted. When Phinn got back to Kinsale House, he'd make sure that the governess took the rest of the day off to do whatever she liked. It was the least he could do. Between himself and a housemaid or two—there was a veritable battalion of them at Kinsale House—they'd take good care of Christopher and Tom.

"Crikey! What's that?" cried Tom, interrupting Phinn's musings. The boy's voice was wreathed in wonder as he stared at the Crystal Palace, a magnificent construction of iron and glass which lay alongside Rotten Row and dominated the southwest end of Hyde Park. Three times the size of St Paul's Cathedral, the majestic building housed a spectacular trade show, suitably dubbed the "Great Exhibition." Whenever Phinn laid eyes on it, he always thought that the sparkling glass edifice resembled a huge mythical creature—a shining dragon perhaps—slumbering in the sun. It truly was an awe-inspiring sight.

"It's the Crystal Palace," explained Christopher. "It's got ever so many wizard things to see inside. Pink glass fountains and stuffed giraffes and tigers and a coat made out of poodle fur.

You can even see photographs of the moon! And over there"—he pointed toward the Serpentine—"are dinosaur statues. Miss Davenport called it a Dinosaur Court."

"Bleedin' 'ell," whispered Tom.

"So you've vis-visited the exhibition with your ma—I mean, you visited the ex-exhibition with Miss Davenport?" Phinn asked Christopher.

"Yes, and my godmama, Lady Grenfell," said the boy. Then his expression changed—grew melancholy. "But she's in heaven now."

"Oh, I'm so sorry to... to hear that, Christopher," said Phinn gently, even though curiosity began to prick.

The boy's godmother had been a noblewoman? But then Christopher did speak with a refined English accent just like his mother. And he was certainly well educated and au fait with social etiquette. Even more so than Phinn. It certainly sounded as if Miss Davenport and her son had been *very* well-connected at some point. But now she was a Parasol Academy governess...

Phinn wasn't sure what to make of this new tidbit of intelligence that Christopher had innocently shared about his late godmother. But he wouldn't press the child for further information lest he cause distress. That was the last thing he wanted to do. He understood loss and grief all too well.

Aloud he said, "I-I haven't been inside the Crystal Palace, but I think that's something we-we should all do together. And soon, before... before it ends next month."

"Cor blimey, I would love that," declared Tom.

"Me too," agreed Christopher.

"Done," said Phinn. "I will speak with Miss Davenport about organizing an excursion when... when we return home." The boys were still chattering excitedly about the prospect of seeing the Crystal Palace exhibition when Phinn steered his phaeton over to Lord Hartwell. Marcus, who'd well and truly "flogged" them, had already reined in his gelding beneath a large elm tree at the end of Rotten Row.

Marcus dismounted as Phinn helped the boys down from the phaeton. "Well, you lot took your time," the viscount said with a grin. "I was starting to think I should have brought lunch with me. I could have eaten it while I waited."

Phinn laughed. "Back... back home, you'd be called a blatherskite," he said.

"Blatherskite?" Marcus snorted. "Better that than being a slowpoke. My seventeen-year-old sister can drive a phaeton faster than you drive yours, Kinsale. I was about to send out a search party for you."

Phinn just shook his head and laughed at the good-natured ribbing. One thing he enjoyed about his interactions with Lord Hartwell was that he never reacted to Phinn's frequent moments of stammering. He never had. It made Phinn feel... comfortable. Like he could be himself. It was the same when Phinn was with Miss Davenport.

Well, not *exactly* the same way. But he felt seen and heard and valued by both of them. And for that he was grateful.

Phinn turned his attention back to Christopher and Tom, who'd started playing a game of fetch with Brutus. The pug was having the time of his life, running pell-mell after a stick from the elm tree. Phinn smirked to himself. Better a stick than a mauve velvet rabbit.

Even though Phinn had told himself that he wouldn't go digging for information about Mina Davenport and her son, he suddenly found himself asking Marcus, "Do you, by any chance, hap-happen to know of a Lady Grenfell?"

"Grenfell, Grenfell..." Marcus frowned and lightly tapped his riding crop against his thigh. "I can't say that I do. I could ask around if you like." He gave Phinn a considering look. "Any particular reason?"

"No, it's a name... a name I heard recently," said Phinn. "It's not in connection with anythin' specific though."

Marcus shrugged. "If you say so."

Phinn cast his gaze toward Rotten Row, watching the passersby. He really should leave well enough alone. Mina Davenport's history, and the identity of her son's father, really was none of his business.

If only he could shake off the idea that there was something wrong in her world...

He should really begin ferrying the boys and Brutus back to Belgravia before the crowds in Hyde Park got too thick. And then Phinn blinked in surprise. But who should be riding past on a fine black steed but the same golden-haired fellow with the distinctive "Sir Walter Raleigh" style mustache and beard that Phinn had spied outside of Hatchards? The same man who'd apparently startled Miss Davenport. So much so, she'd tried to hide from him.

Phinn's "goolies" still contracted painfully at the memory.

"Marcus," Phinn said in a low voice, "do you see that fair-haired chap ri-ridin' by on that strappin' black stallion... Do-do you know him by any chance?"

The viscount narrowed his gaze as he studied the man. "Yes, I do. Well, I know *of* him. I believe it's Sir Bedivere Ponsonby."

Sir Bedivere Ponsonby. "And what-what do you know. Specifically?"

Marcus cocked a dark brow. "You really are full of interesting questions this morning, aren't you?" When Phinn frowned, the viscount conceded. "All right. All right. Sir Bedivere, by all accounts, used to be a decent enough chap. He once held a commission in Her Majesty's Navy a few years back. I believe he also might have done some navigational work farther afield for the Admiralty's Hydrographic Office—something to do with magnetic surveys perhaps?—but don't hold me to that. At any rate, several months ago, the fellow apparently went off the rails. And by quite a bit."

Phinn's curiosity spiked. "In what way?"

"Rumor has it that he became a vainglorious prat. A total tit. He was suddenly filled with delusions of grandeur and claimed that he wanted to navigate the Northwest Passage—a sure and idiotic way to die if you ask me—ostensibly to impress Queen Victoria. But who really knows. The last I heard, he'd set sail from Bristol—this would have been about a month ago perhaps?—en route to the Arctic. Dashed insane. But perhaps he came to his senses because it looks like he's back in London."

Phinn frowned. He'd been in Bristol a month ago? So had Phinn. "Do you know the name of his vessel?"

Marcus frowned. "Something ridiculously grandiose like his ideas. The *Gallant*? Or the *Valiant* maybe?"

The *Valiant*... Phinn recalled that the *Kinsale Cloud*'s captain had complained about a massive ship—a discovery vessel—that had hoved into Bristol Quay and almost sideswiped the *Kinsale Cloud* when it had docked alongside them. Miss Davenport had apparently boarded the *Kinsale Cloud* in Kinsale, but where had the *Valiant* set out from? Ireland as well? Or had it just been returning from its failed voyage to the Arctic?

Phinn hardly knew, and speculating further seemed like a fruitless exercise. Perhaps Miss Davenport and this Sir Bedivere Ponsonby had nothing to do with each other at all. Perhaps it was all a coincidence and Phinn was simply trying to put mismatched puzzle pieces together that would never fit.

"So, when are you going to put in an appearance at one of high society's balls, my good man?" asked Marcus. "Your governess has worked wonders on your speech. It's damn near perfect. So not being able to talk to the ladies can't be your excuse."

Phinn grimaced. "I-I don't know how to waltz," he confessed. "Or perform any other sort of fancy dance."

Marcus gave him a considering look from beneath the brim of his topper. "Surely this governess of yours could teach you that too. Or you could just stand at the edge of the ballroom, looking tall, dark, and broodingly handsome. Women like that."

Phinn gave a snort of laughter. "I'm not sure about the handsome bit, but . . . but I'm sure I could do broodin'. And I suppose that's be-better than being thought of as a great lummox with no social graces whatsoever." Truth to tell, Phinn really had no desire to rub shoulders with his so-called peers, or court well-bred young ladies. He wasn't like Marcus, who was in the market for a wife. Not yet at any rate.

He certainly didn't want to think about the fact that the only woman he wanted to be around was the delectable Mina Davenport. He really was quite obsessed with her.

"You constantly underestimate your worth, my friend," said Marcus, clapping him on the shoulder. "You have a social conscience and those in power could learn a thing or two from you. I, for one, can't wait to see you make your next parliamentary speech. It's scheduled for the next sitting in a fortnight, isn't it?"

"Aye," said Phinn, trying not to feel sick at the thought of it. "I've been wor-workin' on a draft for the last week. Would you . . . would you mind readin' through it when it's finished? As you know, I'm not the most eloquent of men. I'd-I'd value your opinion."

"Of course I wouldn't mind," said Marcus. "Actually, why don't you drop by Hartwell House and read it aloud to me when you're ready? I have this feeling you're going to create quite a stir. But in a good way, mark my words."

"Are-are you sure?"

"I'm positive."

Talk briefly turned to Marcus's progress—or lack thereof—in finding a suitable bride and then the viscount said, "Speaking of brides—and I should have mentioned this earlier—the Duke of St Lawrence and his new duchess, Emmeline, are back from Kent. According to the note Xavier sent this morning, they arrived in London late yesterday. I'm sure Xavier would be more than happy to look over your speech as well. Two heads are better than one and all that."

Phinn was inclined to agree. He was about to ask Marcus if he'd like to schedule another training session at the Belgrave Boxing Saloon—and that perhaps Xavier might like to join them—when he felt a tug on his sleeve. It was Christopher. Beneath the brim of his ridiculously large sailor's hat, the boy's face was looking decidedly pale. "Can-can we go home now, Lord Kinsale?" he asked.

Phinn crouched down. "Are-are you not feelin' well, lad?"

The boy worried at his lower lip. "My belly does feel a bit funny. So . . . so I think I've had enough of Hyde Park, and I'd like to go back to Kinsale House if that's all right."

Phinn frowned. "O' course we can go home." When he straightened, he noticed that Sir Bedivere had just ridden past again, heading back in the opposite direction. But the baronet seemed completely oblivious to their small group beneath the elm tree.

But did Christopher know the man? Was that the real reason Christopher's belly suddenly felt "a bit funny"? Phinn bent down again and said quietly, "That blond-haired gentleman who just rode by on a big black horse, do-do you know him? Or . . . or does your mama?"

Even though the boy shook his head, his large blue eyes were fearful. "I'm not sure who you mean, my lord," he said.

Phinn grasped his shoulder lightly. "You-you know you

can tell me anythin', lad. I'll look after you and your mama. I care about you both, very much."

Christopher looked Phinn in the eye. "I like you too, my lord. So does Miss Davenport. Do you... do you think you might ask her to marry you, one day?"

Phinn's heart contracted. "I'm not... I'm not sure, Christopher." And that was the truth. Then he posed another question. It was something that had been niggling him for some time, like a wee burr in his shoe, but he hadn't been game enough to ask Christopher. "Why-why do you call your mama, Miss Davenport?"

"Because she asked me to," said the boy. "Because she's my governess. And Tom calls her Miss Davenport too. She said it would be easier for everyone if we just did that."

Phinn nodded. "I expect so." It probably didn't mean anything that "Miss Davenport" rolled so easily off the boy's tongue. As though he was used to calling his mother that. No doubt it hadn't been easy for the lad to keep up the pretense that his mama was only his cousin. The scandal associated with being an unwed mother was not easily forgiven by society. Phinn understood the need for secrecy.

But still... Phinn had never heard young Christopher call Mina Davenport "mama" even by accident.

As he drove Christopher, Tom, and Brutus back to Kinsale House, Phinn wondered if he should have a frank talk with Miss Davenport about his concerns and suspicions regarding Christopher's father and about Sir Bedivere Ponsonby. And that the boy had let slip that his late godmother had been someone named Lady Grenfell.

But what if his suspicions were baseless? Questioning Miss Davenport's integrity—trying to unearth her secrets— might upset the governess and cause her to withdraw. And Phinn didn't want to do that, upset her, especially if she *were* in some sort of strife. Tom wasn't the only one who needed to learn to trust those in his life. Phinn wanted Miss Davenport to be able to trust him too.

Perhaps, in a quiet moment, he could simply reinforce the idea that he would help and support her, no matter what.

Not just because he needed her help to transform him into an articulate gentleman. It was more than that. He *did* care for Mina Davenport. Rather a lot. A *dashed* lot.

No, a feckin' lot... which was probably far more than he should.

Chapter 25

*Concerning Euphemisms and Failed Cucumberfication;
Followed by a Reunion Wherein Some Much Needed
Advice Is Given...*

She had the entire afternoon off!

Mina couldn't quite believe it. In fact, she hadn't even had to ask Lord Kinsale. As soon as the marquess returned from Hyde Park with Christopher and Tom and Brutus, he sought her out in the schoolroom, where she'd been waiting for the boys.

"It occurred to me, Miss Davenport," he began, his eyes as soft as moss-green velvet, "that you've been wor-workin' for me for weeks and have gone above and beyond during that time. Yet you... yet you haven't had one minute to yourself. And given the fact you stayed up so late last night, helpin' me with Tom... and then spend-spendin' time with me... givin' you the rest of the day off is the least I can do."

Mina couldn't stop the blush that crept into her cheeks. "Spending time with me" was undoubtedly the hugest euphemism in the history of euphemisms for the "late night shenanigans" (as Frobisher had put it) that Mina had shared with her employer. Their "kissing lesson"—clearly another euphemism if Mina were completely honest with herself—might have been a once-only event, but she couldn't stop going over it in her mind. Locking it away in her heart—as she'd promised herself she would do—suddenly seemed like an impossible feat. Especially since Lord Kinsale was being so thoughtful and kind. *Again.*

He was the most amazing man in the entire world and she suddenly wished with all her foolish heart that she could be his. His Mina.

It appeared that she had fallen hopelessly in love with her employer and that any attempts to "cucumberfy" herself were bound to fail. Indeed, they'd failed miserably already.

"Thank you, my lord," she murmured, reminding herself that there were children present in the schoolroom; Christopher and Tom were presently sitting on the Turkish rug before the fire, playing with Christopher's recently returned set of toy soldiers. The children were her priority and her messy personal situation—or rather, her terribly inconvenient and totally unprofessional attachment to her employer—did not matter. "Your generous offer has actually come at an opportune time," she added. "My dear friend, Emmeline, the Duchess of St Lawrence, has arrived back in London and she has invited me to St Lawrence House to take tea. At three o'clock this afternoon in fact."

"Make sure you have as much cake as you like," said Lord Kinsale softly. "And . . . and do *not* feel guilty about it. Not-not one wee bit. As your employer, I insist."

Mina smiled. "I promise you that I will enjoy my cake with alacrity."

The marquess's smile warmed Mina all the way to the tips of her toes. "As you should."

Ack. You two are soppier than a syrup cake with extra syrup on top, complained Brutus, who was sitting on the window seat, watching them.

Well, don't watch or listen then, returned Mina, casting the pug a narrow look. *And what's wrong with syrup cake? I thought you liked cake.*

Sausages are better. Brutus sniffed the air. *Got any more in that pocket o' yours?*

Mina ignored his question and turned back to the marquess. "I should be back in time to supervise the boys' dinner."

Lord Kinsale's brow creased with a slight frown. "You have the whole day off, remember? That includes this evenin'. I'll make sure Mrs. Aldershot assigns a pair of maids of your choice to take care of Christopher and Tom in your absence."

"Thank you. But..." Mina drew a breath. "But won't you require me for another... another etiquette and elocution lesson tonight? I know it won't be long until you make your parliamentary speech."

"As much as I would enjoy that," said Lord Kinsale, "no. Not tonight. I have... I have other plans."

"Oh... Very well then." Mina's heart sank and she tried to ignore the feeling of disappointment tightening her chest. She knew that Lord Kinsale had seen his friend Lord Hartwell this morning in Hyde Park, so perhaps he'd been issued with an invitation to a high society soiree or ball or dinner party. Meeting Lord Kinsale's eyes, she forced a smile. "Whatever you do, I hope you have a wonderful time."

Lord Kinsale smiled back, his eyes gleaming. "I'm sure... I'm sure I will. Speakin' of plans, I did won-wonder if we might take Christopher and Tom to see the Great Ex-Exhibition at the Crystal Palace in the next day or two? It's clo-closin' next month, and neither Tom nor I have seen it yet."

Mina blinked in surprise. "You haven't? Oh, you must, my lord. It's truly amazing. I took Christopher several months ago and he loved it." And then her stomach rather than her heart sank as she contemplated how dangerous it would be to take Sir Bedivere's ward to such a well-attended event. The crowds inside and outside the Crystal Palace were always large. What if Cheavers and his men were there, watching and waiting? Or even the baronet himself paid a visit?

But then she reminded herself that Cheavers—from what

she'd overheard last night at Fitzwilliam House—had yet to employ the men needed to search for her and Christopher; it might take him a few days to organize that. He'd also said he would deploy them in various parks around London. So they would be spread quite thinly. Indeed, Lord Kinsale had just taken Christopher to Hyde Park and nothing untoward had occurred. As far as she knew.

Aside from all that, hadn't she taken the boys to various parks over the last few weeks without incident? Although, her senses had been on high alert and her heart had been in her mouth a great deal of the time. Especially after the close encounter with Sir Bedivere at Hatchards.

But it's not as though you are defenseless, Hermina Davenport.

You are a Parasol Academy governess.

She was equipped with spells and self-defense skills, and as the Parasol Academy clearly stated, she was prepared for anything (even if she wasn't quite as prim and proper as she used to be).

She certainly couldn't keep Christopher locked up and hidden away forever. That wasn't fair on the poor child either.

No, she would just have to trust that it would be difficult to pick out little Lord Fitzwilliam in a crowd. And if Sir Bedivere or one of his henchmen did, she would be able to deal with any threat effectively, just as she was trained to do.

Although, *she* might be easy to pick out. Cheavers apparently had a photograph of her. It was a pity she couldn't employ the *Glamify* spell again. But then she'd appear different to everyone, including Lord Kinsale. So that clearly wasn't an option.

Mina's apprehension must have shown on her face as Lord Kinsale said, "You-you look worried all of a sudden, Miss Davenport. If you'd prefer not to go . . ."

"Oh no." Mina smiled brightly. "It will be a marvelous excursion and I think we should go sooner rather than later. Tomorrow even, if that suits you, my lord."

"It does," said Lord Kinsale. "I shall secure tickets today."

"Huzzah!" cried Christopher.

"Wizard!" exclaimed Tom. "I mean, cor blimey!"

Brutus yapped three times and twirled around on the window seat. *I love Hyde Park. There are so many trees to cock a leg on. An' ducks an' pigeons an' squirrels to chase.*

The boys and the pug had clearly been eavesdropping. But Mina didn't mind. It was lovely to see everyone so happy.

She might be as tired as could be, but she was happy too. Despite all the terrible things that might happen, they hadn't yet. So she would embrace the here and now and all the wonderful, delightful things that filled her heart with so much joy. Like seeing the bright smiles on the faces of two orphaned children from very different worlds who'd become firm friends. Or the wicked glee dancing in a rumbustious pug's eyes. Or the boundless kindness of a nobleman who'd come from the humblest of beginnings and wanted to use the unexpected gift of his privilege to help those who weren't so fortunate.

She would embrace it all . . . even if she'd never have what her heart truly desired: an Irishman with shamrock-green eyes whose kisses were the most glorious thing she'd ever tasted.

"Governess alert! Governess alert!"

Mina laughed as the Duke of St Lawrence's pet raven, Horatio Ravenscar Esquire, greeted her in the grand entrance hall of St Lawrence House in Belgrave Square. She'd met him at Emmeline and Xavier's wedding in June and found that he was both personable and vastly entertaining.

It's so lovely to see you again, Horatio, she said via her mind as she handed her bonnet, cloak, gloves, and Parasol Academy umbrella (the afternoon had turned inclement) to a waiting footman. *I trust you had a wonderful time at the seaside.*

The raven spread his enormous wings, then soared from the chandelier above her head down to one of the carved newel posts at the foot of the townhouse's grand sweeping staircase. *The absolute best*, he declared. *Although it's good to be back in London.*

At that moment, there was a squeal of childish outrage followed by a shout, and then a girl cried, "Gadzooks, Bartholomew and Gareth! Don't you dare feed my monarch caterpillars to Aristotle! I have a hard enough time keeping Horatio away!"

When Mina looked up the staircase to the landing, it appeared that Xavier and Emmeline's oldest adopted child, ten-year-old Miss Harriet "Harry" Mason, was trying to wrest a glass jar from the clutches of one of her younger brothers— Mina thought it might be the middle sibling, Bartholomew. The youngest child, Gareth, who was holding a terrapin in his hands (perhaps the aforementioned Aristotle) looked on with an expression of bored resignation; it seemed as though he was used to this sort of thing and had little time for it.

Mina was suddenly grateful that Christopher and Tom hadn't yet had any disagreements that had descended into a bout of fisticuffs. She was just about to intervene when Emmeline appeared on the landing in a swirl of cornflower-blue skirts, the perfect foil for her flaming copper-red hair.

"Goodness gracious, Harry and Bartholomew," Emmeline said in a firm voice that contained the perfect blend of gentle admonishment and disappointment. "What are you thinking, behaving in this way? And look, we have a visitor!" She sent Mina a bright smile as she waved a hand at the entry hall. "It's my darling friend, Miss Davenport."

Bartholomew immediately relinquished his hold on the jar of caterpillars. "Sorry, Mama. Sorry, Miss Davenport," he said, looking shamefaced. "Sorry, Harry. It's just that Aristotle is hungry and Horatio"—he shot the raven a reproving look— "scarfed down all the mealy worms and crickets."

"Yes, my apologies, Miss Davenport," said Harry solemnly as she peered over the top of her spectacles. "And to you, Mama. But Bartholomew"—she addressed her brother—"there are plenty of insects and snails in the garden. Why ruin my biology project?"

"Bartholomew," said Emmeline gently, "Aristotle tells me that caterpillars give him indigestion. He much prefers snails and crickets."

So do I, said Horatio, ruffling his feathers. Emmeline must have heard the interjection too, as she sent the raven a small smile.

Turning back to Bartholomew she said, "Why don't you and Gareth take your terrapin out to the pond to keep Archimedes company? I'm sure he'll find plenty to eat on his own."

"Archimedes?" asked Mina as she approached the bottom of the stairs.

"That's my frog," said Harry. "He and Aristotle are the best of friends."

"All right," said Bartholomew with an exaggerated sigh. "Come on, Gareth. Let's go and find Archimedes."

"I believe it's still raining, so I'll send Miss Bellweather down to help you put on your mackintoshes and Wellington boots," Emmeline said as she began to descend the stairs. "Miss Bellweather is the children's new governess," she explained to Mina, "from the Parasol Academy. She just started today and is still settling in."

Mina smiled to herself. It sounded as though Miss Bellweather might have her hands full with Harry, Bartholomew, and Gareth. But then Emmeline had managed splendidly. She'd even won her employer's heart and found true love. Just like a fairy tale.

The boys trooped down the stairs, Horatio fluttering after them, to gain access to the townhouse's back garden while Harry disappeared with her rescued caterpillars.

Emmeline, as soon as she reached Mina's side, threw her arms around her in an enthusiastic hug. "My darling, darling Mina," she declared, pulling away and holding her at arm's length. Her bright blue eyes were glowing. "Just look at you, my friend. Three months is far too long to spend apart from each other."

"It is," agreed Mina, blinking rapidly to clear a sudden rush of unexpected tears. "Far too long. Especially because of your wonderful news." Her gaze dipped to her friend's waist and she squeezed her hands. "Congratulations to you and Xavier," she whispered so any staff lingering about the hall wouldn't overhear. "I'm so excited and happy that you two have a baby on the way to add to your beautiful family. I couldn't think of a more deserving set of parents."

"Thank you," returned Emmeline softly, her eyes misty with joy too. She quickly brushed away a stray tear that had slipped onto her freckled cheek before adding, "But come"—she hooked Mina's arm through hers and tugged her toward a grand set of double oak doors on one side of the entry hall where a pair of liveried footmen stood at attention—"let's talk privately in the drawing room where there's also afternoon tea waiting for us. Xavier's cook, Mrs. Punchbowl, has made a decadent chocolate cake and three kinds of petit fours for us to try."

"A cake *and* petit fours?" Mina laughed as they entered the opulently furnished drawing room, which was a study in soft green and cream and the warmth of gleaming wood. "Good heavens. I won't need dinner tonight."

"I firmly believe that one cannot live on tea and cucumber sandwiches alone," asserted Emmeline. "And don't worry if it's not all eaten." She gestured at the sumptuous spread—the enormous chocolate cake and several tiered, fine bone china cake stands laden with petit fours and delicate tarts and tiny choux buns and ribbon sandwiches—which had already been set out on a table before the fire along with a tea set. "Between Horatio and the children and the servants, it will be gone by this time tomorrow."

"Your husband won't partake in any of the feasting?" asked Mina as she settled herself into a striped silk shepherdess chair.

"Oh no," said Emmeline as she began to pour them cups of tea. "Darling Xavier is more of a black coffee and plain fare man." She grinned as she handed Mina a steaming cup made just the way she liked it. "Which leaves more cake and pudding for me. And this one." She patted her waist. "It's a good thing that Xavier doesn't mind that my waist is expanding at such a great rate of knots."

Mina laughed. "Of course he wouldn't. He's entirely besotted with you. And why wouldn't he be?"

Emmeline began slicing up the cake that was a magnificent, mouthwatering combination of chocolate sponge layered with mousse and raspberries. "Well, it's a good thing that the besottedness is mutual," she said with a soft smile. "I think being so in love is rather like this cake. It's rich and delicious and brimming with abundant joy. And untold fun," she added as she plated a perfect slice for Mina and handed it to her. "I never thought that marriage could be like this."

"I'm nothing but happy for you, Emmeline," said Mina. And she meant it. Emmeline's first, short-lived marriage to a ne'er-do-well playwright—a man who'd left her with nothing at all after his untimely death—had only brought her frustration and sorrow. But Xavier, the Duke of St Lawrence—who by all accounts had been an eccentric loner—had turned out to be the man of her dreams.

Emmeline chatted for a while about the family's extended sojourn at the seaside in Kent, and how thrilled Xavier had been to be awarded the commission for the enormous clock that would grace the top of St Stephen's Tower at the new Palace of Westminster. "He's actually meeting with the Astronomer Royal at Greenwich as we speak," said Emmeline proudly. "I cannot wait to hear when the construction of the clock will commence. Hopefully soon."

Naturally, the conversation turned to Mina's newest position, working for the Marquess of Kinsale. Emmeline had met the Irish nobleman once before, albeit briefly, only a few days before she married Xavier. "He seems like a lovely man," she said. "And it was such a shame that he couldn't attend our wedding. I understand he had pressing business at his estate in Ireland. Xavier certainly speaks very highly of him. But, I must say"—Emmeline cast a quizzical look Mina's way—"I didn't know that he had a ward. Neither did Xavier."

Mina put down her overflowing plate of afternoon tea treats; she'd suddenly lost her appetite. Indeed, it seemed like now was the time to confess all to her friend about her pickliest of pickly situations.

So she did. Mina drew a deep breath and poured everything out to Emmeline. She told her about little Lord Fitzwilliam and Lady Grenfell's prophetic dream and Mina's deathbed promise to the dowager countess that she'd protect her godson "no matter what." And about Sir Bedivere Ponsonby and his ensorcelled ring and how he wanted to spirit his ward off to the Arctic. She told Emmeline about her suspicions that the baronet was being controlled by Evil Queen Mab—and that for some unfathomable reason, the Fae queen wanted Christopher. And of course, how Mina, for all intents and purposes under the eyes of the law, had kidnapped the boy off the *Valiant* and that her teleportation attempt had gone horribly awry, so she'd ended up on Lord Kinsale's ship. But more than that, Lord Kinsale believed Christopher was her son and that she was an unwed mother.

While Mina had also confessed that the marquess had ostensibly hired her to teach Tom Fleet, a pickpocket from the streets, he'd really, secretly wanted her to help him with his stammer and to give him etiquette lessons. Which she'd been doing, all the while keeping up the pretense that Christopher was hers. And that she felt horrible about it and was as guilt-ridden as could be.

She didn't dare own up to the fact that in the early hours of the morning, she and Lord Kinsale had kissed. Not yet, at least. Emmeline had enough to grapple with.

Emmeline, of course, listened carefully throughout, only stopping Mina every now and again to ask a pertinent question or two. She was particularly interested to learn that the Fae had provided Mina with a previously unheard-of *Glamify* spell on two occasions.

When Mina finished recounting her troubles, she released a huge sigh. "It's all such a huge mess, Emmeline, and I don't quite know what to do. About any of it. Especially now that Sir Bedivere is back in London and doubling his efforts to locate young Christopher. And... and I'm so sorry that I've just burdened you with my tale of woe. To be perfectly honest, if you showed me the door, or contacted Scotland Yard or even Mrs. Temple to report my misconduct, I wouldn't blame you in the slightest."

Emmeline snorted. "What nonsense. As if I'd ever abandon my very best friend—a good person and brilliant governess with the noblest of intentions—in a time of great need." She suddenly reached out across the small space between their shepherdess chairs, took one of Mina's hands, and gave it a reassuring squeeze. "You certainly have landed yourself in the middle of a right royal pickle though," she said.

"So"—Mina released another shaky sigh—"what should I do now? Lord Kinsale and I are taking Christopher and Tom to the Great Exhibition tomorrow. But what if Sir Bedivere is out and about? Or Cheavers and one of his minions?"

Emmeline frowned. "In my opinion, the worst thing you can do is act like anything is amiss. You'll raise the marquess's suspicions that something *is* wrong if you go to ground. Besides, Sir Bedivere, whether he's wearing an ensorcelled ring or not, can't be everywhere at once. If he *did* visit Hyde Park it would probably be for an early morning ride. And nothing happened today when Lord Kinsale took Christopher and Tom for a jaunt about the Park, did it?"

"Not as far as I know," said Mina.

"The truth is," continued Emmeline, "you could run into Sir Bedivere, or this Cheavers chap or his men, anywhere. Even though you spotted the baronet outside Hatchards, he didn't notice you or his ward. He's really searching for two very small needles in an impossibly large haystack if you really think about it."

"The fact that he *didn't* see us is probably down to luck more than anything else," said Mina dolefully.

"Perhaps," said Emmeline. Her expression grew thoughtful. "When you go to the Great Exhibition, I suggest you wear your Parasol Academy coalscuttle bonnet—the brim is nice and deep—and shield your face with your Parasol Academy umbrella or parasol as much as you can. And maybe sport some 'against regulation curls.' If you have an abundance of ringlets festooned about your temples and cheeks, it will help to obscure your face. My lady's maid can show you how to style them with a heated curling tong or curling papers, if you like. Oh, and throw a shawl over your uniform to hide the distinctive frogging on the bodice."

"All wonderful ideas," said Mina. "I'll make sure Christopher wears a wide-brimmed hat again. And that he doesn't bring his purple velvet rabbit along. Cheavers and his men will be on the lookout for it, I'm sure of it. I suppose that's the best I can do."

Emmeline agreed. "I'm still intrigued by this *Glamify* potion that mysteriously manifested in your uniform pocket when you needed it," she said. "And on two occasions. It seems to me that the Fae *are* on your side. Why else would they have sent you such a unique magical tool? I do think you should confide in Mrs. Temple. And soon. You might be surprised by her reaction. Your concerns about young Lord Fitzwilliam's safety are valid. Surely she wouldn't condemn you for doing your utmost to protect the boy."

"Perhaps," said Mina. She wished she could be sure. She picked up her discarded plate and nibbled at a tiny strawberry tart. It immediately brought to mind the Victoria sponge that she and Lord Kinsale had feasted on last night, and her cheeks grew as warm as the fire burning in the nearby grate.

"You know, it always amazes me that our magical pockets do seem to know what we need so that we might discharge our duties effectively," she said when she'd finished the tart. "For instance, an elocution book, entitled *The Governess's Guide to Fluent Speech Instruction,* materialized in my pocket the very first time I planned on conducting a lesson for Lord Kinsale. I hadn't asked for it. It . . . it just appeared. And it has been most helpful. Lord Kinsale's stammer is hardly noticeable now. Especially after ki—"

Oops. Mina clamped her lips shut to stop herself saying the quiet bit out loud. With her linen napkin, she dabbed the corner of her mouth. Would it be wicked of her to suggest that she and Lord Kinsale kiss again tonight, just to see if kissing really *was* a "treatment strategy" that facilitated fluent speech?

But he has other plans, remember?

Mina swallowed her maudlin sigh along with a sip of tea.

Emmeline reached out and touched her hand again. "You're in love with him, aren't you?" she said softly. "Your Lord Kinsale."

Mina couldn't stop the tide of heat that flooded into her cheeks. Nor could she hide the truth from her best friend. "How-how did you know?" she murmured.

Emmeline smiled gently. "It's obvious, my darling Mina.

There's a certain look in your eyes whenever you talk about him. A particular wistful warmth in your smile. Do you ... do you think he's in love with you too?"

Mina did let her sigh escape this time. "To be perfectly honest, I'm not sure. It's true we've spent a great deal of time together, alone at night as I've helped Lord Kinsale with his speech and to master all things 'manners.' We've both asserted we're friends. But..." She met Emmeline's compassionate gaze. "But last night, we kissed. It was actually my first kiss. With anyone."

To Mina's surprise, Emmeline squealed and clapped her hands together. "I knew it. I knew it," she exclaimed, her eyes dancing with unconcealed delight. "How was it? Was it wonderful? Lord Kinsale is so very handsome in a rough and rugged sort of way, so I'm sure he must be very good at kissing. And you so deserve a first kiss that's lovely."

Mina couldn't help but laugh at her friend's exuberant reaction. "It *was* wonderful," she admitted. "But we both decided that it must be a once-only event."

Emmeline threw her an incredulous look. "Whyever would you make a decision like that? If you love him, and you suspect his feelings align with yours, how could one kiss be enough? For either of you?"

"I know. I know. It does sound idiotic when you put it that way," said Mina. "But I can't ignore the fact that I've deceived the poor man. The whole time I've been under his roof, working for him, cultivating a rapport with him, helping him with his stammer and giving him etiquette lessons, I've been living a complete lie. I-I want to be honest with him, more than anything, but I simply can't. How can I tell him the truth about how Christopher and I came to be on the *Kinsale Cloud*? Because if I do, then I'd have to divulge the Parasol Academy's sacrosanct secrets. And you know as well as I do that revealing the Academy's association with the Fae might anger them. And then the Academy will lose their Fae charter and Parasol nannies and governesses won't be able to use magic anymore. Children everywhere will be less safe. There's so much more at stake than my feelings and Lord Kinsale's."

Compassion and understanding lit Emmeline's eyes. "If you went to Mrs. Temple though, if you explained that you and the marquess are in love, she might grant special dispensation for Lord Kinsale to learn about the Parasol Academy's secrets. Because of the exceptional circumstances you've found yourself in." Her mouth quirked with a smile. "Stranger things have happened. Indeed, I've come to learn that the Fae sometimes move in mysterious ways and that happy-ever-afters *are* entirely possible. But to arrive at that place, sometimes we must make difficult decisions and take chances. We must risk all for what we believe in. Because in the end, it might just be worth it."

Mina knew Emmeline was alluding to her own situation. Of course, it had all worked out. She'd found true love with her duke. Her only real "crime" in the eyes of the Fae had been to use magic in front of her employer, and that had been forgiven due to "exceptional circumstances." But Emmeline had never stolen a child away from their legal guardian and then told endless untruths to cover it up. "As I said, I'll think about confiding in Mrs. Temple," she said.

Emmeline nodded, seemingly satisfied with Mina's response. And then the subject was dropped entirely as Xavier, the Duke of St Lawrence himself, walked in.

As soon as Emmeline's husband entered the room, he commanded attention. Attired almost completely in black, he was tall and lean with sharply cut features and an abundance of unruly raven-black hair. When his frost-blue eyes locked with Emmeline's, his wide mouth, which seemed habitually set in an uncompromising line, lifted into a warm smile. A moment later, his penetrating gaze settled on Mina, who'd risen to her feet to curtsy, but he waved her back down with a gloved hand. "Miss Davenport, I assure you there's no need for such formalities," he said in his rich deep voice. "Any friend of my wife's is a friend of mine."

My wife. Those two simple words sent an unexpected quiver of envy through Mina. Not because she coveted her friend's husband. Far from it.

Xavier was undoubtedly a delightful man, but it was in that moment that Mina realized that she wanted a husband too. And not just any man. She wanted Phineas O'Connell, the Marquess of Kinsale. She wanted a blissful happy-ever-after with the man she'd fallen head over heels in love with. She wanted a family—children—with him. She wanted to grow old with him.

She wanted it all.

She loved being a governess, but in her heart of hearts, she knew it would never be enough to satisfy her. The problem was, Mina wasn't sure if the things she truly desired would ever be attainable. It was like longing for the pot of gold at the end of a rainbow—she could yearn for it all she liked, but securing such a precious gift seemed like an impossible feat.

At some point, Lord Kinsale would find out how deceitful she'd been. And when he looked at her and the soft light in his green eyes faded—as it undoubtedly would—she didn't think she would be able to bear it.

Chapter 26

In Which Another Invitation Arrives; And Mysterious Ways, Waltzing, and Flying Figs Are Featured...

When Mina arrived back at Kinsale House, it was to discover that her presence was required by the marquess after all. But not in the way she'd expected.

When she entered her bedroom at a quarter past six, she found a piece of parchment pushed beneath her door. In fact, it was the Marquess of Kinsale's personal stationery. And written on that stationery was the following:

Miss Hermina Davenport,
The Marquess of Kinsale cordially invites you to a soirée.
Where: The Kinsale House ballroom
Dress: Your favorite gown (Though, I'm rather hoping it isn't your Parasol Academy uniform.)
Time: 7:00 p.m. sharp
RSVP: Not required, but I do hope you will attend.
Yours faithfully,
Kinsale

A soirée?
What on earth did Lord Kinsale *mean* by that?

Mina worried at her lower lip, even as her heart did an excited little jig. Perhaps . . . perhaps the marquess wanted to practice speaking without stammering in front of a larger audience than just one unremarkable governess.

But then, why ask her to attend at all? Of course, he might simply need a friendly face in the crowd.

Odd though, that she hadn't observed an increased level of activity when she'd arrived back at the house. There weren't servants or footmen rushing about in a mad flap, ensuring that everything was extra neat and tidy. She hadn't noticed any extravagant flower arrangements or other decorations in the entry hall or musicians arriving to provide entertainment. But then, it might only be a small affair.

A "welcome back to London" dinner perhaps, for the Duke and Duchess of St Lawrence? Surely Emmeline would have said something though.

It was all quite a mystery.

As for gowns—favorite or otherwise—that weren't Parasol Academy issued... Mina frowned as she sorted through the meager contents of her wardrobe. She had three dresses to choose from, and to be perfectly frank, they were all rather ordinary except for one.

It was a very pretty, entirely frivolous gown of pale lemon silk covered in a pattern of tiny pink roses and spring-green leaves. Frothy white lace adorned the *en coeur* neckline and cascaded from the three-quarter-length sleeves—it was the sort of dress one might wear to a country dance or perhaps even an afternoon tea with a duchess. Mina's mother and sister had made it for her—it must have been a labor of love considering the voluminous skirts and the intricate needlework. Mina had worn it but once—to Emmeline and Xavier's wedding in fact, and it seemed a shame not to wear it again. And if there were any guests at Lord Kinsale's soiree who'd also been in attendance at the Duke and Duchess of St Lawrence's wedding, so be it. Mina wasn't wealthy and it was the best she could do at short notice.

Although, it was fortuitous that Emmeline's lady's maid had expertly arranged Mina's hair into a becoming coiled braid at the back of her head while her face was tastefully framed by two small bunches of ringlets. It wasn't Mina's usual "look" by any means—and certainly not "regulation" as per the *Parasol Academy Handbook*'s uniform guidelines. But the style was eye-catching all the same and Mina thought it rather fetching.

It didn't take her too long to attend to her toilette and change into her lemon-and-rose-patterned gown and matching silk pumps. But when Mina looked at herself in the looking glass above her dressing table, her cheeks turned a bright shade of pink. She'd forgotten how much of her flesh was displayed by the heart-shaped neckline. Her shoulders were exposed and so was her ample cleavage. (Good heavens, sometimes she really did wish that her breasts weren't quite so . . . so plump.)

Perhaps she should wear a shawl. And then Mina looked herself in the eye and told herself to stop being such a prudish miss. Her mother had had a hand in creating this gown and she was as conservative as could be. (Although, *she* was the one who'd reminded Mina about *Jane Eyre* when they'd been discussing Lord Kinsale's marital status.)

Pushing all thoughts of governesses who married their employers to the very back of the broom cupboard in her mind (where they belonged), Mina dabbed a tiny bit of rose-and-jasmine-scented eau de cologne behind her ears and on her wrists (because one *ought* to smell nice when attending a soirée). When she glanced at the mantel clock, it was ten minutes to seven.

What to do, what to do for ten minutes?

Mina crossed to her bedside table and retrieved *The Governess's Guide to Fluent Speech Instruction* from the top drawer. Perhaps she could have a quick look through the section on "Exercises for Reducing Tension in the Oral Musculature." Because surely there wouldn't be anything about kissing as being a legitimate "exercise" to promote stammer-free speech.

But there was!

There really was!

Mina's mouth dropped open as she read: *Exercises that involve light lip pursing or puckering, or even soft sucking movements and gentle tongue thrusting—such as mouth-to-mouth kissing between consenting adults—may prove useful for some individuals who stammer. While positive results—that is, reduced moments of stuttered speech—may be quite marked initially, the effect might only be temporary. Nevertheless, it is a therapeutic technique worth trying (especially since such an activity is undoubtedly pleasurable. Any activity that cultivates feelings of well-being should never be dismissed).*

Mina had been through this guidebook from cover to cover—pored over its pages, in fact, as she'd devised novel treatment sessions to help Lord Kinsale manage his stammering—and she was absolutely certain that she'd never read this piece of advice until now.

It was almost as though the guidebook was giving her permission to kiss Lord Kinsale.

It was, without a doubt, an astonishing turnup for the books. Or in this particular case, a guidebook that had magically turned up in the pocket of her governess's uniform.

When Mina quit her bedroom a short time later, she'd decided that if the marquess wanted to kiss her again, she had a perfectly legitimate reason to say yes.

Who was she to question any advice provided by the Fae? Perhaps Emmeline was right and they did move in mysterious ways.

"She's on 'er way, milord," Tom whispered dramatically over his shoulder to Phinn. "She's almost at the bottom of the stairs." The boy was filling the role of lookout, peering out a narrow crack between the ballroom doors into the hallway beyond.

Phinn gave a nod. "Thank you, lad," and then Tom scampered across the polished floor to join him and Christopher and Brutus beneath the gas chandelier in the center of the dance floor.

Was it stuffy in the ballroom? Or was he just overthinking things? *Sweet Jaysus*, Phinn prayed he hadn't started to sweat.

He ran a finger around the inside of his stiffly starched collar, then tugged at the cuffs of his snugly fitting evening jacket of fine black wool that his new tailor—the one recommended by Frobisher—had recently created for him. His entire body—every muscle, every tendon—was taut with nervous energy while his blood thrummed with sweet anticipation.

He'd engineered this "soiree" tonight for several reasons. He wanted Tom and Christopher to attend an occasion akin to a family dinner, to make them both feel truly welcome and at home at Kinsale House.

He wanted to waltz with Miss Davenport—or at least *try* to waltz. Feck, he'd be happy to shuffle about the floor with the woman.

Most of all, he wanted to spoil the governess. To make her feel valued. To show her how much he appreciated all the wonderful things she'd done for him and for Tom. And for being a wonderful mother to Christopher.

In honor of the occasion, Christopher and Tom had both donned their best clothes—white cambric shirts and neckties, silk waistcoats and velvet jackets, knickerbocker trousers, fine wool stockings, and polished patent leather shoes. At Phinn's suggestion, Frobisher had trimmed Tom's shaggy mane of sandy hair into something approaching respectable. The boy had been reluctant to undergo a haircut at first, but he eventually agreed when Christopher admitted he'd recently had one and he now much preferred shorter locks.

Even Brutus had allowed one of the footmen to bathe him and dress him up for the evening. He sat at Phinn's feet, sporting a sky-blue bow around his stocky neck—Frobisher had agreed to sacrifice one of Phinn's neckties to the cause.

"Right, everyone. Are . . . are we ready?" murmured Phinn. The boys nodded, Brutus wagged his curly tail, and Frobisher, who sat at the pianoforte—Phinn had recently learned that the valet was quite the pianist—placed his fingers on the keys, ready to play.

And then a moment later, the two attendant footmen swung the doors wide and Miss Davenport appeared.

She hovered on the threshold, suspended in perfect stillness for a second or two. Then her hands flew to her glowing cheeks as she released a surprised gasp. Her bright hazel gaze danced over the ballroom that had been transformed into something that Phinn imagined might resemble a fairy bower. At least, that had been his intention.

His punching bag and any other exercise paraphernalia had been removed. Instead, hothouse flowers spilled from enormous vases that graced the tops of marble pedestals placed at regular intervals around the room. The window pelmets and crystal chandelier were festooned with ivy and fragrant roses and blooms Phinn really didn't know the name of.

Even the floor—all of it from wall to wall—had been chalked with an intricate floral design by professional "chalkers" (Phinn had had no idea such a job existed, but Frobisher had insisted it was necessary). While Smedley and Mrs. Aldershot had complained that the chalk dust would be almost impossible to remove from the cracks in the floorboards, Frobisher had declared that it was the height of sophistication to have a ballroom floor decorated in such a fashion. It was definitely a must-have for a soirée.

Phinn was frozen too as he took in the wonder of Miss Hermina Davenport in a pretty rose-patterned gown—a gown that displayed a surprising amount of her glorious cleavage. If he were a perfect gentleman, he wouldn't have let his attention drift to the twin smooth-as-cream mounds rising above the froth of white lace at the bodice's sweeping neckline. But he wasn't perfect—he was a man who was utterly entranced by a chestnut-haired siren whose hazel-hued eyes he'd quite happily drown in.

"Lord Kinsale," Miss Davenport breathed at last. Her gaze met his across the room. "This . . . this is magnificent. You've turned the ballroom into a-a garden. It's-it's beautiful."

Not as beautiful as you. The words hovered on the tip of Phinn's tongue, but he didn't let them loose. Not because he was stuck in a moment of stammering. He was simply aware that there were two children, his valet, a pair of footmen, not to mention his dog, all watching them.

Aloud he said, "As you know, Miss Davenport, I'm not one for entertainin' much. Well, not at all if I'm bein' perfectly honest. But it seems a . . . seems a shame not to use this room for its intended pur-purpose. I know it's technically still your . . . your day off, but"—Phinn drew a calming breath to quell the sudden rush of tightness in his chest—"I was hopin' you might agree to dance with me." He grinned. "O' course I don't know how to waltz—at least not yet—but if you wouldn't mind shufflin' around the floor with me, I might be able to manage that without steppin' on your toes. Just for the fun o' it . . . Before dinner . . . ?"

When Miss Davenport didn't say anything, Phinn gestured toward the pianoforte. "Frobisher"—the valet sent the governess a little finger wave—"has agreed to play for us."

Miss Davenport stared at Phinn for a moment longer and then her lovely mouth lifted into a smile that made Phinn's heart caper as though he'd already begun to dance. "My goodness. I'm fairly flabbergasted, my lord. So please forgive my momentary inability to form a coherent response. And of course I'd love to dance with you." Turning to the boys she said, "Tom and Christopher, you can help us stay in time if you like. Clap your hands, or stamp your feet, or skip about in time with the beat of the music. That way Lord Kinsale and I are less likely to misstep. And Brutus"—she sent the pug a warning look—"you may also bounce around the room however you like, but promise me you won't get under our feet. We don't want anyone to end up with a sprained ankle or worse."

To Phinn's surprise, the dog gave a yip as if he'd understood Miss Davenport perfectly and had quite happily agreed to comply with her direction.

Miss Davenport laughed, then looked at Frobisher. "Do you know Schumann's 'Of Foreign Lands and Peoples'? It's quite slow and lyrical." After Frobisher replied that yes, he did, she caught Phinn's gaze. "I think it will be the right tempo to shuffle to. Or at the very least sway."

Phinn chuckled. "You . . . you think I'm really going to be that bad?"

She shrugged a half-bared shoulder and her eyes sparkled. "My lord, you're the one who keeps telling me that you cannot dance and that you're afraid you'll stand on my toes."

Phinn winced. "I'll do my best not to."

Miss Davenport moved closer, and Phinn slid one hand around her waist, his palm resting lightly upon her back. He could feel the stiff bones of her corset against his splayed fingers and he silently cursed all women's underthings to Hades. As he enfolded Miss Davenport's right hand in his, she curled her other hand about his shoulder and he couldn't suppress a surge of intense longing.

His natural instinct was to pull the beguiling governess into his arms, as close as could be, but decorum required they keep a little distance between their bodies. Just as decorum required him *not* to ogle her impressive décolletage. Which was no mean feat given the fact the pace of Miss Davenport's breathing had increased even though they hadn't begun to dance. In fact, her breasts were rising and falling in the most delightful but distracting way. Perhaps he wasn't the only one affected by their close physical proximity.

And then Frobisher began to play the piano and Miss Davenport began to sway from side to side, as elegant as could be, with her skirts gently undulating with her movements, Phinn following her as best he could. They swayed on the spot for a minute, and then she began to lead him in a small circle beneath the chandelier. "Right, left. Step to the side. Right, left. Step to the side," she gently instructed. She smiled into his eyes. "That's it, my lord. We'll have you waltzing in no time."

"I'm afraid I'm-I'm as stiff as a board," he mumbled.

"Only a little," she said. "You need to become looser in the hips. Imagine you're dancing about a boxing ring, evading punches. Try to step lightly, bend your knees a fraction, and rock your hips from side to side. Like me."

Gah. Miss Davenport talking about the rocking of hips, both his and hers, was not helping Phinn relax. If anything, he might even be growing stiffer. Then he sternly reminded himself that he and Miss Davenport were not alone.

Indeed, the boys were arm in arm, laughing and skipping merrily about the room raising small clouds of chalk dust, while Brutus was madly racing in circles around the perimeter of the ballroom as though he were chasing an imaginary rabbit. Surely the pug was growing giddy.

Although, Phinn would own that he was already a trifle giddy. His head was awhirl with strong feelings that were all centered around the gorgeous woman in his arms. Aside from desire and the overwhelming urge to protect Mina Davenport from all things hurtful, there was admiration and an achingly sweet tenderness blooming inside his chest that was more than just a fond regard. It was a warmth, a yearning, and a light buoyant sensation that was even more uplifting than the bright melody floating about them. It was . . . it was joy.

It felt right.

He studied Miss Davenport's lovely countenance. "You've arranged your hair diff-differently," he observed softly. "I-I like it."

"You do?" she said, her cheeks pinkening to the same rosy hue as the blooms on her gown. "I thought it might be too much. It's certainly not a regulation Parasol Academy style. Plain, simple, and practical is what I'm used to."

"It's your day off," said Phinn firmly. "You should be able to dress how-however you like. Do whatever you like." God, he hoped that kissing him might be on the list of things she liked. After they'd finished dancing and had partaken of dinner, after Tom and Christopher had gone to bed, he wondered if Miss Davenport might permit him to kiss her again. Not just to see if kissing helped lessen his stammering, but because he very much wanted to.

No, he *needed* to kiss Mina Davenport. He especially wanted to learn that this deep longing inside him wasn't one-sided. It was probably "against Parasol Academy regulations," but right now he didn't give a flying fig about the Academy's rules.

More than anything, he rather hoped Miss Davenport didn't give a flying fig either. He supposed he would soon find out.

CHAPTER 27

*In Which a Post-Prandial Experiment Is Conducted;
Sweet Dreams (of a Thoroughly Scandalous Nature) Are
Encouraged; And a Decision Is Reached . . .*

After Mina had tucked Christopher into bed and he'd begun to drift asleep, she cast the Guardia Nimbus spell. Despite the ever-present threat Sir Bedivere presented—despite her persistent misgivings about what might happen on the morrow when she took the child to see the Great Exhibition—Mina was humming with quiet contentment. She didn't think that she'd had a more wondrous day in her entire life. It had been filled with bright and unexpected pockets of pure delight. And all thanks to Lord Kinsale.

Her heart was trembling with delightful anticipation—indeed it was as fluttery as a swarm of magical *Guardia Nimbus* butterflies—as she quit Christopher's bedroom. She couldn't wait to see what the rest of the night would bring. Or more specifically, what Lord Kinsale might have in store for her.

He'd gone out of his way to spoil her completely and she didn't know what to make of that. It hadn't just been her, though. Lord Kinsale had spoiled the boys too.

After the dancing had concluded in the ballroom—and hadn't she felt so very special, being held in the marquess's arms as they gently swayed around the exquisitely decorated floor?—Lord Kinsale had ushered her, the boys, and Brutus into the dining room where a sumptuous feast awaited them. They'd all been seated at one end of the vast dining table—even Brutus had his own chair that was piled up with several cushions so he could reach his plate—when several footmen began to bring in platter after platter of delicious treats.

Lord Kinsale had declared it was a dinner to welcome Tom and Christopher to Kinsale House, and to thank Miss Davenport for all her tireless work helping him and the boys, and Mina was nothing but touched. The marquess, in her absence, had asked Tom and Christopher to choose their favorite dishes for dinner, and it seemed Mrs. Dunkley had outdone herself. There were platters of beef and pork sausages, a roast chicken, and jugs of rich onion gravy (all of which pleased Brutus). A large bowl piled high with colcannon—an Irish dish that consisted of creamy mashed potato that had bacon, buttery cabbage, and leeks folded through it. There was another bowl brimming with crispy duck-fat roasted potatoes and a loaf of fresh sourdough bread to soak up the gravy. And last but not least, not one but two puddings to choose from. A delicious sticky toffee pudding and a decadent trifle—sponge fingers were layered with custard, whipped cream, raspberry jelly, poached peaches, and sprinkled with toasted almond slivers.

To drink, there was lemonade and ginger beer for the boys and champagne for Lord Kinsale and Mina.

By the end of dinner, Mina was sure the hook-and-eye fastenings of her corset might burst. Fortunately, once the feasting was done, they all repaired to the drawing room for an hour of rousing parlor games. "Squeak, piggy, squeak" and "duck, duck, goose," and "Simon says" had them all laughing fit to burst as well. However, by nine o'clock both Tom and Christopher were beginning to yawn, so Mina declared it was bedtime. While one of the footmen took Brutus up to Lord Kinsale's suite, Lord

Kinsale read the boys a story. Then he helped Mina tuck Tom and Christopher into bed before he invited her to meet him in the library. Just to talk.

"Only . . . only if you want to," he said in a voice that was both warm and soft once they'd retreated to the hallway outside the boys' bedrooms. "I know you must be exhausted after last night. And-and tomorrow will be another busy day given we're ta-taking the boys to see the Great Exhibition."

Mina bit her lip. It was true that she was exhausted. But the marquess had given her the most magical day. She really didn't want to refuse such a simple request.

And she also wanted to share with the marquess what she'd come across in her little green elocution book about kissing exercises. But they couldn't discuss such a thing out in the hall right by the boys' bedrooms. And it wasn't as though she could invite the marquess into her bedroom. And the idea of using the schoolroom to discuss kissing felt odd too.

On an impulse, she reached out and touched Lord Kinsale's forearm. "I do wish to . . . to talk," she said. "But not in the library. I have somewhere closer in mind. Somewhere private."

The marquess's eyes gleamed with interest. "You know I'm more than ha-happy to put meself in your very capable hands, Miss Davenport."

There was a small, rarely used parlor—a music room of sorts—just opposite the schoolroom. Once a pair of gas lamps had been lit, their soft golden glow revealed an old upright pianoforte against one wall, a glass-fronted bookcase that was full of old sheet music, a bare fireplace, and a small sofa upholstered in the same burgundy damask that hung at the windows.

"So, Miss Davenport"—Lord Kinsale's wide mouth stretched into a slow smile as Mina closed the door—"what-what shall we talk about now we're alone?"

He was lounging against the closed lid of the piano, his arms folded over his impressive chest, all studied nonchalance. But

Mina could sense a change in him, that beneath his relaxed veneer, he was ever so slightly on edge. Like a hungry beast waiting to spring into action.

A delicious shiver passed over her as she dared to move closer. "I think we both know what we came here to discuss," she said softly.

Lord Kinsale reached out and touched one of the ringlets framing her face. "The kiss... the kiss we shared last night, perhaps? And its... its effect on my speech?"

"Yes," said Mina. And then she shared what she'd read in her guidebook about the therapeutic benefits of kissing—how it relaxed the oral musculature which then facilitated smoother speech. "So you see, we really should kiss again tonight. To see if we can replicate the same results. And perhaps we can measure how long the positive effect lasts."

Lord Kinsale's mouth tilted into a roguish smile. The exact sort of smile that made Mina's heart race. "Well, I'm game if you are, Miss Davenport," he murmured, his voice a warm purr that seemed to stroke along her spine. "Or... or may I call you... may I call you Mina?"

Mina's cheeks warmed. "I'd love it if you called me that."

Lord Kinsale raised a hand and his fingertips lightly traced a path down the side of her face. His thumb brushed over her fevered cheek. "Mina, I'd love... I'd love it if you'd call me Phinn. Because I've been Phineas O'Connell for a lot long-longer than I've been Lord Kinsale."

"Are you sure?" she whispered. It seemed so very intimate, breaking another one of society's rules. *But what could be more intimate than kissing?* she reminded herself. She really needed to stop being so prim and proper.

The marquess's eyes locked with hers. "Mina, the only thing that I'm *more* certain about in this particular mo-moment is my overwhelmin' need to kiss you."

"Then, Phinn," Mina murmured huskily as she slid her hands around Lord Kinsale's neck, "you most definitely should."

And he did. He pulled Mina in, lowered his head, and covered her mouth with his.

Oh yes. Yes, yes, yes. How silly she'd been to think that just one kiss with Lord Kinsale would ever be enough.

This kiss was everything a second kiss should be and more. Unlike last night's sweetly tempered lesson when Lord Kinsale—Phinn—had been focused on gently showing her what to do—this kiss was hungrier. A little wilder. A little more passionate. And Mina loved it.

Lord Kinsale's mouth moved against hers with assuredness. With purpose.

This kiss felt possessive. Like a claiming. The slide of his lips was firm yet languid. His tongue delved and stroked and teased deeply, each slick caress bolder than the last. It seemed as though he was determined to stoke her desire. To teach her all about pleasure. And Mina welcomed it all. Unlike last night, she wasn't timid in her responses. Her lips, her tongue, knew what to do. Her body knew what it wanted.

She wanted him. She wanted *everything*.

Glorious heat rushed through her veins. Desire gently pulsed and throbbed in all her secret places. Her breasts, between her thighs. And her hands, they seemed to have a mind of their own. They began to explore Lord Kinsale's—Phinn's—beautifully strong body. She brazenly reached beneath his evening jacket, her fingers seeking his hardness and furnace-like heat.

Yes, Phineas O'Connell, the Irishman, was intriguingly lean and hard and hot everywhere she was soft and rounded and yielding. And his masculine scent—a delicious blend of fresh things like wintergreen and pine needles combined with the heady richness of leather and musk—invaded her senses, making her burn and melt.

Lord Kinsale's hands began to roam over her body too. The hand that had so tenderly framed her face slid to the exposed flesh of her shoulder and he gently pushed her sleeve down farther, baring her upper arm. His mouth followed, raining a path of hot yet velvet-soft kisses down her neck to her shoulder. He laved the spot where her pulse fluttered beneath her ear before his lips grazed along her collarbone. When his tongue brazenly flickered into the deep valley of her cleavage, Mina moaned and clutched at his shoulders. Her breasts felt heavy. Her nipples ached, the taut tips straining against her corset. Her inner thighs were slick, her lower belly liquid with wanton, wicked, wonderful desire.

What was this man doing to her?

She'd never felt like this before. So needy and wanting and so out of control. Her head was spinning, her body was pulsing, aching, yearning for . . . for things a Parasol Academy governess shouldn't want. If she ever needed a *Cucumberfy* spell, the time was right now.

"Mina." Phinn groaned her name. He sounded desperate and needy too. Indeed, as one of his hands grasped her bottom and pulled her hips against his, she couldn't fail to notice how affected he was. Even through the layers of her crinoline skirts she could *feel* him. His body was hard and stiff *everywhere*.

Mina loved that she'd inflamed this man's passion to blazing proportions. Her ardent kisses, her body's enthusiastic responses, her own desire were clearly feeding his.

But somewhere at the back of her brain, her sensible side was whispering, urging her to take care. She should stop this amorous encounter before it went any further. Before they both caught fire and went up in flames. And surely they'd achieved what they'd set out to do.

They'd kissed. Now they needed to see if said kissing had had the desired effect on the marquess's speech.

Phinn—Lord Kinsale—seemed to be of the same mind too. He dragged his lips along hers one last time, then his shoulders rose and fell with a heavy sigh. "We should probably stop here, Mina. The last thing I want to do is take advantage of you. I would never try to coax you into doin' things that you'll regret. Things that have lastin' consequences. Things that would hurt you. You don't need that from me or any man. It wouldn't be fair or right."

Mina nodded and smoothed his rumpled hair away from his furrowed brow. Guilt squeezed her chest because she couldn't correct his erroneous belief that she was an unwed mother.

"You're right," she said softly, notes of remorse and melancholy creeping into her voice. "We should stop before this leads us into territory that's even more dangerous and forbidden than kissing. At least for someone like me."

He gathered her hands and pressed them against his chest, where his heart lay. Indeed, Mina could feel it beating, thudding steady and true. "I want you to know that you mean so very much to me," he said, his emerald-green eyes holding hers. "These intimate interludes we've shared are not just exercises to teach you to kiss. Or experiments to see if kisses can fix me stammer for a wee while. They're more than that. They're . . . they're special in a way I can't clearly articulate. They're not inconsequential. They're moments I'll always cherish, even if we must end things here."

Oh . . . Oh my. Mina's heart swelled with a different kind of fervent longing and bittersweet ache, and it seemed she was the one momentarily stuck for words.

"You speak sense," she said when she managed to rein in her surging emotions. "And it would be sensible for us to refrain from . . . from meeting like this. You are a marquess who wishes to make a difference in the world. I know you can ill afford any scandal to be attached to your name. As for me . . . I am but a governess and as much as it pains me to do so, I need to exercise care. This sort of thing—an amorous tryst even in secret—cannot happen again."

Lord Kinsale nodded. When he spoke, his tone was heavy with disappointment. "I know. You, Hermina Davenport, are nothin' but sensible. It's-it's one of the things I most admire about you."

Oh, but she wasn't sensible at all. She was as foolish as could be. She hadn't guarded her heart like a prudent and oh-so-proper Parasol Academy governess should. She'd lost it entirely to this wonderful, generous man whose kisses made her burn and want and hope for more in this life.

But he was also a man she'd deceived. A man she must somehow distance herself from. If not physically, at least mentally and emotionally.

No doubt it would be an impossible feat.

She was about to take a step away from Lord Kinsale when he reached out and caught her chin with his fingers. It seemed he was reluctant to let her go too. "Before you leave, allow me this one last boon, me darlin' Mina," he said in a dark-velvet voice. "Promise me you'll think of me—how it would feel to still have me lips and me hands on you, bringin' you pleasure—when... when you go to bed."

Mina's whole face, indeed, her entire body from the top of her head to the tips of her toes flooded with wicked warmth. Could he mean what she *thought* he meant? That he wanted her to fantasize about him as she abandoned all notions of what was prim and proper and decorous and ladylike and slide her own hand beneath her nightgown to relieve the pulsing ache in her most private, feminine place? Of course, she had already done so before, on several occasions (just last night in fact)—she wasn't a statue made of porcelain or marble. She was a flesh-and-blood woman of six-and-twenty who was hopelessly, irrevocably in love. And the man that she loved—the man at the very center of her deepest desires—was now asking her to do it. For him.

"I will, Phinn," she murmured huskily. She couldn't, didn't want to say no.

Lord Kinsale's answering smile was all things wicked and

wolfish. "I'll be thinkin' o' you too when I climb in me own bed. Goodnight, Mina." He stroked the back of his fingers, ever so gently down her burning cheek. "I wish you the sweetest o' dreams." And then he quit the room.

"Good night, Phinn," Mina whispered after him.

But in the morning, he'll be Lord Kinsale again. And you will simply be Miss Davenport, the governess, not Phineas O'Connell's "darlin' Mina." That's what Mina told herself less than a minute later as she shut her bedroom door and leaned her feverish forehead against it.

Because she couldn't have more than what she'd just had. Not when she hadn't been honest with the man about what she'd done, and was continuing to do, to protect Lord Fitzwilliam from his guardian and Evil Queen Mab.

Perhaps Emmeline was right. She should seek out Mrs. Temple and tell her everything.

She couldn't go on like this any longer.

Tomorrow, after they'd been to the Great Exhibition, she'd send a te-ley-gram to the headmistress, asking for an appointment as she urgently needed to seek the headmistress's counsel.

Whatever happened after that was in the lap of the Fae.

Chapter 28

In Which a Visit to the Great Exhibition Turns into an Even Greater Exhibition . . .

The next morning dawned, gray and dismal and as rainy as could be, and Mina wondered if they should postpone their excursion to see the Great Exhibition. But when Tom and Christopher both grumbled, and Lord Kinsale pointed out that there was always a chance of rain in London, she couldn't say no.

In any event, the fact that it *might* be raining in Hyde Park brought Mina some small measure of reassurance as she helped the boys to get ready. Children in mackintoshes and rain hats and galoshes would be everywhere, making them all look the same. Umbrellas, which concealed faces, would be everywhere too, making it virtually impossible to distinguish one adult exhibition-goer from another.

Although, Christopher had been particularly pouty when she'd asked him to leave Mr. Hopwell at home. She couldn't take the chance that Cheavers or his men might spot the distinctive toy—after all, they were on the lookout for "a small blond boy with a purple velvet rabbit." But when Mina had mentioned the treasured toy might get wet, thus spoiling the velvet, Christopher had complied, tucking the rabbit into his bed.

The inclement weather also gave Mina the perfect excuse to take her Parasol Academy umbrella along. She'd been remiss in not taking it with her on far too many occasions of late. But not today. If Sir Bedivere or Cheavers or any of his hired minions came near her or Christopher, she'd be sure to jab them with the pointy end. And if the Point-of-Confusion failed, a short, sharp whack to the nether regions would fairly incapacitate a man for at least a few minutes, which would be enough time for her and Christopher to get away. (She'd witnessed as much in Hatchards when she'd accidentally felled poor Lord Kinsale.)

Of course, she'd attempted to disguise her appearance further—well, as much as she could without using a *Glamify* spell. After all, Cheavers did have a photograph of her and no doubt knew she'd be wearing a Parasol Academy uniform when out and about. So she'd done as Emmeline had suggested and had framed her face with an abundance of ringlets, then crammed on her coal-scuttle bonnet so the bunches of curls partially obscured her cheeks. Last of all, she'd thrown a voluminous dove-gray shawl over her shoulders, securing it in place with a pearl brooch. Hopefully her navy wool uniform could pass for an unremarkable day gown rather than scream, "Looky here. It's a Parasol Academy governess!"

If any other Parasol Academy nannies or governesses *were* about, they were sure to give her side-eye. They might even report her to Mrs. Temple for breaching the Academy's strict uniform protocols. But it was a risk Mina had to take.

The promise Lady Grenfell had extracted from her echoed inside Mina's head. She'd protect Lord Fitzwilliam, no matter what.

That's what she told herself again as Lord Kinsale's coach neared Hyde Park's Albert Gate.

"What-what shall we see first, boys?" asked Lord Kinsale. He'd been subdued throughout the short carriage ride from

Kinsale House to the Park, looking out the window and occasionally patting Brutus, who lay beside him on the leather seat. Tom's eyes lit up with excitement. "Christopher tells me there's some wicked stuff inside the Crystal Palace. Like a tree made out o' knife blades, and false teef made out o' hippopotamus ivory. And stuffed tigers and frogs and cats and dogs, and even somefink called a dodo bird!"

Brutus lifted his head from his front paws. *Stuffed dogs? What the bejeezus? Ye'll not see me settin' me paws in a place that stuffs dogs. I'd be the dodo.*

Mina pressed her lips together to suppress a laugh. *They're established taxidermist exhibits, Mr. Brutus. No one is going to seize you and cart you off to turn you into a pug display.*

The pug snorted. *Well, that's all right then. But if I see any stuffed rabbits, they better watch out. Because I'll be seizin' them an' rippin' 'em to pieces.*

Mina gave an inward eye roll. Thank goodness Christopher had left Mr. Hopwell at home in his bedroom. To Tom she said, "We can indeed visit all of those exhibits. And the Dinosaur Court."

Lord Kinsale caught Mina's eye. "If you don't mind, Miss Davenport, I might also visit the ag-agricultural displays to see if there might be any useful . . . any useful innovations to employ on me estate back home in Ireland."

Mina offered the marquess a smile. This man was nothing but thoughtful. She couldn't imagine that English absentee landlords took such an interest in their Irish estates and the well-being of their tenants.

It was also clear that the positive effects of their kissing session had worn off. But still, after all his hard work, Lord Kinsale's speech was so smooth, his stammer was barely noticeable.

Mina suddenly wondered how long he would actually need her for elocution and etiquette lessons. There would come a time—

fairly soon, she imagined—when Kinsale House's schoolroom would be her only domain. And that was only if Tom stayed. While Tom did seem more settled now, it was still early days. Trust took time to build, especially in one so young, who'd never really had anyone he could count on. But Lord Kinsale appeared to be doing all that he could to make the young boy feel welcome. It was just one more thing that Mina could add to her ever-growing list of "Things Hermina Davenport loves about the Marquess of Kinsale."

Mina permitted herself a small sigh as she looked out the carriage window and watched the passersby entering Hyde Park. More than ever, loving Lord Kinsale yet not being able to be with him was so very hard to deal with on top of all the other monumental issues she was trying to manage. Every time she looked at him, she thought about their kisses and the wicked yet wonderful things she'd fantasized about in her bed. Her dreams last night had been even more salacious. She was a lather of lust and longing and guilt and confusion. If it were at all possible, she'd seek another post. But she'd never find someone as considerate as Lord Kinsale, who'd take Christopher in as well.

Mina's fingers tightened around her umbrella as the carriage drew to a complete halt. She suddenly felt like a piece of porcelain that contained a tiny fissure, but the crack was about to spread, and very soon she would splinter entirely. As soon as she got through this visit to the Great Exhibition, she would contact Mrs. Temple.

It was time.

"Miss Davenport, are you all right?"

It was Lord Kinsale. Mina summoned a smile as she met his concerned gaze. "Yes, I'm perfectly fine, my lord. I'm just concerned about the weather. Let's hope the rain holds off."

A footman was helping the boys to alight from the carriage

when the marquess murmured, "I'm-I'm sorry if everythin' feels awkward after last night. I... I trust we can go back to bein' just friends? Like we used to be?"

"Of course, my lord," she lied. Could Lord Kinsale tell that her smile was as brittle as could be? That she was about to crack beneath the strain? He had a particular look in his eyes—it wasn't just worry, it was more than that. It was clear he cared for her, at least a little. But somehow, that made everything feel worse because she was such an enormous liar.

He handed her down from the carriage and for a moment, Mina thought he was going to tuck her hand into his elbow. But then he stepped away and called Brutus to heel while Mina made sure the boys' rain hats were pulled low on their brows. A light mizzling rain had started, so she put up her umbrella and lowered her head, hoping her bonnet's brim and curls would sufficiently hide her face.

The decision was made to see the Dinosaur Court first before the rain got any heavier. The group of four enormous concrete statues stood by the banks of the Serpentine, and despite the drizzle, at least half a dozen children were climbing all over them—sitting on the great beasts' backs or swinging from their necks or crawling beneath their undercarriages while their adult "minders" looked on. Mina explained to Tom that the "monsters" as he'd called them, were really replicas of ancient creatures that lived thousands of years ago. "One's called a *Hylaeosaurus*. Another is named a *Megalosaurus* and there are two *Iguanodons*."

"I'm not even go-goin' to begin to try to pronounce those names," said Lord Kinsale by her ear.

He'd leaned beneath her umbrella and for a moment, Mina closed her eyes to savor the scent of his utterly gorgeous cologne. The drift of his warm breath against an exposed sliver of her neck between the edge of her bonnet and her uniform's high collar was the sweetest of tortures too. "I'm sure you could," she murmured, as an acute wave of longing washed over her.

"Perhaps . . . after we'd shared a kiss," he returned in a low voice that sent a delicious shiver down her spine. "Sorry. I . . . I shouldn't have said that." He straightened and clasped his gloved hands behind his back. "But I thought you'd like to know that our . . . our experiment's positive effects lasted for . . . for a whole half hour. I stayed up a while, rehearsin' me parliamentary speech and for the most part, I was flu-fluent. It was quite remark-remarkable. Some might even say miraculous."

"It does indeed sound remarkable," said Mina, returning her attention to Christopher and Tom, who'd wandered closer to the dinosaurs. A footman, the one who'd helped the boys out of the carriage, stood nearby, keeping a watchful eye out too. Brutus, who'd followed the boys, sat close to Christopher's galoshes. "It's a pity we—" She broke off, but Lord Kinsale knew what she'd been going to say.

"I know," he murmured. "It's . . . It's a pity we can't kiss all the time." Mina felt Lord Kinsale's gaze on her and she couldn't help herself—she turned her head. And when her eyes met the marquess's, he smiled so beautifully, her heart somersaulted in her chest. "Mina . . . what if . . . what if there was a way that we *could* make that happen? What if . . . what if we threw all caution to the wind and we just decided that nothin' else mat—"

At that moment, there was a loud shriek. *Christopher?*

Oh, dear God! Mina's head whipped over to the commotion taking place in front of the *Megalosaurus*. And her eyes nearly popped out of her head. Brutus and Christopher were involved in a tug of war over Mr. Hopwell.

Mr. Hopwell! What on earth was the stuffed toy doing here? Hadn't Christopher left it in his room at Kinsale House?

The pug's teeth were firmly buried in one of the mauve velvet rabbit's legs while Christopher had a hold of the toy's ears.

"Let go, Brutus!" the boy cried, his face red with exertion as angry tears spilled down his cheeks. "Let go!"

All the while, Tom was waving a stick at the pug and yelling, "You bleedin' li'l blighter! You li'l gobshite! Let go!"

Mina and Lord Kinsale both started forward at the same time—they only had to cross ten yards of wet, manicured lawn to reach the kerfuffle. But the lawn was slippery underfoot and a moment before the marquess—his stride was naturally longer than Mina's—reached the warring boy and pug, Christopher slipped, lost his grip, and fell backward onto his bottom.

And Brutus was off, a tan-and-black streak of lightning across Hyde Park.

Oh no! Not another wild pug chase!

"Brutus!" yelled Lord Kinsale as he followed in hot pursuit.

"Save Mr. Hopwell, Miss Davenport," cried a frantic Christopher, who'd already scrambled to his feet.

"Don't worry. I will." Mina threw her open umbrella to the footman—it would only slow her down—picked up her skirts and bolted after the marquess and his thieving, runaway dog. "Look after the boys," she cried over her shoulder to the gaping servant.

She *had* to rescue Mr. Hopwell. The mauve velvet rabbit was so very precious to darling Christopher. He'd be inconsolable if the pug actually did rip it to pieces. And then of course, the sooner she got the toy back, the better. Sir Bedivere knew his ward had a toy purple rabbit.

If Cheavers or his hired men were in Hyde Park and noticed it . . .

Lord Kinsale was a swift runner, but courtesy of her Parasol Academy training, Mina was faster. Spurred on by rising panic, she quickly caught up to the marquess and then sprinted past him. Brutus, the wee gobshite, was flying over the ground, his small black ears and Mr. Hopwell's long mauve ones flapping wildly in the breeze.

Mina hurled a mental command at the dog. *Brutus! Stop right now!*
Ha! As if I would! Ye'll never catch me, taunted the pug.
This feckin' rabbit is a goner.
Not bloody likely. Even though her thighs and lungs were burning, Mina would not give up. She forced herself to run even faster, hurtling across the wet, muddy grass, praying she wouldn't slip and topple over.

The pug was keeping to the banks of the Serpentine, skirting the edge of the enormous lake, so it was easy to keep track of him. Mina was grateful he hadn't scarpered off into the knots of park visitors and exhibition-goers. There was a very real chance she would lose sight of him altogether then.

But it seemed Brutus was flagging. After his initial burst of speed, his stocky little legs appeared to be growing tired as he started to slow down. Despite her own fatigue, Mina's determination spurred her on. The pug was only a yard or two away now. If she increased her pace, if she threw herself forward and rugby tackled the dog...

She did. With a cry, she hurled her whole body at Brutus and one of her gloved hands came down on his back. The pug stumbled, went down, and as Mina fell to the ground, she yanked the mauve rabbit from the dog's jaws.

Thank the Fae.

Chest heaving, rescued rabbit in hand, she rolled over to her back, preparing to push herself up into a sitting position. *Ack.* It seemed she'd landed on a particularly boggy part of the Serpentine's banks. But before she could even assess the damage to her person, she heard a masculine shout.

"Feck! Look out, Miss Davenport!" The next thing she knew Lord Kinsale was skidding in the mud but four feet away from her, arms flailing, booted feet sliding like he'd hit a patch of ice. And then he plummeted to earth headfirst, his face landing squarely in the middle of her lap.

Her *lap*. Right between her legs.
Oh. My. God.
Mina gasped. Not because Lord Kinsale had hurt her, but because of the shocking, thoroughly outrageous reality of having a man plant his face right in her most private of places in the most public of places. And public it was. Mina sensed a small crowd of onlookers had gathered about. She could hear the titters and appalled gasps and whispers slipping out from behind gloved hands and from beneath umbrellas.

As Lord Kinsale raised his mud-streaked face from between her spread thighs, his dark hair dripping in his shamrock-green eyes, she knew her own face was burning with mortification.

"Mina . . . I'm so feckin' sorry," he breathed raggedly. He was still out of breath like she was. But the rapid rise and fall of her chest and the wild thudding of her heart wasn't just a result of her mad sprint, but a symptom of something else—the feelings a prim and proper lady "must not name." Because what sort of a woman would she be if she'd already secretly entertained the idea of having Lord Kinsale between her thighs? That the whole notion wasn't all that shocking or outrageous at all?

A Parasol Academy governess certainly shouldn't think that way.

She tried to scramble up as Lord Kinsale lurched to his feet, and somehow, one of the marquess's gloved hands came into contact with her bodice, leaving behind a large muddy handprint on her left breast. It stood out starkly against the pale gray of her shawl.

Could this situation get any worse?

By the time Lord Kinsale had helped Mina up, her cheeks were so aflame with embarrassment even the cold rain couldn't put them out.

But at least she had Mr. Hopwell.

"Are-are you all right?" asked Lord Kinsale, standing between her and the crowd to shield her from all the snickers and prying eyes. "You took quite a tumble."

Wrenching off her stained shawl, Mina nodded. "Apart from a few bruises and my ruined reputation, I'm fine," she said with a pained grimace. Then she glanced about. "Did you see where Brutus went? I hope he doesn't get lost."

Heedless of the mud on his gloves, Lord Kinsale dragged a hand through his hair. "That feckin' dog," he muttered. "If . . . if he does get lost, it will be his own feckin' fault. But I suspect he knows his way home. It's less . . . less than a mile to Eaton Square from here."

"We'd best get back to Christopher and Tom then," Mina said. She wrapped the filthy but largely intact Mr. Hopwell in her shawl. "I'm sure Christopher is eager to hear the good news that his rabbit is safe."

But Mina wasn't so sure that *she* wasn't in danger. And Christopher. As she and Lord Kinsale retraced their steps to the Dinosaur Court, a creeping sense of dread invaded her. Even though she hadn't noticed Cheavers in the crowd—his distinctive bristle-brush facial hair would be sure to stand out—one of his hirelings might be lurking somewhere in the Park, watching.

Just as worrying was the fact she'd spotted several Parasol Academy graduates in their distinctive uniforms. And they'd certainly have spotted her, in the mud, with a man's face in her lap and his handprint on her breast.

What's more, they would have *seen* that Mina was from the Parasol Academy even if they didn't know her personally. While she'd pulled off her soiled shawl to repair her appearance somewhat, she'd inadvertently revealed her uniform. And Lord Kinsale, just before he'd fallen on her, had cried out her name.

There was no doubt in her mind that Mrs. Temple would be hearing about this. And given the crowd, there was every chance it might even end up in the newspapers. Others might recognize she was from the Parasol Academy. Certain people might even identify the Marquess of Kinsale.

This incident was a monumental scandal in the making and there was nothing at all that Mina could do to stop it.

She just prayed that her name wasn't linked to Lord Kinsale's in the papers—or by anyone who worked for Sir Bedivere who might have been on the lookout for her and Christopher in Hyde Park—because if the baronet heard about the connection, he would know where to find her... and his missing ward.

Only the Fae knew what would happen then.

Chapter 29

Concerning Wobbly Jelly, Muddiness, and Mussing; And the Consequences of Scandal...

The carriage ride back to Kinsale House was painfully awkward and quiet. Two sullen boys, a muddy and mortified governess, one brooding muddy marquess, and his chastened muddy pug did not make for convivial company. Indeed, Mina thought the atmosphere was as dark and ponderous as the rain clouds now blanketing London and releasing a veritable deluge.

Tom and Christopher were, of course, disappointed beyond measure that their Great Exhibition adventure had ended before it had even really begun. Promises that they would be taken on a sunnier day did not seem to mollify either of them.

Christopher, when questioned, revealed that he'd snuck Mr. Hopwell under his mackintosh when they'd been getting ready for their outing and Mina hadn't been looking. The boy reported that he didn't want his rabbit to miss out on all the fun and that's why he'd brought him along. But Mina rather suspected he was still being plagued by Queen Mab in his dreams, so he'd brought the much-loved toy along for comfort. She couldn't blame the poor child for that.

As for Brutus, he was as unrepentant as could be. He'd told Mina that he knew Christopher had concealed Mr. Hopwell beneath his clothes—the pug had caught the toy rabbit's scent—and so when the rabbit had fallen out, he'd pounced. Lord Kinsale had been right and the pug had been making his way home to Eaton Square. Mina had caught sight of Brutus trotting along Sloane Street, so she'd made Lord Kinsale stop the carriage to let the dog in.

"You're too soft on the wee bugger," Lord Kinsale had complained as the pug had jumped up onto the seat beside his master. Nevertheless, he'd run a gloved hand over Brutus's sodden, muddy back as the dog lay down and put his head between his paws.

Mina suspected that the only way to assuage Brutus's natural tendencies would be to provide him with other sorts of toys he could quite happily rip and pull and shake to pieces. Perhaps a rope rabbit might do the trick. But it was a project she'd tackle later. She had more pressing problems to deal with right now.

As soon as she repaired to her bedroom, which she did immediately upon returning to Kinsale House, she employed the *Unsmirchify* spell on Mr. Hopwell, and then to restore her governess's uniform, and indeed her entire appearance to what it should be—prim, proper, and perfectly presentable. Even her "non-regulation" ringlets disappeared and her sleek, neat bun returned.

And then Mina did what she didn't want to but most definitely had to. She pulled out her ley-spectacles and a piece of parchment and hastily penned a te-ley-gram with her te-ley-pen—a special fountain pen filled with blue Faerillion ink, used expressly for the purpose of writing leygrams—that she'd send to the headmistress of the Parasol Academy.

> *Dear Mrs. Temple,*
> *Would it be possible to meet with you this afternoon? It seems I urgently require your wise*

counsel about several matters of great importance. Matters which are directly related to the safety of a child and indeed, the preservation of the Parasol Academy's pristine reputation, which, I greatly fear, may be at risk because of my actions—actions which I take full responsibility for. I am currently at Kinsale House but I'm certain my employer would grant me leave to visit you at the Academy's headquarters.
I await your direction.
Yours sincerely,
Hermina Davenport

Mina sighed shakily as she put down her pen on her writing slope. Then, before she could change her mind—because internally, she was trembling like a barely set jelly—she folded up the parchment, slid it into an envelope, then cast the Fae spell that would send the leygram straight to Mrs. Temple's office. "*Leygram Sendio, Felicity Temple,*" she whispered and the magical telegram promptly disappeared in a puff of shimmering silvery-blue mist.

If that missive didn't catch Mrs. Temple's immediate attention, nothing would.

Now, while Mina waited for the headmistress to respond, she just had to face Lord Kinsale, who'd requested her presence in the drawing room as soon as she was ready.

Ready? Ready for what? That's the operative question, Mina's mind whispered as she descended the stairs to meet with her employer.

Although, deep down she *knew* what was about to happen.

It seemed her wobbly-as-a-jelly state was not likely to end for at least another few hours.

There was going to be a scandal. Of *epic* proportions.

Phinn knew that, right down to his very bones. Indeed, he'd

known it from the very moment he'd accidentally fallen face-first straight into Mina Davenport's lap.

He'd known it was an absolute certainty as he'd risen to his feet, covered in mud, and had then recognized several faces of fellow peers in the crowd—gentlemen he'd encountered at White's and Boodle's and other places about town. Men who were sniggering at what he'd done and Miss Davenport's thoroughly besmirched state. And besmirched in more ways than one.

Every part of him had vibrated with the need to wipe the knowing smirks off their faces with his fists. But he hadn't, and while he'd attempted to physically shield Miss Davenport from those leers and horrified whispers in those awful moments, obscuring the crowd's view of her with his own body probably hadn't done much at all.

He didn't even want to think about the fact that he'd been a complete eejit and had made everything that much worse by calling out Miss Davenport's name right before he'd ruined the governess's respectability in an irreparable way.

He still couldn't quite believe he'd planted his face right between the governess's thighs!

Good God.

No, feckin' hell. And how doubly unfair that his most treasured fantasy had been turned into a waking nightmare? He'd dreamed of being between Miss Davenport's thighs for so, so long, but not in *that* way.

There was no question in Phinn's mind: There was only *one* thing he could do to ensure that Miss Mina Davenport's reputation wasn't completely and utterly ruined forevermore. There was only one course of action he could take to protect her.

Which was why he'd summoned her to the drawing room as soon as she'd de-muddified herself. To give her the chance to bathe and change in peace, Tom and Christopher, still as glum as could be—poor lads—were currently ensconced in the kitchen with Mrs. Dunkley, scarfing down cake and warm milk to drown their sorrows.

Cake and warm milk would not be enough to quell Phinn's jitters, though, considering what he was about to do. As he waited for Mina Davenport, impatience and nerves gnawing at his gut, he poured himself an Irish whisky.

Sweet Jaysus, his hands were shaking as he sloshed a good measure of the potent alcohol into a crystal tumbler. He tossed it back, then raked his hand through his hair, which was still damp from his own bath.

There'd been something about Miss Davenport's demeanor in the carriage on the way back to Kinsale House that had set alarm bells clanging at the back of Phinn's mind.

While she'd no doubt been upset about the whole embarrassing "Hyde Park" incident, he had the feeling there was something else going on, like he was on the brink of finding out something quite significant about Mina Davenport. Something she didn't want him to know.

The mantel clock was just striking half past two when there was a knock on the drawing room door. A moment later, Miss Davenport entered and curtsied most formally, which rankled Phinn no end. He didn't want the woman he admired so very greatly—the woman he, in fact, adored—to act so subserviently around him. But then, if he had his way, she wouldn't be curtsying for much longer.

"I hope I haven't kept you waiting, my lord," she said, watching him with wary eyes. Miss Davenport wasn't usually so guarded in his presence, so it made Phinn even more determined to find out what was really going on in that clever mind of hers.

She'd donned a fresh uniform and restyled her thick chestnut hair into the plain-as-could-be bun that she typically wore. Indeed, her appearance was "Parasol-Academy-immaculate" and Phinn had the sudden, almost irresistible urge to sweep her into his arms and muss her up. Her hair, her bodice, her skirts, her composure. Everything. He wanted her unguarded and vulnerable and flushed and breathless and messy and *his*, goddammit.

Hopefully soon.

Aloud he said, "No. Not-not at all, Miss Davenport," then motioned for her to come into the room. The footmen stationed outside in the hall had already closed the double doors. "Please, take a seat. We . . . we have much to discuss."

"Yes . . ." The governess approached the hearth and chose the settee closest to the fire. She sat primly, straight as a ruler with her hands folded neatly in her lap. Phinn didn't fail to observe that her knuckles were white and her countenance was as pale as parchment.

What was she so frightened of? Surely not him?

Frowning, Phinn took the leather wing chair closest to her. "Miss Davenport. Mina," he began. "I feel as though we need to have . . . have a frank talk after what transpired this afternoon. There's no get-gettin' round it. It's a scandal in the makin'."

She raised her eyes to his. "I agree," she said, lifting her chin, her expression nothing but stoic. "It was indeed unfortunate that events unfolded the way that they did. And perhaps it was foolish of me to try to save Christopher's rabbit. But then neither you nor I could have predicted that you would"—Miss Davenport's cheeks turned as red as holly berries—"that you would trip over and land . . . well, in such an eyebrow-raising fashion. While it was all a terrible accident, and no one's fault, given there were so many witnesses to our mishap, there *will* be consequences."

Pausing, she drew a breath. "With that in mind, I have contacted Mrs. Temple to let her know what has happened. I expect she will shortly reach out to me—either to meet with me here at Kinsale House or she'll summon me to the Parasol Academy. I was seen—in uniform—by other Parasol Academy nannies and governesses, and if this incident ends up in the newspapers, as I fear it will, Mrs. Temple will need to control the damage. The Academy has a Royal Charter bestowed by Queen Victoria herself, so maintaining its pristine reputation is paramount." She dropped her gaze to her clasped hands. "My lord, I strongly suspect that I shall lose my license to practice as a governess in the Parasol Academy's name. I-I thought you should know that, considering you hired me, in part, because of my credentials."

Phinn's chest tightened. He didn't like seeing Miss Davenport brought so low. And this entire debacle really wasn't her fault. It made him even more determined to fix things. "I-I do understand the gravity of the situation, Miss Davenport... Mina. Which is why I'm goin' to propose a solution to help manage the scan-scandal. To perhaps even put... put it to bed entirely."

She lifted her gaze to his. "How? What could you possibly do to make it all go away?"

He smiled and his heart began to thrum with sweet expectation. "I thought the answer was obvious, my darlin' Mina. You'll marry me."

Chapter 30

In Which Messes Are Cleared Up; And Proposals and Confessions and Magical Sparks Are Made...

What? Mina, shocked to stillness, could only blink. Then she inhaled a shaky breath and surreptitiously pinched the inside of her wrist. No, she wasn't dreaming. She hadn't misheard. Lord Kinsale *had* just suggested they wed.

"Marry you?" she repeated as the wave of incredulity that had hit her began to ebb. "You... you can't possibly mean that."

"Oh, but I do," said Lord Kinsale. "In fact, if you recall, I'd be-begun to propose that we throw all caution to the wind and do just that... marry. When we were at-at the Dinosaur Court. But then Brutus struck before I could finish sayin' what-what I really wanted to." His chest expanded as he inhaled a breath. "The words I've been hold-holdin' in me heart for days. Actually, for weeks if I'm bein' tru-truly honest."

Oh my. Mina again couldn't quite believe what she was hearing. But while her heart wanted to soar with joy, her guilt—the fact that Lord Kinsale didn't know the truth about her situation—weighed it down, keeping it firmly anchored in a deep well of leaden despair. "Lord Kinsale, I can't let you do this," she said, her tone heavy with remorse. Indeed, every word she uttered felt like she was dragging it out of her chest. "I know that marrying you would save me from scandal. But . . . but it wouldn't be right—"

Lord Kinsale swore beneath his breath and raked a hand through his hair. "I'm . . . I'm makin' a complete mess of this proposal, aren't I?" he said. Then before Mina knew what he was about, he got down on bended knee in front of her. "Mina Davenport," he said, looking straight into her eyes. "I haven't rehearsed all of what I'm . . . what I'm about to say, so please forgive me . . . I mean *my* stammers." Drawing a deep breath, he continued, "My darlin' Mina, how do I love thee? Let me count the ways."

"You love me?" whispered Mina, her heart tripping over itself with awed delight. "You-you have a list of things you *love* about me?"

"Aye, I do." Lord Kinsale's smile lit his emerald-green eyes. "Ever since I read that poem by Elizabeth Barrett Browning, I started makin' a list in me head. Not consciously at first. But-but I have one all the same."

Oh. Oh, heavens above. Mina had never been more touched by anything in her entire life. But then the cold hard truth reared its ugly head and she bit her lip as tears threatened. "But you can't. You can't love me," she said, her voice cracking. "Not really. You-you don't know me. You don't know about the things I've done. What . . . what I am. Which is a terrible, terrible liar."

Lord Kinsale's brows plunged into a frown. "What-what do you mean?"

"I mean," said Mina, dashing away a tear that had spilled onto her cheek, "that from the moment we met on the *Kinsale Cloud*, I've been deceiving you. I've been perpetuating a big fat lie about my past. And about Christopher. He's . . . he's not really my son. He's actually my former charge, the orphaned

Viscount Fitzwilliam. And I was tasked by his late godmother, the Dowager Countess of Grenfell, just before she passed away two months ago, to-to keep him safe from his guardian, Sir Bedivere Ponsonby. I've been hiding Lord Fitzwilliam for weeks and weeks and nobody knows about any of this except my dear friend Emmeline. In fact, she only found out yesterday. And now you know too. Even... even Mrs. Temple doesn't know what I've done. Although"—Mina pulled a breath into her tight lungs—"she will very soon."

Lord Kinsale joined her on the settee, then scrubbed a hand down his face. "So-so just to be clear, you're tellin' me that young Christopher isn't your child, but a viscount in hidin'? That you, in fact, removed him from the care of his legally appointed guardian?"

"Yes," she whispered. "In the eyes of the law, I've technically kidnapped Lord Fitzwilliam."

"But... but why? What sort of danger is the lad in? Does it"—Lord Kinsale's green eyes glittered dangerously—"does it have somethin' to do with the fact that this Sir Bedivere recently set sail for the Arctic? To-to chart a route through the feckin' Northwest Passage?"

Mina blinked in astonishment. "Yes. Well, mostly. Sir Bedivere was determined to take Christopher with him. In fact, the *Valiant* had already set sail for the Arctic with the poor boy on board when I"—*Ack, how to put this!*—"intercepted the vessel. But"—Mina frowned in confusion—"how-how did you know about any of that?"

Lord Kinsale's mouth flattened. "I... I saw the bastard outside Hatchards. Right before you-you ducked down and accidentally whacked me fair in the groin. I suspected you were tryin' to avoid the man, so... so yesterday, when he rode past me in Hyde Park, I asked me friend Lord Hartwell if he knew him. And Hartwell bas-basically told me that the baronet is a 'tosser,' as the English would say, and that he owned a ship named the *Valiant* that had sailed forth from Bristol, headin' to the Arctic Circle . . . about the same time that the *Kinsale Cloud* was returnin' to Bristol."

Mina's stomach had turned into a butter churn. "Did Sir Bedivere see Christopher?" she whispered. "When you were in Hyde Park yesterday?"

Lord Kinsale shook his head. "I-I don't believe so. But the lad . . . the lad was actin' a bit oddly. Right after Sir Bedivere rode by a second time, Christopher told me his stomach felt fun-funny and then he asked if we might return . . . return home."

Dear Lord. What another near miss that had been. Mina swallowed to moisten her dry-as-ashes mouth. "I feel so guilty about everything. About breaking the law. About deceiving you and the Parasol Academy. But young Christopher's life was placed in danger. The Arctic is no place for a child. And a deathbed promise is the sort of promise one must not break."

Lord Kinsale's eyes filled with compassion. "I understand, lass. This Sir Bedivere sounds like he's gone quite mad."

"Not quite. He's—" Mina broke off and bit her lip. Oh, she so wanted to tell Lord Kinsale everything. But if she mentioned Queen Mab and the baronet's ensorcelled ring, the marquess would think *she* was mad.

Lord Kinsale suddenly reached out and touched her hand. Squeezed it gently. "Mina, I . . . I want you to know that I will do my utmost to pro-protect you and young Christopher from Sir Bedivere. I can-cannot imagine that any authority in this land—that Queen Victoria herself—would allow a young peer to be . . . to be taken on such a perilous voyage. I do have one question though . . . one that's been plaguin' me since the day we first met. How-how did you and Christopher end up on me ship? If the boy was on the *Valiant*, headed north for the Arctic, and the *Kinsale Cloud* sailed from Kinsale in Ireland . . . and none of me crew saw you sneak on board . . ." He shook his head. "I do know the *Valiant* returned to Bristol soon after we did. It's just... It's like... It's almost like you and Christopher magically appeared on the *Kinsale Cloud*. But-but that's impossible." Lord Kinsale's gaze locked with Mina's. "Isn't it?"

Mina's breath hitched. What was Lord Kinsale really asking her? Was he actually asking her if she could perform magic? "I don't... I don't know what you mean."

"But... but I think you do," asserted the marquess. "And it's not just how you came to be on me ship that puz-puzzles me. The night you rescued Tom from the clutches of that drunk-drunken lout—the fellow was obnoxious one moment, and then the very next, he was as do-docile as a lamb after you jabbed him with your umbrella and spoke an odd word. Some-something about being perplexed like 'Per-Perplexio'? And then he was. And the way you manage to magically pull all... all manner of things from your pockets. Like-like sausages for Brutus, or-or mousetraps, or sweets, or marbles, or packs of cards. And when I saw you leavin' Christopher's bedroom the other night when we went lookin' for Tom, there seemed to be a soft pur-purple mist that drifted out into the hallway after you. At the time, I dismissed it, tellin' meself that maybe the lad's window was open, and fog had crept in. But the fog didn't descend until later. And it's ne-never purple. Why, even your hair, which was dish-disheveled and muddy a short time ago, is now dry and per-perfectly styled in a record amount of time, while... while mine is still damp from me bath. It's... it's too incredible and defies any and all rational explanation."

"Oh," said Mina with a wince. Apart from her teleportation mishap aboard the *Kinsale Cloud*, she'd always tried so very hard to use her magic discreetly, as per the Academy's strict protocols. But it seemed she hadn't quite succeeded. In fact, she'd failed completely. She'd been about as discreet as a stage magician with an assistant shouting to the audience, "Watch Miss Hermina Davenport, Parasol Academy governess, perform another Fae spell right before your very eyes!"

"Yes, oh," said Lord Kinsale. His tone, like the look in his eyes, was uncompromising. His suspicions were aroused and it appeared he wasn't going to let her off the hook about anything. "And o' course, I still can't fully explain how your kisses magically make me stammer dis-disappear. At least temporarily. Can you?"

Mina blew out a sigh. "Well, I do think the act of kissing *does* relax one's oral musculature. So *that's* a perfectly logical explanation of sorts. I really don't think there's any magic involved even though it seems that way."

"But the rest? Do-do you have logical explanations for any of those things?" The set of Lord Kinsale's jaw was suddenly anvil-hard. "And please don't lie to me, Mina. I think... I think the time for bein' completely honest with each other has arrived."

"Are you... are you really asking me if I can perform magic?" she whispered.

Lord Kinsale's mouth hitched in a wry smile. "I'm... I'm an Irishman. I believe in curses and ghosts and shape-shiftin' goblins called púca. And wailin' banshees, and leprechauns and pots o' gold at the end o' rainbows. I even believe in faeries, me darlin' Mina. O' course I'm askin' you that."

There was nowhere to hide. And Mina was so very tired of hiding the truth from this wonderful man. *The man that she loved.*

So she inhaled a fortifying breath and took a leap of faith, knowing that Phineas O'Connell would catch her. That he would listen and believe her and that he would never laugh at her or let her down. "Yes, my lord," she said. "I can perform magic. While I'm not a magical creature or being, like any of the ones you just named, I was trained to use the magic of the Fae in the course of performing my duties as a Parasol Academy governess."

Triumph flared in Lord Kinsale's eyes. "I knew it!" he declared. "I feckin' knew it. You're a wonder, Mina Davenport, and I'll nev-never regret the day that fate or the Fae or the north wind sent you into my life." Leaning forward, he gave her a resounding kiss. Even though it was brief and fervent, it sparked bright joy inside Mina. "So tell me, how did you end up on me ship? I'm bloody dying to know."

"Well," she began, "Parasol nannies and governesses can travel between places by a magical process called teleportation." And then she told Lord Kinsale everything. About how te-ley-portation worked, but how it had somehow gone horribly awry when she'd tried to spirit Christopher off the *Valiant* and back to Bristol. How Sir Bedivere was being controlled by the evil Fae Queen Mab, through his ensorcelled silver and obsidian ring. But whether Queen Mab had an ultimate purpose beyond using the baronet to "steal" Christopher, she knew not. She told Lord Kinsale about the Parasol Academy's Fae Charter and that her uniform had magical pockets and that she possessed both an umbrella and parasol that could render assailants "pleasantly confused" for a minute or two when poked with the magical tip. And how she'd been casting a protective *Guardia Nimbus* spell over Christopher's bedroom every night to prevent any sort of supernatural minion from Queen Mab's court sneaking into his room and taking the boy.

Lord Kinsale listened to everything Mina told him, asking questions every now and again to clarify anything he didn't quite understand. When she'd finished, he leaned back against the settee, folded his arms, and gave her a measured look. "It sounds to me like this Queen Mab wants Christopher for herself and . . . and to leave a changeling in his place."

"You know about changelings too?" asked Mina

"Aye. O' course I do!" said Lord Kinsale. "The lore is as old as Éire itself." He cocked a dark brow. "In all your time trainin' at the Parasol Academy, did-did you ever learn where this Queen Mab's court is? Because if Lady Grenfell and Christopher both dreamt about a place of snow and ice, and Sir Bedivere was hell-bent on ferryin' the boy to the Arctic, then . . . then maybe that's where this evil Fae queen is."

Mina sighed. "Believe me, I've wondered that too. But the only one who probably would know for certain would be Mrs. Temple."

"Who you've been reluctant to approach. And for good reason." To Mina's surprise, Lord Kinsale shivered. "I've said it before and I'll say it again. That wee woman even frightens me."

Mina couldn't help but laugh. "Oh, Phinn, I can't imagine you being afraid of anything or anyone."

Lord Kinsale suddenly reached out and gently caught her chin between his fingers. "What did you call me then, Miss Davenport? Did I hear you call me Phinn, just like you did last night?"

Mina blushed. "I-I might have," she murmured.

"And why would you be callin' me that, lass?" The light in the man's eyes was as soft and beguiling as his voice. "Could it be that you're rethinkin' your refusal of me marriage proposal?"

"I didn't *refuse* exactly," said Mina. "I simply said that I couldn't let you propose because you didn't know the truth about me. And now you do."

Lord Kinsale smiled. "Aye, I do. If I recall correctly, you also didn't let me finish tellin' you about all the things I love about you."

"No. No, I didn't. You could tell me now. If . . . if you still feel the same way. I'd understand if you didn't tho—"

She got no further as Lord Kinsale—darling Phinn—pressed a finger to her lips. "Hush now. O' course I still feel the same way. In fact, I think I might love you even more. Not only are you beautiful and clever and kindhearted, but you're fiercely brave and noble. And it's clear you'd risk anythin' for those you care about. I think I've been under your spell from the moment I found you in me wardrobe aboard the *Kinsale Cloud*."

"Truly?"

"Truly." Phinn smoothed away a stray lock of hair from her cheek. "So do you have any other objections? Are . . . are there any other reasons why we shouldn't wed?"

"Apart from the fact that I'm a governess and you're a marquess?" said Mina. She had to make sure that Lord Kinsale knew what might lie ahead for him. What was at stake. "Because people are bound to gossip and say unkind, perhaps even cruel things. And the last thing I want to do is harm your reputation. Not when you've been working so very hard to earn the respect of your peers."

Lord Kinsale snorted. "Regardless of any gossip whispered behind me back, I'll . . . I'll still have a voice in Parliament that *will* be listened to. I'm big and loud and I can tone down me accent when I need to. I can even control me stammer now." His expression softened and his eyes glowed with warmth. "All because of you, Mina. And even though I bear the title marquess, deep down, I'm still Phineas O'Connell, a simple man from County Cork who's . . . who's fallen in love with the finest English rose he's ever set eyes on."

"Oh, Phinn." Mina's voice caught. "You say the loveliest things. Things that take my breath away."

The crooked smile Mina loved so much, tugged at the corner of Phinn's wide beautiful mouth. "I'm a man who's always struggled with expressin' me thoughts," he said softly, "but-but with you, Mina, I can be meself. I can speak me heart and me mind and quite honestly, I cannot imagine a life without you in it. Your smiles, your laughter, your every word and sigh completely captivate me, and . . . and I cannot bear the thought of not havin' you by me side, in me arms, and in me bed for the rest o' me days. You are, quite simply, my everythin'. Marry me, my darlin' Mina. Please say you'll be mine." But then Phinn's brow pleated. "Unless . . . unless of course you don't . . . you don't feel the same way . . ."

"Oh, Phinn. Of course I love you," breathed Mina. "With my entire heart. Like you, I've kept the secret of how I feel locked away for weeks. I was so very frightened that when you found out that I'm not the woman you thought I was, that you'd be so very angry. That you'd feel betrayed. So I told myself that you and I could never ever be together. That the idea of an 'us' was impossible. But it seems I was very wrong." She caught Phinn's scarred hands and brought them to her lips. Her eyes locked with his as she said, "Phineas O'Connell. I love you more than you will ever know, and I would be honored to be yours and to share a life with you. Nothing would make me happier."

And then Phinn gave a loud whoop, gathered her close and kissed her without restraint. His mouth moved urgently, his tongue plunged and stroked deeply, and Mina kissed him back just as ardently. There was fire in this kiss. It spoke of passion and joy and adoration and the everlasting bond that she and Phinn were forging together.

She loved being a governess, but this, being in Phinn's arms, knowing she was loved so fiercely—that she'd somehow captivated this man's heart—was everything. Even though she'd been living a lie, he'd seen through all the artifice to her true self. He knew her and trusted her and whatever trials they may face in the coming days, Mina was certain that they could count on each other to get through them. It was a truth as immutable as the rising and setting of the sun and the turning of the world. Love made everything right and whole and beautiful.

Phinn pushed her down onto the cushions of the settee and very soon, Mina found she wanted more than kisses. Her body was aflame and pulsing with need, so when Phinn began to undo the buttons of her bodice so he could kiss her neck and shoulder and décolletage without restraint, she whispered, "You can go lower . . . if you want to."

Phinn growled, low in his throat. "Oh, I very much want to, sweetheart. But"—he searched her gaze—"are you sure about this? We can wait until after we're wed."

Mina bit her kiss-swollen lip. Desire was humming through every part of her from head to toe so she wasn't about to say no. "The door's shut?"

Phinn grinned as he released another button. "Aye."

"And Tom and Christopher are being looked after?"

Another button slid free, revealing the edge of Mina's corset and lace-edged chemise. "Aye. When they've finished their cake, Frobisher will take them to the ballroom and entertain them by playin' tunes and marbles and whatever else they'd like to do."

"And . . . and Brutus?"

"After one of the footmen gives the wee sod a bath, he'll be confined to the house until further notice."

"Not the terrace?" Mina laced her fingers around Phinn's strong neck.

"No." Phinn was down to the last button. "I don't trust the bugger not to roll around in the mud in the back garden just to spite me."

"He loves you, you know. He thinks that you're—" Mina broke off. *Blast.* She did not want to be talking about her ability to mentally communicate with blinking Brutus. Not when the man she loved was in the process of undressing her.

But Phinn had noticed as he looked up and frowned. "And how would you know what me dog thinks, Mina? Don't tell me you can hear his thoughts."

Mina winced. "All right. I won't tell you that."

"Sweet Jaysus." Phinn's eyes crinkled with mirth. "I'm not sure whether that would be a nightmare or feckin' hilarious."

Mina laughed. "A little of both. And just so you know, he can only hear my thoughts if I let him."

"Thank God for that," said Phinn with a roguish grin as he hooked two fingers into the top of her corset and chemise and tugged them down, revealing one of her breasts. "Because your thoughts are about to get all kinds o' wicked. Just like mine are, because feck me"—he ran a fingertip lightly around one of her nipples, making it furl into a tight pink bud—"you're more gorgeous than I ever imagined."

Mina swore she blushed all over as Phinn's frankly admiring gaze drank her partially naked state in. But she also felt beautiful and adored and desired and ready for whatever wicked journey this man was about to take her on.

As Phinn lowered his head and kissed Mina where she'd never been kissed before, teasing the aching point of her nipple with his lips and clever tongue and the rough pads of his fingers, she was aflame with desire. "Oh Phinn," she moaned as he transferred his attention to her other breast. Everything he did to her set off sparks that sizzled through her veins, radiating delicious heat throughout her body. "Why . . . why haven't we done this until . . . until now?"

He lifted his head and arched a dark brow. His eyes fairly smoldered as he said, "Damned if I know, darlin'." He lifted a hand and waggled his fingers. "Just wait until you discover the magic I can do with these."

But Mina *didn't* find out because just as Phinn was sliding a hand beneath her skirts and was heading straight for the slit in her drawers, there was a volley of rapid knocking upon the drawing room door. "Lord Kinsale? Miss Davenport? Are you in there?"

Oh no. It was Meddley Smedley!

Phinn voiced what Mina had been thinking. "Blast and feck and blinkin' hell," he muttered as he sat up and raked a hand through his thoroughly disheveled hair. Mina, as she sat up too, attempted to haul up her corset and chemise. "What the hell do you want, Smedley?" he all but barked. "I'm busy!"

"There's a Mrs. Temple here to see Miss Davenport. She says it's most urgent and cannot wait," called back the butler. "I've shown her to the library."

"Well, have Mrs. Aldershot organize a tea tray for her," returned Phinn tersely. "And tell Mrs. Temple that Miss Davenport will see her shortly. Oh, and don't let anyone else in without checkin' with me first!"

"Of course, my lord. And yes, the distraction of a tea tray is a good idea. It will keep Mrs. Temple busy while you and Miss Davenport straighten yourselves out."

What? Mina's jaw dropped open. "The cheek of the man," she whispered, her face burning with fiery indignation. "He better not have been peeking at us through the keyhole." At least she'd been reclining on the settee and the chair's back would have shielded her scandalous state of dishabille from prying eyes. But still.

Phinn's expression was like thunder. "If he was spyin', he'll rue the day he was born." Casting his gaze over Mina, he grimaced. "I'm afraid I've made a terrible mess o' your hair and uniform."

Mina grinned. "Oh, I can fix that in a jiffy. I can fix your attire and hair too."

"How?" asked Phinn. "You have a spell for that?"

"I certainly do." Mina reached into her governess's pocket and pulled out a small feather duster. "Prepare to be unsmirchified."

Phinn sat back and pulled Mina across his lap. "Does it hurt?"

"Being unsmirchified?" She shrugged a shoulder. "It might tickle a little. But nothing worse than that." Then she sighed. "Although I'm afraid that a Parasol-Academy-perfect appearance will not save me from Mrs. Temple's wrath. Now *that* will hurt."

Phinn tucked a lock of Mina's hair behind her ear. "Maybe she'll surprise you. I mean, it doesn't matter if she revokes your license to practice as a governess now, because you're about to become the next Marchioness of Kinsale."

"True," said Mina. "But what if she has me arrested for kidnapping a child?"

Phinn cradled her face with a gentle hand. "I'm sure she won't. You've told me yourself that the Academy's name and reputation must be protected at all costs. But if she *does* summon Scotland Yard, anyone who tries to arrest you will have to go through me first."

"I love you," said Mina, touching his lean hard jaw. "Your faith in me lends me strength. Now close your eyes." And when Phinn did, she waved her magical duster over them both as she whispered, "*Unsmirchify.*"

A soft white glow immediately enveloped them and a soft wind ruffled their hair and clothes. And when Phinn opened his eyes, he gave a low whistle. "How feckin' brilliant is that?" he murmured, looking down at Mina's gown, which was all done and up and looked like it had just been pressed. His hair and cravat and anything else that had been rumpled were now perfectly in order.

Mina laughed. "It is a handy spell, I'll give you that. Although"—she pushed the magical feather duster back into her pocket as she climbed to her feet—"I doubt I'll have access to Fae magic for much longer. As soon as my license is revoked, I'll just be plain and ordinary Hermina Davenport from Ablington."

Phinn rose too. "You'll never be plain and ordinary to me," he said with fervent sincerity and then he kissed her softly on the lips. "Now"—his expression firmed—"let's go and face Mrs. Temple together and sort out what's to be done about the problem of Sir Bedivere Ponsonby. Like you, I won't be lettin' Christopher get returned to that prat's care. Not . . . not unless he can be un-ensorcelled."

Chapter 31

Wherein a Number of Disclosures Are Made and Truths Are Revealed; And There Is a Surprising Reflection...

As Mina made her way to the library with Lord Kinsale, she rather thought that she knew what it might feel like if one were being led to the gallows. Phinn's hand might be at her back, and he might have offered her a reassuring smile when she looked up into his eyes, but that didn't stop her being assailed by a sudden attack of nerves. Her heart was thudding erratically against her ribs, her knees had jellified, and the pit of her stomach was filled with stone-cold dread.

It didn't matter that she would voluntarily surrender her license to practice as a Parasol Academy governess. What mattered was that she was about to expose her duplicity to a woman she greatly admired and respected. A woman who would decide whether Mina would be forgiven for breaking a countless number of Academy rules and putting both the Fae and earthly Royal Charters at risk, or whether she would be held to account in some way.

Emmeline Chase might have been forgiven for her rule breaking, but she hadn't technically committed any crimes in the eyes of Scotland Yard. Whereas Mina technically had.

The law was *not* on Mina's side.

Mrs. Temple was waiting for Mina by the library fire. She wasn't seated—an ominous sign to Mina's way of thinking—but stood on the hearthrug, gloved hands folded primly in front of her neat waist, ostensibly studying the gilt-edged mirror above the mantelpiece. The tea tray Mrs. Aldershot had provided, sat upon a low table, completely untouched—clearly also not a good sign.

When Mina and Phinn entered, the headmistress turned, and her fair eyebrows climbed toward her hairline. "Lord Kinsale." As she curtsied, her pale gray crinoline skirts, as lustrous as pearls, gently shimmered. "I was not expecting you to join Miss Davenport and me for our meeting. But"—her ever-perceptive gaze transferred to Mina—"considering the unfortunate incident that transpired in Hyde Park earlier this afternoon involved both of you—yes, I've heard about it already, Miss Davenport—I suppose it's best if we kill two birds with one stone, as the expression goes."

"I think that 'unfortunate incident' might be a wee bit o' an understatement, Mrs. Temple," said Phinn with a wry smile. "More like an epic disaster. And it was all me own fault. I was the one who er . . . fell on top o' Miss Davenport. It was an accident, pure an' simple o' course. And she was only doin' her duty, makin' sure that me . . . me blighter of a dog didn't ruin wee Christopher's purple rab—" He broke off and a bright red flush spread across his face. "Mina, I'm sorry, lass," he murmured. "Me mouth ran away with me and—"

Mina placed a hand on his arm. "It's all right, Phinn," she said softly. "Mrs. Temple is going to find out that Lord Fitzwilliam—"

It was Mrs. Temple who interrupted this time. "That Christopher, Lord Fitzwilliam, has been with you, Miss Davenport, ever since Sir Bedivere Ponsonby attempted to take his ward to the Arctic a month ago? That you stole aboard his ship, the *Valiant*, and then rescued the poor child from a terrible fate?"

She arched a brow. "Yes, I know about everything—well, just about everything—in regard to the young viscount's whereabouts and what's been happening. And what a terrible business it is. In fact, I would go so far as to call it a crisis."

If Mrs. Temple had suddenly sprouted a fish tail and turned into a mermaid, Mina would have been less surprised. When she managed to make her jaw work again—it had become unhinged and fallen open during Mrs. Temple's last series of pronouncements—she asked, "But how? How could you know about any of that? And if you did know I'd removed Lord Fitzwilliam from Sir Bedivere's care, why didn't you say anything? Especially when Lord Kinsale hired me as a governess?" She suddenly grew indignant. "I've been fretting for weeks about what to do. I do rather think it's unfair of you, Mrs. Temple, with all due respect, to waltz in here and tell me you've known all along about Lord Fitzwilliam and the danger he's been in but then you've never offered me your support." She shook her head as a sense of betrayal crept through her chest, tightening her lungs. "Of all the things that have happened lately, I find this so very hard to reconcile."

"I agree," said Phinn gruffly. "As you English would say, it's just not cricket."

The headmistress's expression softened. "I understand, Miss Davenport. And I'm so, so sorry that everything has been handled in such a 'hands-off' fashion by me and the Academy. But rest assured, I've been monitoring the situation *very* closely and know how difficult it's been for you. Right from the very beginning, in fact, when Lady Grenfell tasked you with caring for her godson just before she passed away. And I know about her"—she glanced at Lord Kinsale before returning her attention to Mina—"her dream, shall we say?"

Mina frowned in confusion. "But how? Lady Grenfell never left Highwood Hall in Hertfordshire when she fell ill. She was very weak and confined to her bed."

"She wrote to me," said Mrs. Temple. "In her letter, which arrived by special courier, she told me that she was gravely ill and that she feared for her godson's safety because of a dream she'd had, warning her that her godson would be taken to a... a frozen realm. And that Sir Bedivere, who was suddenly acting out of character, would be the one to take him there. It was only a brief missive, but she said that if she took a turn for the worse, she would ask you, Miss Davenport, to care for Lord Fitzwilliam to protect him from such a fate. Indeed, when Sir Bedivere came to the Academy demanding to know who your new employer was after he'd sacked you, Miss Davenport, I refused to say a word because I knew that Lord Fitzwilliam was actually residing at Kinsale House too.

"I also suspected that Sir Bedivere wouldn't give up trying to locate his godson. When the baronet's private detective, Cheavers, had men try to break into the Academy to discover where you now worked, Miss Davenport, I had already put extra protections in place to prevent that. You've always had the Academy's tacit support, even though I couldn't in any way acknowledge what was going on."

"But why?" asked Mina, thoroughly confused. "You could at least have hinted that you knew what I'd done and that I had the Academy's approval."

"If Scotland Yard learned that I was a party to your actions—which were, and still are, technically illegal—I would have been held accountable too," said Mrs. Temple. "As headmistress of the Parasol Academy, I'm duty bound to protect its interests, and it cannot fall foul of the law. At the very least, we'd lose Queen Victoria's support. At worst, such a monumental scandal would result in the Academy being shut down completely. And as you well know, that would put children everywhere in danger."

Mina nodded. She did understand in a way. After all, it was the reason she'd delayed talking to Emmeline about her "pickly" problem for so long. She hadn't wanted to drag her friend into anything illegal either.

"Truth to tell," Mrs. Temple continued, "there's great concern in *other* quarters that—" Breaking off, the headmistress gave a small huff of annoyance. "I feel as though we're beating about the bush and not addressing the main issue. Which we must. Because after your very public and very scandalous display in Hyde Park today, I suspect it won't be long before Sir Bedivere comes looking for you here, Miss Davenport. Things seem to be coming to a definite head." She eyed Phinn. "Lord Kinsale, you seem to be aware of young Christopher's true identity, so I'm assuming Miss Davenport has shared with you the reason why she took her former charge away from his guardian?"

Phinn nodded. "Aye. I do. My fiancée has told me everything about the lad and Lady Grenfell and Sir Bedivere. I know about his ensorcelled ring and the Parasol Academy's ties with the Fae." He cocked a brow as though in challenge. "If-if that's what you were alluding to when you mentioned there was 'concern in other quarters.'"

"I see," said Mrs. Temple, and Mina held her breath as she studied the headmistress's expression. It shifted from the realm of grave to puzzled then outright surprised. "Fiancée?" she repeated, her gaze darting to Mina. "Pray tell, when did this happen, Miss Davenport?"

Mina's face heated. "Just before you arrived, Mrs. Temple, Lord Kinsale proposed to me. And I"—she lifted her chin proudly—"I have accepted."

"Not just to save Miss Davenport from having her reputation ruined—because of the Hyde Park mishap—but because I love her," added Phinn. He caught Mina's eye and smiled. "With me whole heart. And yes, Mrs. Temple, during the course o' our discussion about getting married, she felt compelled to disclose everything about Lord Fitzwilliam. And the fact that she can perform magic and that the Parasol Academy is affiliated with the faery folk." He shrugged a wide shoulder. "As I told Mina, I'd already guessed that somethin' quite out o' the ordinary was goin' on with her when she and wee Christopher mysteriously appeared aboard me ship, the *Kinsale Cloud*, a month ago. You... you cannot blame her for confirmin' me suspicions that magic was involved."

"Considering that I love Lord Kinsale too, I had to tell him the truth," said Mina. "I couldn't in all good conscience say yes to his proposal if he didn't know the secrets I've been keeping from him. It wouldn't have been right."

"Well," said Mrs. Temple, "I must say, that makes things a bit easier for me and the Parasol Academy in terms of managing any scandal associated with the Hyde Park mud mishap at least." Then to Mina's surprise, the headmistress beamed. "Let me be the first to offer you both my heartfelt congratulations."

Oh... Mina blinked in surprise. "Thank-thank you," she said. "Of course, I understand I'll have to tender my resignation, surrender my Parasol Academy governess's license, and cease employing the magic of the Fae—"

"About that," said Mrs. Temple. "As I mentioned before, I believe, there is a crisis afoot. And the Fae agree with me. In light of the unprecedented and perilous times we are in, I think it's best if Good Queen Maeve herself explains the situation and what is at stake."

"Queen Maeve?" breathed Mina. If someone had tried to knock her over with a feathered *Unsmirchify* duster right now, they would have succeeded. "Is that even possible?"

Mrs. Temple laughed. "Why of course it is. I talk to Queen Maeve regularly, seeking her counsel."

"But... But what about the Parasol Academy's rules?" asked Mina. "I've broken so many, including the fact that I've disclosed a good deal of the Academy's secrets to Lord Kinsale. Won't Queen Maeve be angry?"

"In the past, perhaps," said Mrs. Temple. "But not right now. Not when it seems that her sister, Queen Mab, appears intent on stealing Lord Fitzwilliam. That she's the one who's been orchestrating Sir Bedivere's actions through his ensorcelled ring. But I'm sure Her Majesty will be able to explain it better than I can." She looked at Phinn. "Would it be possible to secure the library door before I summon Her Majesty? I'd rather no one enter during our conversation. It must be conducted in private."

"O' course," said Phinn. As he locked the library door, Mrs. Temple asked, "I trust both Lord Fitzwilliam and Tom Fleet are being looked after while we speak?"

"Yes," said Mina, and she explained the arrangements Phinn had made. "I believe they'll be perfectly safe and content for the moment."

"Aye," agreed Phinn as he returned to the fireside. "And the front door is always manned by a pair of footmen, so if Sir Bedivere decides to show up on me doorstep lookin' for Mina or Christopher, I'll hear about it straightaway. And . . . and he'll have me to answer to."

Mrs. Temple inclined her head. "Very good," she said. "Now, just one last thing before I summon Queen Maeve." She reached into her silk gown's pocket and to Mina's surprise, withdrew a *Parasol Academy Handbook*, a great feat in and of itself given the size of the tome. "Lord Kinsale," she said gravely, "I'm going to ask you to swear an oath."

After donning a pair of ley-lensed spectacles also pulled from her pocket, Mrs. Temple opened up the *Handbook* to a page toward the end. "It's all here," she continued, pointing at a particular paragraph. "Just pop on these special glasses"—she passed Phinn the ley-lenses—"place your right hand over your heart, and then you'll simply state what's written here. That upon your honor as a nobleman and a gentleman, you will *never* reveal the Parasol Academy's secrets, or anything to do with the Fae Realm, to anyone at all. Or words to that effect."

"Well, considerin' I'd rather not risk gettin' turned into a rat or a frog or a newt, I'd be more than happy to," said Phinn, sliding on the ley-spectacles then placing a large hand upon his chest.

Once he'd made the pledge Mrs. Temple had asked of him, she nodded her approval. "In light of recent events, I feel as though we need to create honorary memberships for the true loves of Parasol Academy alumnae," she said. "But that is something for another day. Right"—she took back her spectacles and put the *Handbook* down on the table where the untouched tea tray sat—"let us talk with Queen Maeve."

With a fascinated gaze, Mina watched as Mrs. Temple crossed to the gilt-edged mirror above the marble mantelpiece, the one she'd been studying when Mina and Phinn had arrived. The headmistress removed one of her white silk gloves, pushed it into her pocket, then lightly touched her bare fingertips to the glass. And then she began to sing an incantation, one that Mina had never heard before.

Felicity Temple's voice was as sweet and light as any songbird's as the melody floated into the air. Mina couldn't quite catch any of the words, but she could tell it was a Faerillion spell. As Mrs. Temple sang, the mirror's surface began to ripple and shimmer like water; it was as though a breeze had drifted across a moonlit pool.

A moment later, tender sprigs sprouting flower buds and delicate green leaves emerged from the mirror and curled about its gilt edge. The vine-like branches spilled forth, twining around the mantelpiece and its array of porcelain vases and marble busts. When the blossoms opened, revealing their soft pink and white petals, they released a deliciously sweet fragrance that smelled exactly like spring.

Phinn reached for Mina's hand and gave it a gentle squeeze. But when she chanced a glance at her fiancé's face, he was as transfixed by what was happening before them as much as Mina was.

The strange rippling of the glass surface ceased as soon as

Mrs. Temple finished her melodious incantation. Peering into the mirror was like looking into a shifting, silvery-lilac mist, and Mina couldn't see anything much at first. Excitement and not a small degree of apprehension bubbled inside her. She wanted to move closer to the mirror so she could finally see the much-venerated Good Queen Maeve, but she was also a trifle fearful. The last thing she wanted to do was upset the powerful Fae Queen. Well, any more than she possibly already had, considering her rule-breaking spree.

It certainly wouldn't hurt to curtsy.

And then all at once the veil of mist dissipated and the most breath-stealing creature Mina had ever seen materialized in the mirror.

Beside her, Phinn gave a low whistle as though he too were overcome with awe, and Mina couldn't blame him.

Her Royal Highness, Good Queen Maeve, was breathtakingly beautiful with a flawless porcelain complexion. Her dark brows, elegantly arched, were set above lavender-gray eyes fringed with long dark lashes. Her nose was straight, her forehead high and noble, her cheekbones sculpted. Her lips were full and the hue of ripe summer berries, and her cheeks were tinted with the softest hint of rose-petal pink. Upon her pale lilac hair, which framed her face in waves before tumbling to her slender shoulders, sat a delicate crown of small white flowers—hawthorn blossoms perhaps.

And her ivory-white gown—from what Mina could actually see of it because the Fae Queen was only visible from the waist up—appeared to be rendered from gossamer-thin silk that sparkled as though sprinkled with stardust. She sat regally upon an intricately wrought wickerwork throne threaded with ivy and more hawthorn blossoms. And were those almost-transparent lilac wings at her back, shimmering ever so slightly?

When Mrs. Temple curtsied, most gracefully, Mina was prompted to do so too. Phinn tilted his large body into a respectful bow.

"Felicity Temple, you have summoned me," said Maeve with a warm yet regal smile. Her voice brought to mind delicate, lovely, tranquil things like the tinkling of tiny silver bells or water spilling from a fountain. Or the whisper of a gentle breeze through long grass or the boughs of a willow tree. The sigh of a wave against a sandy shore. Mina might still be overwhelmed with awe, but at the same time, she was also strangely comforted. Her instincts told her that she could trust this ethereal being.

"Yes, Your Majesty," said Mrs. Temple. "And as you see"—she gestured toward Mina and Phinn—"we have company. May I introduce Miss Hermina Davenport and her fiancé, Phineas O'Connell, the Marquess of Kinsale?"

"Ah, Hermina Davenport," said Maeve. As her lavender-gray eyes settled on Mina, a shiver passed across Mina's skin. It felt as though the Fae Queen could see right into her heart and mind. But then the odd sensation passed and Mina felt like herself again—well, *almost* like herself apart from the sense of quiet wonderment surrounding her. "Congratulations to you and your Lord Kinsale on your engagement. I take it this is a recent development?"

Mina curtsied again and Phinn inclined his head in acknowledgment. "Yes, it is," he said. "Very recent. And thank you, Your Majesty." He placed a hand lightly upon Mina's back. "I'll take good care 'o Miss Davenport."

"I'm sure you will," said the Queen with a gracious smile. "Now, Miss Davenport"—her brows dipped into a solemn but kind frown as she addressed Mina—"you have been through some trials, all courtesy of my sister, Mab. And you have performed admirably, going above and beyond to protect young Viscount Fitzwilliam. Do not ever doubt that."

"Thank-thank you, Your Majesty," said Mina when she managed to summon her voice. Then she pulled back her shoulders and asked a question that had been burning the tip of her tongue. "But, I must ask, Your Majesty, how do you know all this about me? And what is your sister's endgame? Why has she enlisted Sir Bedivere Ponsonby, Lord Fitzwilliam's guardian, to take him north to the Arctic? Is that the location of your sister's court?"

The Fae Queen sighed. "It is a very long and complicated tale, as these things often are," she said. Her gaze shifted to Phinn. "Lord Kinsale, I suspect our faithful servant, Mrs. Temple, has already asked you to pledge an oath with regard to protecting the Fae Realm's secrets?"

Phinn inclined his head. "She has, Your Majesty. I will not breathe a word to anyone."

Queen Maeve smiled in such a charming fashion, color bloomed in Phinn's cheeks. "I trust your word, Lord Kinsale. I *know* you have a good heart. Now, to best answer your questions, Hermina Davenport"—her attention moved back to Mina—"I must go back in time to when the Parasol Academy was first founded. And even beyond that."

And so, she explained that for centuries, both she and Mab visited the Earthly Realm quite regularly, crossing over from the Fae Realm in places where the veils between the worlds were thin.

Mab's kingdom was located in ancient Caledonia. "Or as you humans now call it, Scotland," said Maeve, "whereas my realm is in Britannia, or as you would say, England, Ireland, and Wales. The problem was, Mab, despite my words of caution and eventually vehement disapproval, took great delight in manipulating humans for her own amusement. On occasion, she would, in fact, have her elvish courtiers steal human children from their parents, leaving changelings in their place."

"A terrible practice indeed," said Mrs. Temple. "It happened to the younger sister of my great-grandmother, Verity Truelove. She was taken when she was but a wee child of five."

"Yes," said Maeve. "And your very brave great-grandmother, through her resourcefulness and cleverness, managed to rescue her sister from Mab's Caledonian court. Which is why I asked Verity to establish the Parasol Academy all those years ago."

"Pardon me ignorance," said Phinn, "but what does Mab actually want with human children?" He shuddered. "I hope to God she doesn't want to bake them into pies like certain so-called faery tales mention."

Maeve's expression grew grave. "Not quite. But she does want to fill her court with servants from the Earthly Realm—to serve as handmaidens and pages and footmen, the poor wee mites. That would be the fate awaiting Lord Fitzwilliam, because make no mistake, she wants the young viscount."

"But why?" asked Mina. "Why has she fixated on Lord Fitzwilliam? That's what I've been struggling to understand all this time."

"I think it's partly to do with the fact that he's a child of noble birth," said Maeve. "You see, unbeknownst to humankind—because of course it's never been recorded in the annals of human history—Mab replaced certain elevated persons of influence and rank within the English Court with changelings. Namely, King Richard the Third, Anne Boleyn, Edward the Fourth, and Charles the First. Mab also supplied her changeling subjects with ensorcelled items of jewelry so she could control them and, in turn, their descendants, if they ever put them on. I believe Mary, Queen of Scots's ill-fated advisor Rizzio, while not a changeling, also wore an ensorcelled pendant about his neck."

"Like Bedivere's silver and obsidian ring?" asked Mina. "Lady Grenfell, Lord Fitzwilliam's godmother, told me it was a family heirloom that once belonged to Charles the First."

"Yes. Lady Grenfell was correct," said Maeve. "And as far as I know, Charles the First was the last noble child Mab successfully abducted. She did attempt to infiltrate the royal nursery and steal one of Queen Charlotte and King George's children. It was then that I resolved to take action. That enough was enough."

"That's when you founded the Academy?" asked Mina. "So that there would be nannies and governesses who could employ Fae magic to help protect their charges?"

"I did," said Maeve with a decided nod. "But more than that, I finally amassed enough magical strength to exile Mab to the Arctic, where she has been imprisoned for the last ninety years."

"Oh," murmured Mina as pieces of the puzzle she had been struggling to make sense of, fell into place. The woman of ice and snow in Christopher's nightmare, and Lady Grenfell's prophetic dream, had indeed been Mab. "So, is that why Sir Bedivere has been trying to take Lord Fitzwilliam so far north? I always thought his quest to navigate the Northwest Passage was a ruse."

"Yes, I'm certain it is too," said Maeve. "Because I surrounded Mab's prison with powerful wards—wards constructed from strong leyline forces running through the earth—it has been well-nigh impossible for her to send her elvish minions out into the world. Although, I fear that she's been chipping away at the wards with her dark magic, trying to create a fissure. The wards, unfortunately, are not perfect and sometimes chinks do form because water—even ice—can unexpectedly warp and weaken the leyline energy."

Mina frowned. "Perhaps that would explain why my teleportation attempt went wrong when I was aboard Sir Bedivere's ship? Perhaps the leyline energy was distorted by the River Avon?"

"It could very well have been a factor," said Mrs. Temple. "When I have a chance, I shall adjust the Parasol Academy curricula to reflect that. That teleporting over water may have unexpected results."

"A sound idea," said Queen Maeve. "But if we may return to the subject of Sir Bedivere, I believe Mab *has* found a small fissure in the wards because when the baronet began to wear his ensorcelled ring, it seems she was able to reach out and control his actions directly. She's essentially recruited him to bring Lord Fitzwilliam to her Arctic prison. So"—she caught Mina's eye—"to answer your earlier question—why is Lord Fitzwilliam Mab's target?—my ever-ruthless sister has simply seen an opportunity and taken it."

Phinn folded his arms across his chest and rocked back on his heels. "But even if Sir Bedivere and young Lord Fitzwilliam managed to reach the Arctic unscathed, how could they break through the wards?"

Maeve's wings fluttered as she adjusted her seat upon her throne. "The wards, essentially, were designed to keep my sister and the supernatural members of her court—her Fae servants—contained. So humans, in theory, should be able to cross them." She sighed, a soft shivery sound, and her expression grew troubled. "Truth to tell, I greatly fear that this latest abduction attempt by Mab—by using ensorcelled humans rather than the Fae to carry out the kidnapping—is only the beginning."

A tremor of apprehension slithered down Mina's spine. "How so?" she asked.

"I'm starting to wonder if Lord Fitzwilliam's attempted abduction is a test of sorts," said Maeve. "And Mrs. Temple does too."

"I do," agreed the headmistress. "Indeed, both Queen Maeve and I are concerned that Mab is plotting something even more sinister. That perhaps she wishes to steal even more noble children, perhaps even Queen Victoria's children from the royal nursery."

"Whether to create havoc in the Earthly Realm for her own perverse enjoyment, or for some unforeseen reason, it is not yet clear to me," added Maeve, her tone as solemn as could be. "But there is trouble brewing. I can sense it."

Mina didn't doubt it. "What I would like to know," she said, "is how can we stop Sir Bedivere trying to take Lord Fitzwilliam to Queen Mab? I'm certain it won't be long before the baronet comes knocking on the door of Kinsale House, looking for his ward. And the law is on his side."

"Aye, we need a plan to stop that happenin'," said Phinn fiercely. "Because there's no way on earth that I'll... that I'll let that wee lad get carted off to some frozen hellhole to serve an evil Fae Queen."

"I agree, my lord," said Mrs. Temple. "In fact, Queen Maeve and I have been discussing strategies for some time. And we *believe* that we've come up with a solution."

Queen Maeve nodded. "For weeks I've been searching through the books in my palace's library, looking for an answer. But it wasn't until a few days ago that I came upon a very old tome written in ancient Faerillion that described a way to destroy an ensorcelled item. The text also indicated that once this had been achieved, the wearer of said item should no longer be subject to the capricious whims of the item's creator. They will be free of the enchantment and their free will and former temperament will be restored."

The Fae Queen caught Mina's then Phinn's eye. "When the opportunity arises, and it will," she said, "you must remove Sir Bedivere's silver and obsidian ring from his person. Of course, that will not be easy, because a human who is ensorcelled often possesses preternatural strength. Confusion spells do not seem to work either."

"Yes, I discreetly tried one out at the Parasol Academy when Sir Bedivere visited, but it did not work," said Mrs. Temple.

"Physically relievin' the baronet of his ring shouldn't be a problem," said Phinn, rolling his shoulders and flexing his fingers.

Maeve laughed. "I've no doubt you could, Lord Kinsale." Transferring her attention to Mina she continued. "As soon as the ring is off Sir Bedivere's hand, then you, Hermina Davenport, must destroy it with Fae fire. It is the only way."

"Fae fire?" repeated Mina. She'd never heard of such a thing.

"It's very powerful, ancient magic," said Mrs. Temple. "And from what I understand, a Fae wand fashioned from hawthorn wood is the only conduit."

"Just like any other magical tool, the hawthorn wand will materialize in your uniform's pocket precisely when you need it," added Queen Maeve. "And of course, to summon the fire, you must also utter the required spell."

Excitement sparked inside Mina at the thought she had been tasked to use such potent magic by the Fae Queen herself. "Which is, Your Majesty?"

Maeve smiled. "*Faerillion Flambosium*," she said in her lyrical voice. "I know it's quite a mouthful, but I have every confidence that when the moment is right, you will employ it."

Mina felt herself blushing. "Thank you for your faith in me, Your Majesty. I'm . . . I'm ever so grateful for the other magical gifts you've provided, on occasion, to assist me with discharging my duties. The *Guardia Nimbus* spell has no doubt provided an extra degree of protection against elvish kidnapping attempts while Lord Fitzwilliam sleeps. And the *Glamify* spell has been most useful too."

"*Glamify* spell?" Mrs. Temple arched a brow. "Goodness, even *I* haven't heard of that one. Pray tell, Your Majesty, is that another magical tool we can add to the *Handbook*?"

"Most definitely," said Queen Maeve. And then she sent Mina a mischievous smile. "I might even consider adding a spell that renders one as cool as a cucumber when required? Considering the alarming rate at which the Parasol Academy's best nannies and governesses are finding their true loves and then resigning . . ."

How . . . how did she know that? Mina was momentarily flummoxed. Could Maeve read minds? It seemed the Fae Queen's powers were more far-reaching than Mina ever could have guessed. But then she emitted a laugh. "I think the addition of a *Cucumberfy* spell wouldn't go amiss."

At that moment, there was a frantic knocking at the door

and Frobisher called out, "Lord Kinsale! My lord! You must come quickly."

Mina's heart all but froze while Phinn cursed beneath his breath. Even the dauntless Mrs. Temple, who always seemed "cucumberfied," appeared rattled.

"He's here." Queen Maeve's voice was no more than a soft-as-silk susurration as a lilac mist began to envelop her. The delicate blossom boughs that had sprouted from the mirror, curled in on themselves and vanished. "Courage, Hermina Davenport and Lord Kinsale," she whispered. "I know you will not fail." And then the mirror's surface rippled and the Fae Queen disappeared from view altogether.

Mina and Phinn exchanged a speaking look—one of concerted determination—before Phinn strode over to the library doors and flung them open. A white-faced Frobisher stood on the other side.

"What's happened?" Phinn demanded, his voice gruff.

But Mina, cold dread snaking down her spine, already knew what the valet was going to say even before he spoke the words. "Smedley let a fellow by the name of Sir Bedivere Ponsonby into the house, my lord, and now he's trying to leave with young Christopher."

Chapter 32

Wherein There Is Much Ado in the Ballroom ...

As Mina and Phinn charged from the library, Mrs. Temple keeping pace, following swiftly, it sounded like all hell had broken loose in the nearby ballroom.

Shouts and curses and barking spilled through the open doors and bounced down the hall. Not a footman, or Smedley for that matter, could be seen.

"Let go of 'im, you bleedin' gobshite. You sodding geezer," yelled Tom. "I'm warnin' you! I'll smack you in the goolies!"

"Yes, let go, you gobshite!" cried Christopher. "I don't want to go to the North Pole! You bleeding well can't make me."

"Ow, you little brat." That was Sir Bedivere. "That hurt!"

Beneath all the insults and vociferous protesting was a chorus of sharp yaps and vicious growls. Brutus was clearly doing his bit, too, to hamper the baronet's efforts to make off with his ward.

When Mina and Phinn burst into the ballroom, it was to discover that Sir Bedivere had seized Christopher by the back of his coat collar and was dragging him toward the door, along with Brutus; the stocky little dog had sunk his teeth into the baronet's trouser leg and was tugging with all his might. Unfortunately, it did indeed appear to be the case that Sir Bedivere possessed a degree of preternatural strength as Queen Maeve had warned. Even though Tom was valiantly attempting to thwart the baronet's progress by vigorously whacking him about the backside and the backs of his legs with a poker, Sir Bedivere, for the most part, seemed immune to the blows.

Nevertheless, Christopher was also doing his best to resist his guardian. He was flailing his arms and kicking out with his legs and generally squirming about like a hooked fish.

There was no sign of Smedley, but Mina was certain that Phinn would deal with him later.

It was definitely Sir Bedivere who had to be dealt with first. And hopefully once and for all.

Phinn seemed to be of the same mind too. "Unhand Lord Fitzwilliam right this instant," he bellowed, crossing the wooden floor in a handful of ground-eating strides. But as he reached out for Sir Bedivere's arm, the one holding Christopher, Tom jabbed the baronet's nether regions with the poker.

With a howl of pain, Sir Bedivere released his ward to clutch at his groin. While Tom's poker blow to the baronet's "goolies" hadn't felled the man, he was at least momentarily stunned. Enough so that Phinn immediately seized the opportunity to crash-tackle the baronet to the floor. Christopher, now free, scampered backward toward Mina and Mrs. Temple. Tom Fleet, still brandishing the poker like a sword, darted across the room to join them too.

"Are you all right?" Mina asked the boys, running her gaze over them both, looking for any signs of injury. Both Christopher and Tom nodded, then after Tom surrendered his poker to Mina, Mrs. Temple bent down and said in a low voice, "Why don't you both come with me, and I'll take you somewhere safe?" Catching Mina's eye, she murmured, "I'll teleport them to the Academy. I can feel Mab's presence. She's growing stronger. It's why it's grown so cold in here."

Mina glanced about the ballroom and was shocked to see that a light dusting of frost was forming over everything—the windowpanes, the chandelier, the marble fireplace, and even across the floor. The tiny ice crystals glittered as sharply as diamonds, hurting Mina's eyes.

Turning back to Mrs. Temple, her breath misted in the air as she whispered, "I can feel her too. You and the boys had best make haste."

"Are we going for a ride in the magic cupboard?" asked Tom as the headmistress took the children's hands and led them into the hall. "Christopher told me all about it. It sounds like wizard fun."

Mina looked back to Phinn and Sir Bedivere, who were still locked together as they wrestled on the ice-crusted floorboards, both of them attempting but failing to gain the upper hand.

Indeed, Mina's heart was in her mouth as Phinn and the baronet rolled to the side and Sir Bedivere landed an almighty blow to Phinn's jaw that nearly knocked his head clean off. As Phinn's head snapped to the side, blood sprayed from his split lip.

Mina winced in sympathy. *Ouch.* Poor darling Phinn. She could try to whack Sir Bedivere with the poker again, but there was a risk she'd injure her fiancé too.

Even so, she moved closer, her booted feet crunching through the frost until she was but a handful of yards away. If there was any chance at all to help Phinn get that cursed ring off Sir Bedivere's hand, she would take it.

Brutus, who seemed to be oblivious to the icy cold, was dancing excitedly around the wrestling men and emitted an encouraging bark as Phinn landed a counterpunch, right in the middle of Sir Bedivere's nose. *That's it, Cutthroat O'Connell. Pummel the feckin' bastard into next week. Hand his arse to him on a plate. Knee him in the nuts. Show him who's the boss.*

The grunting men rolled again, and this time Phinn landed

on top. Even though one of Sir Bedivere's hands was at Phinn's throat, Phinn managed to deliver another powerful punch, this time to the side of the baronet's head. Sir Bedivere's eyes rolled back, the hand squeezing Phinn's throat fell away, and Phinn immediately pounced.

"Mina," he cried, ripping off Sir Bedivere's silver and obsidian ring. "Catch!"

The ring flew through the frosty air toward Mina and she caught it in one hand. "I have it!"

Casting the poker to one side, she immediately dashed across the ballroom to the fireplace. Was it her imagination, or did the ring feel like a small lump of ice that was so cold, it burned the tender flesh of her palm?

Fresh logs and kindling had been stacked in the grate, ready to be lit, and Mina tossed the ensorcelled ring on top of the pile.

Now, to destroy this feckin' thing once and for all.

As Mina plunged her hand into her governess's pocket in search of the hawthorn wand she'd been promised by Queen Maeve, Mab's black eye blazed to life in the ring's obsidian stone.

It glared at Mina so fiercely, with so much malice, Mina's heart stuttered and her blood felt like it was turning into a sluggish, icy slurry in her veins. Her thoughts became muddled, like her head was filled with freezing fog.

Traitor. Weakling, hissed a voice inside her mind. Then came a softer plea as Mab's frost-tipped eyelashes fluttered inside the ring's dark depths. *Put me on . . .*

A wave of dizziness suddenly assailed Mina, and she was possessed with the sudden urge to reach out and do just that. Her half-frozen fingers twitched . . . but then she thought of darling Phinn and Christopher and Tom and Emmeline and Mrs. Temple and her own mother and sister. Everyone she loved, even blinking Brutus.

Gritting her teeth, ignoring the almost overwhelming lure of

Mab's ring, Mina squeezed her eyes shut and whispered "Believe." And then all at once, her cold fingers closed around something hard and smooth and slender in her pocket. The wand!

"Mina? Anytime you w-w-want to destroy that feckin' ring is good with me," called Phinn from behind her. "Bloody Sir Bedivere is stir-stirrin' and I'm not sure how m-m-much longer I'll be able to hold him. He's-he's a strong bastard, I'll give him that."

Mina glanced over her shoulder. Sure enough, the baronet was coming to.

"Sorry," she returned, then hastily withdrew the carved hawthorn wand of light golden-brown wood. Pointing it straight at the ensorcelled ring, Mina gathered her courage, narrowed her gaze and glared straight back at Mab's eye.

"*Faerillion Flambosium,*" she declared in a ringing voice . . . and before she could inhale a breath to triumphantly add, "you wicked cow," there was a bright burst of blinding light within the fireplace, and the ring was engulfed in eye-searing flames of violet and azure blue.

"Thank the Fae," murmured Mina as she stepped back a few paces. Although, it seemed that Queen Mab was not best pleased with having the tables turned on her. As the tongues of magical Fae fire devoured the logs and everything within the fireplace's bricked maw, the silver and obsidian ring let out a shrill and furious scream that rattled the windows and the crystal chandelier and indeed, the whole house. In fact, it was so intense, Mina clapped her hands over her ears and stumbled backward . . . straight into Phinn's waiting arms.

He held her close, Mina's back to his front, and as the last shreds of Mab's cry faded away along with the layer of frost encrusting the room, he murmured, "Well-well done, lass." His deep voice, as warm and soothing as a smile, caressed the shell of her ear. "You . . . you did it."

"*We* did it," Mina whispered as she turned in Phinn's arms. Framing his beloved face in her hands, she frowned as she examined his injuries—his split and swollen bottom lip, a grazed cheekbone, and a nasty-looking purple bruise had begun to flower along his jaw. "Heavens, look at you, my poor, darling man. I'd kiss you but for the fact I'm worried I'll hurt you."

Phinn gave a small snort. "I've had worse. What's more, a bit of a sore lip sure as hell won't stop . . . won't stop me from doin' this." And then he gently cupped Mina's cheek, lowered his head and claimed her mouth in a tender, soft-as-velvet kiss.

Oh. Mina wrapped her arms around Lord Kinsale's strong neck and let herself melt. *Melt into Phinn.* Just knowing that she need never stop kissing this man—the man she loved and would soon marry—was making her heart brim with unfettered joy and delight.

But of course, *this* particular kiss had to end because there were so many things that needed to be sorted out. One of which had just started cursing and making groaning noises behind them.

Phinn had heard the baronet too. Drawing back from Mina, he sighed then gestured over his shoulder with his thumb. "Do you have any idea what the hell we should do about Sir Bedivere?"

"That's a very good question," said Mina. She and Phinn turned to discover that the baronet had pushed himself up to a sitting position. His forearms rested on his bent knees, and his head hung low. Brutus sat nearby and a low growl emanated from the pug's throat every time the man made the slightest movement.

As Mina and Phinn made a cautious approach, Sir Bedivere looked up and regarded them both—and Mina winced in sympathy. Courtesy of Phinn's punches, he *was* rather a mess. One eye was empurpled and almost swollen shut, and his nose was bleeding. He wiped away the trickle with his sleeve then frowned in apparent confusion at Mina. "Miss... Miss Davenport?"

"Yes, it's me, Sir Bedivere," she said. Gesturing at Phinn she added, "And this is my fiancé, the Marquess of Kinsale."

The baronet's brow creased. Then he grimaced and gingerly touched his swollen eye. "So I suppose it was you who knocked the living daylights out of me, Lord Kinsale? Although from what I recall, it seems like I deserved it." His troubled gaze met Mina's. "Have I really been such an utter prat all these weeks?"

"What do you remember?" asked Mina. It would be a relief indeed if Sir Bedivere *did* actually recall at least some of what had gone on. And if he was willing to acknowledge his behavior had been odd, bordering on unhinged, it would be even better.

Sir Bedivere staggered to his feet. "It's all a bit of a blur to be perfectly honest, but I recall there was this godawful woman with black eyes who kept hounding me in my sleep. And that bloody ring." He visibly shuddered. "She made me put it on and then I couldn't take it off, no matter how hard I tried. It's like I've been living in a nightmare. I've not been myself. At all. And oh, God." His mouth twisted and his voice was tinged with remorse as he added, "My poor ward. That poor child. He must be terrified of me. No wonder he called me a gobshite."

So Sir Bedivere *did* seem to remember *some* things. "Yes, he's been through quite a lot," agreed Mina. "But rest assured, Lord Fitzwilliam is safe and well. And the cursed ring that you've been wearing, it's gone now. Destroyed. So that horrid woman won't be plaguing you anymore."

"Who *was* she?" The baronet seemed genuinely perturbed. "She made me buy a ship. She kept telling me that she wanted my ward."

Mina sent him a kind smile. "I think it's best if we all visit the Parasol Academy. Mrs. Temple, the headmistress if you recall, might be able to help with . . . explanations. And you'll be able to see Christopher—that's where he is at the moment."

Of course, she didn't want Sir Bedivere to take Lord Fitzwilliam away—in fact the very idea made her heart ache terribly—but unless the baronet agreed to relinquish his guardianship, there was little Mina could do.

Sir Bedivere was frowning. "Has my ward been at the Parasol Academy since he went missing from the *Valiant*?"

"No, he's been residin' here at Kinsale House," said Phinn. "With-with me own ward, Tom. Miss Davenport has continued to act as Lord Fitzwilliam's governess."

Mina summoned a reassuring smile. "Lady Grenfell asked me to look out for him while you . . . while you were unwell."

"Thank heavens you did," said Sir Bedivere, his expression the epitome of harried. "Good God. What was I thinking, trying to cart little Christopher off to the North Pole? The North Pole! Who on earth would want to go there? I think even the walruses and polar bears don't want to be there."

Mina couldn't help but laugh. "I think you might be right."

Phinn lightly clapped the baronet on the shoulder. "Why . . . why don't I have my valet assist you with tidyin' up, and then we'll visit the Parasol Academy. Then we can sort out what to do . . . to do about your ward."

"Yes . . ." Sir Bedivere rubbed his furrowed brow. "Dashed if I know what to do, though. I've made such a complete mess of things. If Christopher were older, I could send him off to Eton or Harrow. They'd do a good job of educating him at least." He released a doleful sigh. "No doubt I've been blacklisted by the Parasol Academy after all"—he waved his hand around the ballroom—"this. Perhaps I'll have to employ that tutor Meecham again."

Mina gasped. When the baronet looked up and saw the expression on her face—she couldn't hide her horror—his frown deepened. "What's wrong with Meecham?"

"Well, aside from the fact he thinks nothing of rapping a child's knuckles if they make a simple mistake," said Mina, "don't you think Christopher deserves to live somewhere where he feels safe and cherished and wanted? Not an encumbrance or nuisance?"

Sir Bedivere looked at Mina, his expression thoughtful. "He's been happy here with you and Lord Kinsale, Miss Davenport?"

She lifted her chin. "I believe he has. Very much so. He looks up to Lord Kinsale and he's found a very best friend in the marquess's ward, Tom. And I... I've come to care for Christopher rather a lot. More than I can say, in fact."

"Aye, me too," said Phinn. "In many ways, I feel like we've grown into a... a family of sorts. It-it might be unconventional in some respects, but that doesn't mean it isn't a home filled with love and laughter." He caught Mina's eye and smiled. "At least I like to think so."

"Well then," said Sir Bedivere. "I have a lot to consider moving forward. When Christopher's parents asked me to be his guardian, when he was but a wee babe, I of course agreed. The late Lord Fitzwilliam was a close friend of mine and I've only ever wanted his son to be happy. Perhaps it's time for Christopher to decide what he wants."

"And the money you've had access to, managing Christopher's trust, that's not a factor?" asked Mina.

Sir Bedivere gave a small snort. "Perhaps if I were still planning on navigating the Northwest Passage, an insane venture sure to end in financial ruin, not to mention disaster. But no, I have sufficient wealth, so that's never been a consideration." He grimaced. "Well, until I put on that cursed family heirloom."

Hope bloomed inside Mina's chest. She was so very relieved that the un-ensorcelled baronet was willing to consider the idea of relinquishing his guardianship. If Christopher wanted to live with Mina and Phinn and Tom at Kinsale House, no doubt there would be quite a long-winded bureaucratic process that would have to be slogged through in the Chancery Court. But in the end, it would be worth it.

After Phinn delivered Sir Bedivere into Frobisher's capable hands, Mina asked her fiancé about one other matter that was niggling at her like a thistle in her stocking. "Is there anything we should do about Smedley?" she asked. "He expressly disobeyed your direct order not to let Sir Bedivere in. And while I know it might have been difficult to stop the baronet from barging his way into Kinsale House when he was under Mab's control, it was Frobisher who raised the alarm."

They were in the hall outside Phinn's suite of rooms. Nevertheless, Phinn glanced about to see if they were alone before he responded. "Aye, we should," he said. "I've lost count of the times he's behaved in high-highly questionable ways. Not to mention his continued lack of respect. Not-not just for me, but for you too." He caught Mina's hand and kissed it. "We'll deal with him as soon as we return from the Parasol Academy. None of us, Tom and Christopher included, need that sort of dis-disagreeable presence in our lives."

Mina couldn't have agreed more.

With all her heart she hoped that Phinn's dream—which was hers too—could become a reality. That she and the marquess, Tom and Christopher, and even Phinn's wee beastie of a pug, could be a true family.

Finding out what the future held for all of them was only a trip to the Parasol Academy away.

Chapter 33

In Which Any Confusion Is Dispelled (Not Spelled); And Rubbish Is Effectively Dealt With...

"Of course, I would love to live with you, Miss Davenport. And Lord Kinsale and Tom, forever and ever," Christopher had declared in Mrs. Temple's office at the Parasol Academy when Mina had asked the boy who he would like to reside with if he had a choice.

And just like that, any confusion about where Lord Fitzwilliam stood on the issue had been cleared up. Sir Bedivere had confirmed he would support an official change in guardianship through the Chancery Court. Mrs. Temple had even offered to have a quiet word with Queen Victoria about the matter; if the Queen herself lent her support to the change, then it was likely that it could all be made official within a handful of weeks rather than months.

Mrs. Temple had also pulled Mina aside for a quiet word. "I think that for the time being, it would be best if you retained access to your magical tools," she'd said. The headmistress had reasoned that a break with the usual protocol—that a Parasol nanny or governess who resigned her commission had to give up practicing Fae magic—was justified given that Queen Mab might still continue to chip away at the protective wards keeping her contained in her Arctic prison. Hopefully Good Queen Maeve would soon be able to make those wards "watertight" so her sister would no longer pose a threat to Christopher, or any children at all.

"Only time will tell though," she'd concluded. "Until then, Miss Davenport, I would recommend that you continue to cast a *Guardia Nimbus* spell each night. And one for young Tom Fleet. He's Lord Kinsale's ward and after this afternoon, Mab could very well focus her attention on him too. I'm certain Queen Maeve would concur."

Mina had readily agreed. As always, she would do whatever she could to protect any child in her care. And Christopher and Tom were so very special to her. She knew Phinn felt the same as well. To think that very soon they would be a family made her heart glow.

As for Sir Bedivere and the fact that he now knew quite a lot about the Parasol Academy, including the existence of the Fae, he happily agreed to swear an oath of secrecy on the *Parasol Academy Handbook*, just like Phinn had. "Even if I hadn't taken an oath, I would never say anything about Mab or the Fae or the Academy," he'd said. "I'd be locked up in an asylum somewhere if I admitted to anyone I'd been ensorcelled by a cursed ring." Chagrin colored his voice as he added, "Now I just have to work out what to do with this dashed ship I bought. Although, I could do with a vacation, so maybe I'll set sail for somewhere warm before winter sets in. The Caribbean or Mauritius or Tahiti perhaps." He shivered. "Certainly no place where I could be turned into an icicle."

Despite the fact a dismal gray evening was descending over London, the mood in the Marquess of Kinsale's carriage on the way back to Eaton Square was exuberant. There was much discussion between Mina, Phinn, Christopher, and Tom about having a celebratory "picnic" dinner consisting of all their favorite dishes—namely colcannon and sausages and cake—right in the middle of the drawing room floor.

Although upon arriving home, it was to discover there was another surprise awaiting Phinn and Mina. As the carriage pulled up outside Kinsale House, they were greeted with the sight of Meddley Smedley and Mrs. Alderot ordering a pair of footmen to lug their trunks, various carpetbags, and several valises out to the front portico.

"Go-going somewhere?" inquired Phinn after he'd helped Mina and the children to alight.

Mina, who'd spied Frobisher lurking in the entry hall along with Brutus, quietly beckoned the valet over to usher the boys inside. Christopher and Tom didn't need to hear a discussion which was bound to turn unpleasant.

Smedley looked down his hawkish nose at Phinn. "After Mrs. Aldershot and I heard from some of the other staff about what happened between you and Miss Davenport in Hyde Park this afternoon, we have decided we can no longer afford to work here. *Your* reputations might be sullied, but we refuse to let that happen to ours."

"I see," said Phinn, narrowing his gaze.

"And what have you heard, exactly?" challenged Mina once the children were safely out of earshot. "Because listening to gossip does you no credit, Smedley." She turned her attention to the housekeeper, who was wearing an expression that was a cross between superior and belligerent. "Nor you, Mrs. Aldershot."

The woman sniffed. "That's rich coming from the likes of *you*, Miss Davenport. I thought Parasol governesses were supposed to be exceptional rather than common."

"You might be lea-leavin' me employ, Mrs. Aldershot," snapped Phinn. "But I'd have a care with how you . . . how you address me fiancée." When the housekeeper gasped, his mouth lifted into a wry smile. "Yes, this afternoon I proposed to Miss Davenport and she's con-consented to be me wife. So you'd best not insult the woman who could provide you with a ref-reference."

Smedley gave a snort. "Marchioness or not, I doubt a reference from *her*"—the butler's derisive gaze raked over Mina—"would be worth the paper it's written on. I certainly shan't be seeking one from you, my *lord*. Your predecessor would be horrified—"

"Enough!" growled Phinn, stalking up the front stairs until his nose was only inches from Smedley's. Given his bruised jaw, swollen cheek, and split lower lip, the Marquess of Kinsale exuded the energy of a man who should not be crossed. Indeed, the butler had turned as white as a sheet. "I'll-I'll not hear one more word from either of you. In fact, bo-both of you can wait on the pavement for a hansom cab. Not . . . not on me doorstep."

Transferring his gaze to the two footmen manning the front door he added, "I'd like you to move their trunks and other baggage down the stairs. Right n-n-now in fact."

"But . . . but it's started raining again," complained Mrs. Aldershot. And indeed it had. The dark clouds that had amassed above the square looked like they were about to release bucketloads. "We'll get soaked. So will our luggage."

Mina, who'd already retreated to the shelter of the portico, arched a brow. "Well, considering you no longer work here, that's not really Lord Kinsale's problem now, is it?" she said.

Good riddance to bad rubbish, I say, growled Brutus from the doorway. He looked up at Mina. *And I don't mean you, Miss Davenport. Since the master is goin' to marry you, I've decided ye're agreeable enough. Well, as long as ye keep those sausages comin' out o' yer pockets.*

Mina smiled. *I've decided you're agreeable enough too, Brutus. And I* will *always* reward good behavior.

The pug returned his gaze to the butler and housekeeper,

who were now fuming on the pavement. *Do you want me to cock me leg on their luggage? Maybe that valise or that carpetbag? Or on Meddley Smedley's trouser leg? A pug must do what a pug must do when nature calls*, remarked Mina. *There might even be a sausage in it for you.*

Brutus gave a yip of excitement as he barreled down the stairs, and as Mina took Phinn's arm and her fiancé escorted her into Kinsale House, it was to a chorus of outraged exclamations and curses from the butler and housekeeper.

For once, Mina was not going to reprimand the pug for exhibiting bad manners. Because sometimes, bad manners were called for when dealing with nasty bullies like Smedley and Mrs. Aldershot.

As Brutus had so aptly stated: Good riddance to bad rubbish.

CHAPTER 34

In Which a Spell Is Cast and Magic Is Made...

The *Guardia Nimbus* butterfly that rested above Christopher's head, lazily flapped its lilac-hued wings as Mina softly closed the bedroom door.

After a rousing evening of drawing room picnicking and parlor games, both Christopher and Tom were exhausted. In fact, when Phinn read the boys a bedtime story at half past eight, it was Tom—usually the more energetic of the pair—who'd nodded off first in the additional bed that had been set up on the opposite side of Christopher's room. The boys, now the very best of friends, had decided that they would love to share the same bedchamber, and neither Mina nor Phinn had had any objections.

Indeed, the *Guardia Nimbus* spell would also protect Tom. A butterfly with soft lavender wings had settled upon his pillow, just above his head when Mina had cast the spell. Mina prayed that Mab wouldn't be able to deploy any elvish kidnappers to the children's room, that the wards of her prison would hold, but nevertheless, and in accordance with Mrs. Temple's recommendation, it wouldn't hurt to employ extra precautions to ensure both boys were as safe as could be throughout the night.

But Mina didn't want to think about the Fae or Mab or her minions any longer. Especially when she turned to face Phinn, who'd been waiting for her to emerge. He'd ditched his constrictive coat during the drawing room shenanigans and was dressed informally in his shirtsleeves, a black silk waistcoat, loosened cravat, and dark trousers. And the way he was regarding her, with such tender adoration, Mina was tempted to pinch herself to make sure she hadn't fallen asleep and was dreaming.

Gathering Mina into his arms, he kissed her gently. "If I hadn't just seen you cast that spell with me own eyes, I wouldn't have believed such a thing were possible," he said, his voice threaded with quiet awe. "What an absolute marvel you are, Hermina Davenport. And you're all mine."

She laughed softly and touched his poor bruised jaw. His cheekbone still bore a graze, but a special ointment that she'd found in her uniform's pocket had helped to heal his split lip. "I am. Completely yours. But the magic"—she waved a hand at the bedroom door—"that's all thanks to the Fae."

"Darlin' Mina," he said, tracing a gentle fingertip down her cheek. "In my eyes, you *are* the magic."

Oh... Mina swallowed as her throat tightened with so much love, she didn't think she could speak. She placed her hands against Phinn's solid chest to reassure herself this beautiful man was real. And indeed he was. She could feel his heat and the steady thump of his heart beneath her palm. "Phineas O'Connell. I think I've been waiting for someone like you my whole life," she murmured huskily. "You're a gift I never expected to receive and I will treasure you every single day, now and always."

Reaching up, she kissed Phinn, and his mouth was soft and warm and welcoming. When they drew apart, and Mina met his gaze, an emotion—something akin to speculation or a question perhaps—flickered in the depths of his gorgeous green eyes. And Mina knew what he was going to say, and she knew what her answer would be, even before he spoke.

"Would you consider spendin' the night with me in me suite?" he asked as he laced his fingers through hers. "We haven't really had time to speak about when we should wed, but . . . but I will readily confess that I would like nothin' more than to marry you sooner rather than later. O' course, we can wait to share a bed—"

Mina pressed a finger to his lips. "Phinn, my darling man, I would love to spend the night with you. I cannot wait for you to show me everything there is to know about lovemaking."

He lifted her hand and kissed her knuckles. "Truly? You're not just sayin' that? Because I'm a man and impatient and—"

"Truly," she said with a smile. "I think from the moment you caught me in your arms aboard the *Kinsale Cloud* I've been wondering what it would be like to be with you . . . in that way. Besides"—she looked up at him through her lashes—"I'm dying to learn about the magic you can do with these." She waggled her fingers at him.

Leaning into her, Phinn's lips grazed the shell of her ear. "Wait 'til you see what I can do with me mouth, my darlin' Mina," he whispered, his breath a hot caress that sent a shiver of delicious anticipation through her, straight to her lower belly.

His fingers still threaded through hers, Phinn tugged her toward the staircase at the end of the hall, then they were rushing down to the next floor where his rooms lay. Oh, how breathless she felt and so very light, simply bubbling with so much excitement and expectation and fierce joy, she thought she might burst.

Frobisher had already retired for the night, and Brutus, his belly full of sausages and cake, was fast asleep and snoring on the rug before the sitting room fire. Which was a relief, to say the least. Mina did not want any interruptions. Not when Phinn was about to teach her all about physical love, both the giving and the taking.

Mina and Phinn tiptoed past the pug, into the bedroom, and as soon as the door snicked shut, Phinn was kissing her. His hands were in her hair, stroking down her spine, framing her waist, cupping her bottom through her skirts, everywhere. His increasingly bold caresses were expertly awakening Mina's desire, sending ripples of delicious sensation through her entire body. Making her moan and shiver and want like she'd never wanted before.

She quickly found herself pushed up against the bedroom door's panels, straddling one of Phinn's muscular thighs. As she kissed him back with a matching passion, her eager hands traced over his wide shoulders, broad chest, and the swell of his biceps, wanting to learn the shape of his lean, hard body. In Mina's eyes, he was an Adonis. And she wanted him so very badly.

Desire was an insistent pulse between her thighs and she had the shocking urge to rock against Phinn's leg. To ease the building ache there. And Phinn noticed.

Breaking the kiss, he stared down at her. The corner of his mouth inched into a smile that was pure devilry. "Could-could it be that kisses are not enough for you, lass?"

Mina toyed with Phinn's black cravat. "I think you can tell that they aren't."

Phinn's eyes gleamed. "Well, what say we remove some of these troublesome clothes"—he ran a finger down the line of buttons at the front of her far too prim and proper uniform—"because they're only gettin' in the way of us both findin' pleasure?"

Mina's face heated but she wasn't about to naysay the man she loved. Not when she wanted fewer layers of fabric between their bodies too. "I want that more than you could possibly know." It wasn't a lie. She boldly slid her hand beneath Phinn's waistcoat and reveled in the feel of his ridged torso beneath the skin-warmed cambric. "In fact, just last night while I touched myself," she whispered, "just like you asked me to, I was fantasizing about being naked in your arms. Of your bared body covering mine, claiming me. I can't wait to be joined with you."

Phinn closed his eyes and Mina swore she could feel his aroused manhood jerk against her thigh. "Mina," he groaned, "if... if you keep talkin' like that, lass, I'm goin' to come undone even before I unfasten the buttons on your feckin' gown."

Heavens. She, Mina Davenport, was really having that much of an effect on this strong-as-Hercules man? What an undeniably heady thrill. Although she was but a novice when it came to bedsport, it gave Mina the confidence to take things further. She tugged Phinn's shirt from the waistband of his trousers, then pushed her hand beneath where her fingertips found taut, hot flesh. "Well, we'd best strip now, before it's too late."

A growl rumbled in Phinn's chest, and Mina felt it all the way to her toes. He began to undo the fastenings of her bodice, but when his fingers slipped, he swore and grumbled about the "feckin' ridiculous number of cursed wee buttons" he had to deal with. A second growl of frustration heralded the yanking apart of said bodice—fabric ripped, buttons flew, and a bolt of pure lust, wild and primal and instinctual, arced through Mina, straight to her core.

It wasn't only Phinn who was becoming undone. She was too.

Gripping Phinn's head, she kissed him fiercely and then they were stumbling toward the bed. Her gown was pushed off her shoulders, down her arms, and within moments, it had pooled on the floor along with her petticoats. Phinn's waistcoat, cravat, and braces soon followed, joining Mina's uniform in the pile of discarded clothing. He toed off his shoes, pulled off his socks, but when he threw off his shirt in one swift movement, Mina paused in her efforts to shed anything else of her own.

Of course, she'd seen Phinn sans shirt on two other occasions, but nothing could compare to being this close to him when he was completely bare from the waist up with no towel or robe to hide any part of him. She bit her lip as she devoured the sight of this exquisite male specimen... this man that loved her and she would soon marry.

He was so well-made, so perfect in every way, from his mountainous shoulders to his heavy pectoral muscles with their bronzed nipples, to his washboard of an abdomen (good Lord, she really could count the ridges of muscles there), Mina's breath caught in her lungs. And then there were his huge biceps and corded forearms and large hands—hands that would soon be exploring her own body.

Even the dusting of dark hair on his chest and the intriguing line of it that arrowed down into his trousers were mouthwateringly mesmerizing to Mina. As for Phinn's rampantly aroused male member... it stood to attention, tenting the fall of his trousers like a flagpole. To think she'd soon get to see that part of him too. And later, that impressive hard length would slide deep inside her and she truly would be his...

Mina swallowed. When she raised her eyes to Phinn's he was watching her, an expression of tender concern on his ruggedly handsome face. "You can change your mind about this any time, Mina. I clearly can't hide how badly I want you. But I'm a large man, everywhere, and if the sight of my... my unruly cockstand is givin' you second thoughts, we can do other things. Things that just bring *you* pleasure." He gave her a half smile. "I can wait until we're wed."

Mina placed a hand on his bare chest. "I love how unruly your... your cockstand is," she murmured. "To see you so aroused, arouses me too. And you should know by now, I'm no shrinking violet."

"My brave, beautiful Mina." Her hair, which had become hopelessly mussed during their kisses, was falling down around her face and he tucked a loosened lock behind her ear. "Life with you is going to be the most amazin' adventure."

She smiled. "And to think we've only just begun."

"Aye." Phinn's smile was slow and all kinds of wicked as he slid the straps of her chemise down, baring her shoulders completely. Leaning into her, he placed a hot, open-mouthed kiss on the side of her neck as he began to slowly and methodically release the fastenings at the front of her corset.

As he worked, his fingers brushed her nipples, making them peak impudently through the thin lawn of her chemise, and when his smoldering gaze lingered there, frankly admiring the sight of her breasts, a burning blush rose in her throat and swept over her face. An unexpected feeling of uncertainty fluttered in her belly.

Why was she suddenly so damned self-conscious and more missish than a room full of Parasol Academy graduates? Good heavens, the man had fondled and kissed her bared breasts but a few hours ago. And in the drawing room!

Phinn's hands had rucked up her chemise to her waist as though he were about to untie the ribbon securing her drawers. But perhaps he'd sensed the rising tension in her body as he paused. "You're beautiful, Mina," he murmured, his gaze catching hers. "Don't ever doubt it."

"I . . . I know I'm being a ninny," she returned, her voice breathy with nerves. "And I wasn't expecting to be beset with last-minute jitters. It's just . . . it's just that I've never been completely naked in front of anyone before. Especially not a man." She released an awkward laugh. "And you're so beautiful and perfect and I'm . . . well, let's be honest, I'm a little curvier than I would like to be. Courtesy of my penchant for cake, no doubt." She couldn't contain a sigh. "So much for my much-professed bravery."

"Hey . . ." Phinn cradled her hot cheek, stroking there with the pad of his thumb. "You're not a ninny at all. You're feelin' vulnerable and there's nothin' wrong with that. But... but your curves are gorgeous. Delectable in fact, and don't you ever think otherwise. Truth to tell, I'm bewitched by you, always have been, and... and I meant it when I said you're beautiful." His other hand skimmed down her side to her hip, his caress warm and reassuring. "Every bit o' you. But-but if you don't want me to remove anythin' else, that's all right too. Just say the word." His mouth hitched in a wicked smile. "Believe me, I can work around clothes."

Mina held his gaze. How she loved this man. How he seemed to read her so well, and how he understood her and never judged her about anything at all. "No. We can keep going. When we come together, I don't want there to be any sort of barrier between us."

Phinn's mouth hovered above hers. "Then that's how it will be, oh love of mine," he murmured before his lips brushed over hers in the softest of kisses. Then his hands were unpinning her already tumbledown bun until her locks were free and spilling down her back and about her shoulders and over her breasts. Whether he'd done so to create the illusion of a veil that partially shielded her nudity, or whether he just wanted to see her as no one else ever had, with her hair unbound, she wasn't sure. But nevertheless she appreciated the care he was taking with her, more than she could say.

A few moments later, when Mina's drawers were gone and she stood before Phinn in nothing but her chemise and stockings and shoes, he sank to the floor and began to unbutton her half boots. And then he found her Parasol Academy knife, strapped to her ankle. From beneath the tumble of dark brown hair across his brow, he looked up at her, his green eyes agleam. "I don't think you'll be needin' this anymore," he said, amusement brimming in his voice as he unfastened the strap and removed the sheathed weapon.

"You never know. It might come in handy for peeling apples or opening letters or even shaving. It's very sharp," she returned.

He rubbed a hand over his jaw where his night beard was growing. "Are you tellin' me I need a shave? Because you know I'll do it for you." He grinned. "I... I can wake Frobisher."

Mina aimed a frown at him. "Don't you dare. Aside from the fact I'm practically naked, I've waited weeks for this, Phineas O'Connell. I'm willing to endure the rasp of your whiskers when you kiss me."

"What about if I kiss you here?" He was still kneeling on the floor, looking up at her as he slid a hand up her leg, slowly, slowly over her stocking-clad ankle, then her calf, coming to a halt at her knee. And then he turned his head and kissed her on the inner side of her lower thigh, making her gasp. Even through the fine wool of her stocking, she could feel the heat of that burning kiss.

"Or here?" Phinn's hand traveled higher, lightly caressing the bare skin above her stocking until he paused at the top of her inner thigh. His thumb grazed the sensitive flesh there, and Mina bit her lip in an effort to stifle a moan. "Would... would you let me kiss you here, Mina?" he asked again. "Or even here?" This time, his thumb brushed against the damp seam of her sex and Mina did moan. "Even though me jaw is rough with whiskers?"

"Yes," she whispered. She was breathless. Practically panting. All her nerves had fled and desire was rushing through her, full force. "Yes. You can kiss me anywhere."

Phinn smiled wolfishly. Then grasping the hem of her chemise, he pulled the flimsy lawn garment up, up, up as he rose to his feet, and when she raised her arms to help, he tugged it off completely. "Darlin', I'm going to kiss you *every*where."

And then he fitted his mouth to hers and as he kissed her deeply, he picked her up as though she weighed nothing at all and carried her to the bed. As he gently laid her on the green silk counterpane, he followed her, never breaking the kiss. The silk was cool against her bare back and bottom and the tops of her legs.

Phinn drew back, and after he peeled off her stockings and tossed them onto the floor, he hovered above her, bracing himself on his strong arms. His green gaze wandered over her nudity in a leisurely sweep, enflaming her need to blazing proportions. Her apprehension, her doubts were all burnt to cinders by the hunger in his eyes. A hunger that was in stark contrast to the way he slowly, almost lazily smiled, then dipped his head and began feasting on one of her breasts. He grasped the plump flesh with one hand while his soft-as-velvet tongue swirled around and around the straining peak. And when he caught the taut bud between his lips and gently suckled . . . Mina clutched at his shoulders as a whimper escaped her. *Sweet heaven.* She could get addicted to this, these glorious sensations of being adored and worshipped and pleasured.

Phinn was clearly taking care of her first. He might be aflame with lust too, but it was *her* satisfaction that mattered to him. It made her love him all the more.

When Phinn transferred his attention to her other breast, Mina arched restlessly against him. Desire was an insistent pulse between her thighs and when her sex brushed his erect manhood, she couldn't contain her moan.

Sensing her need, Phinn transferred his weight to one arm, and as he continued to lavish attention upon her breasts, one of his large hands stroked over her softly rounded belly until she could feel his fingers flirting with the cluster of silken curls hiding her mound.

Raising his head, he caught her gaze. "Do . . . do you want me here, Mina? Touching you? Kissing you?"

"Yes," she whispered, parting her thighs for him in invitation. "You know I do."

His smile was pure sin. "I'm not sure who's goin' to enjoy this more. Prepare to be pleasured, sweetheart." And when he slid one long finger down where she was slippery and aching with want, where she needed him most, she gasped at the exquisite sensation.

Ooooh. Mina closed her eyes as Phinn stroked and caressed and teased her most intimate place.

How did he know that when he touched her sex like that, so knowingly and perfectly, delicately circling that tiny throbbing nub that she alone had explored, that her desire would build and build and soon she would be swept up in a maelstrom of swirling bliss?

But then to her frustration, he stopped, and she whimpered in protest.

"I'm . . . I'm going to kiss you here now," he whispered. His voice was rough as he softly slid a fingertip along the damp furrow of her sex. "Explore every bit of you."

She nodded, for the moment too breathless to speak. Oh, how wanton and wicked she was becoming. She'd never felt so alive. "I want you to," she confessed when she found her voice. "I've been thinking about it since . . . since this afternoon. When you fell face-first into my lap."

Phinn's mouth kicked into a wicked smile. "I'm glad I'm not alone then. I haven't been able to stop thinkin' about it either."

He kissed her briefly but tenderly, laved each nipple, then moved slowly down her body, his mouth roaming over her with studied purpose. His lips grazed across her ribs in teasing and tickling brushes. His tongue traced over the outline of one hip then the other before flickering over and around her navel, making her shiver. And when he settled at the end of the bed, his hands gently coaxed her legs apart so she was completely open to him.

Oh my. She should be awash with self-consciousness. But she wasn't. The heated intensity of Phinn's gaze, the naked hunger of his expression as he looked at her *down there*, his soft words of praise as he murmured how wonderfully wet and ready she was for him, made fresh desire bloom low in Mina's belly.

Dropping her head back on the pillows, she closed her eyes and gave herself over to Phinn... the man she loved, who would soon show her heaven.

Phinn settled his shoulders between Mina's splayed thighs. He was determined to make this experience so very wonderful for her, if it was the last thing he did. He was throbbing, burning up with the need, but *his* release didn't matter right now. This decadent act he was about to perform was all about showing Mina, this woman he adored, the profound pleasure that making love could bring.

Indeed, this was a "first" of sorts for him too. Never before had he made love with someone who he did actually love. Any carnal relations he'd had in the past had been very much about living in the moment. It had been about having fun and finding immediate gratification with willing women who only wanted that too. It hadn't been about forming an intimate and loving connection like this experience truly was.

So when Phinn placed soft, lingering kisses on the silken skin of Mina's inner thighs, he reveled in the sounds she made—all the tiny intakes of breath and sighs. And the way she shivered and her fingers slid into his hair and tightened upon his scalp, all of those things provoked a hum of satisfaction in his body.

With his tongue, he tasted the dew-drenched petals of her sex, teased the tiny pink bud where her pleasure was centered, with calculated swirls and delicate flutters. In his quest to show Mina true pleasure, he would leave no part of her untouched or unloved.

To prepare her for their joining, he slowly slid one of his

fingers inside her, delving and then plundering gently in a steady rhythm. And when she moaned and arched her hips, pressing herself to his mouth, he added another finger. The "Oh yes . . . yes, Phinn" that tumbled from her lips in response to his intimate stroking was the sweetest thing he'd ever heard.

Her panted breaths, the scent of her, the taste of her on his tongue, the feel of her hot and wet silken flesh clasping his fingers so tightly, was simply magical to Phinn. It seemed Mina was being swept away by the magic of the experience too. When he drew on her core, suckling with gentle insistence, her desire rose swiftly to claim her. As pleasure broke over her, she cried out and gripped his head, pulling his hair almost to the point of pain, but Phinn didn't mind in the least. He exulted in the evidence of her satisfaction and as she basked in its aftermath, he crawled up her body and gathered her into his arms and basked in the wonder of her too.

When Mina's breathing returned to a pace that resembled normal, when pleasure's glow began to ebb, she lifted her head from Phinn's chest and pressed her lips to his stubbled jaw. "Thank you," she murmured. "You certainly didn't overexaggerate your talents when it comes to lovemaking. I think I was practically teleported to another plane of existence."

Phinn chuckled softly and the deep rumble in his chest was music to Mina's ears. "I'll take that as a compliment," he said. Pushing himself up onto one elbow, he stared down at her. "But just wait until you see where I can take you with this." He shifted his hips and the jut of his "unruly cockstand" made Mina's pulse flutter with excitement.

"We should definitely do something to rectify your lack of satisfaction, Phineas O'Connell," she said as she boldly reached between their bodies and gently clasped the rock-hard length of him through his trousers. When Phinn groaned and pushed himself into her hand, another thrill skittered through her.

"Sweet Jaysus, lass. Keep-keep that up and you'll . . . you'll be havin' to cast that *Unsmirchify* spell o' yours," he said through gritted teeth.

"Well, perhaps you should get rid of your trousers," she suggested, running a finger along the waistband before toying with the straining buttons. "I must say, your new tailor is to be commended though, because honestly, I have no idea how you haven't burst the stitches on these."

Phinn laughed as he rolled off the bed. "Neither do I," he said as he swiftly undid the rest of the fall front then shoved down the garment in question. When he straightened and Mina took in *all* of him, she couldn't contain her gasp.

Oh. My. Lord. Phinn's erect member was as breathtakingly impressive as the rest of him. As Mina's eyes returned to Phinn's, he grinned almost sheepishly. "It's . . . er . . . I'm not . . ." Drawing a deep breath he said, "I told you I'm large."

"Yes, yes, you are," she murmured huskily. But she wasn't afraid. If anything, her craving for this man to claim her fully had only sharpened. She reached out her arms in invitation, wanting his big, beautiful body to cover hers. She wanted his mouth on hers. His hands loving her. His manhood moving inside her, driving her to the brink of pleasure.

"If . . . if you can, try to relax your muscles so your body opens to me," Phinn murmured as Mina lay down and he slid over her. "I'll be as gentle as I can, but . . . but when I first enter you, it will likely be uncomfortable."

Mina pushed the thick sweep of Phinn's hair away from his brow. "Don't worry about me," she whispered. "I might be a virgin, but courtesy of my Parasol Academy training, I'm tougher than you might think. I can endure some temporary discomfort."

"Even so"—Phinn ran a finger down her nose—"the idea of hurtin' you pains me more . . . more than I can say."

Mina cradled Phinn's jaw, touched that he cared so much

about her comfort. "It will be worth it," she returned softly. Then she smiled. "And you can always kiss me better, later."

He released a husky laugh. "Aye," he said as he shifted, taking his weight on one arm. Then he gently coaxed her legs apart and settled between her thighs. "I promise that I will." As he bent his head and kissed her tenderly, Mina felt him notching the broad, velvet-smooth head of his long, hard length at her untried entrance. "Are-are you ready for me, lass?"

She curled her fingers around his broad shoulders. "Yes," she whispered, and then Phinn inhaled an unsteady breath, tilted his hips, and pressed forward.

Mina bit her lip to stop a whimper of pain escaping. There was no denying it. This was going to hurt. But as Phinn gently rocked his hips, nudging into her inch by slow inch, he whispered words of praise and encouragement in her ear. How brave she was. How beautiful. How sweet. How wonderful she felt. How much he loved her. And even though there was pressure and stretching and burning and, at one point Mina thought she might burst, at last Phinn was fully sheathed inside her body.

"You're in?" she whispered. "All the way?"

"Aye." He pressed his sweat-sheened forehead to hers and it was then that Mina realized he was trembling. "And God, you feel so, so good, lass. But I . . . I don't know how long I can hold still . . . while you get-get used to me."

A wave of tenderness washed through Mina. "I'm already used to you. I do feel rather . . . full. But the truly painful part is over."

"Thank God," he breathed. "So-so I can move?"

She kissed him. "Yes. Yes please. I want that."

And so he did. He began to stroke in and out of Mina, ever so slowly and carefully at first. The sensations he aroused in her felt strange—an odd sort of discomfort, or perhaps a delicious sort of friction that bordered on pleasurable. And then Phinn's measured thrusts grew faster and harder and deeper and they *did* feel good. Actually, better than good. They felt incredible. It was like she was riding a wild stallion, racing so very, very fast toward a precipice. The familiar, coiling tension that heralded her peak was building, spiraling tighter and tighter and she wrapped her legs about Phinn's sturdy thighs and clutched at his broad back to match his feverish pace.

Oh, she was almost there.

And so was Phinn. He was breathing heavily, raggedly as his powerful plunges grew faster still. "Come with me, Mina," he entreated, his voice hoarse, desperate. Sliding a hand between them, he massaged the exquisitely sensitive bud at the apex of her sex . . . and that was enough to send Mina over the edge into ecstasy. As she came apart on a pleasure-drenched cry, Phinn quickly followed her. Shuddering, groaning, he collapsed on top of her, his hot breath gusting against her neck.

"My sweet, sweet Mina." Phinn shifted his weight and rolled to the side, bringing her with him so they lay facing each other, skin to skin. Heart to heart. "How I love you."

She smiled and reached out a hand to stroke his beloved face. "Can you count the ways?"

His answering smile was so full of tenderness, Mina's breath caught and her throat tightened with emotion. "Darlin'," he murmured, smoothing a strand of hair away from her flushed cheek, "the list of things I adore about you is endless."

And when he kissed her, Mina showed Phinn exactly how much she adored *him*.

Epilogue

In Which an Irishman Makes His Voice Heard; And an English Rose Finds Her Voice, Too...

Much to Mina's relief, the only thing that had made the newspapers about the Marquess of Kinsale and Miss Hermina Davenport, had been the announcement of their engagement. There was no mention of any sort of scandalous "muddy" goings-on between the marquess and the Parasol Academy governess in Hyde Park. No allusion to any unfortunate falls or "not manners" face-planting in laps. Phinn's and Mina's and the Academy's reputations had remained unsullied. Mina did wonder if Mrs. Temple had waved her figurative magic wand and had somehow performed a miracle, because the press hadn't breathed a word.

Everyone that Mina and Phinn had shared their engagement news with had been overjoyed. When they'd visited St Lawrence House, Emmeline had squealed and hugged Mina. Xavier had been somewhat more restrained when he'd congratulated Mina and Phinn—although Mina had detected a gleam of genuine warmth in his blue eyes as he'd smiled at her and then offered his gloved hand to Phinn to shake.

As for Mina's mother and sister... After Mina sent a telegram to Rose Cottage, Edwina Davenport and Dorothea, thrilled beyond measure, jumped on the very next train to London. They'd resided at Kinsale House until Phinn had generously installed them in their own fully furnished townhouse in Kensington just after the wedding.

Exactly one week after their engagement had been announced, Mina and Phinn, both of one accord, were married by special license in St Paul's Church in Knightsbridge. Emmeline had acted as matron of honor, and the very handsome, thoroughly rakish Viscount Hartwell had stood up as Phinn's best man. Brutus had even participated in the ceremony—he'd been tasked with the role of ring bearer, and Christopher and Tom, both pageboys, had dutifully led the pug down the aisle, Mina and Phinn's wedding bands tied to a bright blue satin ribbon around the dog's stocky neck.

Mrs. Temple had attended the ceremony and wedding breakfast too, and Mina *did* wonder if the headmistress might actually be harboring a reluctant attraction to Lord Hartwell. Although the two hadn't really spoken—not that Mina had noticed at any rate—an uncharacteristic blush had crested Mrs. Temple's cheekbones when the viscount had once sent a curious, perhaps even speculative glance her way. Mrs. Temple had promptly looked away from Lord Hartwell and her expression had shuttered. The change had been so abrupt, it was almost as though she'd cast a *Cucumberfy* spell on herself. In any event, Mina thought it had been *most* curious. She hadn't noticed any sort of tension between the two at Emmeline and Xavier's wedding in June, but then, Mina had been so focused on her best friend's happiness that day, no doubt she'd been oblivious to anything else.

As for Phinn's much anticipated parliamentary speech... he'd made it the following week after their nuptials, when Parliament had commenced its second session for the year in October. While Phinn maintained his maiden speech in May had been an utter disaster, this speech, he'd proclaimed with a huge grin when he'd emerged from the House of Lords chamber, had been "grand." Mina, who'd been watching from the public gallery, thought her handsome, fiercely determined yet noble-hearted husband had performed admirably, and she'd never been prouder of anyone in her life. Especially since he hadn't tried to hide his Irish accent.

"I'm an Irishman and there's nothin' wrong with that," he'd told Mina before he'd entered the chamber. "If me accent is not to their likin', well . . . well that's on them, not me."

Mina wholeheartedly agreed.

Of course, Phinn's word-perfect speech delivery had probably been helped by the fact that he'd kissed Mina quite thoroughly in the carriage on the way to Westminster. And then he'd kissed her again before he'd entered the chamber and she'd headed up to the public gallery to watch.

Even though Phinn would no doubt attest that Mina's kisses were pure magic, Mina still believed that kissing per se wasn't *really* magical—that it was simply the case that when she and Phinn kissed, his whole body relaxed, allowing him to achieve greater fluency for a short period of time. In any event, she *knew* beyond a shadow of a doubt that Phinn could confidently employ all the techniques they'd worked on to improve his stammer. He'd rehearsed and read his speech about tenancy rights and agrarian reform over and over again until it was cemented in his mind. He knew how to relax his body and make sure he slowed his speaking pace. He knew when to pause and take a breath and use gentle articulatory contacts when producing certain speech sounds. Mina truly believed that *all* of these things had helped him to deliver a smoothly spoken and assured speech. One that had earned him many a "hear, hear" of approval from fellow peers.

Time would tell if the Marquess of Kinsale's proposed Irish tenancy reforms would pass into law, but at the very least the process of change had been started. Phinn and Mina had also discussed ideas for future reforms related to improving the treatment of children in orphanages and workhouses. "If... if I earn the moniker of 'that Irish rebel,' so be it," Phinn had said to Mina one night while they were cuddling in bed. "The main thing is, my peers are beginnin' to listen to me and are no longer dismissin' me as an ignorant lout with nothin' but-but stuffin' for brains. I *will* make a difference."

Mina was certain that her clever husband would.

So it was on a fine blustery day in early December, just after Parliament had finished sitting before Christmastide, their little family—Phinn, Mina, Christopher, Tom, and Brutus—had set sail for Ireland on the *Kinsale Cloud*.

Edwina and Dorothea Davenport were on board too. When Phinn had first suggested to Mina that her mother and sister might like to join them for their first family Christmas at Kinsale Castle, Mina had been nothing but touched. Although she had added a small warning. "Don't let my mother convince you that the castle needs redecorating and that she should have a hand in it," she'd said. "Otherwise it will end up looking like the Covent Garden flower market. You've seen Rose Cottage and their Kensington townhouse."

Phinn had laughed. "I promise I won't. I especially won't listen to her if she starts harpin' on about anyone's cake or puddin' consumption. In fact, I'll-I'll be packin' her back to Gloucestershire fast-faster than you can say Ablington Railway Station."

Dorothea, who'd resigned from her post at the Ablington Parish School, had taken to helping the new, very agreeable Parasol Academy governess, Miss Blythe, with Tom and Christopher's lessons. Although Miss Blythe was perfectly capable of doing so, Mina still cast the *Guardia Nimbus* spell each night after Phinn read the boys their bedtime stories, just to be on the safe side. Mrs. Temple had helpfully provided Mina with a spool of the same silver Fae thread that Emmeline had been provided with when she'd surrendered her Parasol Academy nannying license; it meant Mina could sew magical pockets into all her gowns, so she'd always have magic on hand to protect her "boys" (as she'd taken to calling Christopher and Tom) if she needed to. Even though Mab was no longer an immediate threat, according to Mrs. Temple, Good Queen Maeve still wished to err on the side of caution until she was absolutely certain that her sister's Arctic prison was impenetrable.

Mina had also discovered why Brutus had taken against Mr. Hopwell so vehemently. It turned out that Mrs. Temple had "ensorcelled" the toy rabbit in her own way. She'd confessed all to Mina in a quiet moment during Mina and Phinn's wedding breakfast at Kinsale House. "You probably don't know this, Lady Kinsale," she'd said, "but after I received Lady Grenfell's letter of warning, I teleported to Highwood Hall in the middle of the night and secretly placed a magic 'locating' crystal—an amethyst in fact—inside Lord Fitzwilliam's velvet rabbit. I suspected that the boy would always keep it close, so it might be a way for me to keep track of his whereabouts should Sir Bedivere attempt to take him to the Arctic as Lady Grenfell had feared. That's how I also knew that he'd been on board the *Valiant* and the *Kinsale Cloud*. And then of course, in Ablington before you began working for Lord Kinsale."

Mina, to ensure that Christopher's rabbit would no longer be the focus of Brutus's ire, had removed the amethyst. And the pug and Mr. Hopwell had been living in perfect harmony ever since. Which had worked out quite well, all things considered.

A fact that Mina was reminded of when Brutus crossed the deck of the *Kinsale Cloud* to where she stood, wrapped in a fur-lined cloak of crimson wool with her husband's strong arms around her. The sky over the Bristol Channel might be gray and lowering, the sea might be choppy and the icy wind might be nipping at her cheeks and tugging at her hair and clothes, but Mina had never been happier.

Got any pups in the oven yet? the pug asked, pointedly staring at Mina's middle.

She rolled her eyes at the dog. He'd really become quite obsessed with the idea that his master and new wife might be producing their own "litter" before too long. *You know that you'll be one of the first to know should that happy circumstance eventuate,* Mina told him. *You don't have to keep asking. Besides, I thought the idea of your master and me 'breeding,' as you put it, was objectionable to you.*

Brutus gave a snort through his black snub nose. *It's not the idea of ye havin' pups, milady. It's how you humans beget them that's the objectionable part.*

After Mina and Phinn had wed, Brutus had, in fact, taken to sleeping in the boys' bedroom. Mina, of course, had been quietly relieved. If the dog was at the end of a long hallway on the floor above, it meant that she didn't have to be as careful with masking her thoughts when she and Phinn were intimate. When the pug had announced his decision to Mina, he'd even said, *I've got excellent hearin', milady. And I don't want to hear you two goin' at it hammer and tongs on yer weddin' night. Or ever for that matter.* He'd given a dramatic shiver that had even set his curly tail aquiver. *It's enough to give a dog the willies.*

Before Mina could respond to Brutus, Phinn's arms tightened around her. "You're . . . you're talkin' to me dog, aren't you?" he asked, his voice warm and low in Mina's ear.

Mina turned in his arms. "How do you know?"

He grinned. "Brutus gets a certain look on his face. And so do you."

"We do?"

"Aye. He looks disgruntled and you look mildly disapproving." Phinn raised a dark brow. "What . . . what did he say?"

She laughed. "You really don't want to know, my darling husband."

Phinn lifted her chin with a gloved finger. "Tell me. It-it can't be that bad."

Mina pushed her hands into Phinn's greatcoat, seeking his heat. It had begun to snow and tiny snowflakes were settling on her husband's dark hair and wide shoulders. "Well, if you insist... He asked if I had a pup in the oven. I do think he's very excited about the prospect of being an 'uncle.'"

Phinn chuckled. "The cheeky sod. At least he hasn't heard us at night." His mouth slid into a wicked grin. "Or at other times for that matter." Leaning in, he whispered in her ear, "I'm-I'm lookin' forward to christenin' the bed in our cabin a bit later on when everyone's retired for the night, me darlin' lady-wife."

I can hear you two, you know, grumbled Brutus. But as Phinn kissed Mina, the pug ambled off to where Tom and Christopher stood a few yards away, catching snowflakes on their tongues as Miss Blythe looked on. Mina's mother and Dorothea had opted to stay below to take tea and try the cook's excellent Bath buns and pound cake. So aside from Brutus, there really was no one who would look askance at them for stealing a kiss or two. They were practically newlyweds after all. And this trip to Ireland could be looked on as a belated honeymoon. That's how Mina was viewing it anyway.

After a while, when they drew apart, Mina captured her husband's gaze. "You know, I've decided I have a new favorite romantic hero. It's no longer Mr. Rochester."

Phinn laughed. "So, milady, you've decided that a man who locks his wife in an attic and attempts bigamy is *not* hero material?"

She smiled. "Not to mention the fact that he *doesn't* fancy Ireland. What a foolish man."

Phinn's hands pushed beneath her cloak and he pulled her even closer. "Well, what about Mr. Darcy? Or Mr. Knightley? Or . . . or Heathcliff?"

Mina raised a gloved hand and ticked off what she thought of each suggestion. "Too stuffy. Too prudent. Too vengeful."

Phinn's mouth inched into the most heart-stopping smile Mina had ever seen. "So who is it, me darlin'?"

Looking up at her handsome husband through her lashes, she whispered, "You, my lord. Since the moment we met on this ship, it's always been you."

And if anyone on deck—Christopher, or Tom, or Miss Blythe, or the crew, or Brutus—objected to the passion of the Marquess and Marchioness of Kinsale's kiss—Mina did not give a flying feck.

Afterword

Dearest Reader,

I'd just like to have a quick word about stuttering as the hero of *The Governess's Guide to Spells and Managing Misfit Marquesses*, Phineas O'Connell has a significant stammer or stutter. If you've read Book 1 in the Parasol Academy series, *The Nanny's Handbook to Magic and Managing Difficult Dukes*, or read my author bio, you might have also taken note that before I became an author, I was a speech pathologist for many years. During my speech pathology career, I worked extensively with pediatric clients with a range of communication difficulties including stuttering. Not only that, but one of our daughters, when she was young, had a stutter for a time which she received speech pathology treatment for, and her disfluency did resolve. So it's safe to say that I had both personal and professional past experience to draw on when depicting Phinn's stuttering and the challenges it presented for him in the context of the mid-nineteenth century . . . with a slightly alternate history.

During the course of *The Governess's Guide to Spells and Managing Misfit Marquesses,* you'll see that Phinn trials various methods to improve his fluency. His speech does become more fluent or "smoother" as the story progresses, but I wanted to make it clear that there really isn't any magic involved. His stutter isn't miraculously fixed by Fae magic. Rather he actively employs particular techniques to control his disfluency. But of course, this is a cozy fantasy historical romance novel, and the intervention strategies described in this book—*especially* the effects of kissing—are not meant to be a "how-to guide" on current speech pathology practice in this area, at all. For further information on disorders of fluency, diagnosis, and evidence-based stuttering treatment, I would point readers in the direction of the following professional speech pathology organizations: American Speech-Language-Hearing Association (ASHA), Speech Pathology Australia (SPA), or the Royal College of Speech and Language Therapists (RCSLT) in the UK.

In conclusion, past-speech-pathology me and current-author me hope that I've succeeded in portraying Phinn's challenges with achieving fluency in a way that is both sensitive and respectful. After all, everyone deserves to have a voice and to achieve their goals in life. Everyone deserves to be accepted and loved for who they are. *Everyone* deserves a happy ever after.

Amy Rose Bennett

Keep reading for an excerpt of
The Nanny's Handbook to Magic and Managing Difficult Dukes

Emmeline Chase, twenty-five-year-old widow and new alumna, may be more high-spirited than the Academy would like. Few graduates, however, could turn a mismanaged teleportation onto a duke's rooftop into an offer of employment. But Emmeline's circumstances, along with her desperation to support her bankrupt, incarcerated father, have made her dauntless. Which seems the primary qualification to work for expert horologist Xavier Mason, Duke of St. Lawrence, and manage his three rambunctious wards. Yet Emmeline soon discovers that the nobleman's heart-melting voice and captivating mind present an entirely different sort of trouble. She cannot risk losing her license by fraternizing with her employer . . .

Xavier's wards have sent two nannies packing in a month thanks to frogs, firecrackers, and general mayhem. In addition, Xavier's professional reputation is on the line. He's already considered odd, with his talking raven companion and his fascination with timekeeping instead of pleasure-chasing with his peers. Charming, vivacious Emmeline seems intrigued with his quirks—but Xavier must have absolute peace to design London's "King of Clocks" for Westminster Palace before the competition closes. Emmeline can no doubt restore order. As long as he doesn't fall under her spell . . .

Yet, with a possible saboteur in their midst, and the attraction flaring between them threatening to become a deliciously disastrous distraction, a touch of magic may be required . . .

Chapter 1

Concerning the Nanny's Plight; Spilled Tea, Dickens on Toast, Cucumber Sandwiches, and Jelly; A Teleportation Cock-Up of Magnificent Proportions; And an Unexpected Encounter with a Raven...

The Parasol Academy, Sloane Square, London
Spring 1851

At the age of five-and-twenty, Mrs. Emmeline Chase had come to the realization that, much like her unruly red hair—which seemed to do whatever it liked unless ruthlessly pinned into submission—she would never be *quite* the right amount of prim and proper to satisfy Polite Society. Indeed, even though Emmeline had just graduated from the Parasol Academy for Exceptional Nannies and Governesses, it was common knowledge within its ranks that she *sometimes* struggled to comply with the Academy's exacting standards of etiquette, despite her best efforts.

So when Emmeline spilled her half-finished cup of tea down her snow-white nanny's pinafore and, without thinking, exclaimed, "Blast and drat and dickens on toast," in the middle of the Academy's refectory, it really shouldn't have been a surprise to anyone. Nevertheless, there were more than a few censorious glares from teaching staff sent her way, along with a flurry of horrified gasps from fellow Academy graduates and the latest cohort of up-and-coming students. There was definitely a titter or two.

Her cheeks flaming, Emmeline blew out a frustrated sigh and blotted ineffectually at the unsightly brown splotch with a linen napkin.

"It's just because you're nervous," murmured her bookish, fiercely intelligent friend, Hermina "Mina" Davenport, who was seated beside her. "Everyone knows you're not your usual bright self. No one would blame you for spilling a bit of tea given the circumstances."

Of course, Mina's thick chestnut hair never misbehaved regardless of the circumstances, thought Emmeline. It was always as smooth and glossy as the polished surface of the elegant oak dining table at which they sat. A hurricane could hurtle through the Parasol Academy and Mina would still look completely unruffled. But Mina was so sweet and supportive, Emmeline couldn't begrudge how perfectly poised she was. Or how clever. She would always be grateful she had such a steadfast friend.

Emmeline drew a breath and offered Mina a smile. "I suppose you're right. Although, when it's time for me to leave, I fear my knees won't support me. They're already quivering like a barely set jelly."

In less than an hour she would be attending an interview for a nannying position—her first ever since she graduated from the Academy a fortnight ago. And Emmeline needed the job more than she needed a spotless pinafore, or hair that behaved, or knees that didn't knock together. Because if she *didn't* secure a permanent position with decent wages, she had no idea how she would be able to continue to pay off the turnkey at Newgate Prison where her father was currently incarcerated. This week's payment was already late . . .

Emmeline's situation might not have been so dire if her

ne'er-do-well late husband, Jeremy, hadn't frittered away everything they had, leaving her nothing. She also couldn't rely on her brother, Freddy, to come up with the money. After all, it was *his* fault that their father's antique clock store had fallen into bankruptcy in the first place.

The fact that Emmeline's father was in prison for unpaid debts was the only thing that Mina didn't know about Emmeline. No one at the Academy knew either. And Emmeline's secret had to remain exactly that. Secret. Because who would employ a nanny whose father was locked away in one of England's most notorious prisons?

"You didn't even touch your luncheon," said Mina, her clear hazel eyes soft with understanding.

Emmeline grimaced at the neat row of cucumber sandwiches on her porcelain plate. The Academy's cook obviously used a set square to cut each one into a perfect equilateral triangle. "I hate being so wasteful, but my stomach's full of rampaging butterflies at present."

Mina touched Emmeline's forearm. "You'll be fine. You're one of the bravest, smartest people I know, and I'm certain you will get this job."

Emmeline smiled back at her friend. "Thank you. I wish I had your confidence—"

"Mrs. Chase?"

Emmeline looked up to find the relatively new headmistress of the Parasol Academy, Mrs. Felicity Temple, standing right in front of their table.

Oh, double blast and drat and a bucketload of botheration as well. At least Emmeline remembered to swear in her head this time. Although, according to the *Parasol Academy Handbook*'s guidelines in Chapter 2, which pertained to nanny and governess etiquette, "botheration" and any of its variations were permitted, along with: oh my; oh dear; my goodness; good gracious; good heavens; heavens above; for mercy's sake; and on the odd occasion, by Jove, or by Jupiter. Unfortunately, "drat" was too close to "damn" so its use was discouraged.

Even though Mrs. Temple was only thirty years old (and styled herself "missus" because she was a headmistress, not because she was or had ever been married), there was an unmistakable air of authority about her. A marked steeliness in her bearing. In fact, up until six months ago, Mrs. Temple had been employed by none other than Her Majesty, Queen Victoria, in the Royal nursery, and everyone at the Academy was in complete awe of her.

Yet there was a soft gracefulness about Felicity Temple too. Her pale blond ringlets perfectly framed her heart-shaped face, and her petite frame was always immaculately attired in a haute couture gown. Indeed, there were occasional whispers in quiet corners of the Academy that Mrs. Temple might just be the *teeniest* bit vain given she always kept a rather ornate silver and crystal-encrusted hand mirror upon her office desk. Emmeline didn't believe such talk though. In her mind, the headmistress was the epitome of everything the Academy stood for: prim and proper and prepared for anything.

Right now, Emmeline feared she might have to prepare herself for a public drubbing of the verbal kind. She swallowed to moisten her dry mouth. "Yes, Mrs. Temple?" she ventured in a suitably polite tone. The refectory had grown as hushed as a church hall as there was a collective holding of breath.

"May I see you outside?" the headmistress asked quietly. But, to Emmeline's relief, there was no hard edge of disapproval in her voice, and the expression in her gray eyes was thoughtful, perhaps even compassionate. Perhaps she would simply express her disappointment and issue Emmeline with a stern reminder about the "rules."

Emmeline could but hope. She inclined her head in acquiescence. "Yes, of course, Mrs. Temple."

As she put down her napkin, Mina gave her hand a reassuring squeeze and murmured, "Good luck."

Emmeline nodded her thanks as she pushed unsteadily to her feet. Truth to tell, she was grateful her knees *didn't* give out as she followed the headmistress into the deserted corridor outside the refectory.

When Mrs. Temple came to a halt by the door of the study hall, she gave Emmeline a smile. "I'm not going to reprimand you for using impolite language, if that's what you're concerned about, Mrs. Chase."

"Oh . . ." Emmeline pressed a hand to her stomach to help still the rioting butterflies within. "Thank you, Mrs. Temple. I assure you that I *do* know which particular exclamations are permitted as per the *Parasol Academy Handbook*."

"I know you do." Mrs. Temple gave her another reassuring smile. "Just like I know that you're nervous about your upcoming interview with Mr. Culpepper Esquire. I can practically see that you're quivering in your half boots. But you really shouldn't be so anxious. I'm confident that you'll do very well." Her smile widened. "As long as you remember *not* to say things like 'blast' and 'drat' and 'dickens on toast.' Especially in front of the Culpeppers' two young children."

"I promise I won't," said Emmeline. "And thank you for your understanding." She might not be perfect, but it seemed the Parasol Academy's headmistress didn't think she needed to be absolutely perfect all the time either.

"Now," said Mrs. Temple as she examined Emmeline's uniform, "let's see what we can do to remedy your attire so that you won't be late for your appointment." She withdrew a small feather duster from the pocket of her dove-gray silk skirts, then murmured, "*Unsmirchify*," as she made a grand sweeping gesture down the front of Emmeline's pinafore.

A soft incandescent glow enveloped Emmeline's person for a brief moment, and a warm breeze, almost like a sigh, gently swirled around her, ruffling her clothes. When she looked down at herself, she could see that the tea stain had magically vanished; the white linen of her pinafore was spotless once more.

She smiled at the headmistress. "You're too kind, Mrs. Temple. Although"—she glanced toward the arched window at the end of the hall that revealed a bleak leaden sky—"I do hope my uniform can survive the trip to Bedford Square." She didn't have any spare coin to afford a hansom cab or even an omnibus fare at present, but she couldn't very well tell Mrs. Temple that.

"Of course, you have my permission to teleport to your interview," said Mrs. Temple. "It's official Academy business after all. There's a Metropolitan Police box at the northern end of Bedford Square you can make use of to conceal your arrival. Then it will be but a short walk to the Culpeppers' residence."

Emmeline nodded. Te-*ley*-porting, which harnessed the secret leyline magic of the Fae, was just one of the many magical tools a Parasol nanny or governess had at her disposal to discharge her professional duties. But one had to be discreet about it. Teleporting out in the open where members of the general public might see one mysteriously disappear or materialize as if from nowhere was frowned upon and one of the worst breaches of the Academy's rules. As per the guidelines in Chapter 1 of the *Parasol Academy Handbook*, strictly guarding the Academy's unconventional practices was of paramount importance, so cupboards and wardrobes and pantries and, on occasion, Metropolitan Police sentry boxes, were the preferred "vehicles."

Although, as Emmeline understood it, access to police boxes for the purpose of teleportation was a relatively new practice. The Academy had recently been granted a Royal Charter by Queen Victoria, so an "arrangement" with Scotland Yard had been established. Needless to say, Parasol nannies and governesses still had to be judicious with exercising such a privilege. Anyone who was careless with the Academy's secrets risked having their training cut short or even their Parasol nanny or governess accreditation revoked. Such an eventuality was something that Emmeline could ill afford.

Emmeline farewelled Mrs. Temple then hastened to the Academy's dormitory on the floor above. Once she'd donned her navy-blue cloak, her coal-scuttle bonnet, and had retrieved her Academy umbrella from the stand near the door, she was ready. *Well, as ready as I'll ever be*, she thought. She checked her Academy-issued silver pocket watch, which kept perfect time, and noted she still had half an hour to make it to her interview. *If* she successfully teleported to Bedford Square without making a hash of it . . .

Tel-*ley*-porting was *always* a discombobulating experience. And when Emmeline lost her focus, that's when things tended to go spectacularly awry. That's when she ended up in places she wasn't supposed to be. That didn't happen often, thank goodness, but when it did (like that one time she'd ended up in the middle of the Thames and had to be rescued by the River Police), it proved to be all kinds of mortifying and inconvenient, to say the least.

But not today. She couldn't afford to lose her focus, today of all days.

Emmeline dug out her pewter leyport key from her pocket, then crossed the room with sure strides to the wardrobe she shared with Mina. Even though the door wasn't locked, she needed to use her key to open up the leyline portal. Without it, the wardrobe would be an ordinary closet, not a conduit for teleportation.

The wardrobe's interior was cloaked in deep shadow, but when Emmeline pushed all the clothing aside, a small but bright light glimmered at the very back like a beckoning candle flame at the end of a long dark tunnel. The key had sparked the leyline magic to life.

Emmeline inhaled a deep breath, bracing herself for the journey. The process was simple enough in theory. All she had to do was step inside the wardrobe and focus on the leylight while simultaneously picturing herself where she needed to be. She'd whisper the required Fae incantation to set the magic completely aflame and then she'd be on her way.

"Keep calm and nanny on," Emmeline murmured as she hopped into the wardrobe, her eyes fastened on the flickering leylight flame. No sooner had she conjured up a mental image of Bedford Square and murmured, "*Vortexio*," when there was a sudden flare of blinding light. A familiar but also unsettling *whoosh* filled her head, and then a strange sensation of whirling weightlessness—like one was spinning around inside a Catherine wheel—engulfed her.

And then the movement and the rushing sound stopped, leaving Emmeline panting and slightly dizzy. Even though she'd closed her eyes at some point, she could sense that the intense white leylight had faded away.

Inhaling a bracing breath, she dared to crack open an eyelid... and when she discerned *exactly* where her derriere had landed, her stomach pitched and she uttered a string of curses a lot worse than *blast and drat and dickens on toast*.

She was not in a stone police box. She was not even in a wardrobe or cupboard.

She was on a roof. A roof!

Another wave of dizziness assailed Emmeline and she clutched at the rain-slick tiles beneath her gloved palms to stop herself accidentally plunging to a quick and untimely death.

Was she at least in Bedford Square?

There was only one way to find out. Emmeline forced herself to open her eyes and then she very carefully adjusted her seat so that she could peer down at the cherry-tree-lined square below. Belgrave Square according to the sign. *Not* Bedford Square.

Blooming hell with bells on. Had she said the wrong word in her head? Belgrave and Bedford both started with *B*. Had she conjured up the wrong mental image because Belgrave Square was close to the Parasol Academy in nearby Sloane Square? She must have. What a monumental cock-up. What a complete henwit she'd been.

The mildly startled pigeon perched upon the row of chimney pots to Emmeline's right stared at her as if in complete agreement with everything she'd thought. A soft empathic coo was followed by a ruffling of its gray feathers, but then the bird took off, winging its way over the London rooftops to whatever its destination might be... unlike Emmeline, who was well and truly stuck on a most precarious perch for a human—four stories up with no foreseeable way down.

Emmeline couldn't help but mutter, "Lucky blighter," as the pigeon became a mere speck against the cloud-shrouded sky. And then she fell to contemplating her options and her future, which hopefully wouldn't be short-lived.

One: Stay stuck on this roof forevermore. While Emmeline hadn't envisioned a future as a nanny weathervane, she reasoned that it was a slightly better fate than her next logical option...

Two: Fall and become a rather unfortunate splat on the cobblestone square far below. Emmeline shuddered. Although that particular outcome *would* be far from ideal, at least it would be over with quickly. But the drawback was that she'd never see her dear father, who rather depended on her, again. Or her brother for that matter. Or darling Mina. Becoming a "splat" wasn't a good choice in the big scheme of things.

Three: Call out and hope someone would be moved to rescue her. There did appear to be a Metropolitan Police box at the other end of the square, but Emmeline doubted her voice would carry that far. And the bobby might be anywhere.

What she needed was an impossibly long ladder. Even a

long rope would do at a pinch. While Emmeline's training had equipped her with the ability to scale a tree or a wall should she need to rescue a trapped charge, or even a charge's far-too-curious cat, she'd still need a rope and possibly a grappling hook to lower herself to safety.

In certain circumstances, Emmeline could simply reach into her uniform's magical "nanny pocket" to procure whatever she needed to manage a difficult situation. But as per Chapter 4, Section 2 of the *Parasol Academy Handbook*, she could only produce "necessary items" from said pocket, "while in service to a child in her care, or in certain situations, a child in need." Getting oneself stuck on a rooftop because you were distracted and failed to discreetly teleport from one location to another did not signify.

Emmeline blew out a heavy sigh and frowned at the toes of her kid half boots. Her fourth consideration was probably the most important of all. If she did survive this massive teleportation blunder, she hoped to God that Mrs. Temple didn't hear about it. She'd already been in enough trouble for one day.

"Remember, you're a Parasol Academy nanny, Emmeline Chase. You're prim, proper, and prepared for anything. Exactly like Mrs. Temple," she sternly reminded herself as she somehow shoved down her nerves, much like one would shove down a mouthful of castor oil. Her nerves had gotten her into this mess to begin with, so she had no time for them at the moment. "You will work out how to get down from here without breaking your neck. You will not sully your reputation or the Academy's by drawing undue attention to yourself. And you *will* secure that nannying job. Failure is *not* an option."

Emmeline examined the impressive townhouse she was presently seated upon. It was entirely on its own at one corner of the square. Craning her neck to look behind her, she spied two whitewashed wings that jutted off the main edifice. Each wing had numerous casement windows. Perhaps she could attract the attention of one of the townhouse's occupants. Well, if they looked outside.

Taking a deep breath and tightening her grip on the slate tiles, Emmeline carefully swung one of her legs over to the other side of the steeply sloped roof, then proceeded to inch herself along the ridgeline toward the row of chimney pots and the nearest wing. She supposed she could always lob her umbrella at one of the windows. She was a good shot, and surely that would arouse someone's notice.

There! A movement—a dark sort of fluttering—in one of the windows on the second floor caught Emmeline's attention. Someone was watching her, she was sure of it.

Emmeline made herself let go with one hand then waved madly. "Hulloooo," she called. "I say, hullooo!"

What the deuce? What on earth are you doing up there? sounded a voice in her head. An avian voice with a distinct rasp that reminded Emmeline of a distinguished gentleman who was fond of pipe-smoking. The sort of man who'd don a velvet banyan and prop his leather-slipper-clad feet upon a footstool with a brandy at his elbow and the latest copy of the *Times* spread out before him.

Emmeline dared to lean forward a little more as she squinted at the windowpane in question. *It's all rather complicated,* she replied to her all-but-invisible conversational partner. She suspected that he *was* a bird of some kind. Aside from dogs and horses, birds were the easiest animals for Parasol Academy graduates to communicate with by thought alone. Cats, on the other hand, were altogether too aloof and not likely to respond at all.

As you can see, I'm in a bit of a pickle, Emmeline continued in what she hoped was a friendly manner, not a panicky, Oh-Lord-I'm-going-to-die fashion. *Is there anyone inside the house that might be able to help me? If someone could summon a chimney sweep, I could climb down his ladder...*

I see . . . I suppose I could do that . . . As long as you're not up to anything nefarious . . . Suddenly the casement window swung open, and a rather magnificent raven appeared on the window ledge. Cocking his head, his dark inquisitive gaze met Emmeline's. *I hope you'll excuse my impertinence, but what is your name? It's not often that I come across someone like you. An* animalis sussurator *or animal whisperer, so to speak. You are a rarity, indeed.*

Animal whisperer . . . Emmeline liked the sound of that. Not all Parasol Academy graduates could telepathically communicate with animals. The ability seemed to be a side effect of using Fae magic and you either developed it as a skill—like learning to play the pianoforte or speak another language—or you didn't. And like any other skill, once you had attained it, you possessed the ability for life. At least that's what Emmeline had learned during her Parasol Academy training.

Casting a smile at the raven—it wouldn't do to appear rude—she responded to his question. *My name is Mrs. Emmeline Chase and I'm . . .* She drew a fortifying breath. *I'm a nanny with certain singular talents.* She didn't think it would be wise to elaborate further on that score—disclosing she had magical abilities would certainly ruffle feathers in more ways than one—so instead she asked, *And to whom am I speaking?*

The raven puffed out his chest and his glossy black feathers gleamed like polished ebony. *Horatio Ravenscar, Esquire. At your service, madam. I shall summon my master. I shan't be long.* And then, with an elegant flap of his enormous wings, he disappeared.

Emmeline released a shaky sigh of relief. Things were looking up after all. Well, as long as Horatio Ravenscar's master wasn't an arrogant, snobbish pain-in-the-derriere who refused to help her. She didn't like playing the role of damsel-in-distress. And she really should curb her unruly tongue, even in her head. She was in Belgravia. Not Cheapside, where her father's store had been. Or Shoreditch, where Freddy's struggling music hall, the Oberon, was located.

But then, Horatio's master wasn't going to employ her. Mr. Culpepper of Barclays Bank would. All going well. If only she could get down from this infernal roof.

Visit our website at
KensingtonBooks.com
to sign up for our newsletters, read more from your favorite authors, see books by series, view reading group guides, and more!

Become a Part of Our
Between the Chapters Book Club
Community and Join the Conversation

Betweenthechapters.net

Submit your book review for a chance to win exclusive Between the Chapters swag you can't get anywhere else!
https://www.kensingtonbooks.com/pages/review/